NIGHT MOVES

Olivia Lively Mysteries

Final Draft

Night Moves

NIGHT MOVES

An Olivia Lively Mystery

SHELLEY BURBANK

Encircle Publications
Farmington, Maine, U.S.A.

Encircle editor: Cynthia Brackett-Vincent

Book and cover design by Deirdre Wait
Cover images © Getty Images

Author photograph by Nicholas Andrews, SDHeadshots

Published by:

Encircle Publications, LLC
PO Box 187
Farmington, ME 04938

info@encirclepub.com
http://encirclepub.com

Chapter One

● ● ● ● ● ● ● ● ● ● ● ● ● ● ●

If cleanliness was next to godliness, then Olivia Lively's chances of a heavenly afterlife were slim.

Sitting at her desk in the Lively Investigations office, Liv sliced open yet another envelope, scanned the contents, and placed the invoice in her to-do tray. The stack of papers tilted at a precarious angle, and when she reached for the next piece of mail, her elbow grazed the paperwork. Correspondence slithered off the desk and onto the floor.

Liv scowled. It was official. She'd filled her inbox to overflowing.

In the mellow, late-afternoon light falling through the room's dusty window, the room looked like a hoarder's den. Old takeout containers filled the trash bin. Lipstick-stained coffee cups cluttered the area around the coffee machine. A disorganized stack of case folders teetered next to the credenza. Notebooks, invoices, and hastily-scribbled sticky notes littered the desktop.

She bent to retrieve the fallen correspondence and tossed the disorganized handful onto the desktop. A shiny, slippery postcard advertising an amateur dance contest at a local strip club skittered toward the edge of the desk. She snagged it, held it up, and scanned the closeup of a woman's shapely thigh cinched with a purple garter belt. A little, gold, triangular charm dangled from the satin elastic. Typeset in a garish, golden-yellow font, the copy announced "All ladies welcome!!! $500 in Cash and Prizes!!!"

"Good to know I have options if this private investigation thing doesn't work out," she muttered aloud as she tossed the postcard in the bin and reached for the next letter in the pile.

The mess represented more than simple growing pains for her one-woman firm in Portland, Maine. Riding high on her big win in the recent Tedeschi-Falwell plagiarism case, she'd foolishly accepted more work than she could handle alone.

Now she was floundering. Drowning in cases. Caught in the sucking vortex of her own success.

If you don't hire some help soon, Lively Investigations will fail.

She believed the voice in her head. Unfortunately, her cash-flow trickled at the moment, despite all the new clients and publicity. She didn't have time to work on the cases she'd accepted plus handle administrative tasks like invoicing. Paying bills eroded her account balances even further. At the end of the day, she couldn't afford a temp, let alone a full-time assistant.

She was thirty years old and in pretty good shape thanks to yoga and a daily run around Portland's Back Cove, but after weeks of craziness following her last case as well as the arrest of her slimy ex-boyfriend Rob Mickelson, she wasn't feeling or looking her best.

Too much caffeine. Too many takeout meals. Not enough Veuve Clicquot.

She scraped at a dried blob of ketchup on her L'Agence dark-wash jeans. She wore them with a blue-striped, ruffled shirt, a tangle of delicate gold necklaces, and pumps. Her brunette pixie cut was in need of a trim. She'd chewed off her red lipstick hours ago. Her mascaraed eyes burned.

She leaned back in chair, crossed the navy Ferragamo pumps on top of the desk, and rubbed her fingers over her eyelids. *You can't go on like this.*

Working ten- and twelve-hour days just to keep up, she'd given up all semblance of a private life. Case in point: the previous Thursday, she'd called Jasper, her boyfriend of three months, to cancel yet another date.

He teased her. "Are you trying to break up with me?"

"Very funny." She kept him on speakerphone as she continued to scan an investigation report for typos. It was due the following day to attorney Patrick Ledeau who had become one of her best clients. She corrected a comma splice and hit save. "This is just a rough patch," she said. "It'll get better soon."

He hesitated a beat too long. "I want to believe you."

Irritation shot through her. As an on-call cardiothoracic surgeon, he sometimes canceled dates or cut them short. He didn't apologize for it, and she didn't expect him to. She wanted the same kind of respect. For her. For her work. For her goals.

Society allowed a man to prioritize *his* work while expecting a woman to prioritize *her* relationships.

The double-standard infuriated her.

"Believe it. Don't believe it," she'd snapped. "That's up to you."

"Hey. Joking. I don't want to fight with you, Liv."

She addressed an email to Patrick, attached the report, and hit send. "Good. Me, either."

A pause. "Are you typing?"

"Just sending an email. I'm all yours now."

Another pause. "If only that were true." His tone was wistful, and guilt slammed into her gut.

The real kicker was she didn't know if she even wanted to be. All his. All anybody's. Ever.

After another minute of stilted conversation they hung up, no good-night, nothing resolved.

The following morning he'd shown up at her apartment with flowers and a double-espresso latte. Without a word, she'd opened the door wide, and they'd practically combusted when they kissed.

"See," she'd murmured against his mouth. "Absence makes perfect."

He'd laughed at her malaphor, scooped her up. Two hours later, he'd left placated, but wary. Since then, tension quivered between them like a guitar string plucked by a frustrated hand.

Now in the stuffy confines of her gross office, she sniffed and caught a whiff of failure in the air.

Or maybe it was just that her Chanel No. 5 had worn off.

Giving up on the stack of endless paperwork, Liv reached instead for the cleaning spray. If she failed—if they found her dead at her desk with a stack of overdue bills at her elbow and an overdrawn account at the bank, the victim of her own poor choices—at least her office would be tidy.

And she'd storm those pearly gates after all.

●　　●　　●　　●　　●

Singing along with her favorite Puccini arias, she spent the next hour stacking papers into neater piles and wiping surfaces free of grime. She washed and dried coffee mugs and arranged them next to the coffee maker. She ran her little red carpet sweeper over the floor. Finally, wrinkling her nose, she tied up the reeking trash bag. She pulled the bag from the bin and lugged it through the reception room toward the office door. She held the bag at arm's length and lunged into the short, dim hallway.

And smacked into a wall.

A six-foot four-inch wall dressed in beige chinos and a light blue polo shirt.

Liv ricocheted and stumbled backward in her heels. She grabbed the doorframe as the trash bag tumbled to the floor. Her heart thudded. A memory of her sleazy ex, Rob Mickelson, accosting her in this very hallway flashed through her mind, but when she looked up, she recognized a friendly and familiar face.

"Donovan Ferguson! What are you doing lurking in my hallway?"

"I wasn't lurking. I came by to ask you for a favor." He looked at the trash bag. "But maybe this isn't a good time?"

She unlatched her fingers from the doorframe and straightened. Her heart rate slowed. She ran a hand through her hair and hoped he wouldn't notice the ketchup stain on her jeans.

"It's, uh, fine." She bent down and lifted the bag. "Housekeeping day. Let me get rid of this, and I'll meet you in my office. Straight through reception to the second room. Make yourself comfortable. I'll be right back."

She tossed the bag into the dumpster. A swarm of flies rose into the air. The rusty, metal door creaked and shut with a bang, and the flies dispersed. She hustled back to the office where she found Van struggling to open the window. Her face heated.

"I'll get that. You sit." She threw the safety bolt and cranked the window. "Want some coffee?"

He took a seat in front of her desk. "Sure. Black's fine."

She popped a K-cup into the machine. "This is a surprise. It's been, what, nine—ten months since we've seen each other?"

"Has it been that long?" He propped an ankle on his knee. "Time flies, I guess."

They'd grown up in the same West End neighborhood, attended the same K-12 day school, and bonded as slightly off-kilter, non-athletic kids in high school. She guessed he'd had a crush on her, but she'd always gone for the bad boys. Last fall, she ran into him at a Coyne School fundraiser, and he invited her to lunch to catch up.

They met at Nosh, a quirky cafe on Congress Street. Van brought his dog, a light-brown, curly-haired mix named Busterdoodle, and they'd sat outside enjoying bacon-dusted fries, soaking up the autumn sun, and chatting about old times. She'd decided Van and dog were well matched: beige and slightly goofy. Basically harmless.

The French roast spluttered. She held the mug out to him. "So, how're you doing?"

He took it by the proffered handle. "Okay. You?"

"Good." She sat behind her desk. "Lots of business ever since that Mason Falwell thing this spring."

"I heard about that. Congratulations."

"Thank you." She crossed her legs. "Are you still at Holt & Compton?"

He shrugged. "It's a good company."

That was another thing about Van, she thought. No adventurous spirit. He'd joined the environmental engineering firm right after graduate school and was now in middle management. He'd married someone a few years ago—a social worker—and moved into an upscale subdivision in a posh coastal town just north of the city.

Her mother still mentioned how Liv had let Van "get away." She told Tiffany she didn't consider it a loss.

"How's Alice?" Liv asked now.

Van winced. "Actually, that's why I'm here. I think she's cheating on me," he said. "With my brother."

Liv felt her mouth drop open. "With *Alby*? You're kidding."

"I wish I was joking, but I'm afraid it's true."

Albert "Alby" Ferguson was Van's older brother. She remembered him from high school, two years ahead of them. Lacrosse star. Prom king. Golden boy. The parents had doted on the eldest son, she recalled, while Van had been treated like an afterthought. Like Prince Harry, Liv thought. A spare.

She noticed Van's hand trembled as he sipped his coffee. Poor guy. Distress seeped out his pores like sweat.

"I hope I'm wrong," he said. "Last night she told me she decided to take a two-week vacation up at the chalet. Said she enrolled in an online writing class and needed to be alone. I don't believe her. I think she's going to meet him. Could you drive up to Carry Over on Monday, stay for a few days, and check things out?"

"Oh, I don't know, Van." Liv recalled the family's summer home and the small lake, Duckbill Pond, situated at the foot of the mountains in Carry Over Township. It was at least three hours north of Portland. Plus mixing business and friendship could be tricky. "I'm really swamped right now."

"Turn it into a vacation. There's a cabin for rent right across the lake from our place. I know the owner. I've already called, and it's available next week. I can make the arrangements as soon as you say yes."

"It's kind of last minute."

"Five thousand dollars."

Liv's eyebrows shot up. "That's too much!"

"No, it's not. I'm asking for a week of your time, on short notice. It's totally worth it. To me." Tears filled his eyes. "This is my marriage we're talking about, Liv. It's obvious you're busy, and this is sudden, so I'm willing to compensate you for the inconvenience. Just say the word, and I'll write you a check for two-thousand right now." He pulled a checkbook from his pants pocket. "Three grand more when you give me your final report. Will you help me?"

She hesitated. She had no time to go trotting up to east puckerbrush or wherever, but she did a quick calculation in her head and realized the amount he'd offered wasn't so extreme for an entire week of her time. Five-thousand dollars would fix her cash-flow problem. She'd be able to hire an assistant, at least for the summer.

Tempting, she thought. *Very tempting.*

"Let me take a look at my schedule." She opened her calendar app and scanned her calendar. With a little creative rearranging and a couple all-nighters this week, it might be doable. Zeroing in on one item, she made a face.

Except for Tuesday evening.

Jasper's parents were flying in from the Midwest, and he'd made dinner reservations at Fore Street, one of Portland's excellent restaurants. She squinted at the screen and calculated whether or not she could make the trip from Carry Over to Portland and back again without compromising the job.

Three hours on the road to get to Portland. A couple hours for dinner. Then coffee at Jasper's place before driving those three hours back.

Plenty of time for Alice to engage in a romantic rendezvous.

It wouldn't work. She couldn't take Van's money and disappear for eleven or twelve hours during prime *cinq à sept* time. The corners of her mouth curved up. She loved the French colloquialism for an extramarital tryst, finding it both elegant and descriptive. Jasper, however, wouldn't be amused when she told him she couldn't make it to dinner.

Her smile faded. She'd deal with it. She'd make him understand that she had to sacrifice her personal life for her business sometimes, especially now that she was on the cusp of real success.

Lively Investigations had to come first, she'd explain, and she'd promise to make it up to him later. Somehow. Any way he wanted.

She turned from the screen. "I'll do it." She handed Van a pen.

"Listen," she added as he filled in the amount and signed his name. "If I had to bet, I'd say the chances Alice and Alby are doing the nasty are slim to none."

"Noted."

"But she *could* be meeting someone else up there. In which case, you'd want to know, right?"

He ripped off the check, handed it to her. "Definitely. I need to know what I'm dealing with so I can fix my marriage."

Fixing a marriage rarely began with hiring an investigator, Liv thought, but with five-thousand dollars on the line, she'd be wise to keep that thought to herself.

Later, when everything went sideways, she wondered if she should have said something after all.

Chapter Two

• • • • • • • • • • • • • •

L iv pulled a notebook from a drawer and asked Van the first of
many uncomfortable but necessary questions. "What made you
suspect Alice was seeing someone else?"

"She's been acting weird. Distracted." He paused. His shoulders
drooped. "Flushed."

"Maybe she started going to a tanning salon."

He squirmed. "Not that kind of flushed."

Liv nodded, chagrined to have caused him further distress. She
was getting punchy, and it showed. "Um, okay. Is there anything
else that makes you think she's having an affair? Phone calls she
takes in the other room? Odd expenses on the credit cards?"

"Not really," Van mumbled.

"Well there must be someth—"

"She stopped sleeping with me, okay?" Van rubbed his face.
"This is so awkward."

"I've heard it all, believe me."

Van's knee jiggled. Blotches on his skin rose from the collar of
his polo shirt, covering his neck.

Liv pretended not to notice, kept her tone neutral. "Let's assume
she is having an affair and that's why she stopped sleeping with
you. Why Alby? Isn't he married?"

"Divorced. Since December. He and Emsley finalized right
before Christmas."

"Oh. I hadn't heard."

Albert Ferguson had married an artist, she recalled—a somewhat reclusive sculptor if she remembered correctly. They were both active in the Portland art scene.

The story of Alby Ferguson's success was legendary in town. When he was in his mid-twenties, eight years ago or thereabouts, he'd made a fortune on Wall Street. The specifics were murky. He cashed in, moved home to Portland, and opened an art gallery in the Old Port. He appeared in Portland's society columns, perfectly attired, smiling into the camera at this or that fundraiser, charity auction, art opening, or performance, sometimes with his wife, sometimes with friends.

The idea of Alby Ferguson having an affair with his sister-in-law seemed far-fetched.

She must have looked skeptical because Van said, "I know how crazy this sounds, but I have proof. Well, sort of."

"Yeah?" Liv kept her pen poised above the notepad. "Shoot."

"Thursdays are a half-day at her office. Several times she mentioned seeing a friend after work, but she didn't specify who. Last Thursday, I saw them together. Alby and Alice. I happened to be near her office building around noon and saw her get into his car. She came home for dinner and never said a word about meeting him. That's when I knew."

"You just happened to be outside her office building at the time she got off work?"

Van looked sheepish. "Okay, full-disclosure. I wanted to see this *friend* for myself, so I went to the sandwich shop across the street and waited for Alice to leave work. I sat at a table near the window to watch. She stood on the sidewalk, Alby's car pulled up at the curb, and she hopped in."

"Did you confront her? That night, I mean?"

"No." He sighed. "This is my wife and my brother we're talking about. If I accuse them of... of... *this* and I'm wrong, it will be a total mess. That's why I'm hiring you. Maybe I'm imagining things. Fine. Great. They'll never know I suspected them. I'll forget about it, and we can get on with our lives."

Sure, Liv thought. *But your marriage will still suck.*

She uncrossed her legs, reminded herself not to be judgmental. As someone who'd dated more than her share of damaged men, she was the last person to pass judgment.

"Is there anything else?"

"Yes. When she told me about going to Carry Over, I questioned her about the class. Before now, she'd never mentioned taking up writing. As far as I know it's never been an interest of hers. She mumbled something about creative outlets and turning thirty, blah blah blah. I'm pretty sure it's just an excuse to meet Alby."

Liv frowned. "Maybe your attitude explains the bedroom troubles."

The splotches spread to his cheeks. "I'm a good husband!"

"I'm sorry. I'm sure you are."

She watched the tension drain from his shoulders, the color in his cheeks subside.

"Anyway," he said, "It sounded pretty suspicious to me. We do have internet at the chalet, but not DSL. It's slow. Goes in and out a lot. Taking an online class would be difficult."

Liv took a note. "Could she use a hot-spot with her phone?"

"No cell service. We've called the provider many times, but they say there's nothing they can do. There are lots of dead spots up there in the woods. The chalet happens to be in one. Don't worry, though. The cabin you'll be staying in gets a decent signal. Most of the time. At least that's what the owner tells me."

"The chalet has a landline, I assume?"

"Yes."

"Okay. Let's think this through a bit. You said she's planning to be there for two weeks. Have you talked to Alby? I mean, do you know if he's going to be out of town, too?"

"I haven't asked him. We don't talk that much."

"Fair enough." Their conversation evolved into reminiscing about high school and band and other classmates, and Liv felt an unusual glow of nostalgia. A half-hour later, she showed Van to the door.

As they walked through the dreary reception room, she noticed the slight limp in Van's left leg. He'd sustained a knee injury playing football with his older, stronger brother as a pre-teen, she remembered. Because of that injury, he'd never been an athlete in high school and had gravitated toward music instead. Alby, meanwhile, earned trophies and attention for his physical prowess.

She mused now on the vicissitudes of life, the chance circumstances that set you on your path. They reached the door, and Van thanked her again. He gave her a bear-hug and she patted his back. "I really hope you're wrong about this, Van."

He stepped away, face glum. "Yeah, me, too."

• • • • •

She pulled an all-nighter.

After depositing Van's check into her bank account, Liv zipped over to Whole Foods for a salad and a large energy drink. She ate the meal at her desk, Mozart's *Don Giovanni* soaring from her computer speaker, while scanning Alice Ferguson's sparse social media profiles. She was an infrequent poster.

A few photos of Busterdoodle and Van. Someone's birthday party with cake and candles. Pictures of the beach, of waves crashing against a rock pier, of sunsets. Flowers in a backyard border. A motivational saying on a pink background. A plate of charcuterie. A meme from *The Office*. A meme from *Gilmore Girls*. A photo and post about a French Country armoire. A recipe for tortellini soup. Just basic bland stuff posted by someone without much interest in social media.

Liv could relate. She kept a bare-bones business page for Lively Investigations that included an address, a phone number, and a link to her website but not much else. So much on socials was vapid. When it wasn't, it was cringy. At worst, it was incriminating.

People had no idea how much information an investigator—or a bad actor—could gather and use against them just from a few social media profiles. Not to mention the creepers she called the "Hello Dear Guys."

She scrolled down the feed, finding no pics or mentions of Alby except one family shot of the Ferguson clan in front of a giant Christmas tree. Parents Gavin and Tanya with Alby, Van and Alice, plus aunts and uncles and assorted cousins.

Everyone wore matching L.L.Bean flannel shirts and grinned big toothy smiles at the camera. Busterdoodle, tongue lolling out halfway to his chest, and a couple of more dignified brown Labradors sat at their feet.

They looked, she thought, like an aspirational, downeast Maine version of the Kennedys.

Liv took notes on the legal pad. She flipped the page and copied names from Alice's list of friends. Maybe there were rumors going around regarding Van and Alice's marriage. People—not just women—loved to gossip. She'd found men to be just as chatty as their female counterparts, but of course the stereotype of the gossipy woman persisted.

Misogyny springs eternal, she thought, tapping her fingers on top of her desk and frowning at the list. It was shorter than you'd expect for someone in the Ferguson's social sphere.

Alice kept to herself, it seemed. Or she didn't make friends easily. Or, unlike most people these days, she kept her private life private.

In other words, Alice might be just the kind of person capable of conducting an extramarital affair and keeping it under wraps.

Liv labeled a manila file folder, placed her notes into it, and slid the folder aside. Switching to digital filing was another task she could give an assistant.

A sharp pain stabbed her neck, and she realized she'd been staring at the screen, focused and still, for too long. If she wanted to make it through the night, she'd better get up and move.

She stood and cycled through a few yoga poses. Sun salutation. Lion's breath. Triangle. Feeling looser—but also sleepier—she sucked down a cup of coffee before tackling the mound of paperwork on her desk.

By 2 a.m. she'd organized everything into piles, topped each pile with a neon-colored sticky note, and paid all the bills. Ignoring the renewed tightness in her shoulders, she sent second notices on overdue invoices to several pokey clients. When that was done, she emailed her current clients and, citing an emergency, pushed deadlines back a week. For the inconvenience, she offered an apology and a ten percent discount on her services for the rest of the year.

Maybe that was overkill, she thought, but reputation and word-of-mouth mattered. If any of her clients said they couldn't wait, she'd refer them to another agency.

But it would kill her to do it.

Just before sunrise and punchy with exhaustion, she called it quits.

She'd made a huge dent in her work and still had a couple days to tidy up loose ends before she left for Carry Over on Saturday morning. Satisfied with her progress, she locked the door to the office and walked down the dim, narrow hall feeling lightheaded and strangely buoyant.

Low, security-only lights cast gloomy shadows in the cavernous Fiber Fox Cooperative makerspace from whom she rented her office suite. She strode past the off-set printers, weaving looms, and rows of industrial sewing machines, her heels echoing on the worn wood floor boards, but she felt secure. Fiber artist and entrepreneur Amanda Fox had finally taken Liv's advice and installed outside lights, surveillance cameras, and a good alarm system.

The first pink light of morning tinged the sky as she stepped into the parking lot. She breathed in the morning air, the scent of the ocean carried in on cool, summer currents, and felt happiness swell like a balloon in her chest. Yes, she'd been brought up by her hospital administrator father and socialite mother to enter into a privileged and cushy adulthood after college, but she'd fought for independence and a grittier, more satisfying career as a female private investigator instead.

Sure, there were challenges—like growing too fast and overextending herself—but she possessed the determination and intelligence to meet those challenges and thrive. What were a few nights of lost sleep if it meant a boost to Lively Investigations? She thought of her business as her baby. She'd do whatever she could to ensure it survived and grew into the boutique agency she envisioned.

Liv allowed herself a moment of giddy, exhausted pride as she crossed the shabby parking lot toward her car. A seagull screeched from its perch on the dumpster. It was then she remembered she'd have to break the news about Tuesday to Jasper. Her mood deflated.

She'd think about that later, she decided, slipping into the car. She yawned and pulled out of the lot. Right now, she just needed some sleep.

Chapter Three

• • • • • • • • • • • • • • •

Her cell's ringtone woke her from a deep sleep. She thrust out her hand, scrabbled for the phone, and opened one eye to check the display. Nine-twenty a.m. *Ugh.* She put the phone to her ear. "H'lo."

"Why didn't you tell me Jasper's parents will be in Maine next week?"

Liv wiggled to a sitting position and rubbed her face. "Hi, Mom."

With just over four hours of sleep and another long day ahead of her, the last thing she needed was to argue with Tiffany. She winced. "I didn't know you'd be interested?"

As expected, the voice on the other end rose two octaves. "Of course we're interested! I could have planned a nice dinner for the six of us. The Temples will think we're rude. Honestly, Olivia, sometimes I wonder about you."

That made two of them.

Liv kept her voice to a placating *sotto voce.* "They aren't going to think you're rude. They're coming here in order to spend time with their son, not me. Certainly not you and Dad."

Tiffany's signature gold bangles clinked. "You sound weird. Are you still in bed?"

"I was literally up all night. Working. I got home just before sunrise."

Silence. Liv dreaded a lecture about sleep hygiene and wrinkles, but Tiffany let it drop. Her mother was nothing if not focused.

"Do they know about you?"

"Who? Jasper's parents? Yesssss."

"And do they know your family lives in Portland?"

"I suppose so."

"Then they want to meet us." Paper rustled as Tiffany flipped through her datebook. "What does their schedule look like? Maybe there's still time to salvage the situation."

Liv slumped against her pillows, put her phone onto the bed, and silently screamed. She picked it up again. "That's a nice thought, but it's not going to work."

"Why not?"

"Because I'm going out of town next week."

A beat. "You're going out of town next week."

"I just got a big case. It's not ideal timing, but the situation requires immediate attention. I'm heading up north Saturday morning, and I'll be there all week."

"How convenient. Have you told Jasper?"

"Tonight. I'll tell him tonight." *Or tomorrow. Yeah, tomorrow would be better.*

Silence.

"It's a very important case," Liv repeated.

"Well, if it's really important…"

The sarcasm grated on Liv's already jumpy nerves. She felt like she was thirteen again, sparring with Tiffany about clothes or black eyeliner or skipping her sailing lessons in order to go to the arcade in Old Orchard Beach with a public school boy she met at Hot Topic in the mall.

Liv knew Tiffany disapproved of her private investigation business, an occupation she regarded as one step below cleaning toilets for a living, but would it kill her to be supportive once in a while?

"Mom, I'm sorry, okay? I didn't tell you about Jasper's parents because I was worried about meeting them. And then I got this case yesterday and it's…"

"Important. Yes, you've been quite clear." Tiffany's bracelets clinked again. Her voice was cool. "Why don't you want to meet them?"

"I don't know. It's, uh, so soon. We've only been dating since April. Just over three months. What if it doesn't work out?"

The cool evaporated. Alarm sounded in the older woman's voice. "Why wouldn't it work out? What have you done now?"

"I haven't *done* anything. I'm just not sure it's going to be a long-term kind of thing."

Tiffany sighed and Liv pictured her disappointed frown. "Olivia, listen to me. You're thirty years old. Most of your friends are married already, starting families. Look at Ashleigh. It's time for you to grow up, take on some adult responsibilities, and settle down."

Liv made a face. Her best friend, Ashleigh, was pregnant. With twins. Lately, she'd been so focused on all things maternity and babies, their girl's nights out and shopping weekends and marathon phone conversations had dwindled to texts and occasional brief and unsatisfactory calls.

Hurt stabbed at Liv's heart. Tiffany always did have a knack for hitting the sore points. She pushed back. "Just because I'm not ready to make a life-long commitment to a man you happen to like," Liv told her mother, "doesn't mean I'm not responsible."

"You're being immature and selfish. As usual."

"And as usual, you're upset because I'm not doing exactly what you want, when you want."

"Did you ever stop to think it's because I'm worried about you? I want you to be safe. I want you to be taken care of. Is that so horrible?"

Guilt softened Liv's response. She supposed this was Tiffany's way of showing love. What was that stuff Ashleigh always talked about, love languages? Something about recognizing the other person's preferred way of expressing and receiving love like touch or quality time. Normal ways like that.

Her mother, Liv thought, had developed a love language all her own: benevolent harassment.

"Mom, I appreciate that. I really do, but I can take care of myself. I have to live life my own way."

"Oh, believe me, I'm aware."

Mother and daughter sighed in unison. A few seconds ticked by. Finally, Tiffany broke the silence. "If there's a problem between you and Jasper, you should talk to him about it. Nothing good comes from keeping secrets. Believe me, I have stories."

"You have stories? What kind of stories?"

Tiffany ignored that question. "Jasper's a good man, Olivia Rose. Take my advice for once. Talk to him."

Chapter Four

● ● ● ● ● ● ● ● ● ● ● ● ● ● ●

"Omigod, what is that stench?" Liv dropped a canvas grocery bag by the door of Jasper's apartment and put fingers beneath her nose. It was Friday, late afternoon. They'd planned to spend the evening together at his place after a hectic work week for both of them. Though they'd spoken on the phones several times, she still hadn't told Jasper about her upcoming trip.

Jasper, chopping something on a large cutting board in the galley kitchen, turned his head to grin at her. "Kimchi. I'm experimenting with a new recipe. Don't worry. You don't need to eat it."

Tall and gangly with dark, tousled hair and blue eyes that crinkled at the corners when he smiled, Dr. Jasper Temple looked more like a television doctor than a real one. Her parents had played matchmaker in the spring, and despite Liv's initial doubts, she'd been able to give the good doctor—and commitment—a chance.

At least, she was trying.

They shared a love of the *X-Files*, cryptozoology, and all things sci-fi, supernatural, and strange. She liked that he knew his way around the kitchen. He liked that she knew her way around the bedroom. They complemented each other, she thought, but sometimes she worried. Uneasiness crept into her like fog.

She took off her shoes and crossed the floor in bare feet. The tile was cool against her hot soles. Jasper watched her with a gleam in his eyes as she sashayed toward him in her little white linen dress. She felt weak at the knees. Even a little dizzy because, despite her misgivings, he had that effect on her.

Or else it was the fish sauce.

She made a face, deflecting her emotions with humor as she approached. Fumes rose from the prep surface in front of him. "Ugh. It smells like Lucifer's outhouse in here."

"Nice comparison," he said. "Classy."

"Sorry." She tilted her head up for a kiss. "Just thought you should know."

He smiled. After bending down to brush her lips with his, Jasper went back to slicing scallions, easily manipulating the chef's knife with his large hand.

A crockery bowl filled with diced daikon radishes, carrots, ginger, red pepper flakes and garlic—along with the Korean fish sauce and fermented shrimp—sat on the kitchen's trendy concrete counter. Another bowl off to the side contained salted cabbage. Glass canning jars gleamed on the drying rack, ready to be filled.

She wrapped her arms around his waist, pressed her cheek against his back. "That's a lotta cabbage. You're really getting into this pickling thing, huh?"

"Thanks to you."

He was barefoot as well and comfortable in jeans and a white button down shirt. She was pleased to see he'd tied the linen chef's apron over his clothes. She'd commissioned it from Amanda Fox. On the apron front, a stylized graphic of a human heart accompanied the words, "My Heart Beats for You, Doc."

She'd presented the apron to him on his birthday in June along with a book on lacto-fermentation she'd found while combing the shelves of a tiny culinary bookstore in Boston.

Since then he'd been obsessed. He'd experimented with pickles, sauerkraut, dilly beans, and several kimchi recipes, looking for the perfect blend of spices and heat. Glass jars lined a couple shelves of his pantry already.

She peered around his arm as he picked up a crooked brown root. "More ginger?" she said.

"Yeah. I think so. Going by smell."

"Are you sure you haven't burned your nasal receptors into oblivion?"

"What do you know about nasal receptors?"

She put her face against his back again. "Don't forget, my dad's been in the hospital biz my whole life. I grew up tripping over med journals. I was the first girl in my class to know what a prolapsed uterus was."

He laughed. She swatted his backside before stepping to the refrigerator. "Ah, goodie!" She grabbed a chilled, pink-labeled bottle of Veuve Clicquot Brut Rosé and took it to the counter to remove the foil and cage.

She popped the cork, filled a wine glass, and leaned a hip on the counter to watch him massage the seasoning paste into the cabbage. Remembering what she had to tell him, dread welled up inside her.

Maybe her bad news would go over better after some wine and food.

And sex.

But only after he'd showered the stench of fish sauce off him.

"I'm gonna open some windows and air this place out," she told him. She carried her glass from the galley kitchen to the combination dining and living area. Here, a brick wall with two tall windows faced Portland's working waterfront just across Commercial Street. The original exposed beams and pipes added to the industrial vibe of the former shipping warehouse.

A large-screen TV faced a sectional couch in distressed leather, and on another wall, floor to ceiling bookshelves held an impressive collection of sci-fi and fantasy novels along with medical books and cryptozoology accounts.

Near the books, a full-sized skeletal model named Horace held a cigar between his grinning teeth. Jasper had covered Horace's round skull with a jaunty Portland Sea Dogs cap. Liv wandered over and adjusted the cap for no other reason than nerves. She tapped the flute with her fingernails. She knew she had to tell Jasper about her impending trip up north. Her chest tightened, and suddenly she found it hard to breathe.

She strode to the windows and opened them as much as they'd go. She took a deep, cleansing breath as a salt-tinged breeze stirred the floor-length, white sheer curtains.

From this vantage point, she could see boats chugging in the harbor and several islands out in the bay. The ferry churned toward the terminal at the end of Franklin Street while seagulls wheeled overhead. A soft, haze of clouds low on the horizon hinted at a nice sunset.

An idea came to her. "Hey," she called, turning her back to the window. "Looks like a nice sunset. Why don't we pack a picnic and go out on the ferry? We can get some ice-cream on Cliff Island, maybe see some seals if we're lucky."

In the kitchen, a drawer opened and shut. "Sounds like fun," Jasper said, "but my parents fly in on Monday, remember? I thought we'd do the ferry thing that night."

Guilt gnawed at her chest like some radioactive rodent. He wanted this visit to be special, and she was going to spoil everything. But it couldn't be helped, she told herself. Five thousand dollars was too much to pass up. "That sounds nice," she said, her voice faint.

She heard glass jars rattling and then a self-conscious chuckle. "Just wait until my mother finds out I've been making pickles. For fun, no less. Her eyes are going to pop out when she sees the pantry."

"Mmm-hmmm."

He wandered into the room. Even wiping his hands on a dish towel and smelling like fermented fish guts, he radiated good, clean, All-American Boy Scout. She felt sick when he added, "They're very excited to meet you, by the way."

She winced.

"Don't worry. They're gonna love you." He walked over and gave her shoulders a squeeze. She had to force herself not to shrug his hands off her. A wild feeling came over her, like she wanted to race to the door and fly away and not look back.

She took a deep breath and gathered her courage. If she didn't tell him now, when he'd given her the perfect moment, it would make things much worse later on. "It's not that. I have to tell you something, and you're not going to like it."

His hands dropped from her shoulders, and his voice went wary. "What is it?"

"I can't make it on Tuesday. Something's come up."

He stared at her for a second. "You're bailing." He said it as a statement, not even questioning it.

"I'm not bailing. Well, I am, but not the way you think. I have to go up north to this place called Carry Over Township. I'll be gone the whole week."

"What for?"

"A case."

"Right." Jasper stepped away from her, threw the towel over his shoulder, and stalked toward the kitchen. "Whatever, Liv."

She followed him. "Look, I know you really wanted me to meet your parents, but this came up suddenly, and the guy's desperate. He's an old friend. He needs my help."

She didn't want to tell him that Lively Investigations—that *she*—needed money. Maybe it was pride or ego or whatever, but she wanted to be self-sufficient. Taking Van's case solved the problem. Jasper didn't have to like it. In fact, she kind of resented having to explain herself to him.

"What am I supposed to tell my parents?"

"The truth. That I had to go away for work."

"So you want me to lie."

"No, I..." She narrowed her eyes. "Wait a minute. You think I'm making this up?"

"I don't know, Liv. What I *think* is that you're freaked out about meeting my parents and found a convenient reason to cancel. Couldn't you drive home Tuesday afternoon and head back up Wednesday morning?"

She pointed at him around her near-empty glass of pink bubbly. "One, I've been hired to watch and report on someone's activities. It's a three-hour trip—each way. That leaves too much of a time gap for this job. And two, yeah, okay. You're right. I think it's too soon to meet your parents. There. I said it. We've only been dating three months. You're pushing me."

"I've met your parents," he countered. He turned, picked up the knife, and began chopping again.

"That doesn't count. You met my parents before you met me, and the three of you conspired…"

He interrupted. "Fine. You made your point." He put the knife down on the counter. "I'm really disappointed. This is the first time my folks have been to Maine. I took a few days off from work to show them around, and I really wanted you to meet them."

"I'm sure they'd rather spend time alone with you. I'll meet them next time. What's the big hurry?"

"It's just dinner, Olivia. Not a marriage proposal."

A silence, heavy and fraught, fell between them. Finally, she said, "I know you're upset, and I'm sorry, but I'm not going to change my mind. I'm doing this for my business. It's important to me."

"More important than I am, obviously." His mouth tightened. He wiped his hands on the apron. "I'm going to take a shower."

"Do you want me to stay?"

"Do what you want. That's how you operate anyway."

He scraped the vegetables into a bowl, put the bowl in the refrigerator, and slammed the door shut. She crossed her arms as he untied his apron, balled it up in his hands, and threw it onto the counter.

She heard him stomp up the stairs to the primary bed and bath suite, listened as the water blasted from the tile shower system's rainfall head and multiple sprays.

She could stick around, she thought. Could try to cajole and appease him after he cooled off. But she really didn't want to talk to him any more. She frowned. If he couldn't understand her business was just as important to her as his career was to him, then too bad. He could spend the evening alone packing kimchi into glass jars and see how he liked it.

She hoped he'd be satisfied with his solitary—and stinky—Friday evening.

She rinsed her glass and left it to dry on the small metal rack next to the sink. She put on her shoes and picked up her canvas bag and went home.

Chapter Five

• • • • • • • • • • • • • •

The next morning, Saturday, Liv woke early and packed for her week at the lake.

She gathered a true crime book she'd been wanting to read plus notebooks, pens, and a journal Ashleigh had given her for her last birthday. Maybe she'd actually try writing about her thoughts and feelings every morning as Ash suggested.

Remembering her fight with Jasper, she made a strangled noise in the back of her throat. She felt guilty for bolting the previous night, on top of feeling guilty for reneging on dinner with his parents.

To be honest with herself, she knew he was right about her. She wasn't all in on the relationship, no matter what she claimed and how hard she tried. If keeping a diary helped her figure out why she couldn't totally commit, it might be worth the time and effort. Jasper might be worth the effort.

Suddenly, she missed him. The missing felt like a small ache in the space between her ribs. She wondered if he was still in bed, if he was lying awake thinking about her, missing her. Regretting the fight, as well. Part of her wished she could go to him, slide into bed and curl up at his side, run a hand along his hip and kiss the tender spot at the nape of his neck…

Let it go, her impatient inner voice scolded. *You have work to do.*

She grimaced and set the journal on top of the book. The damage was done. Best to concentrate on the case, earn the money she needed, and worry about making up with Jasper later.

She gathered her laptop, a tablet computer, and a few key pieces of investigative equipment. Binoculars. A camcorder. Power banks. Extra phone. Cords. Sig P365 handgun and holster. She placed all these into her travel bag—smooth, luxurious chestnut leather—and set the bag beside the door. A small cross-body held her usual wallet, keys, pepper spray, and lipstick.

She'd begun folding clothes into one of her late grandmother's vintage Louis Vuitton suitcases when the door buzzed. She strode down the hall and peeked at the monitor screen she'd installed next to the door. Her heart thumped when she saw Jasper standing outside, a morose look on his face. She pressed the button to let him in, heard him bounding up the two flights of stairs two steps at a time, and opened the door.

"Hey," he said, huffing mightily as he reached the landing. "Glad I caught you. Can I come in?"

She stepped aside. Now that he was here, her doubts came rushing back. She gave him a wary look. "I'm packing."

"Can we talk about last night?" He followed her to the bedroom. He smelled good, like expensive cologne and fabric softener. Her body hummed in response.

So she wouldn't throw herself into his arms, she turned her back and placed a pair of jean shorts into the suitcase. She folded her favorite Ralph Lauren sweater, the one with the dog on the front, and put that on top of the shorts. "If you have something to say, say it."

"Are you going to look at me?"

She whirled, hands on hips. "Okay, I'm looking."

He was still breathing hard from his dash up the stairs. *Boy needed to do more cardio,* she thought.

He cleared his throat. "Look. I'm still upset, but I didn't want you to go away for a week with this hanging between us. I'm sorry about how I reacted last night. I was surprised. I thought we were on the same page here."

She tried to sidle around him. "'Scuse me. I need some socks."

He grabbed her by the hips and held her still and looked her in the eyes so intently she couldn't look away. He pleaded. "I'm sorry if I misread your signals or that you misread mine. I thought I was very clear about my intentions all along. I want to be in a committed relationship. With you." He shook his head. "No. That's not right."

"You don't want to be in a relationship with me?" she said.

"I want to get married."

Still anchored to him at the waist, she reared her head back and stared at him. "You're joking."

He laughed at the look on her face. "Not right this minute or even this year, but yes. I guess I need to know we're heading in that direction."

She had no idea what to say. He took that as an opening. He slid an arm up to her shoulders and pulled her closer again. He felt warm and strong and forceful, and she melted just a little. He said, "I'm crazy about you, Olivia Lively. I think you're a little bit crazy about me, too. Meeting my parents seemed like the next logical step."

Desperate for clarity of mind—which was pretty impossible smooshed up hip to hip like that—Liv shrugged herself out of his grasp and stepped back. "Jasper…"

"Don't say anything right now. I know you aren't ready. I didn't know it yesterday, but now I do. We haven't really talked about our timetable, and…"

"Our timetable? It's only been three months!"

"You're right. After you left last night, I realized I'd been a jerk. We should have talked. I should have told you what I was thinking and given you the chance to do the same. That's why I'm here. I wanted to catch you before you left so that I could tell you I'm fine with the status quo, at least for now. I'm sorry I shut down instead of talking this out with you last night. That was stupid of me."

"And I'm sorry I bailed at the last minute."

"Apology accepted." He moved close to her again, put his arms around her. "From now on, we talk when we have a problem, okay? I can see us building a life together, and part of that is learning how to disagree without blowing up the entire relationship. We won't always be on the same page, but we do have to communicate."

She snorted but stayed in his arms. "And that's why you came over here this morning? To tell me we need to communicate?"

"Yes. That." He maneuvered her closer to the bed. "And we have unfinished business."

She arched her eyebrows and teased, "Unfinished business like figuring out how to make this right with your parents? Maybe we can fly out and visit them this fall? I'd love to see where you grew up. Plus, you know, crop circles."

"Shhhh." He kissed her, long and deep, leaving her breathless. He pulled away just enough to search her eyes. "So...we good?"

Liv felt uneasy, but she nodded. "Uh-huh."

"Good. Because you left last night before we got to the hot stuff." He let go of her, grabbed the suitcase from the bed, and placed it on the floor. Without warning, he pushed her onto the bright colors of her summer comforter.

She squeaked and sat up on her elbows. "Hot stuff like the kimchi?"

"No. Not like the kimchi."

She grinned as he settled on top of her. His lips hovered above hers.

She whispered, "Well, what then?"

He kissed her again. Hard mouth. Eager tongue. Hand running up under her shirt. Fingers tugging at the button of her soft, faded jeans. Panties next and those fingers of his, precision tools useful for heart surgery and this, this, oh this.

He stopped and got out of bed. She blinked. "Where are you going?"

"Hold that thought."

Flushed and gritting her teeth in frustration, she collapsed back against the pillows. She heard him rummaging in her cupboards and then his bare feet slapping down the hallway. "Close your eyes," he said before he reached the room.

"Okay, they're closed."

She heard him enter the room, felt the mattress move under his weight as he lay beside her. Her breath grew shallow as anticipation built.

"I saw this in a movie once," he whispered. "Open your mouth."

She did. She felt a warm trickle on her tongue, tasted the sweetness of honey, felt his hot mouth closing over hers. And then she was lost.

• • • • •

By the time she left Portland a little after 9 a.m., the sun was sparkling off the Atlantic. Coffee steamed in the cupholder of her Corolla. Vivaldi's *The Four Seasons* soared from her speakers.

Exhilarated, body humming with recent pleasures, she opened her window and headed inland up I-95 to Waterville to catch Rt. 201 west toward Caratunk and The Forks. Three hours later, she stopped for groceries at the tiny local market in Carry Over Township.

Carry Over was an unincorporated village nestled in the great expanse of western Maine wilderness. The market offered basic groceries, ice cream, hot coffee, and pizza by the slice or whole. Near the entrance, a beat-up local newspaper box sat beside a DVD rental kiosk. Two gas pumps squatted in the middle of the parking lot.

She filled her tank, picked up a paper, and went inside. She loaded a cart with necessities and chatted about the weather with the sole cashier, a middle-aged woman with a sleeve of tattoos, a partially-shaved head, and a nice smile. Supplies procured, she followed printed-out directions to the rental cabin on Duckbill Pond.

The small cabin sat on a half-acre of woods situated off a narrow, winding camp road. The dirt road ran three-quarters of the way around a small, clear, spring-fed lake rimmed by towering white pines. Cabins and camps of various sizes and vintages dotted the shoreline. What looked like logging trails intersected the road in several places along the way.

She found the cabin's key in its hiding place and opened the door. She moved through the cabin, inspecting the open kitchen/dining/living area, the small bathroom, and the surprisingly large bedroom. The decor trended more toward 1985 meets side-of-the-road chic than crisp, modern cottage, but there was a cozy screen porch overlooking the water plus comfy old chairs, a sofa, and a newly repainted dining set in a pretty soft green.

The smell of lemon furniture polish mingled with the scent of pine-needle sachet pillows tucked here and there. She went into the cozy bedroom and turned down the blankets. The linens were stiff, as if they'd been line-dried in the sun. A faded peach and aqua quilt had been folded across the bottom edge.

She went back to her car for her bags and groceries. She packed the small fridge with the food, tucked her clothes into the chipped antique dresser, and wandered outside to make friends with a family of crows strutting around the yard.

They flapped into tree branches to caw at her as she made her way to the dock. Staring across the lake, she lifted her binoculars and studied the Ferguson's sprawling log chalet directly opposite the cabin.

Situated on a sloped lot, the chalet appeared to be three stories if you included the partial daylight basement. Beneath a soaring, peaked roof, a wall of windows and two sets of glass French doors faced the water. The views must be incredible from that room, she thought.

A small bass fishing boat chugged toward her, engine at a low rumble. The smell of the pine trees mingled with the scent of the pond, a soft, slightly-muddy perfume. Liv sucked in a deep breath, inhaled the fresh, Maine air, and felt her shoulders completely relax for the first time in months. *No wonder Alice wanted to come up here for a week or two,* she thought. *It's heaven.*

She turned her attention to the chalet again, taking in more details. A short, one-story wing extended off the main body of the chalet near the driveway. A deep deck belted the entire front. The deck created the roof for a portico-type parking space and a screened-in porch on the basement level. Squinting, she spotted Alice's green Subaru parked in the shadows of the portico.

Liv lowered the binoculars. Was Alice there to write, as she'd told Van? Or to indulge in passionate love-making with her brother-in-law?

After it retreated down the lake, the bass boat's gentle wake rocked the floating dock like a cradle. Listening to the sound of water lapping gently against the wood, Liv wondered how likely it was that Van's suspicions were justified.

If handsome, wealthy, socially-connected Alby Ferguson was having an affair, wouldn't the woman be a stunning model type, not his brother's mousy social worker wife?

Of course, she mused, sometimes the quiet ones surprised you.

Liv understood all too well about extra-marital affairs. She'd been with married men on a few occasions. Unwittingly once. Not so unwittingly a couple other times. She wasn't proud of it.

She'd always been drawn to the bad boys, maybe as a reaction to her privileged upbringing or maybe just genetic disposition. Their uninhibited, risk-agreeable, fallen-angel vibes did it for her. At first, anyway. Inevitably she realized all that bravado hid a streak of insecurity or narcissism or just plain mean, and she ended it.

Ashleigh once asked her if there'd been any abuse in her past, and she'd said no. She hadn't experienced anything more traumatic than accidentally locking herself in a steamer trunk as a young child. While this led to a fear of being stuck in tight, dark spaces, it had nothing to do with her predilection for dangerous, unstable, unavailable men. She simply found vanilla rather bland.

She squinted at the chalet, sunlight bouncing off the top floor windows. Maybe Alice craved the same kind of excitement? Seven years into marriage with beige, boring Donovan with his beige, boring job and beige, boring dog might have pushed her over the edge into an affair.

Liv winced at this ungenerous thought. Poor Van. Boring or not, he was a nice guy. If Alice was cheating on him, with his brother or someone else, he deserved to know the truth. Hopefully she'd be able to give her old friend the answers he needed.

Perhaps in the solitude and quiet of the deep, Maine woods, she'd find some answers in her own heart, as well.

Chapter Six

• • • • • • • • • • • • • •

Later that afternoon, Liv situated a musty-cushioned chaise on the dock and slathered sunscreen onto her arms and legs. Sunlight danced on the water. Breathing in the scent of coconut sunscreen and lake and pine needles, she perched a straw hat on top of her head, slid sunglasses over her eyes, and opened her true crime book. Every third page, she looked up and peered at the chalet across the lake through her high-powered binoculars.

A couple hours passed before Alice emerged onto the chalet's deck.

Liv sat up and refocused the lenses. Alice wore a plain navy tank suit with a navy and white striped sarong tied around her hips. Big, dark Jackie Onassis-style sunglasses and a floppy striped hat obscured her face.

Liv tracked Alice's movements as she made her way down the stairs and unspooled a long hose from beneath the deck. Alice drew on a pair of gardening gloves and watered each of the flower beds, spray glittering in the sun, and coiled the hose again.

Sounds of boat motors and loud, happy conversations and the splashing shrieks of kids jumping off docks interrupted the quieter call of birds and the slap of waves against the dock.

When Alice finished the garden chores, she removed her gloves, tossed them onto the deck, and strolled to the gravel beach in front of the chalet. Liv followed Alice with the binoculars as she shed the wrap, waded into the water, and breast-stroked to a small, square float anchored a few yards off-shore.

Liv grabbed her camera and, making sure the timestamp option was activated, snapped a few pics while Alice sunbathed. Ten minutes later, Alice made a graceful, shallow dive off the float, swam back to the beach, picked up her wrap, and returned to the chalet. Alone.

Using her cell phone, Liv called Van to report. She was pleased that, as promised, the cabin had reception.

"Alice is the only one here," she said, telling him about his wife's solitary swim. "And she's keeping the plants watered."

"Keep watching," he said. She heard Busterdoodle barking in the background. "Quiet, you goof!" Van yelled. In a regular voice he said, "Sorry about that."

"What's up with your dog?"

"Squirrel in the backyard."

"Loud," she said, laughing. "Does he do that often?"

"Only when he sees them." Van chuckled, too. "Call me tomorrow."

· · · · ·

On Sunday, after an hour of fruitless surveillance from the dock, Liv went for a long run.

She stayed on the narrow camp road that squiggled down to clusters of cabins and wound around the lake and made sure to pass the Ferguson place. All was quiet at the chalet. Alice's car remained under the portico, no other vehicles in the driveway. Next door, a few neighbor kids cannonballed off a dock, and the scent of mesquite plumed into the air as someone messed around with an egg-shaped smoker grill.

When she called Van to give her daily report, he thanked her for keeping him posted. "I hope you're managing to enjoy yourself a little too," he said.

"I haven't been this relaxed in months," she told him. "I should be paying you."

"Nah," he said. "You're doing me a solid. If it turns out I'm wrong, it will be worth every penny."

She could hear the smile in his voice and felt guilty for thinking he was such a dud all these years. "You really are a good guy, Donovan Ferguson," she told him.

He chuckled. "I wish you'd known that in high school."

"Girls are stupid in high school. Alice picked well."

"I've tried to make her happy. I hope she remembers that."

"Oh, Van. I'm sure she does."

The trite words slipped out of her mouth like a curl of cigarette smoke and drifted across the lake.

· · · · ·

Monday, mid-morning, Liv drove back to the small village center. She checked out a couple of farm stands set up along the side of the road. It was early in the season, but the farmers and homesteaders made the most of early crops and supplemented limited produce with home-baked goods, jellies, and pickles from last year's bounty.

After loading up with raspberries, microgreens, radishes, early cukes, homemade bread, butter, and jam, she pulled into the Carry Over Market to get some bug spray.

The mosquitos, she'd discovered, were vicious at dusk.

She'd just reached into the back seat for a reusable shopping bag when a silver Audi purred into the lot and parked in a spot behind her. Liv froze, eyes tracking the car through the rear window for a couple of seconds. Fearing notice, she turned around and slouched in her seat. Adjusting the rear view mirror, Liv watched the driver's door open. A man emerged, tall, blond-haired, and impeccably dressed.

She recognized Alby immediately—and not only from the photos she'd added to her file. He looked like Van, she thought, but he had a stronger jawline and broader shoulders. He carried himself with a confidence that made him appear like a taller and more handsome version of her friend.

Maybe Alice thought so, too.

Alby rounded the end of the car and opened the passenger door. Sure enough, petite, taffy-haired Alice Ferguson popped up, a big smile on her face. Liv slid further down in her seat, made sure her sunglasses were in place, and watched as the two strolled toward the market. When she felt safe from notice, Liv grabbed her phone, pointed it out the rear window, and took a few hasty photos.

Alby wore a Red Sox cap with a pair of preppy pink shorts and an untucked white shirt rolled at the sleeves. He looked relaxed, strolling next to his brother's wife without a care in the world. No furtive glancing around. As for Alice, her beige, sleeveless linen dress hung to mid-calf, not at all fancy or seductive, and she wore green-tinted sunglasses over her eyes. She carried several cloth totes.

Nothing about their body language seemed especially intimate. They didn't hold hands or even walk close together.

As Liv snapped away, Alby turned his head and said something to Alice. She nodded and answered, and then they disappeared inside the store.

Perhaps they were just being cautious, Liv thought as she kept an eye on the door. The Fergusons had summered in Carry Over for decades. It wouldn't be unusual for Alby, Van, and Alice to be in town at the same time. Alice and Alby shopping for a few groceries wouldn't raise eyebrows with the townsfolk. Holding hands might.

She considered following them inside, but decided it would be too risky. Alby might recognize her and be spooked. She decided to wait in the car.

Fifteen minutes later, Liv took more photos of Alby and Alice exiting the market, canvas bags bulging with purchases. Alby opened the door for Alice, strolled to the driver's seat, and took off, engine revving. Liv pulled out of the parking lot behind them and followed the Audi at a discreet distance to Duckbill Pond.

When the Audi entered the chalet's driveway, Liv continued

down the road. She turned around a few houses down and then drove by again in the other direction. As Alby and Alice lugged the groceries into the house, she slowed. Alby noticed. His eyes locked on her car. She quickly looked away and accelerated, hoping they'd think she was just another lost tourist looking for a friend's lakefront home.

Back at the cabin around noon, Liv called Van to report on the latest development. "I hate to say it, but you might be right. Alby arrived today. I saw them together at the market and followed them to the chalet."

Van let out an expletive.

Liv tried to reassure him. "This doesn't prove they're having an affair. It could be completely innocent. I think you should come up and talk to them."

"What? No."

"Listen for a second. It's Alby's camp, too, remember? Your parents deeded the property to both of you when they moved to Florida, right? It's summer. It's hot. Maybe Alby decided to go up to camp, not realizing Alice was already here. Do you and Alby have schedules planned ahead of time? I mean, weeks blocked out or whatever?"

Van sighed. "My parents come up at the end of August for a couple of weeks, and we all gather for a long weekend at that time. Alby doesn't like Duckbill Pond much. I can count on one hand the number of times he's actually used it. He prefers resort hotels, European vacations, oceanfront cottages, that sort of thing. If he does open it for a weekend with a bunch of his friends or whatever, he always tells me beforehand. I've never known him to be up there on his own. If he's there, it's for Alice."

The words hung between them for a moment. Finally, Liv said, "I'm so sorry, Van."

"I'm staying put. If I come up, they'll just deny everything. Keep an eye on them, okay? I'll confront her—them—when she comes home." Liv thought he sounded resigned, but then his voice tightened. "Friggin' Alby. Always has to be the center of attention. Always competitive. Couldn't even let me have this one thing better than him."

"What do you mean?"

"I don't know. His marriage busts up, so that means I win, or something? He just can't stand to let me beat him at something, so he has to break up my marriage, too, steal my wife if only to prove he can. And the worst of it is, he doesn't care about her. He won't love her the way I love her. He's just doing it to win."

"That's dark," Liv said. "If it's true."

"Oh, it's true. Our whole lives, it's been one big competition. Who's tallest? Who gets the best grades? Who's the most popular? Who gets into the best college? Who has the most successful career? Our whole lives, up until his divorce, the answer was Alby. He just can't stand seeing me come out ahead."

Wow, Liv thought. *Maybe I'm glad I'm an only child.*

Thinking back to her and Van's and Alby's younger years, she realized she'd observed the competitive family dynamic in person. She just hadn't known the boys carried it over into adulthood.

Liv looked across the lake at the chalet, baking in the afternoon sun. What about Alice? Knowing about the competition between her husband and his brother, she'd have to be one cold-hearted snake to betray Van this way.

She switched the cell to her other ear. "So you think Alice is just an innocent pawn in all this?"

"It's lame, I know, but I don't blame her. When have you ever seen a girl, any girl, able to resist my brother?"

"Oh, come on, Van. That's ridiculous. In high school, maybe, but Alice is a grown woman."

"Doesn't matter. I hope when the truth comes out, she'll see him for what he really is and will agree to work on our marriage. I've found a couple of good counselors. Made a list. I still love her. So much." His voice went bitter again. "It's *him* I blame."

Chapter Seven

• • • • • • • • • • • • •

That afternoon, dark clouds gathered and rolled over the lake. Lightning flickered and thunder rumbled low and menacing. Liv smelled ozone in the air as she gathered the chaise and cushions from the dock and stored them under the porch.

Minutes later, the wind gathered force and rain fell in heavy sheets. She ran for cover in the cabin. From the safety of the screen porch, she watched pine branches tossing against the roiling black and purple sky. The power flickered and went out. After fifteen minutes, the thunder receded, leaving only a steady patter of rain on the tin roof.

Chilly, Liv pulled the quilt from her bed and carried it to the porch sofa. She curled up on the plump cushions to listen to the rain, and fell asleep.

When she woke a couple hours later, the skies had cleared and the power was back on. She made herself a cucumber and butter sandwich for supper and washed it down with a glass of good, chilled white wine. Mosquitoes whined against the screen. A red sunset promised fair weather tomorrow.

After washing the dishes, she doused herself with bug spray, strolled to the lake, and admired the stars winking in the now-clear sky. The air smelled as fresh as a laundry detergent commercial. She stood at the end of the splintery dock and lifted binoculars to inspect the Ferguson chalet.

Alby's car was still in the driveway.

A bright planet gleamed just above the peaked shadows of tall pines rimming the opposite shore. A lone boat chugged down Duckbill Pond, a ripple of wake parting the glassy water, and then everything went still and silent as the last of the light faded from the western sky.

Across the lake, two human figures, backlit in yellow light, moved in front of the chalet's French doors. Olivia glanced at her watch. 8:40 pm. She adjusted the focus of her binoculars.

Alice and Alby appeared to be arguing. Alice lifted her hands and made emphatic chopping motions beside her head. Alby clutched at his hair and then let his arms drop as he bent his head. Alice picked up something—possibly a book—and threw it at him. He cringed and ducked, and then he straightened, gesturing wildly again.

What was this? she wondered. *A lover's quarrel?*

Olivia tightened her grip on the binoculars as Alice turned her back to Alby and walked away from him. He followed a few steps behind. She stopped. Held still. He put his hand on her shoulder, and she spun around, throwing her arms around his neck. After a quick embrace, they parted, stepped away from each other, and disappeared into the interior of the house.

Over the next hour, Olivia kept watch. One by one the windows in the house went dark except for one small light in what she assumed was the kitchen. Despite the bug spray, mosquitoes whined in her ear. The smell of the lake wafted over her as the breeze kicked up. A loon called. Chills raced up Liv's arms at that haunting, echoey sound.

At around a quarter to ten, when further activity seemed improbable and she'd just about decided to call it a night, a flash caught her eye. She lifted the binoculars again.

From the chalet, someone carried an old-fashioned type lantern into the woods to the east of the property. Liv followed the oblong shape of the light winking in and out as someone carried it through the trees. They stopped. The lantern glowed steadily.

Liv watched, mesmerized and intrigued. What could they be doing out there? Was it Alice or Alby? And weren't they getting eaten alive by those mosquitoes?

After a few minutes the person returned to the house along the same path. She heard a screen door slam, clap echoing over the water. The light moved across the large windows and then glowed faintly in a smaller window next to the driveway and was then extinguished. She waited another fifteen minutes. The house lay dark and silent. Finally, she lowered the binoculars.

The loon called again. Another answered. And then all was still.

· · · · ·

On Tuesday, predawn, Liv woke to the insistent cawing of the crows. With a steaming cup of coffee in her hand, she wandered out to the dock and watched columns of mist spiral from the water.

As a small bass boat put-putted down the lake, Liv lifted a hand to the fisherman at the wheel. He waved back. Slow, hypnotizing rolls of water spread behind the boat in a widening v. The eastern horizon had lightened, but the sun still hadn't made an appearance.

She looked across the lake. Alby's car was not in the driveway. He—or they—were up early. Very early.

Liv considered the argument she'd witnessed the night before. Apparently Duckbill Pond wasn't paradise for the lovebirds. If that's what they were.

Liv still wasn't convinced. Arguing wasn't exactly love-making. Of course, a heated exchange of words often led to a heated exchange of body fluids, but until she saw incontrovertible evidence of an affair, she'd keep an open mind.

She needed to speak with Alice, but it was too early to knock on the chalet's door. She'd take a run and figure out the best way to approach Alice later.

After a long, sweaty jog and refreshing swim in the lake, Liv pulled jean shorts over her bikini and made herself a peanut-butter and jelly sandwich for breakfast. She stood at the kitchen counter eating the sandwich and sipping a cup of coffee. She considered calling Jasper but figured that might stir up a hornet's nest.

She started a jar of sun tea instead.

Because there was no internet connection at the cabin, she used her cell as a hotspot and logged onto her computer. She spent the next couple of hours on the screen porch working on background checks and answering emails while keeping an eye out for Alby's car across the lake. If he didn't return by mid-afternoon, she decided, she'd pay that visit to Alice.

A few hours later, all caught up on her emails and still feeling relaxed—she'd heard of the benefits of forest bathing and decided those ecotherapists Ashleigh was always talking about might be onto something—she took a closer look at Alby's social media profiles.

His photos tended to be of him dining out, hobnobbing at fundraisers and art gallery openings, and bicycling around New England in races and for fun. That explained his lean physique, she thought. His two cats, Maine Coons named Bam-Bam and Pebbles, made regular appearances on his personal feeds, as well.

She checked his gallery's pages next. Lots of traffic and engagement. Artist receptions. Regular rotation of familiar names on the southern Maine art scene. There were no family photos at all or shots of him with any particular man or woman, not even his ex-wife, Emsley.

Like Alice, Alby kept his private life private.

After snooping through the social media, Liv scanned through her notes. Van's suspicions seemed justified, she had to admit. Alice had lied, telling Van she was meeting "a friend" after work, but Van had seen Alice get into Alby's car instead. The pair then arranged a rendezvous at the family lake house. Alice's disinterest in sex with her husband waved a big, red flag, too.

Is that what happened after seven years with the same person, she wondered? Did marriage eventually kill every last ember of desire?

Liv leaned back in her chair and gazed across the lake. She wondered if she'd ever feel ready for marriage. Committing to a long-term relationship with Jasper stretched her capacity for intimacy as it was.

It wasn't that she hadn't witnessed strong and lasting relationships. Her parents enjoyed each others' company and made a formidable team on Portland's social scene.

Her father, Gilbert, was head administrator of Sharon Medical Center. He'd recently led the hospital through a tricky merger into a MainePatientCare, a state-wide health system that served as an umbrella for multiple hospitals and specialists. Her mother, Tiffany, served on various philanthropic committees, including presiding over the prestigious SMC Ladies Auxiliary.

Her parents were happy, but Liv knew herself enough to know she wasn't like them. She tended toward restless and easily bored. She'd rejected Gilbert and Tiffany's society lifestyle and was unable to see herself in the role of happy housewife. Not without turning into a zombie, anyway. She shuddered, thinking, *a zombie subsisting on anti-depressants and Veuve Clicquot.*

Liv shrugged that image from her mind. Unfortunately, Jasper wanted the life her parents had. She suspected he believed he could bring her around, could tempt her with *X-Files* reruns and hot meals followed by hotter sex, could indulge her business aspirations and would force himself to tolerate the gritty realities of her investigation career, at least in the short term, until she caved. What happened when he wanted to start a family, though? Did she even want children? Was there a way for them both to have the life they wanted?

Waves ruffled gently in the breeze, throwing sparks of reflected sunlight, dazzling to the eye. Yet another boat skimmed past, an inner tube dragged behind it, screaming children hanging on for dear life. The chalet's windows reflected the strong afternoon sunlight, and she forced her thoughts back to the task at hand. She'd worry about Jasper when she returned to Portland.

She picked up the binoculars again. Still no sign of Alby's Audi in the driveway. He'd been gone before dawn and now all day. Come to think of it, she hadn't seen Alice, either.

She shut her laptop and theorized about the lovers' quarrel she'd witnessed the previous evening. Maybe Alby had ended things. Maybe Alice had come to her senses and asked him to leave. Liv could only speculate at this juncture. She needed to ask Alice a few nosy neighbor questions and get some answers.

Her eyes fell on the kayaks stacked on a rack beside the silvery, old dock and decided. She'd paddle over to the chalet and make some excuse for knocking on the door.

She eased herself from the couch, and her muscles ached in a gratifying way from her morning run. She wandered into the kitchen for a glass of water, and her eyes fell on the container of raspberries she'd picked up at the farm stand.

She grinned. She'd use that oldest of old nosy-neighbor tactics and beg for a cup of sugar for a homemade raspberry pie. Liv had never made a pie in her life, but Alice didn't know that.

Liv grabbed an old jelly jar from the cupboard, threw a blue button-up shirt over her bikini top and cut-offs, and examined a faded cotton fishing hat hanging on a peg near the door. It had one rusted hook and a tiny lure pushed through the fabric brim. She placed it on her head and slid a pair of dark sunglasses over her eyes. *Disguise complete.*

Outside, she located a life-preserver and paddles in a storage space beneath the porch and carried everything to the water's edge. Lifting the kayak from the rack beside the lake, she grunted and promised herself she'd start weight training again in earnest when she returned home. Finally, she dragged the kayak to the water where she managed to get herself settled onto the seat without tipping over. With another grunt, she pushed off.

Once she adjusted to the rocking motion of the kayak, she dipped the two-sided oar into the water and paddled across the lake toward the chalet.

Ten minutes later, she pulled up to a sandy area next to the Ferguson's dock. She dragged the kayak safely onto shore, snagged the jelly jar, and walked to the kitchen entrance near the driveway.

The house was built into a slight hill with a daylight basement level overhung by the first-floor deck facing the lake. She knocked and waited. No answer. She tried again, knocking and calling out, "Yoo-hoo! Anyone home!"

Still nothing.

Liv glanced at the crushed-stone driveway. Still no Alby. She walked around to the base of the wrap-around porch. Alice's Subaru Forester was parked in the spot underneath the deck. She felt the hood. Stone cold.

Next, she climbed the steep flight of steps to the deck. "Hello!" she called again. Still no movement inside the chalet. Maybe Alice had gone somewhere with Alby—a day trip to Kingfield or Farmington.

Liv peered through the French doors. The great-room was decorated for the lake in hunter green and dark blue plaids. Canoe paddles and old-fashioned skis hung on the walls instead of art. A looming moose head gazed glaze-eyed above the field-stone fireplace. Creepy, she thought, averting her eyes from the dead animal.

Since she was here on Van's invitation, she could even slip inside if she found a door unlocked. She could poke around while Alby and Alice were away, see if they'd left anything incriminating lying around. Sexy lingerie, for instance. Rumpled sheets in the bedroom. Two sets of discarded clothing on the floor.

She jiggled the handles of the French doors. Locked. She walked to what she assumed was the kitchen window and peeked in. Antique china cabinet on one wall. Tall, white cupboards. A few dishes dried on a rack placed atop the kitchen island. A lantern, probably the one she'd seen bobbing through the woods the night before, sat next to a vase of daisies. Still no sign of Alice or Alby, though.

She was about to give up and kayak back to her cabin when an odd, white shape on the floor caught her attention. She cupped her hands around her eyes and looked again.

What appeared to be a woman's bare foot stuck out from behind the island.

When Liv realized what she was looking at, she gasped. She rapped hard on the glass and yelled Alice's name. No response.

Heart hammering, she backed away and pulled her cell phone from her pocket to call 9-1-1. She looked down at the screen and groaned. Just as Van warned. No cell service. She ran down the steps of the porch and out to the dock. She lifted her phone into the air and looked at the screen. Nothing. Next she tried the driveway. Still no connection.

Liv's thoughts raced. If that was Alice on the floor, she could be injured, unconscious but alive. Van said they had a landline phone. If she got into the chalet, she could assist Alice and call for help.

She ran to the side door, sure it would be locked, and tried the knob. When it turned in her hand, she let out the breath she'd been holding. She flung the door open, raced through a small mudroom and into the kitchen.

Her eyes widened. She skidded to a stop and put a hand to her mouth, holding back a yelp.

There behind the island, Alice lay spread-eagled on the floor, satin-and-lace nightgown hitched up to her knees, eyes open and unseeing. A knife handle stuck straight up from her chest. Blood stained the front of the satin fabric, and one of Alice's hands clutched at the bodice. Liv knelt to feel for a pulse. The woman's skin was cold and rigid, pale as a ghost.

Alice Ferguson was dead.

Chapter Eight

• • • • • • • • • • • • • •

Feeling a little queasy, Liv lunged for the landline phone hung on the kitchen wall. She lifted the receiver to her ear and half expected there'd be no dial tone. She heard, however, the distinctive hum, and breathed a little easier as she dialed 9-1-1. After giving the dispatcher the address, her name, and a brief description of the situation, Liv hung up the phone.

She stood for a moment, considering what to do next. Dust motes floated through the air, glowing in the sunlight, which fell through the kitchen window facing the lake. As a private investigator, she dealt with cheating spouses, process service, and background checks. Not dead bodies. Not murder.

She avoided looking at Alice with that gruesome knife sticking out of her chest.

Remaining calm in spite of the situation, Liv considered what might have happened. When it came to the question of who killed Alice, Alby was the obvious suspect. She'd seen them arguing in front of the windows the previous night. Liv frowned. At least she presumed the two figures had been Alice and Alby. It was just speculation, she realized. Because they'd been backlit, she hadn't been able to make out their faces.

Poor Van, she thought. Pretty soon the authorities would arrive and they'd have to send someone to tell him in person that his wife was dead. That's the sort of news that should be delivered in person.

Liv blew out a held breath, wondering when she should call him and what she'd say when she did. She had no answers for him at this point. She glanced at the ceiling, wondering what she might find on the second floor. In a few minutes, law enforcement would arrive on the scene, and once they did, her opportunity to investigate would evaporate.

Maybe Van wouldn't care now, she thought. Alice was dead. Would it matter if she'd been cheating or not?

"If it were me, I'd want to know," Liv murmured to herself as she looked toward the hallway leading out of the kitchen and listened for the sound of emergency vehicles. No faint sirens yet. Nothing but the cawing of a crow.

Liv knew what she wanted to do, but she hesitated. Walking around the crime scene could contaminate evidence. She didn't want to jeopardize the official investigation.

On the other hand, Van deserved answers, and he'd paid her to get them. He was distraught already, and soon he'd be grieving. The least she could do was assure him that Alice had been faithful before she died, or else she'd confirm his suspicions had been right. Either way, he'd have the cold comfort of closure.

She made up her mind to take a quick look around the chalet before the police arrived. She resolved not to move anything, not touch anything with her bare hands. She'd just… look.

Her eyes fell first to the body. Alice's feet were bare. She wore an ivory silk nightgown trimmed in luxurious, black lace. In the center of her chest, just beneath her breasts, a thick, black handle stuck straight up, the tiniest gleam of steel at the top. Liv glanced at the top of the island. She noted two empty slots in the wooden block knife holder. A small one for the paring knife, and a big one for the chef's.

Liv returned her gaze to the victim, squatted to get a better look. Alice's brownish-blonde hair, shoulder length, spread around her face in messy tangles. Her left arm lay bent-elbowed over her head. The other hand grasped the satin fabric near the knife's handle, as if she'd tried to reach for it, to pull it out.

To make the pain stop.

Feeling queasy, Liv closed her eyes and took a deep breath. She was a private investigator, not a crime scene analyst, but she could do this. She'd focus her attention on details, distance herself from the horror.

When she opened her eyes, her gaze fell on a thin, gold chain around Alice's neck. A charm was attached, dangling on the left side of Alice's neck. Liv scooched for a closer look. The charm was in the shape of a small triangle tipped on its side within a larger one. The delicate gold gleamed in the shadow between Alice's neck and shoulder. Liv squinted as she leaned closer. There was something vaguely familiar about the design, but she drew a blank.

Steeling herself, she took note of Alice's face. Eyes wide open. Mouth open, too, as if gasping for air. No makeup. No seductive mascara on her lashes. No glossy red lipstick. Liv sniffed. No lingering scent of perfume, and nothing putrid-smelling from the body, either, thank goodness.

Blood stained the front of the nightgown, but most of it must have collected inside the body as there was no pool of red on the floor.

Liv stood and scanned the entire scene. The LED camping lantern on the kitchen island indicated Alice might have been the person carrying the light through the woods the previous evening. Her feet were bare but not dirty. Looking closer, Liv noticed a few long scratches on Alice's legs. If she'd moved through the woods that night, branches would have clawed at her calves even if she'd worn shoes or flip flops.

Liv went back to the little entry hall. A pair of pink, rubbery clogs, a bit of brown leaf stuck to the side of one, sat on a worn rug. Liv pulled her phone from the back pocket of her shorts, snapped a photo.

She went back to the kitchen, took a few photos of Alice. A wine glass with a few ounces of some kind of white wine sat on the counter. Another, clean, rested upside down in the dish drain. Two corks lay side-by-side on the island next to a small cheese board. A paring knife rested at an angle on top of the board. Both the board and knife had been cleaned and left out to dry.

Her glance fell on the refrigerator. She slipped off her shirt. Holding it in her hand, she opened the refrigerator door and scanned the contents. The usual condiments. A pound of butter. A carton of eggs. Half and half. Veggies in the crisper drawers and a couple bottles of Chardonnay on their sides, chilling.

Salami, the package unopened. Smoked salmon in a plastic pouch, also unopened. Cream cheese. Pickles. A package of rib-eye steaks.

She shut the door and checked out the freezer. One container of Ben & Jerry's Super Fudge Chunk. Nothing else.

Next, she peeked beneath the sink. There she found an empty wine bottle and a small trash bin. A plastic wrapper from a small block of cheddar sat on top.

Wine and cheese, Liv mused. *Could be a snack for a romantic rendezvous. Or a lone woman's evening meal. But those two glasses—and the argument she'd witnessed through her binoculars from across the lake—suggested the former.*

Liv snapped several more photos of Alice and the kitchen. Moving on, she stepped down a short hallway into the adjoining living/dining area. Here the ceilings soared up to a second-story peak, all exposed beams and pine boards.

A gigantic fieldstone fireplace, complete with moose head, filled the eastern wall. Two sets of French doors led to the expansive deck overlooking the lake. She took a few more photos, but other than a pitcher of wildflowers on the dining room table, the room seemed stale and dead.

Not as dead as Alice Ferguson. Liv shuddered as that unbidden thought popped into her mind. *Morbid humor,* she thought. *A defensive reflex.*

Heading back through the short hallway, Liv stuck her head

into a small powder room. Spotless. No medicine cabinet. Toilet lid shut. Roll of toilet paper nearly full.

She cocked her head, listened for the sound of distant sirens. She heard nothing but the muffled sounds of boat motors, the hum of the refrigerator, and a loud, buzzing insect outside. A cicada maybe.

Since the coast appeared to be clear, Liv moved up the wooden stairs that led to the second floor. Here, several doors opened onto the wide landing overlooking the living room. A railing ran the length of the landing. Liv stepped into the first bedroom. The bedding on the antique four-poster lay smooth, and there were no personal items in the closet or bureau. A thin coating of dust filmed the bedside table.

The second bedroom showed no signs of occupancy, either. No dust, though. Hmmm.

She approached the furthest room, pushed at the half-closed door with her elbow, and slipped inside.

Unlike the tidy public rooms downstairs and the other bedrooms, this one was messy. The bed was unmade, comforter and sheets rumpled at the foot of another four-poster.

A robe draped a petite upholstered chair in the corner. Alice's navy bathing suit and sarong lay crumpled on the floor in front of the open closet where a few linen dresses and shirts had been hung, presumably by Alice.

She checked the drawers and found more women's clothes, nothing to indicate another occupant besides Alice.

But when she looked under the bed, she discovered what looked like a man's dress shirt, white, crumpled as if it had been dropped to the floor and accidentally pushed beneath the bed. She sniffed. The bergamot and lemon scent of Armani Code told her the shirt probably belonged to Alby, unless Alice wore men's cologne.

She remembered the shorts and shirt outfit Alby'd been wearing when she spotted them at the market. The shirt had been white.

She took a photo, straightened, and made a slow turn to take in the entire room. In an alcove formed by a good-sized dormer window, a small desk and a hard-back chair created a charming work space.

The window provided a view of oak and fir trees and the camp road behind them. Books, notebooks, and loose papers had been piled up on the left side of the desk. A mug held a collection of pencils and pens. To the right side of the chair, an old canvas L.L.Bean bag with faded red handles held more books.

A laptop yawned open in the middle of the desk. It was plugged in, and the screensaver changed photos every few seconds. Liv wrapped a layer of shirt around her finger and rubbed the touchpad but nothing happened. Must be heat sensitive. She pulled the fabric tighter and waited for her finger to warm the thin material before trying again. This time the screen lit up. A document opened, topped by a long row of open tabs.

Liv scanned the type. The document appeared to be a scene from a short story or novel. An unnamed man and woman negotiated a contract of some sort. Liv skimmed through the heated argument—the writing wasn't terrible—and then her eyes fell to the final words on the screen. "His fingers felt like silk-covered steel as they lightly grazed her cheekbone. Groaning, he lowered his head to claim her lips with his, and she melted against his…"

The scene broke off mid-sentence. Liv stared at the words, mind racing. So, Alice hadn't been lying to Van, not about the writing, at least. She checked the title of the document. *Calliope & The Viper's Den.* Moving the arrow to the scroll bar, she could see this was the final page of a 232-page document.

Feeling anxious about the time now, she scanned the row of tabs, tapping each one open in turn, but not lingering on any of them. An online thesaurus. Something called Erotiwritica.com.

Liv would look into that one later, but it was obvious to her that Alice was writing, or attempting to write, an erotic novel. She clicked the remaining tabs. A search page for "pole dancing lessons." An article entitled, "How to Write Smutty Romance." An article about the Russian mafia. An article on indie publishing.

Liv frowned. How did the mafia fit in? Maybe the story Alice was writing involved the mob? She supposed some people might find that sexy. "What were you up to, Alice?" Liv whispered in the quiet of the room.

She tapped back to the main document, and now her eyes landed on the blue share button in the top left corner of the screen. She clicked on it and drew in a sharp breath, surprised, though maybe she shouldn't have been. Alice had shared the document with one other person: Alby Ferguson.

She clicked into the document and, scrolling backward, scanned back a few pages to the beginning of the scene.

The characters' passion disguised as anger pulsed from the page. As the scene unfolded, a woman named Calliope paced and argued. Her companion, Nikolai shouted. Calliope offered to fulfill the contract, nothing more. Nikolai, brutal and determined, demanded more. Demanded her allegiance, an alliance that could not be broken except by death.

Alice was pretty good at this stuff, Liv decided. She'd captured the erotic charge between two strong, well-matched individuals. Nikolai's need to control Calliope. Her resistance to that control. The tension both verbal and sexual rising between them.

Finally, Calliope threw her wine-glass at Nikolai, who laughed, stepped aside to avoid the glass, and reached for her. Calliope, feeling chastened by her lack of composure, offered a compromise. Then Liv was back where she started, the graze of the cheek, tenderness, and embrace, which ended in that final, aborted sentence.

Liv felt a pull of regret that she wouldn't be able to read what happened next. Alice hadn't had a chance to write it, and now she never would.

A wailing sound interrupted her thoughts. *The police.* Liv's head whipped up. She'd been so engrossed in the story they'd almost reached the cabin before she heard them.

She swirled the shirt around her body, pushed her arms into sleeves, and ran out of the room and down the stairs. The sirens grew louder. She skidded past Alice's prone body, reached the kitchen door, and slipped outside.

She closed the door behind her. Breath coming in short gasps, heart hammering in her chest, she plunked her butt onto the granite step, warm from sunlight, and watched the first of several official vehicles roll down the driveway.

Get a hold of yourself, she told her beating heart. A pair of Maine State Police officers emerged from their vehicle. *It's showtime.*

Chapter Nine

• • • • • • • • • • • • • •

"Yes, I'm the one who called. My name's Olivia Lively."

The officers nodded. One asked her to stand beside their vehicle. They secured the scene with yellow crime tape and then asked for her information. She answered them in a short, direct manner: phone number, email, place of work, home address, local address. She noticed the raised eyebrows when she mentioned Lively Investigations, the exchange of looks.

One officer, a youngish man with sandy brown hair, scratched his head with the end of his pencil and then tapped the point on his notebook twice. *Dotting his i's*, she thought. *Crossing his t's*.

"Okay, Ms. Lively. That's about it for now. How long you gonna be staying in Carry Over?"

"I'm supposed to be here until Friday." She wasn't sure she'd stay. Not after this. She didn't offer any explanation for her being in Carry Over, and they didn't ask.

The other officer, a red-head who looked like he spent a lot of time at the gym, gave her a hard stare. "Make sure you're reachable. Most likely a detective'll be contacting you for a more in-depth conversation."

She noticed he didn't say interrogation. "Okay. I'll have my phone on me."

More vehicles rolled down the gravel driveway. Ambulance. Medical examiner's van. In the woods, a crow cawed the alarm and another answered. She looked up and watched as the two birds flapped out of a nearby pine and across the lake. She returned her attention to the Staties. The one with the notebook checked his watch, scratched something, presumably the time, into his notes.

He gave her a quick smile. "Take care now, Ms. Lively. Thank you for notifying us. Someone will be in touch."

The ginger-haired fellow gave her another long look, nodded, turned away without another word. They walked up the drive and began talking with the woman who'd emerged from the medical examiner's van.

Tempted to stay but not wanting to attract any more attention, Liv kayaked back to her cabin. Her hands shook and chills washed over her as she made her way across the lake. She diagnosed her symptoms as an adrenaline response.

She shuddered, remembering the scene in the kitchen. Alice's staring brown eyes. Her fingers reaching for the knife handle.

Poor Alice, Liv thought. And Poor Van. And where was Alby?

She felt sick to her stomach imagining what happened. They'd argued. She'd seen it with her own eyes through the binoculars the night before. Maybe Alice wanted to break things off and he'd been so angry he'd plucked that knife from the stand on the counter and killed her. Realizing what he'd done, he packed his things and took off.

She thought about the undisturbed guest rooms, the shirt under Alice's bed, reeking of men's cologne, indicating he'd been sleeping there. The police would surely find it and place it into evidence.

The kayak hit the gravely shoreline, and Liv hopped out into the water to drag it up onto the grass. She stored the oars inside the shell and left the kayak to dry in the sun.

Once inside the cabin, she peeled off her bikini and put on fresh clothes. She wadded the shirt she'd used at the chalet and stuck it into her suitcase in the closet. She felt nervous, jangly.

It was understandable considering she'd just discovered a dead body. Not just anybody, either but the wife of her friend. The friend who'd hired her because he suspected that wife was cheating on him.

With his brother. *Who, let's face it*, Liv thought, *probably killed her.*

She brewed a cup of coffee and wandered to the screen porch to drink it. Curling up on the musty couch, she forced herself to focus on other things. The blue sky. The sparkling water. The fishing boats putt-putting slowly to and fro. All this felt surreal juxtaposed with the brutality of the murder scene she'd stumbled upon.

A vision of Alice's hand clutching the silk cloth near the knife handle intruded. Her throat constricted and bile rose. She gulped her coffee, wincing as the heat seared on its way down. She wondered if the police had notified Van yet. Should she give him a few hours and then call him, or should she wait for him to contact her?

She wasn't sure what to do. This was her first dead body. Being a P.I. in real life wasn't like television. Murders didn't take place on her watch every week on Tuesdays at 8:00 p.m. She wasn't Jessica Fletcher, and her life wasn't anything like *Murder She Wrote*.

At least, not until today.

Liv shivered again and wrapped both hands around the warm mug. Alice Ferguson had been someone's wife, someone's daughter, someone's friend, someone's co-worker. Now she was nothing but a dead thing being trundled off to the medical examiner's office for a forensic autopsy. A piece of evidence to be cataloged. Soon only dust and ash.

Liv stared across the lake. Without the binoculars, the chalet looked distant and innocuous, a vacation home on a pretty Maine lake sparkling in the summer sun. For Liv, though, it might as well have been cast in deep shadow. She brooded. If she'd gone to see Alice last night after witnessing the argument, she might have prevented a murder.

Or you could have been a victim yourself.

Setting the coffee aside, she picked up one of the books she'd stacked beside the chair. Her eyes ran down the page, but her mind drifted. She tossed the book back onto the stack. She couldn't concentrate. Images from the crime scene crowded all other thoughts from her mind.

She stalked to the kitchen to pour herself another coffee. On the way back to the porch, she picked up her notebook and pen. If she couldn't stop ruminating, she might as well record everything she could remember about the crime scene.

The food in the refrigerator. The mess in Alice's bedroom, all the items on the floor and in the closet, the document Alice was working on, the open tabs. Taking notes would help her process what she'd seen and maybe help the detective assigned to the investigation. She expected they'd contact her soon to request an interview.

•　•　•　•　•

An hour later, the coffee had grown cold and she had several pages of notes.

She thought about what to make for dinner. She never really cooked. She'd bought some soup she could heat up on the stove, but the day's heat had accumulated inside the cabin. A cucumber and tomato sandwich then, she decided.

She unfurled her legs, stood up, and stretched. She felt calmer. Clearer. Getting everything out of her head and onto the page had worked. At least for now.

The phone in Liv's back pocket vibrated. Van?

She drew it out and looked at the screen. Just an email notification. She read the email—a referral from one of her business clients asking about a security upgrade—and she typed back a quick note saying she'd call them the next day to schedule an appointment. Lucky she had cell service here, she thought, unlike poor Alice across the lake.

She put the phone back in her pocket thinking about the steep hills and valleys of the region that made cell phone service so spotty. The land was dotted with numerous lakes and ponds, and at least some of the rocky, moss-wrapped mature forest stretched untouched by logging. The Appalachian Trail ran nearby. She'd listened in line at the market as the cashier commented on the increased number of hikers that year—so many unfamiliar faces coming in to restock their supplies before heading north to the terminus of the trail at Mount Katahdin.

Her phone buzzed again. She didn't recognize the number. "This is Olivia Lively," she said.

"Hello, Ms. Lively. This is Detective Karina Briggs from the Maine State Police. I hope I'm not getting you at a bad time."

Liv took a deep breath. *Here we go,* she thought. "It's fine."

"Good. I was hoping I could come by tomorrow to talk about what happened this morning. Would nine a.m. be okay for you?"

"Sure. I'll be here."

"Good," the detective said again. She sounded friendly but confident. Liv pictured an *X-Files* Dana Scully-type.

Thinking about the *X-Files* reminded her of Jasper. It was Tuesday. She should have been in Portland getting ready for dinner with his parents, not talking to a police detective about the body she'd discovered that morning.

It meant something that she'd still rather be here.

"Ms. Lively? Do I have the correct address?" the detective's voice interrupted her thoughts.

"Oh. Sorry. Yes."

"Thank you very much. I'll see you in the morning. Have a good night now."

"Uh, you, too."

Liv pressed the red end-call button on her phone and typed the appointment into her calendar app. Not that she'd forget. It was just habit. One of those anchors that kept your life in place even though circumstances tossed you around now and then.

Like finding a dead body in a kitchen. And being the last person to see the victim alive.

Other than the murderer, of course.

Chapter Ten

• • • • • • • • • • • • • •

Turned out, Detective Karina Briggs looked nothing like Agent Scully, but she was just as sharp.

Liv heard a brisk tap-tap-tap on the cabin's screen door promptly at nine Wednesday morning—as if Briggs had waited on the camp road and timed her arrival to the minute.

Liv opened the door. "Good morning, Detective. Please, come in."

Detective Briggs thanked her and stepped inside. She wore a lightweight gray pantsuit and black, low-heeled shoes. Even with the extra inch or two, she was shorter than Liv in her bare feet.

Briggs wore her long, blonde hair braided and wrapped it into a kind of ball at the back of her head. No-nonsense black-rimmed glasses framed alert brown eyes.

Liv ushered her to the kitchen table. "Would you like some coffee?"

Briggs gave her a slight smile. "That sounds great, thank you."

When they were both seated at the table, mugs of coffee in front of them, Briggs placed a form, a pen, and a recording device on the table. "I'll ask some preliminary questions, and then I'll take your full statement, okay? You won't mind if I record the interview, do you?"

"No," Liv said. "I mean, that's fine."

Aware of the detective's close attention to her demeanor, Liv provided her age, address, place of business, and a few other bits of personal information.

Briggs nodded, not quite smiling but not frowning either. "So, why don't you tell me what happened? Start anywhere and we'll go from there."

Liv explained what she could—without breaking confidentiality—about Van's hiring her to investigate Alice. Then, beginning with her arrival in Carry Over on Saturday, she told the detective everything she could remember about the last few days up to the moment she discovered Alice's body.

Briggs interjected now and then. She nodded throughout, made eye contact, remained warm and non-confrontational.

"Thank you," Briggs said when Liv wound down. "After you found Alice, did you go into any rooms besides the hallway and kitchen?"

Liv had prepared herself for this question and replied honestly. "Yes. All of them. I wanted to make sure no one else was there requiring medical attention."

"Did you touch anything?"

"Not that I remember. Just the kitchen door in and out."

"How long were you upstairs?"

"Just a minute or two."

"Okay." Briggs scribbled some notes. "A couple more questions, if you don't mind, about your professional relationship with the deceased's husband."

She peppered Liv with more than a couple questions. How did she know Donovan Ferguson? Did they meet often? What day had he come to her office? What had he asked her to do? Had she recorded the meeting? What dates and times had she phoned Van? Briggs kept her voice casual, but watched with laser focus behind her dark-rimmed glasses as Liv responded.

As the minutes ticked by and the coffee grew cold, Liv kept her answers shorter, more to the point while her stress level ballooned.

Why was the detective grilling her so hard?

Liv's suspicions grew when Briggs asked the next question. "When you called Van to report that you saw Alice and Albert together in Carry Over, how did he seem on the phone? Angry? Upset? Surprised? Sad?"

"Uh, upset, I guess, but calm. Resigned. Definitely not surprised. I suggested he come up and talk to them."

Briggs lifted her head. "And how did he respond?"

"He told me he wanted to be sure first. Before confronting them, I mean. He said he was worried he'd screw up his relationships with them if he was wrong, so he wanted me to keep watching to make sure before he accused them. Not his exact words. Something to that effect."

Briggs flipped back a page, scanned her notes. "You said you observed no intimate contact between Alice and Albert Ferguson. I'm assuming you told Mr. Ferguson the same thing?"

"Right. I didn't see any intimate contact at the market or at the chalet when I drove by. Later that night, I saw two people arguing and briefly embracing at the chalet, but there was no way to identify them for certain. They were silhouettes."

"Could it have been Donovan you saw arguing with Alice?"

Liv's stomach dropped. So her client was a suspect. That made sense. A high percentage of female homicide victims were killed by spouses or romantic partners. Van hired her to report on Alice's activities. Did that make her a potential suspect as an accessory?

"Like I said, I couldn't actually see faces. I'm sorry I can't be more sure."

After a few more questions, often repeats of those she'd already covered, Briggs finally wrapped up her interview.

She read Liv's statement aloud and obtained her signature. The detective then stood and gathered her recording device, notepad, and pen. "Thank you for your cooperation, Ms. Lively. We may need to speak with you again. Here's my card. Let me know if you're going to be unreachable or traveling,"

As Briggs stepped outside, Liv said, "Do you have any idea where Alby is? I'm sure Van's worried."

"We'll keep him informed. Have a nice day now."

After Briggs drove off, Liv let the door slam. Out of habit, she looked over the water toward the chalet and all the other little cabins lining the shore. Despite the sun overhead, Alice's murder cast a dark shadow over the lake and the town of Carry Over. A crow cawed in one of the pine trees, sinister and portentous. A shiver ran up her back. Someone had killed here.

Only one person had the means and opportunity. Maybe two, if you considered motive.

Liv frowned, considering the possibility that her client, acting on her information, committed cold-blooded murder. If Van decided to drive up to Carry Over to confront his wife and brother, it would have taken him three hours to get here. Liv's last check on the chalet had been just before ten p.m. and she'd gone out to the dock the next morning by what, six a.m.? Eight hours.

It was three hours between Portland to Carry Over. Eight hours was plenty of time for Van to get to the chalet, kill Alice, and flee the scene.

She dismissed the thought as ridiculous. Van had been adamant on the phone about waiting for further information. He wanted Liv to complete her surveillance before he confronted Alice. He would have called to tell her if he'd changed his mind, she was *almost* sure of it.

Liv compulsively checked her phone messages again to make sure she hadn't missed one. Nope. No message from Van.

Feeling troubled, she paced into the kitchen. She hoped he had a solid alibi for his whereabouts Monday night through Tuesday morning or else he was in for some uncomfortable questioning.

Liv reached for a glass and filled it with water. Gulping it down, she pondered what to do next. There was no reason for her to stay in Carry Over any longer. In fact, if she went home now, she could meet Jasper's parents before they left town. Maybe that would make things better between her and Dr. Hottie.

She still wasn't sure about a long-term commitment, but at least she could do this one thing for him.

She'd screwed up dinner, yes, but there was still time to repair the damage. She'd apologize profusely and be at her most charming and parent-friendly. She imagined Jasper's surprised smile when she showed up at his door with a bouquet of flowers for his mother and maybe a jar of that local honey from the farm stand down the road.

Her excitement grew as she washed her glass, dried it, and set it back in the cupboard. She'd get some more raspberries, too, and if she left right away, she'd have time to go home and bake a pie—How hard could it be?—and impress his parents with her domestic skills.

See, the pie would say, *your son is in good hands.*

Though, thinking about it, that might be asking a lot of pie.

Whatever. It couldn't hurt. Liv strode into the bedroom and threw her clothes into her suitcase, anxious now to be on her way. She'd do her best to win the parents over, make up for the missed dinner, and be her most charming self.

If they didn't like her, oh well. She'd never been the kind of girl boys brought home to their mother anyway. She snapped the vintage LV suitcase shut.

At least Jasper wouldn't be able to say she didn't try.

Chapter Eleven

• • • • • • • • • • • • • •

"Surprise, I'm back!"

Jasper's face went blank when he saw her standing in his doorway with a bag full of goodies over her arm, fresh flowers in one hand, and pie in the other.

She wore a dress the color of the summer sky. Constructed from a multitude of fabric flowers sewn onto a sheer, sleeveless, knee-length sheath, the effect was three-dimensional and totally feminine.

The neckline was reminiscent of Jackie O's famous shift dresses, 1960s demur and sweet. Kitten heel sandals in the same blue color, dangly gold earrings, and a quilted white leather carry-all completed the meet-the-parents look.

"Um, hi." Jasper, looking handsome in jeans and a salmon-colored button-down, leaned in to give her a quick kiss. He smelled good, like some new cologne. Citrusy and crisp.

"Mmmmmm. More." She went in for another kiss, but he drew back. Her eyebrows quirked, but she remained silent.

He said, "I didn't expect to see you until next week."

The sound of several people laughing inside the apartment reached her ears, and she raised her eyebrows even more when Jasper glanced over his shoulder.

Standing on her tiptoes, Liv tried to look around him. "I came home early to meet your parents. Carry Over was a nightmare. Are you going to let me in or what?" She nudged him, felt his hand brush her elbow as he tried to stop her.

"Wait, Liv. I should tell you…"

She sashayed into the room. Her heels clicked on the hardwood floor. As the dining area came into view, she stopped abruptly. A gray-haired man and woman sat on one side of Jasper's table. Across from them, a petite, brown haired woman wearing a white, poofy-sleeved cotton dress and a preppy, white headband beamed at her.

Liv's smile faded. *What the hell was Wren Osborne doing here?*

"Olivia, wow. Hi!" Wren said. "Jassy told us you were away on a case."

Liv fought the urge to smoosh her perfect, golden-crusted raspberry pie into Wren's too-smiley face. As if reading her mind, Jasper lifted the dish out of her hand. "Let's put this in the kitchen," he said. "Where it's safe. I'll get a vase for the flowers."

She narrowed her eyes at him. "You do that."

He reached into a cupboard and called out, "Mom. Dad. This is the woman I've been telling you about. Olivia Lively. Liv, meet my parents, Timothy and Brenda Temple. You know Wren, of course."

"Of course. Hello, Wren." Liv's fingers curled in toward her palms.

She'd known Wren since childhood. Their parents ran in the same social circles. Though a year apart in school, she and Wren had grown up taking the same tennis and sailing lessons every summer. Wren's parents enrolled her in a boarding school in Massachusetts while Liv attended Coyne day school in Portland, but they'd seen each other at country club functions and parties over the years.

Entrenched in Portland's social scene, Wren fluttered around the city like an irritating butterfly. Last spring, when Liv and Jasper first started dating, Wren managed to come between them at a crucial moment in the relationship, accompanying Jasper to the annual hospital auxiliary Spring Fling, a fundraiser Liv's mother organized every year.

Jasper and Liv had nearly broken up for good. Now here she

was again. Less like a butterfly. More like mold on the shower tiles.

Jasper's father stood, interrupting Liv's thoughts. Tim Temple's hair was graying blond. He sported a farmer's tan, blunt, cheerful features, and an easy smile. "Nice to meet you, young lady. We've heard a lot about you."

"You, too." She walked closer, held out her hand.

He squeezed it and gave her a wink.

So that's where Jasper got his charm, she thought. She smiled at Tim even though she felt like running for the door. Or lunging over the table and pulling Wren's hair out by the roots and the stupid headband along with it.

Jasper's mother glanced from Liv to Wren and then to the bouquet of shasta daisies, pink poppies, and white phlox Liv held in her other hand. "Aren't those flowers pretty, Olivia. Such cheerful colors."

Brenda Temple's salt and pepper hair had been brushed away from her face and secured in a low ponytail. Laugh lines fanned from the outer corners of eyes the same blue as Jasper's. She wore little makeup—only some pink lip gloss—but she appeared pulled-together and stylish in white jeans and a canary-yellow top. A simple gold cross swung from a delicate chain around her neck.

Seeing it reminded Liv of Alice's triangle necklace, and she repressed a shudder. She looked down at the flowers. "I picked them up at an adorable little farm stand this morning on my way back from my business trip." She shot a look at Jasper who'd finally found a vase. "Let me go to the kitchen and arrange them."

Wren popped up from her seat and snatched the bouquet from Liv's hands, an over-eager bridesmaid during the flower toss. "I'll do it. You sit and chat with Tim and Brenda."

Who died and made you social director?

Liv pressed her lips together to keep the words from escaping her mouth. She studied the table set for four with the white Le Creuset dinner plates and green striped linen napkins Liv had helped Jasper pick out in June. Glasses of iced tea garnished with lemon wheels sat on green ceramic coasters. Tim and Brenda sat on the left side of the table, Jasper and Wren's places across from them.

She *so* hated feeling like a fifth wheel.

She took the seat at the unset foot of the table, placed her bag at her feet, and pasted a bright, fake smile onto her face. She asked the Temples about their impressions of Maine so far.

They mentioned the hot weather and beautiful coastline. They asked her about Lively Investigations. She gave them the usual spiel about her job as an assistant P.I. after college and how she'd discovered not only an aptitude but also a passion for the investigation biz.

She cast quick glances at Jasper and Wren in the kitchen fussing with the flowers. *What was taking them so long?*

"Isn't it dangerous?" Brenda fiddled with the cross at her throat. "Detective work, I mean?" *Like mother, like son,* she thought, feeling a little snarky.

"Rarely. It's mostly a lot of talking to people and online research and paperwork."

"Oh," Brenda murmured, and looked at her husband. He put his arm around her shoulders and gave a squeeze. Liv felt bitterness form in the back of her throat as the conversation died and the three of them looked awkwardly at their plates.

Jasper and Wren laughed together about something, and Liv's eyes narrowed as Wren put a hand on Jasper's elbow. She thought about excusing herself from the table and asking to speak with him privately, but she didn't want to be rude.

Some of her mother's lessons in propriety held tight.

Like vice grips.

Fortified with Superglue.

"Well, you can cut this tension with a cheese slicer," Liv said, forcing a laugh. "I'm so sorry I missed our dinner on Tuesday. I thought I'd surprise the three of you tonight to make up for it. I should have called first."

The Temples looked at each other again. Tim straightened his tie. Brenda sipped her iced tea. Liv stared at them, wondering what they were thinking, and died a little inside imagining.

Jasper and Wren returned to the table. Wren carried the vase of flowers and placed them in the center. "There." Serenely ignoring the awkward atmosphere, Wren took her seat to the left of Olivia and beamed across the table at the elder Temples.

Jasper cleared his throat and sat as well. "Dinner should be ready soon."

He didn't look at Liv. Should she offer to get another place setting herself?

"So pretty," Brenda murmured as she touched one of the petals. "Thank you Wren. And thank you, Olivia, for bringing them."

"No problem. Oh, I almost forgot. I picked up a few little things for both of you. I felt so awful about missing our dinner." She reached for her bag and set it on her lap.

She thumped a jar of honey on the table. "This is organic— complete with comb—from a beekeeper in Carry Over. That's where I was working this week. It's this really small, rustic village up north in the woods. Camping. Fishing. Hunting. Snowmobiling in the winter. That sort of place. I got some jam, too. Plum." She gave Jasper a side-eyed look and set the second jar down with a thump.

She caught Tim's eye and reached to hand him a box. "Jasper said you liked to fish, Mr. Temple. These are flies hand-tied by a guy highly recommended by the locals up there. And this," she said to his mother, "is just something funny, but I thought it might amuse you."

She passed the hand-embroidered sachet pillow to Jasper's mother. The dried pine needles inside the pillow crunched. Brenda turned it from one side to the other and scrunched her eyebrows together. "Interesting."

"Let me see," Wren said. Brenda handed it over. "Oh, how cute! See, one side has a chickadee embroidered on it. It says, 'Maine

State Bird.' On the other is, omigosh, a giant mosquito. 'Maine's Other State Bird,' it says. That's adorable."

Liv shot her a look. "I thought it was kind of funny."

Her eyes traveled to Jasper. He looked like he'd rather be in an emergency heart surgery, wrist-deep in some guy's chest, than here. She said, "I baked the pie myself, Jasper. Raspberry. Your favorite."

She smiled at Wren, but when she spoke, her voice was ice. "Wren. I'm so sorry. If I'd known you were going to be here, I would have brought something for you, as well. Obviously your being here having dinner with my, uh, with Jasper and his parents is a complete surprise."

Jasper caught her eye. He pressed his lips together and shook his head. She squinted at him and made a face.

Tim looked at Brenda. "Raspberry? I thought apple was his favorite? Isn't apple his favorite?"

Brenda slid a sideways glance at her husband. "His tastes have obviously changed."

The timer went off in the kitchen.

Chapter Twelve

• • • • • • • • • • • • • • •

L iv stood. She'd had enough. "Well, that's my signal. The four of you need to eat. It was nice to meet you, Mr. and Mrs. Temple. I hope I can see you again before you fly home." She grabbed her bag. "Walk me to the door, *Jassy*?"

He looked helpless. "The timer..."

Wren hopped up again. "I'll get it."

Jasper's mother looked from Liv to Jasper to Wren and also stood. "*I'll* get it. You're the guest. Wren, you sit here and keep Tim company."

Liv followed Jasper to the door. He opened it, and she stepped outside to the small landing. Glazed flower pots contained various herbs and a couple of cherry tomato plants, and the smell of tarragon and fennel wafted around them.

Jasper shut the door behind them. She studied his face. "Why is it every time we hit a bump in our relationship, Wren Osborne shows up?"

He shoved his hands into his pockets. "You aren't going to hold that Spring Fling fiasco against me now, are you?"

"I baked a pie!"

The corners of his mouth twitched.

"It's not funny."

"It's kind of funny."

He took a deep breath and let it out. "Okay, I know why you're upset, but there's nothing going on between me and Wren. We ran into her at the hospital today when I was showing my parents around. She got all excited—you know how she gets—about how she had tickets to the new show in Ogunquit but couldn't use them herself. She offered to bring them by this afternoon. Somehow that turned into me inviting her for dinner. Or she invited herself." He shrugged. "I don't really remember."

"Was this before or after you told her I was away on business?"

"I'm not sure your name came up."

She huffed. "She's got a thing for you, and you like it!"

"And you're jealous. I do like that. I take it as a good sign."

"Well, don't."

He might find this amusing, but she wasn't in any kind of mood for banter. She whirled and walked up the street to where she'd parked. He didn't ask her to stay.

When she reached the Corolla, she slid into the driver's seat. She blasted WCYY as she headed up Munjoy toward her apartment.

Feeling weary, bitter, and confused, she screeched into her driveway and switched off the engine. It ticked as she stared at nothing and silence enveloped her. It dawned on her that Jasper might only have dated her because of her social background, her father's influence as head of the hospital, and her mother's place as the reigning queen of Portland's philanthropic class. What if when Liv declined to be the woman Jasper hoped she'd be, a woman whose coattails he could ride into Liv's parents' social circle, he moved on to the next best thing?

Bitterness squeezed her chest. She'd always been drawn to men with issues. Sad but true. With Jasper, she'd thought she'd broken her nasty habit.

She put her head on the steering wheel and moaned.

What if Dr. Hottie turned out to be another bad boy in disguise?

• • • • •

She spent the night contemplating her options. By morning, she'd decided to set her worries about Jasper aside. He'd call and apologize or he wouldn't. She'd wait to see what happened and instead concentrate on her business. Which meant using Van's retainer money to reorganize her business and take it to the next level.

The solution to her temporary assistant problem came to her the next afternoon as she passed the leafy, summer campus of Longfellow College. Like a bolt of lightning, the idea struck: why not see about posting an off-campus office job for the remainder of the summer?

Feeling buoyant and tingly, she swung into a parking lot and made her way to Wordsworth Hall to talk to her friend Barbara in the English Department. Cheerful and efficient, Barbara had helped her a couple of times in the plagiarism case in the spring and didn't hold it against Liv for feigning interest in the MFA writing program in order to investigate professor Mason Falwell.

Looking fetching in a dotted yellow sundress, Barbara enthusiastically welcomed Liv's request and promised she'd post the job on the department website before she left for the day.

The next morning, Liv received a call from recent MFA graduate, Marion Plank, asking if the position was still available.

A gifted student in the Longfellow MFA in Creative Writing, Marion had been helpful in the Falwell plagiarism case and had proved herself to be rational and calm. She explained to Liv that she'd been accepted to the law school and needed work to tide her over until the beginning of the fall semester.

"Can you come in for an interview this afternoon? One p.m.?" Liv asked.

"I'll see you then," Marion answered, sounding excited.

The twenty-three year old showed up wearing a pink and black floral skirt topped by a shapeless pink tee that, unfortunately, did nothing to accentuate her figure. Her shiny, pink patent leather Doc Martens, however, gave Liv an immediate rush of shoe-lust.

Liv invited the curvy, dark-haired young woman to have a seat in her office.

"This must be fate." Liv smiled behind her desk. "And I don't believe in fate."

"I don't either," Marion replied. "I believe in serendipity, though."

"Aren't they the same thing?"

"Not exactly. Serendipity is when good things come together unexpectedly, you know, due to actions you've taken."

"And fate?"

"More like predestination. It's not always good."

Liv said in a dry, amused voice, "So you only believe in magic when it's positive?"

"Sure. Why not?" Marion laughed, and Liv thought how nice it would be to have her around the office for the summer.

"So," Liv said. "You majored in poetry, correct? Tell me about your decision to apply to law school."

Marion nodded and explained that she'd volunteered with a writing program for incarcerated women her final semester and now wanted to help that population in a more tangible way than rhymed couplets and iambic pentameter. Meanwhile, she'd taught a few summer classes for the Portland School District.

"You know this is only a temp job, right? I can't promise you anything after these first six weeks."

"It's exactly what I need. The job came at the perfect time. My teaching gig ended last Friday, and student loans for law school won't be available until the end of August. I considered applying for a barista job to tide me over, but this sounds perfect."

"Law school. That's quite an undertaking. Was the LSAT terrifying?"

Marion blushed and looked down at her lap. "Not really. I'm, uh, kind of good at tests."

Liv already knew this. She'd contacted Barbara again right after Marion's call, and the admin had been more than happy to dish about one of her favorite student's transcripts and test scores.

Marion, it turned out, was a genius.

Liv crossed her denim-clad legs. "I'm afraid this job might not be very challenging for you intellectually. It's going to be a ton of filing, answering phones, handling some correspondence, and holding down the fort when I'm out of the office. I can offer you twenty bucks an hour, twenty to twenty-five hours a week."

"That sounds great! I like the secretarial stuff, plus I'm excited to learn more about private investigation work."

Liv shook her head. "I don't have time to train you as a P.I. The job is strictly clerical."

"I get that, but it will be fun to see you in action and learn how you run your business. I pick up a lot from observation. Plus," Marion grinned. "I was a huge *Veronica Mars* fan in high school."

Liv felt another twinge of concern. "It's not that exciting." She sat back, frowning, and looked down at the transcripts in her lap. "I'm afraid you're way overqualified for this job."

Marion went silent for a moment. She sounded deflated when she spoke. "Oh. Okay. Thank you for meeting with me anyway."

Liv smiled. "But it's yours if you want it."

Marion's face lit up. "Yes, I want it! You had me scared for a second. When can I start?"

"How about now? I've got a stack of case files in my office so high you might run away screaming."

"I don't scare easy." Marion stood up. "Lead me to your fortress."

Chapter Thirteen

• • • • • • • • • • • • • •

Over the weekend, Jasper left several messages on her cell. She ignored them and instead spent the time painting the walls of the Lively Investigations reception area a pearly antique white.

She ordered a new sofa in soft gray and a mid-century Lucite table with a swirly base. She took one of her grandmother's antique tables out of storage to serve as the reception desk.

A nice clerk at her favorite office supply store helped her set up a multi-line phone, desktop computer, and printer for Marion.

Standing in the doorway surveying the results Sunday afternoon, Liv crossed her arms and gave herself a delighted hug. With the fresh paint, new furnishings, and some of her favorite art hung on the walls, Lively Investigations finally looked like the boutique agency she'd envisioned.

In fact, she'd be one-hundred percent excited except for the fact that her good fortune was entwined with Alice Ferguson's demise.

On Monday morning, Marion gasped and clapped her hands when she walked into the refurbished reception area. "This is beautiful, Olivia!" she said, settling herself at the desk, running admiring fingers over the antique oak surface. "I can't believe I get to work here."

She spent the next several hours recording answering machine messages, researching workflow management software, and acquainting herself with Liv's accounting system.

On Tuesday, Liv emailed her final report to Van. She wanted to tie up loose ends and officially close the case. It would be a long time before she'd be able to put Alice's murder out of her mind, but she needed to look ahead.

On Wednesday, when Van hadn't responded to the email, she phoned him to make sure he'd received the report.

"I apologize for being incommunicado," Van said, choking on the words. "I haven't been able to read it yet, but I'm sure I'll want to one of these days, you know, when it's not so painful."

"I wasn't sure if I should send it or not, to be honest." She leaned back in her chair and crossed her legs on top of her desk. "How are you holding up? You've probably had a lot to do and to process." As far as she knew, Alby hadn't been found and was wanted for questioning.

Funeral, she thought. *Investigation. Missing brother. Worried parents. Grief.*

"I'm not dealing with all this very well, I'm afraid." Van sighed. "But I haven't forgotten our deal. I'll mail your check this week."

She inhaled sharply. His retainer had been enough to get Marion on board. She couldn't press him for more, not after what happened. "Oh, no, Van. Forget about it. I was only on the job for a few days. Consider us even. I'm just so sorry this happened on my watch." Liv hesitated. "Have the police told you anything about the investigation?"

"Two detectives showed up the day after the, uh…" His voice broke. "Murder. I have a hard time even saying the word."

"I get that. You don't have to talk about it if you don't want to."

"I'm okay. Just hits me at odd moments." He fell silent for several seconds, and then he cleared his throat. "Sorry. Uh, they asked me a bunch of questions. They wanted to know when you and I spoke, if Alice and I communicated at all, where I was that night and the following morning. I know the spouse is always the first person they suspect, but it was awful being grilled like that. I almost felt guilty. Like I'd done it in some sort of fugue state or something."

Liv frowned. "What did you tell them?"

"The truth. After I talked to you, I mowed the lawn and had a couple beers with one of my neighbors. That was around 3:00 p.m.... Later that night, I watched the Sox game and two movies on Netflix. I took Busterdoodle for his late-evening walk around midnight and went to bed."

Liv considered this. Anyone could access a Netflix watch history, but the items weren't time-stamped. "You didn't see or talk to anyone?"

"Not until the next morning around seven when Buster and I went to Dunkin' for coffee and donuts. I picked up a half-dozen at the drive-thru and went home again."

Liv's thoughts raced as Van rambled on about Busterdoodle and a donut hole the nice woman at the drive-thru window tossed to him.

Though he sounded like he was telling the truth, Van didn't seem to have a solid alibi to account for his time that evening. She'd talked with him on the phone at noon, telling him about seeing Alby and Alice together. He'd said he wasn't driving up, but could he have changed his mind after the beers with the neighbor—after the Sox game even—and still made it to the chalet in plenty of time to confront Alice?

She did a quick calculation. Alice had been killed sometime after ten p.m. when Liv saw her walking in the woods. It took a little over three hours to drive between Duckbill Pond and Portland, six hours round-trip plus added time to commit murder in between.

How long would it take to shove a knife into someone's chest and flee the scene?

Not long, she realized. If Van arrived at the chalet by midnight and confronted Alice, leaving her for dead, he could have been back well before daylight and that Dunkin' Donuts run. She felt cold dread settle into her stomach.

But then Van said, "I know what you're thinking. No alibi. The police thought it, too. Lucky for me, a neighbor installed a couple security cameras during the pandemic after some of her packages were swiped off her front porch. She's diagonally across the street from our, er, my house." He choked a little on the words. "The recordings have timestamps that back up my story. Our family's lawyer watched them and said they clearly show me walking Buster around midnight, just like I said."

She did the math. He still could have been in Carry Over by three and back to Portland by seven. Barely, but possible. "What about street traffic?"

"We... I... live on a cul-de-sac. To get out to the main road, I have to drive past the cameras. The videos recorded my car in the morning when I went to get coffee and donuts. Nothing before then. Travis came over to take Buster to the dog park and help me move some furniture just after noon, so you can see his truck coming and going. I showed the police my debit card charge for the Dunkin' run in the a.m. My lawyer thinks they've cleared me as a suspect, but it really stinks being accused of killing my own wife."

He sniffed back tears. "I miss her, Liv. We were having trouble, but I never wanted something like this to happen to her. I can't believe Alby did this and ran away. Maybe it's a good thing he's missing. If I got my hands on him, I might kill him myself."

Liv winced. "I know. It's truly horrible. But don't say things like that around the police, okay?"

A pause. "Sorry. You're right. I didn't mean that. It was a stupid thing to say. Like I could kill Alby. Or anyone. I wouldn't have the guts."

She struggled to find the words to comfort him. "You're too good a man to resort to violence. That doesn't make you weak, you know."

Silence. Another sniff. "Thanks, Liv."

"You're welcome. And it's a relief about your neighbor's camera. They always suspect the husband first." Liv relaxed against her chair. She wished she could get a look at that recording, but no way the authorities would give her access. She was a P.I., not law enforcement.

Didn't matter, she told herself. The police would look at traffic and highway videos as well, she imagined, but it appeared Van had a solid alibi. Plus with Alby still missing and the last person to be seen with Alice, Liv assumed he'd be the prime subject.

It seemed likely Alby and Alice had another altercation after Liv ended her surveillance for the night. Alby must have lost his temper, grabbed the knife, and killed Alice in a fit of rage. Realizing what he'd done, he must have packed his stuff and taken off, most likely to nearby Canada, rather than face the consequences. Typical Alby.

She ventured, "Have the police told you anything about your brother? Where they suspect he might have gone?"

"No idea. My lawyer says they've been talking to a lot of his friends and acquaintances, but Alby knows people all over the world. He could be anywhere, hiding out. As far as I know no one's heard from him. How about you? Have you heard anything official?"

"From the police? No. I haven't talked to them since the detective questioned me up in Carry Over. I'm sure they're working hard to find Alby and get some answers."

Alice's novel popped into Liv's mind, but she hesitated to share that tidbit with Van. She hadn't put anything about Alice's writing in her case report to him. She only knew about the novel because she'd snooped into Alice's computer. When asked about her actions that day, she'd lied to the detective. She couldn't admit—especially in writing—that she'd touched anything at the chalet. If discovered, the state might revoke her P.I. license for misconduct.

Curiosity got the better of her, though. She asked, "Have they returned Alice's things to you? Her computer or anything?"

"No. Should they have?"

"Not necessarily. They might be keeping it as evidence."

Since Van didn't have the computer, she decided to drop the

topic. Alice's writing hardly seemed relevant. She was more worried about Van and his legal standing. "You said you have a lawyer to advise you through all this?"

"My father hired one for the family. He thinks Alby's innocent, of course. He wants to make sure dear brother's reputation remains intact when he returns."

Of course. Poor Van. Once the spare, always the spare. "It's a hard situation for sure."

Van let out a shuddering sigh. "I'm still in shock. Anyway, the police have released her body. Her funeral's next Saturday."

Oh, please don't ask me.

She hated funerals. The thought of being enclosed in a casket filled her with existential dread and loathing. When it was her time to go, she wanted to be scattered on the dune grasses of her favorite beach while a violinist played "The Lark Ascending" by Vaughn Williams.

Van interrupted her gloomy thoughts. "Can you be there, Liv?"

Damn. "Oh, Van. I don't know," she said. "It's really a family and close friends kind of situation."

"Please? You're like family to me. You know that."

Not really, she thought. Part of her wished she'd never agreed to take this case. She'd only done it as a favor.

Plus, the money, her subconscious reminded. *It's the least you can do for the poor guy.*

"All right," she said. "Text me the details. I'll be there."

Chapter Fourteen

• • • • • • • • • • • • • •

That evening troubled thoughts tumbled in Liv's mind.

After work, she went for a satisfying, sweaty run around the cove, soft and shimmery in the hazy July heat. Black tank clinging to her skin, breath taken in small gulps, she chugged up Munjoy Hill. At the top, she breathed hard, hands clasped on top of her head, perspiration running in rivulets down her neck.

Two couples, each with barking dogs in tow, strolled toward each other and began talking in excited voices about a city council decision regarding homelessness and a canine poop problem.

Liv walked the other way.

It seemed like everyone in the neighborhood had a dog these days. She didn't mind as long as their owners picked up after them and kept them from barking at night, but she'd never been tempted to keep a pet. Other than the riding lessons in middle school, she had little experience with animals. *Other than the human kind,* she thought, grimacing and stretching her aching calf muscles.

After a cool shower, she poured herself an ice-cold glass of pinot grigio and plopped her boneless self into her favorite sunroom chair to watch the colors of the sunset fade to indigo. Venus's bright glimmer hovered like a distant firefly over the foothills west of the city.

Wondering how to spend the remainder of her quiet evening at home, Alice's novel popped into her mind. She tapped her fingernails on her glass. Should she have told Van about the book?

No, she decided. No good could come of Van knowing Alice had been writing erotica with his brother.

She sipped her wine, letting the cool, tart flavor sit on her tongue. The police had confiscated the laptop, so they must have discovered Alice and Alby's collaboration. Maybe the detectives would ask Van if he knew anything about his wife's novel-in-progress, and he'd be able to honestly say that he did not. One less complication for both the investigators and her friend-slash-client.

Liv sank deeper into her chair. What intrigued her most was the question of why Alice and Alby had been writing an erotic novel together in the first place. Obviously the two had been up to something with that book, but it didn't prove the two of them had been bumping uglies in the bedroom. They'd been passionate enough to argue that night in Carry Over, yes, but people disagreed about many things, even stupid things. Didn't mean they were having an affair.

Didn't mean they weren't, either. She frowned. Most likely, forensics would check for physical evidence of sexual assault or activity, take photographs, and collect DNA samples. They'd compare samples with Alby's DNA collected from his home or belongings.

His fingerprints would be everywhere, but that proved little. Liv's testimony already placed him at the chalet. Even if they found prints on the knife, it wouldn't prove he was the killer. Someone had sliced some cheese to go with the wine. Alby—if they apprehended and put him on trial—could claim he used the knife to prepare a snack and left it on the counter where someone else picked it up and used it as a deadly weapon. What about a second set of prints? Alice's or even Van's? All the Fergusons had access to the chalet and the knife block. What if the killer wore gloves? Any other prints would be smudged.

In any case, she knew it was rare to convict a killer based on fingerprints alone.

Still, someone had picked up that knife and plunged it into

Alice's chest. She pictured Alice's staring eyes. It was an image burned into her brain. She doubted she'd ever be able to erase it. A shiver went through her. The nature of the murder suggested a crime of passion, the assailant frustrated, possibly humiliated, blind with rage.

Or else staged to look that way? Who could have wanted Alice dead? And why?

She thought about the lamp carried to the woods. What had Alice been doing out there? Hiding something? Meeting someone else?

Alice had been out there only a few minutes before returning to the chalet. Liv had seen the lights in the chalet go dark, and then she'd gone to bed. Now she thought about the men's shirt under Alice's bed. Maybe Alby'd visited Alice in bed that night, acting out erotic scenes of their own. Liv had no way of knowing, and maybe it didn't matter. Not for Alice anyway.

Because when Alice, wearing her pretty satin and lace nightgown, returned to the kitchen later on that night, someone confronted her there. Pulled the knife from the block. Plunged it deep into her chest.

Shuddering, Liv gulped her wine. *Left her there alone*, she thought, remembering Alice's staring eyes. *To die.*

•   •   •   •   •

"When Marion saw that stack of case folders, I thought I'd lost her, but she rallied and dove right in."

Liv rolled down the window of Ashleigh's new white hybrid SUV crossover as they headed down Quebec Street toward East Bayside. Portland gleamed beneath cloudless blue skies and bright sunshine. A perfect Maine summer day.

Ashleigh glanced in her rearview mirror and gave it a quick adjustment. "So you think she's going to work out?"

"Definitely. I'm going to train her on the accounting system this week, and she's going to research VoIP phone services so we can have caller ID and call transfers, things like that." She pushed her rectangular, black Chanel sunglasses up her nose and smiled at her friend. "It's good to see you, Ash. Feels like it's been forever. How are you feeling?"

Despite the open windows, not a hair stirred on her friend's smooth, blonde ponytail. Ashleigh's French-manicured nails gleamed as she kept her hands diligently at ten and two on the steering wheel. Liv had to admit that pregnancy glow looked good on her best friend.

"The end of the school year and this pregnancy wiped me out. Did I tell you I gave my official notice?"

"You said you were thinking about it." Liv kept her voice neutral. "I guess you decided. So... congratulations?"

Ashleigh made a face. "I know you don't approve of me giving up my career, but with twins on the way and the cost of a nanny, it doesn't make sense to keep my job. Besides, I don't want someone else to raise my children. I've wanted this for so long, and you know how much we went through getting pregnant. It might not have happened at all. Don't judge me, please. Just say you're happy for me."

Ashleigh, whose endometriosis had made conception difficult, had earned a master's degree in school counseling and then worked for several years at an elementary school serving underprivileged kids. Brilliant, intuitive, and caring, Ash loved her work. Kids adored her. Parents listened to her. School administrators and teachers respected her.

Was giving up her promising career for mommyhood worth the sacrifice, Liv wondered? She hoped her best friend wouldn't wake up one day in her mid-fifties— empty-nested, kids off to college, eighteen years out of the field—and regret her decision. It happened. Liv had met women like this, and many of them wondered why the heck they gave up all their hopes and dreams for the sake of offspring who couldn't be bothered to call except when they needed cash, a ride, or the down payment for a condo in Tampa after they'd fled frigid New England for sun, sand, and surf.

Since Ashleigh'd made up her mind, though, Liv told her what she wanted to hear. "Of course I'm happy for you."

She turned to look out the window as Ashleigh navigated the narrow streets. Portland bustled in summer with out of state tourists on vacation, kids on summer break, and everyone outside to take advantage of the beautiful weather. Ashleigh put her blinker on several seconds earlier than necessary and pulled into a parking lot.

Liv scanned the premises. A cluster of galleries and shops, all with hip names and fancy awnings, had been carved from an old metal fabrication building. It was all part of the continuing gentrification of the old industrial East Bayside area.

A bougie smoothie place called *Guava or Go Home* boasted outdoor seating in bright colors. Another sign reading *Poppie & Porpoise* had been painted with a little teddy bear riding in a baby-blue hot-air balloon. Liv's stomach sank.

"*Poppie & Porpoise?*" she said as Ashleigh slid the SUV into a parking space. "You mentioned a cute new boutique. You never said it was a baby store."

Ashleigh gave her a bland look and shrugged. "Stop pouting. I need you to help me choose crib bedding, and I heard they have the sweetest gender-neutral designs ever. Come on. You'll love it." She grabbed her Dooney & Burke bag—a "knocked-up" gift from her husband, Trevor—and sailed toward the boutique. In her navy and white polka-dot maternity dress and kitten-heel sandals, she radiated posh-mommy vibes.

Liv followed, feeling betrayed. She loved Ash, her friend who looked like Margot Robbie and talked like Oprah Winfrey with her "live your best life" and "be mindful of the present" and "trusting the process" advice. This, however, felt like a bait and switch.

Liv considered trusting the process right back home.

"Come on, slowpoke," Ash called out. "After you help me choose the perfect bedding, I'll take you to lunch. My treat. Anywhere you want."

· · · · ·

Two hours later, after Ash had cooed over each and every item in the store, Liv shoved their cart toward the oh-so-precious checkout counter where the line was fifteen deep with glowing and drowsy-eyed women.

Ashleigh, unfazed by the astronomical total, whipped out a platinum credit card and beamed as the cashier gently wrapped each item in baby blue tissue and placed it into blue and white striped bags with their cutesy-bear-and-balloon logo.

"See, that wasn't so bad." Ashleigh handed a couple bags to Liv, picked up the rest herself, and floated toward the door on a dangerous combo of buyer's high and pregnancy hormones. "Wasn't that fun?"

"I'd rather be sitting in a car for six hours doing surveillance on some dinglehead cheating on his wife than spend one more minute in this baby bunting version of Hades," Liv said. "Now let's get lunch at Union so I can drown my memory of this place in espresso martinis and a lobster roll."

Chapter Fifteen

● ● ● ● ● ● ● ● ● ● ● ● ● ●

The following day, after an uneventful process service job handing legal paperwork to a defendant in a personal injury case, Liv picked up two lattes at the Coffee By Design on Diamond Street and drove the Corolla back to her nearby office.

The phone rang just as she walked in the door. She felt a spasm of annoyance, but then she happily remembered she had an assistant to screen her calls now.

Sitting behind the new desk in the freshly-painted reception space, Marion clicked the button on her headset like a pro. "Lively Investigations, Marion speaking." She put her hands together and mouthed "thank you" when Liv placed the latte in front of her. "One moment, Ms. Larabee. I'll see if she's available."

Liv raised her eyebrows.

Marion clicked a button to put the caller on hold. "It's Francine Larabee from Raptor Paper. Says she has a job for you."

"Great," Liv said, heading toward her office. "Give me ten seconds and put her through."

Francine was the head of the human resources department at the Raptor Pulp & Paper Company in Fallbrook, a working-class suburb west of the city. Francine had hired Liv several times to handle detailed background checks on upper-level management applicants.

Liv slid behind her desk, popped the tab on her to-go cup, and picked up the phone when it chirped. "Hello, Francine. What can I do for you?"

Francine spoke in her usual clipped tone. "We've been hit with a big worker's comp claim. I'm liaising with our insurance rep and legal team who suggested hiring someone to investigate. Interested?"

"You bet I am. Give me the highlights." Liv pulled out a fresh legal pad and a pen. Raptor was an important client, and moving up from routine background checks to potential insurance fraud investigation was a big step up for Lively Investigations, the sort of case she'd dreamed of handling when she first decided to become a P.I.

Francine exhaled sharply. "Here it is in a nutshell. The employee maintains he sustained permanent damage to his hand after an accident involving a pickaroon tool. These are used to pull logs into a chute in our groundwood plant. He claims he can't feel or move his fingers, but I'm told he's been bragging to coworkers that he's gonna retire on the comp settlement and move somewhere he can play golf and fish year round."

"Sounds suspicious."

"Exactly. Can you meet at the plant around 2 o'clock this afternoon? I'll give you the documents we have and show you around the groundwood facility so you can get your bearings."

"Fabulous. I'll see you at two."

Grinning, Liv replaced the phone handset. Marion cracked the door and popped her head into the office. "Did we get a new case?"

Liv's smile widened. She loved Marion's enthusiasm and the way she took ownership of the job despite the temporary status. It was nice to have someone else around the office, too. "Yes, we did, and it's a good one," she told Marion as she eased the lid from her own latte. "How's the account reconciliation going?"

"Almost done. I'll have reports on your desk by the end of the day."

Liv shook her head in admiration. "Unbelievable. Thank you so much, Marion."

In less than a week, her new assistant had organized the filing cabinets, mastered the billing and accounting software, and hired a service to steam-clean the rugs. She'd replaced the tired old magazines on the coffee table with fresh copies of Longfellow College's most recent literary magazine and a few popular publications she'd picked up at Nonesuch Books in South Portland. She'd even begun scanning old paperwork and organizing a paperless filing system.

The thought of no more file folders made Liv giddy. "You're a miracle worker."

Marion lifted her coffee cup. The flowing sleeve of her kimono-style top looked, appropriately, like an angel's wing. "It's these lattes you keep bringing me, I swear. I'm addicted now, by the way."

"It's more than that and you know it. I really wish I could keep you on permanently."

"No worries. I'll be busy with law school in the fall. I'll help you find another intern before I leave. I promise."

Liv made a face. She didn't want another intern. She wanted Marion.

"Well, let's worry about that when your six weeks are up. Meanwhile, why don't you take your lunch break. I have to be in Fallbrook at two."

"If it's okay with you, I'll just eat at my desk. I have some editing to do."

"Oh! Are you working on some new poems?" Marion didn't talk much about her writing. Liv had been dying to ask but didn't want to pry, so she'd waited for the MFA grad to bring up the topic first.

Marion's round cheeks flushed bright pink. "Not exactly. I'm, uh, working on a novel."

"Oh? What kind of novel?"

"Romantic suspense. A woman moves back to her old family home and accidentally uncovers evidence of a crime. She starts dating the hot safe cracker she hires to open her great-grandfather's basement vault safe as part of her investigation. The perpetrator realizes he could be found out and tries to get her to leave, but when she doesn't run away, he attempts to kill her." Marion shrugs. "It's just for fun, really."

"That sounds interesting." Liv's mind flashed to Alice's erotic manuscript. "You know, I might be able to use your writing expertise on something."

Marion's eyes lit up. "For a case?"

"Sort of. I'm not sure yet if it's anything, but I might need another set of eyes on an unfinished draft that might be relevant to one of my clients. Do you have a problem with, uh, erotica?"

Marion put the hand not holding her coffee on her heart. "Just the opposite. Big *Fifty Shades* fan here. Let me know if and when you want me to help."

· · · · ·

At one o'clock, Liv left the office and drove to Buoy Bagels to grab lunch before her meeting at Raptor. She greeted Ruth, the gray-haired and kind owner of the sandwich shop, who talked her into trying a new item on the menu. Ruth called it The Hawaiian Spams-A-Lot. The gooey sammy featured Spam lunch meat and pineapple rings grilled with melty Monterey Jack cheese on a plain bagel. It was delicious.

Driving north on I-95 after lunch, she took the Fallbrook exit and made her way toward the Raptor offices. Raptor Pulp & Paper's operation was an industrial sprawl tucked beside the Presumpscot River. Some people looked down their noses at mill towns, but Liv understood the company provided good manufacturing jobs in the community, not to mention the basic material used for things people tended to enjoy. Like books. And cards. And pretty wrapping paper.

Better made in Maine, she thought, *than some gosh-awful place overseas where the environmental laws were lax and workers' rights barely existed.*

She stopped at a light a few miles from the paper mill and hummed along with the Albinoni concerto trilling from her speakers. Waiting for the light to change, she tapped her fingers and idly looked around.

She noticed a low, square, beige building squatting next to a busy Dunkin' Donuts. It looked like a warehouse. The entrance was a dark-tinted glass door. No other windows broke the expanse of colorless, corrugated aluminum siding. A large sign towered over the cracked parking lot. On a black background with gold-edged white lettering, the sign read, "The Golden Triangle Club."

The letterboard beneath the name promoted a Thursday Ladies Night with $5 cocktails and a Tuesday Night Cabaret, but it was the double-triangle logo on the sign that caught her attention.

Chills raced up her arms as she recognized the design. *Alice's necklace!*

Her mind jumped back to the junk mail promotion card she'd tossed into the trash just before taking Van's case. No wonder the necklace had looked familiar when she saw it later that week. Why would Alice own a necklace with the same symbol as a strip club?

A horn blared behind her, and Liv realized the light had changed. She tore her eyes from the sign and stepped on the gas. The car behind her pulled around into the left lane and zoomed up beside her. The driver looked over and gave her the finger.

Always fun to be in Fallbrook, she thought. She returned the gesture but slowed down to let him pass. Poor guy was driving a battered minivan with a "My Kid's an Honor Student" sticker on the dented rear bumper. He probably needed a badass moment once in a while to make up for his sad life of carpooling, parent-teacher conferences, lawn mowing, and honey-do lists.

She found a visitor parking space, and exited the car. Heat rolled off the hot top, and sweat popped out on her forehead immediately. Machinery clanked, company vehicles zipped here and there, and from the towering smokestack, thick steam billowed into the sky. "The smell of money," Liv muttered, trying to remember where she'd picked up that Maine quip. Probably an old boyfriend, or maybe even Ashleigh who'd grown up in a paper town in Western Maine and through sheer determination and brains earned herself a full-ride scholarship to Bowdoin College and became Liv's roommate and best friend for life.

Inside the Raptor executive office building, Liv was ushered into an air-conditioned office the approximate temperature of Siberia. Francine, as promised, gave her documentation and a tour of the groundwood facility. The human resources director wore a black pantsuit and crisp fuchsia shirt beneath it and classic black brogues on her feet. Her auburn hair swung along her jawline as she led Liv to a door on the second floor and said to follow her.

The two women stepped along a catwalk situated above the main work area. Liv noticed workers staring up in their direction—some pointing, others scowling. The machinery was deafening, and the stench of wood processing chemicals permeated the air.

Men hoisted short-handled tools with deadly-looking iron curved picks on the end and used them to guide logs down a watery chute. Francine said they were called pickaroons. Liv could see how one could go through a worker's hand and cause some major damage.

"See enough?" Francine yelled after a few minutes.

"For now," Liv yelled back. "Did you say the insurance rep was going to meet with us?"

Francine glanced at her big, square smartwatch. "Yes, she should be here soon. Let's go back to my office."

After a productive thirty-minute meeting, Liv decided to scoot back to The Golden Triangle to take another look at the place. As she wove through afternoon traffic, questions circled through her mind. Why was Alice wearing a necklace with the stripclub's logo attached? Was it just a coincidence or had Alice been involved in something Van was unaware of? Or maybe she really had been having an affair with Alby or someone else… someone connected with Fallbrook's seedy den of iniquity?

Even though she wasn't part of the official investigation, she felt excited about discovering a possible lead that might help the police find Alice's killer.

And give Van the closure he needed.

Chapter Sixteen

• • • • • • • • • • • • • •

Minutes after leaving the paper mill, Liv pulled into the Dunkin' next door to the strip club, ordered an iced coffee, and found a good spot to view the parking lot of The Golden Triangle.

Business was slow, not surprising for a Wednesday afternoon. A few cars and pickup trucks rolled into the lot. The customers were, as expected, primarily male.

She watched from behind her Chanel sunnies. The customers were from all walks of life. Men wearing jeans and baseball caps. A group of young businessmen in suits, ties loosened, and pointy-toed fancy shoes. A couple older guys, silver hair, paunchy and florid-cheeked, who looked as if they'd just finished a round of golf and decided to stop in for some refreshments and gawking on the way home.

As Liv sucked down her iced coffee, a taxi pulled in. Two young women climbed out, laughing. They were thin and well-endowed—implants, most likely—but otherwise unremarkable in minuscule jean shorts and tiny tees and wearing dark sunglasses over their eyes. Dancers, Liv decided. They probably kept their costumes in a dressing room on the premises rather than shuffle them back and forth from home.

When the women disappeared into the club, Liv opened the photo app on her phone and scrolled the photos she'd taken in Carry Over until she found the one she remembered. *Poor dead Alice.*

Pushing the body from her mind, she enlarged the image to reveal more details of the charm hanging from its golden chain around Alice's neck. She squinted back and forth from the phone to the sign outside the strip club. Definitely the same design, but it was possible there was no actual connection. An artist making jewelry and a graphic designer creating a sign could have been inspired by the same design in a book, a collection of images, an ancient symbol.

A coincidence, yes, but not impossible.

She took another long gulp of iced coffee and wondered if she could get her hands on the necklace to see if there were any inscriptions. If the detectives hadn't made a connection between the symbol on the charm and the strip club logo, perhaps they'd returned the necklace to Van along with any of Alice's belongings not tagged as evidence.

She scrolled through the rest of the Carry Over pictures, looking for anything else that might connect Alice to the club, but nothing jumped out at her. She wished she'd taken shots of Alice's computer tabs. Hadn't one been about pole dancing?

Liv caught movement out of the corner of her eye. She looked up just as a glistening black Lincoln eased into a marked parking space directly in front of the club. Two doors opened simultaneously, and a couple of men, sort of lean and foreign-looking with chiseled cheekbones, European haircuts, and dark suits, emerged. The pair adjusted their sunglasses and strolled toward the door. Another man, gigantic and bald, wearing a thick gold chain around his beefy neck, opened the door from the inside and held it for them.

The hairs on the back of her neck tingled.

Liv raised her phone and clicked a few photos of the men before the door to the club swung shut behind them. She scrabbled around in her leather bag on the passenger seat and drew out her binoculars. She tapped the Maine license plate number into a note on her phone to check later.

For a brief moment, she considered going into the club for a look around but decided to wait and talk to Van first. Maybe he knew something about the necklace.

· · · · ·

Following Alice's Episcopal funeral and sweltering graveside service, Liv turned onto Van's street in Larkwood Estates, a cushy development in the seaside town of Pellham just north of Portland.

The houses in Larkwood came in three or four basic designs clad in a choice of tasteful Colonial colors. Slight variations of window placement, porches, porticos, and trims added a thin veneer of individuality. Two- and three-bay garages looked more like stables than car ports.

The whole place oozed upper middle-class privilege, Liv thought as she searched for a place to park, but something about the neighborhood felt over-manicured and artificial, like something on a television reality show.

Cars lined the sidewalks on both sides of the street. She turned around in the cul-de-sac just past Van's house and spied another car pulling away, leaving a spot free. After parallel parking without incident, she smoothed the wrinkles from her black, scalloped-sleeved shift. She'd gone a little too short and sexy for a funeral, but the muggy July weather made propriety less important than comfort. She hated funerals as it was. A girl could only suffer so much.

With strappy Manolos digging into her feet, she made her way to the front door of Van's house, a massive three-story Colonial with classic gray clapboard siding. She stepped into the foyer and gave an audible sigh as blessed air-conditioned coolness enveloped her. A tasteful bouquet of flowers sat on a round, marble-topped table beneath a crystal chandelier dangling from the open, two-story ceiling. A staircase curved to the second-floor hallway. A hardwood floor gleamed beneath a scarlet and navy Persian rug.

The thought crossed her mind that buying and decorating the

place must have cost Van and Alice a fortune. As a social worker, Alice's salary couldn't have helped much. She wondered if Alice came from wealth or if the elder Fergusons had helped the young couple with a down payment or something.

She signed the guest book on the table and followed the low murmur of conversation to the living room. Dark-clad mourners clutched drinks in their hands and spoke in subdued voices. Several people cast sidelong glances in her direction, men with interest, women with raised eyebrows.

She spotted Van in a cluster of people in a far corner of the room. When she caught his eye and gave a little wave, he extricated himself from the knot of consoling friends.

"Van. I'm sorry for your loss."

She leaned in for a breezy air kiss. Instead he surprised her with a bear hug. "Liv. I wasn't sure you'd come. Thank you for being here," he said. His breath, heavy with alcohol fumes, tickled her ear. "It's been a nightmare."

He rocked her back and forth even as she tried to pull away from his grasp. More people turned their heads to watch. She patted his back several times before he let go of her. She put a few inches between them and smoothed the front of her dress. "Are you doing okay?"

"Barely. My parents are here. I think they are less sad about Alice and more concerned about finding Alby."

"Do the police have any leads at all?"

"Not that they're sharing with me." He took her elbow. "Come on. Let's get a drink. We can go somewhere quiet to talk."

He steered them to the drinks cart and poured two glasses of scotch on the rocks. After handing one to her, he led her to a small room off the kitchen. Liv scanned the fancy washer and dryer, the floral rug, and the natural wicker baskets nestled up to a little French writing table and matching chair.

"Pretty," she said.

"This was her work space. Letter writing. Bill paying. Laundry, obviously." Van stuck one hand in the pocket of his slacks, Hugo Boss if she wasn't mistaken. "I told her we could hire someone to handle that for us—the laundry, I mean—but she liked doing it herself." He took a large gulp of the scotch. Ice-cubes rattled as he shook the glass. "I can't believe she's gone."

"It must be hard."

"I just keep asking myself why I let her go up there. I should have begged her to stay home or offered to take her on vacation somewhere. We could be in Oahu right now." He finished off his scotch, red-rimmed eyes staring at her over the rim. "You know, I'd prepared myself for the possibility that she and Alby were having an affair. I understood that meant possible separation and maybe even divorce. But this? It's just…I don't even know how to process it."

"It's a terrible, terrible thing." Liv walked to the desk, ran her finger over the smooth top. Admired the curve of the front and iron pulls on the drawers.

Van noticed. "She had good taste. Not that she always went for the most expensive things. Money didn't really matter to her that much. That's why she was content with her social work job. Helping the immigrants. Getting them services and language tutors and such. She was a good person. She didn't deserve to die this way."

Liv hesitated. "Look, Van. I'm not sure this is the right time to discuss this, but I may have stumbled onto something about Alice. It's not much, so I haven't gone to the police yet, but I noticed something when, well, when I found her. I mean, it's probably just a coincidence…"

Face tense, he interrupted. "Just spit it out, Liv."

"Do you remember her wearing a gold necklace with a double triangle charm attached to it?"

His face registered bafflement. "No. I never bought her anything like that. She didn't like jewelry much, anyway. She rarely wore her engagement diamond. She preferred her plain platinum wedding band. Why?"

"She was wearing the necklace when she died. At the time, I thought the design of the charm looked familiar, but I couldn't place it. And then the other day I was driving over to Fallbrook for a case and saw the same—or what may be the same, I'm not positive—symbol on a business sign. I'm just not sure how or why Alice would be connected to this place."

"What's the business?"

"The Golden Triangle." Liv watched his reaction. She added, "It's a strip club."

He blinked, blank-faced, and shook his head. "I know what The Golden Triangle is, but what does it have to do with Alice?"

Chapter Seventeen

• • • • • • • • • • • • • • •

Liv gave Van a troubled look. "That's what I've been asking myself. Maybe nothing. Like I said, it could be a coincidence. I'd like to get a closer look at the necklace. Have the police returned Alice's things to you yet?"

"No." He rubbed his face with a trembling hand. "They aren't telling us much. Nobody's mentioned a necklace or a strip club."

"If it's any consolation, they won't talk with me, either. All they say is it's an ongoing investigation."

When she'd returned to her office after her discovery in Fallbrook, she'd called Detective Briggs to ask if they had any leads. Briggs gave her the standard we're doing all we can brush-off, and Liv found herself reluctant to mention the triangle charm. "I wish I could tell you more."

Liv spotted a coaster on Alice's desk, set her barely-touched drink on it.

"You don't have any secret contacts inside the state police?" Van attempted to grin. "What good are you?"

"Not much, I guess."

Van reached past her and picked up Liv's abandoned glass. "Do you mind?"

She shook her head.

He took a few gulps, ice cubes rattling. "My parents are half out of their minds about Alby. They keep saying he couldn't have done it, that he's been abducted. They call the police every day with far-fetched theories about crazed drug addicts roaming the western Maine woods or a flannel-shirted serial killer on the loose." He snorted. "You can imagine how likely the police are to tell us anything after hearing that kind of sh...*stuff*. Pardon."

"Don't worry about it, and yeah. A crazed serial killer in L.L.Bean is highly unlikely."

They lapsed into silence. Liv pictured Alice's body, the large knife plunged to the hilt in her chest, the spread of blood on satin. Could Alice's murder have been some completely random crime? A case of wrong place, wrong time?

If so, had Alby also fallen victim? Kidnapped? Taken somewhere else and tortured? Killed? In this era of social media, cell phone cameras, security and traffic monitoring, and surveillance in general, how did a person simply disappear?

She eyed the drink in Van's hand and wished she could take it back.

Van pointed a finger at her around the glass. "They just can't believe their golden boy would do something so violent. No matter what he does, they back him up. They'd sooner believe I committed murder, than Alby. Thank goodness my neighbor has those security cameras or I'd be the prime suspect, and I doubt my parents would even care." He sighed. "I think they only came to the funeral so they could bug the police about finding him. Hard to do that from Florida."

"That stinks, Van."

He held out his free hand. It trembled. "Look at this. My hands won't stop shaking. I'm a mess."

Liv felt a rush of sympathy. If anyone needed a hug right now it was Donovan. She wrapped her arms around him and patted his back. He hugged her back, rocking her side to side. "They'll find him soon," she said, trying to keep her balance on her high heels. "You'll get some answers. It might be hard to swallow, you know, when you find out what happened, but at least you'll have some closure."

"Thank you, Olivia. I feel better talking to you." Van held on as if she were a human life preserver. She felt panic begin to rise as his arms tightened around her, but she forced herself to breathe. The least she could do was lend her old friend human warmth and affection to assuage his grief.

"Van?" Tanya Ferguson, Van and Alby's mother, poked her head into the room.

She wore a tasteful black sheath, black stockings, and sensible black pumps. Her double strand of pearls matched the earrings in her stretched-out, older-lady lobes. Bold, red lipstick bled into the small lines surrounding her thin-lipped mouth.

Van and Liv separated.

The older woman narrowed her eyes. "What's going on here?"

"Hello, Mrs. Ferguson." Liv held out her hand. "Do you remember me? I'm Olivia Lively. Gilbert and Tiffany's daughter? I'm an old high school friend of Van's. I'm so sorry for your loss."

Mrs. Ferguson ignored Liv's greeting and cast a stern frown in Van's direction. "People are asking for you. You'd best return to the living room." She threw Liv a look of pure disgust, turned on her basic, black pumps, and disappeared.

"Guess she still doesn't like me," Liv said.

"Welcome to the club." Van threw back the rest of the drink and nodded toward the door. "Guess we better…"

"Yup."

She followed him into the living room. The crowd had thinned somewhat, but about twenty people still clustered in little groups, conversing in hushed tones.

A very tall, extremely gaunt woman with long, flowing, platinum-blonde hair and bleary eyes staggered around them and headed toward the mini-bar. She looked vaguely familiar, but before Liv could ask Van who she was, a couple in their mid-forties with sorrowful expressions approached.

"Incoming," Liv warned. She put a hand on his arm and squeezed. "I'm out of here. Call me if you hear anything new, or if you just need someone to talk to."

Van nodded in her direction and turned to face the condolences.

• • • • •

Leaving was easier said than done. Several people greeted her as she made her way across the room. They either recognized her from the media coverage in the spring or else remembered her as one of Van's and Alby's classmates at Coyne School. After nodding and smiling and being as agreeable as she could manage, Liv finally reached the foyer.

The platinum-haired woman Liv had spotted earlier sat on the bottom step of the staircase. She lifted a very full martini glass to her mouth, sloshing some down the front of her black lace dress and onto the wide, black satin ribbon cinching her tiny waist. Liv lifted her fingers in a little wave, not expecting a response, and reached for the door knob.

"Are you the one who found her? That whore who was sleeping with my husband?"

The woman wobbled to her feet, spilling more of her drink. She swayed toward Liv in her mile-high, black-beribboned heels. Liv braced herself to catch the woman if she pitched forward. That's all Van needed, she thought. Some drunk chick cracking her head open in his foyer.

"Excuse me?" Liv said.

The gaunt, long-limbed, slightly-familiar stranger managed to keep her balance. "Alice. The woman of the hour." She let out a hoarse laugh. "Even dead she manages to suck up all the attention."

Liv crossed her arms. "Well, to be fair, it *is* her funeral."

The woman raised her near empty glass. "Here's to that."

The movement put her off balance. She stumbled, and as Liv stepped forward to grab her by the elbow to steady her, the smell of vodka, olive brine, and Opium perfume wafted up in a sickening haze.

"Who's your husband?" she asked as she led the woman back

to the staircase and took the glass from her hand.

"You don't know?" The woman gave her a sly sideways glance as she sat, knees tucked to her chest.

"Uh-uh."

"I'm Emsley. Emsley Ballard-Monihan. Alby's wife."

Aha, Liv thought as she placed the martini glass on the marble table next to the guest book. As a stone sculptor, Emsley was somewhat famous in Maine's art world. Though Liv had never seen her or her work in person, she'd read about her. She should have recognized her from her research into the Ferguson clan, but in photos Emsley always wore her hair in a tight bun at the back of her head. She hadn't been so gaunt, either.

Liv remembered that the couple had divorced last winter. Apparently that fact hadn't quite registered with Emsley. At least not in her current state of inebriation.

She sat down on the stair next to Emsley. "You think Alice and Alby were having an affair?"

Emsley rolled her eyes. "Duh."

"Had it been going on for a long time?"

A sly look crossed Emsley's face. "The wife's always the last to know. Haven't you heard that expression?"

"I've heard it."

"Well, it's true. We fought all the time, but that's marriage, you know? We're both stubborn, and we both like to get our own way. I didn't want the divorce, but fool that I was, I believed him when he said there wasn't another woman, that he just couldn't take the arguing anymore. Turns out, it wasn't because of our fighting, at all. He wanted Alice. And Alby always gets what he wants." Her voice was bitter.

"So I've heard." Liv crossed her arms over her knees, mimicking Emsley's posture. "How did you find out? About Alice and Alby I mean?"

"Oh, everyone's talking about it now." Emsley picked at an almost healed scratch on her arm. "How he left me so he could be with Alice. And now he's…"

Emsley didn't finish her sentence. Voices from the living room grew louder as the gathering wound down and people moved toward the foyer. Liv asked, "Now he's what, Emsley?"

She frowned. "I don't know. Gone."

Liv waited for her to say more, but when she didn't, Liv stood. "I should go."

"Me, too. I'm sleepy. I'm going upstairs. Van won't mind. We're family." With that, Emsley wobbled to her feet, and staggered up the staircase one stiletto-clad foot at a time.

Chapter Eighteen

• • • • • • • • • • • • •

L iv woke late Sunday morning following Alice's funeral and dressed for a long run along the Eastern Prom.

Humidity levels had risen overnight, and sticky heat enveloped her as soon as she set out. Despite everything going on with Jasper—they still hadn't talked because she'd refused to answer his calls and texts and he'd finally given up—she felt energized and strangely at peace.

Nothing like a funeral to make you appreciate being alive.

It wasn't just that, though. For the first time in ages, panic didn't set in whenever she thought about her business. With Marion on board and handling administrative work like a pro, Liv had time to concentrate on cases and projects. Several back payments from recalcitrant clients had arrived in the mail that week, and her bank account looked less anemic than it had at the beginning of the month.

If things continued to swing along through the summer, her next quarter would be Lively Investigations' best one yet.

Breathing easy, she looped around Fort Allen Park and past the new restaurant, Twelve. Continuing into the Old Port, she'd made it halfway down Commercial Street toward High when she became aware of a familiar black SUV slowing beside her.

She glanced over. FBI Agent Colin Snow rolled his window and grinned out at her with his crooked, naughty-boy smile, his short, regulation-cut brown hair ruffling on top of his head in the breeze.

One wrist carelessly steering the wheel, he called out, "Lookin' good, Lively."

Her mouth dropped open to respond but he gave her a thumbs up and sped off.

She scowled as she picked up her pace. "Nice to see you, too, Agent Snow."

She hadn't seen Snow since April, when he'd rescued her from a very sticky situation involving her closet, her collection of scarves, and too much champagne in her system. Discreet inquiries revealed he'd gone back to the divisional office in Boston after wrapping up the bank and mortgage fraud case into which Liv had accidentally stumbled.

If Snow was back in town, he must be working on a federal case. Her curiosity level notched up a couple degrees. If she called him, would he answer her questions, she wondered?

Probably not. Aside from a bit of mild flirting, nothing had happened between her and the agent. That didn't mean she hadn't thought about it at the time. Snow had that sweet, edgy something that tempted her like candy laced with Cointreau. She suspected he was a good guy with a few interesting bad boy talents, but she hadn't yet tested her theory. Back in the spring, she'd thought they might indulge the attraction between them, but when she decided to commit to her relationship with Jasper, she'd pushed thoughts of Snow from her mind.

Now, she thought, *Had Dr. Hottie been worth it?*

Her feet pounded on the sidewalk at a moderate pace as she pondered the situation. She and Jasper needed to talk, she decided, if only to end things officially. Trouble was, her feelings about him swung back and forth from wanting to hear him out to hoping never to see him again. It was so unlike her, moods changing like the weather, hot then cold.

Did she love him? She didn't know. Maybe it was simply pride, not love, that had her reeling. She hated failure. For the first time in her life, she'd plunged into a relationship hoping, reaching, for long-term. To have it implode mere months from the start felt like a bad grade on a final exam for which she'd prepared. An up all night in the library highlighting passages and memorizing dates kind of preparation. A give up the keg party to study kind of preparation.

Seeing Wren with Jasper and his parents was the big fat F on her blue book, the red pen corrections pointing out her inadequacies, the call to the principal's office to discuss her uncertain future.

Whenever she thought about that dinner and the four place settings and Jasper's inability to invite her to stay, her stomach hurt, so it was easier not to think about him at all.

In fact, she didn't want to think about it now. Kicking up her pace, she hit Forest Avenue at the edge of the park and rounded onto Marginal Way. Her breathing evened out as she got her second wind, and her body thrummed as she reached the hill climbing toward the northern end of the Prom.

She'd come almost full circle.

Story of her life.

When she reached home, she pulled out her phone and texted Jasper. *I'm ready to talk if you are. How about Wednesday night?*

A minute later she saw the three little dots. She waited. The dots disappeared. They reappeared. *I can make that work. I'll call you Monday to finalize?*

She let out her held breath and typed one word. *Okay.*

· · · · ·

"Olivia Rose Lively, what's the matter with you?" Tiffany Lively glared at Liv over the rim of her martini as Liv approached the cafe table. Liv glanced at her vintage Cartier watch, a beauty she'd found on her favorite online shop several years ago. It was barely noon on Monday.

"Hello to you, too, Mom." She leaned down and gave her mother a kiss on the cheek before slipping into her seat. The air smelled of grilled meat and the salty ocean, a scent particular to the Old Port. Wrought iron tables and chairs nestled behind a fence dotted with flower pots filled with bright blossoms.

The humidity had cleared overnight, and with a breeze coming in off the waterfront, the air was cool. Patrons wearing crisp jeans, pretty sweaters, and colorful suede moccasins or espadrilles chatted over their garden salads, iced teas, coffees and desserts. Everyone radiated the smooth, classic-but-casual vibe of wealthy New Englanders or visitors from away.

Two thirty-something women, each leading a small dog on a leash, followed the hostess to a nearby table. The dogs circled the chairs, winding their leashes. Their owners cooed and untangled them. A nearby West Highland Terrier clad in a tartan sweater barked at the new arrivals. The women giggled and picked up their menus.

Liv turned her attention back to her mother.

Tiffany had called the office demanding to meet her for lunch. It was either that or dinner at the club, so Liv suggested The Garden Cafe at the Regency Hotel. She raised her eyebrows as Tiffany took another sip of vodka and olive brine. "I guess it's five o'clock somewhere?"

Her mother's signature gold bracelets clinked. "Don't start. If I'm drinking it's only because you drive me to it."

"What did I do now?"

"Oh, let's see. Sneaking off into the laundry room with Van Ferguson at his wife's funeral reception." Tiffany's nostrils flared. "What were you thinking?"

The laundry room. Tanya Ferguson. Of course.

"I wasn't thinking, obviously." Liv crossed her legs and tried to look nonchalant. "I mean, you'd have to be insane to go near a washing machine these days considering they're all made overseas and are probably programmed to collect data on America's cleaning habits 24/7. Forget TikTok. Congress should be looking into front loaders."

"You aren't funny."

"I'm a little funny." Liv looked around for a server. When the young woman arrived at the table, Liv ordered an unsweetened iced tea and Cobb salad.

Tiffany said the salad sounded good, too, but no bacon. "I've been told to reduce my sodium intake. My doctor doesn't like the look of my blood pressure," she said while chomping on a large, green olive.

"Is that a dirty martini you have there?" Liv put on an innocent face.

The server smiled. Tiffany noticed and glared at the poor girl. "What are you smirking at?"

"I'll be right back with your tea," the server said, smile wiped from her face.

Liv grimaced at her and mouthed, "Sorry."

The girl rolled her eyes and scurried off.

When the young woman was out of earshot, Tiffany turned back to the original topic. "Donovan's wife has just been *murdered*."

"I'm well aware."

"She's barely in the ground, and you're canoodling with her husband at her own funeral. In the laundry room, of all places."

"It was *after* her funeral, not at it. Emily Post makes it very clear that *after* funerals it is perfectly acceptable to canoodle in front of major appliances."

"Oliv—"

"Mom, relax. Nothing happened between Van and me."

"Oh, really." Tiffany pointed her olive pick in Liv's direction. "Then why did three separate people call to tell me they saw the two of you sneaking off together?"

Liv shrugged. "Boredom?"

"Tanya Ferguson told Clarice Martin she caught the two of you in a clinch and who knows what would have happened if she hadn't walked in at that moment. Of course, Clarice had to call *me* to gloat under the guise of 'I just thought you should know.'"

114 · SHELLEY BURBANK

Tiffany made a face and quoted her friend in a smarmy, nasal tone.

Liv laughed. "I thought you liked Clarice Martin."

"Oh, please." Liv's mom waved the toothpick. "She's a moron." Tiffany gulped down the rest of the martini and popped the last olive into her mouth.

The server arrived with Liv's iced tea and both salads. Tiffany and Liv went silent. The server asked if they needed anything else. "No, thank you," mother and daughter said in unison. A tiny dog yipped.

"You should steer clear of Donovan," Tiffany continued when the server disappeared. "The man's wife has just been murdered under very suspicious circumstances, which is scandalous enough, but his brother's also a fugitive from justice. That family is completely toxic right now. You need to think about your reputation, Olivia."

"I'll try to remember that."

Tiffany stabbed her fork into a piece of hard-boiled egg, frowned at it, and dropped it back onto her plate. She looked around the dining area. The corners of her mouth turned down. "I can't eat. Who are all these people with the dogs?"

Liv rattled the ice cubes in her tea, and looked around. There did seem to be a lot of dogs around, many dressed up in preppy sweaters and bejeweled collars. Kind of like their owners.

She turned her attention back to her mother and felt a pang of guilt. Tiffany seemed genuinely upset and worried. Once again, she'd caused her mother pain and frustration. At age thirty, she should be over that, but she didn't do these things on purpose, she argued with her conscience. They just sort of… happened.

"Listen, Mom. I'm sorry people are calling you about Van and me having a private conversation at his wife's funeral. I'm sorry you're embarrassed. He was grieving. I gave him a hug. It was totally innocent. If anyone mentions it again, remind them that he and I are old school friends, he's going through a terrible time, and I'm simply trying to help."

Tiffany picked up her fork again. Her bracelets clinked as they slid along her arm. She stabbed a piece of tomato with more force than necessary. "Well, next time try to help a little less."

Chapter Nineteen

• • • • • • • • • • • • • •

Back at her office Liv chalked the whole lunch experience up as just another disappointing parental interaction and let it go.

She sent Marion off to lunch and then, determined to get some work done on the Raptor worker's comp case, she pulled the case folder from her credenza and reacquainted herself with the details.

The employee, Raymond Booker, had been injured while pulling logs in the groundwood facility two winters ago. Booker's coworker had accidentally put a pickaroon through Booker's hand while both struggled to lift a frozen, jammed log into the grinder.

Scheduled on light duty after the accident, Booker now claimed continued pain and permanent disability, and he was suing the paper company for negligence and unsafe work conditions. According to scuttlebutt around the facility, Booker had been bragging about the lawsuit and how he'd never have to work again. He planned—rumor went—to move to Florida where he could fish and golf year round.

So far, the comments were just hearsay. Liv's job was to investigate and document, tag-teaming the legal team who would take it from there.

Settling more comfortably into her office chair, she pulled up one of her favorite playlists, a collection of piano concertos, for background noise while she studied the paperwork. She examined the incident report, the hospital statements provided to the paper company, the ambulance bill, and medical reports. She jotted notes on the date of injury and scrutinized time-sheet records from before and after the accident to look for patterns.

One thing stood out. Several times a year, mostly in the spring and winter months, he took vacation days or called out sick on a Friday, Monday, or both. This pattern hadn't ended with his injury.

Liv bit the end of her pen and squinted her eyes. Spring and winter meant fishing season in the state of Maine. Booker talked about moving to Florida to fish. Maybe she could scour social media and find some photographic evidence of him using his hand.

She logged onto Booker's primary social media site and examined his public feed. Not much to see there. He either didn't post much or he was smart enough to manage his privacy settings. She clicked another link and grinned. He'd overlooked the privacy setting for his friend list. Onto a yellow legal pad, she scribbled the names of various guys who looked like outdoor camping and fishing types and proceeded to check their socials as well.

After an hour or so, she hit pay dirt with a bunch of photos taken at some kind of winter ice festival in central Maine. The early-March event ran late in the ice-fishing season. A bunch of men, bearded and wearing knit caps and snowmobile boots and plaid jackets, posed for numerous photos and short videos: holding up fish in front of ice shacks, drinking beer while standing around on the ice, playing a game called IceHole judging by the merch on display.

She scrolled until one photo popped out at her. "Gotcha!" she said out loud as she clicked on the photo to enlarge it.

There was Raymond Booker lugging a giant ice auger with his injured left hand.

Liv took a screenshot of the page and copied the photo to her files. For future reference, she took note of the men tagged in the photo—she'd contact them for interviews as potential witnesses. Hot on the trail, she decided to head over to Fallbrook to check out Jorgies, a hole-in-the-wall bar and grill patronized by mill workers who might know something about Booker and the rumors going around about the lawsuit.

• • • • •

"So, you gonna give me your numbah or what?"

Liv shook her head and finished her Bud Light longneck. She gave the guy—trim, forty-something, kinda handsome with a full head of salt and pepper hair—a smile. "Not today, but maybe I'll see you around."

"Aw, come on. We had a nice time talkin'. I'll buy ya dinnah and you can tell me more about ya'self. How about Chinese? I know this place with great spareribs and those crab rangoons."

The bartender, a chestnut-haired woman with droopy eyes and a pretty smile, strolled over. "Cisco, you talking about another establishment while sitting in mine?"

The man looked abashed. "Sorry, Nina. Your pierogies are great. You know I love 'em, but I'm tryin' to entice the beautiful Olivia here to go out with me."

Liv slipped from her stool and slid a twenty across the scarred surface of the bar. "Some other time, okay? Beer's on me. Thanks, Nina."

She headed to the bathroom down a short, dark hall and thought about how places can surprise you. She'd expected a dismal, depressing dive. Instead she'd encountered a warm, welcoming atmosphere, friendly people, and a promising menu.

Jorgies was located on the first floor of a narrow, four-story building rising from the center of Fallbrook's traffic circle. The only natural light seeped through a leaded, diamond-paned window near the front entrance.

Dark wood walls were covered with framed photos of the mill over its ninety-year history. Yellow glass shades over the lights cast a warm glow, but the wooden tables and chairs were heavy, scored with dings and scratches. Liv figured the space had been redecorated around 1976.

Despite the retro decor, the place radiated cheer. Filling the tables, workers just off from their day-shift talked and laughed. Good smells of onion, pepper, meat, and spices wafted from the kitchen. The menu, Liv discovered to her delight, included not only the typical hamburgers, grilled sausages, fries, and onion rings, but also homemade pierogies, roasted beet soup, and hot potato salad.

She was definitely coming back to sample these Eastern European dishes. And soon.

Investigation-wise, she'd made some progress. Her companion at the bar knew of Raymond Booker and the accident, though he hadn't met Booker personally.

"Divorced, is what I heard," Francisco Diaz told her after they clinked bottles and she asked him what he knew of the groundwood worker. "No kids. Not very social. He's been on light duty, sanitation stuff since the accident. Moppin' down the latrines, emptyin' waste bins, that sorta thing. I see him around tryin' to do stuff one-handed. Musta hurt like a son-of-a-gun when that pickaroon went through his hand."

She'd asked him a few more questions, and they'd chatted for fifteen minutes or so. Several other Raptor workers stopped by to greet Cisco who wasn't bashful about pumping them for information on Liv's behalf. They never asked why she wanted to know. Didn't care, she surmised, or if they did suspect she was digging around on the company's behalf, maybe they also didn't agree with the lawsuit.

Whatever their lack of curiosity indicated, nobody seemed to know much about Booker other than what Cisco'd told her, anyway. They all confirmed they'd seen him trying to mop or vacuum floors one-handed. Nobody she spoke with knew him personally or saw him outside of work hours.

Liv washed her hands and touched up her red lipstick in the ladies room. As she stepped into the dining room, a familiar-looking man exited the swinging doors from the kitchen.

He wore tight-fitting black jeans, a black jacket with a vaguely European cut, and he carried a money bag emblazoned with a local bank logo in his hands. Liv frowned. She'd seen him before. That close haircut, the sharp cheekbones and jawline.

She remembered something about a dark car. He'd been with another man, and she'd seen them approaching a building. She just couldn't quite remember where.

As she followed him through the restaurant to the door, it came to her, and a tingle went up her spine.

It had been at The Golden Triangle the day she'd noticed the symbol matching Alice's necklace. She'd seen this guy and another who looked a bit like him exiting a dark Lincoln and walking into the club.

She left the building and pulled on her sunglasses against the late-afternoon glare. She watched as the man with the money bag used the cross-walk to reach the Lincoln she remembered. He'd parked the vehicle on the other side of the two-lane circle, and he barely glanced at traffic as he swung the driver's side door open and got in. The tinted windows hid him from view as the car slid away from the curb, went around the circle, and disappeared.

• • • • •

Later that evening, sitting with her laptop in her sunroom, fresh air wafting through the screens, Liv sipped a mug of chamomile tea and punched the license plate of the Lincoln into a database. Steam curled around her face as she inhaled the sunny, mellow scent and squinted at the laptop screen.

She frowned. The car was registered to something called Zebri Investments, LLC. She typed the LLC into the Maine.gov corporate name search and discovered the corporation listed a registered agent, a lawyer located in Saco. She clicked through to articles of incorporation and requested a copy. The LLC's owners were listed as Anthony Zee and Leo Zee.

Brothers? Cousins?

She did a quick internet search of both names and nothing much other than their addresses and phone numbers popped up. They both lived in Fallbrook now, but former addresses indicated they'd each moved around a bit. Neither appeared to be on socials.

Next she typed Zebri Investments, LLC into her search engine and scanned through several articles. Staring at the screen, she slowly lowered her mug and placed it on the small table beside her where it cooled as she read.

According to multiple reports, Zebri Investments owned several businesses in Fallbrook, including Jorgies and The Golden Triangle. A landscaping company, an ice-cream stand, and a hardware store were also listed as Zebri properties.

Because of the logo, it was the club that interested her.

Newspaper articles spanning several years reported on disturbances of the peace connected with the club as well as arrests for indecent exposure, car break-ins, assault, drunk driving, and disorderly conduct. None of the articles named the Zees as owners. If they or their company had been charged with any criminal activity, the media hadn't reported it.

The nightclub appeared typical of other establishments of its kind. People went there to drink, hook up, watch the girls, and get lap dances. Some got into brawls. Some engaged in a little thievery. Some got behind the wheel when they shouldn't.

But patrons breaking the law didn't mean the club was doing anything illegal.

Reaching for her tea, Liv discovered it was stone cold. The lights of Portland sparkled below her. She slapped the laptop shut.

Her real cases required her attention. She shouldn't be wasting time investigating connections for a case being handled by the police—no matter how intriguing. Her phone rang. She glanced at the number on the screen. It was Jasper.

"Are we still on for Wednesday?" he asked when she picked up.

"If you still want to see me."

"Picnic in the park?"

"Fine with me. We can hit the food trucks."

"Sounds good. I'll bring a bottle of something if you bring the glasses and a blanket. See you at six-thirty?"

"Okay. See you then."

She stood, tossed the phone onto the chair cushion, and walked to the windows. Nerves jumped in her stomach. She wanted to clear things up with Jasper. The only problem was, she didn't have a clue as to what she wanted the outcome to be.

Maybe she'd know when she saw him.

Chapter Twenty

• • • • • • • • • • • • • •

"You're just going to have to trust me." Jasper, expression serious and eyes intent, leaned toward her.

"Said every liar and scam artist in the history of humanity." Liv made a face and tried to look away, but he reached out to gently hold her chin in place.

"Hey. It's me. I'm here. I want to be with you. Not Wren. Not anyone else. What can I do to make you believe me?"

They sat on a blanket on the Eastern Prom. The air had turned sultry and smooth again, pink in the sky like strawberry ice-cream with whipped cream clouds floating on top. From their vantage point they could see the food trucks downhill in the parking lot and the sailboats bobbing in the sparkling water near launch. Two shrimp sandwiches from Vy Bánh Mì and a sweating bottle of sparkling rosé sat between them on the blanket.

But first, *The Talk*. An appetite killer if ever there was one.

She jerked her chin and his hand fell away. "For starters it would help if she didn't pop up every time you and I have a disagreement."

He sighed and clasped his fingers around one bent knee. He looked toward the ocean as he spoke. "I told you. My parents and I ran into her at the hospital when I was showing them around. She said she had tickets to a show in Ogunquit but couldn't use them. Mom and Dad seemed excited about it, so she offered to bring them over. My mother invited her to stay for dinner."

"Your mother."

He turned toward her again. "Yes. My mother. She's from the Midwest. Midwesterners do things like invite people to dinner on the spur of the moment. They are *nice*."

Was he implying Maine people weren't? Mainers were known to be crusty and sardonic, true, but they were hospitable. At least toward people who deserved it.

She looked away and squinted at the ocean. "The thing is, Jasper, you didn't invite me to stay."

The hurt welled up as she spoke the words. How hard would it have been to bring another place setting to the table? He'd been punishing her.

She wished he'd just admit it. Instead, he blamed her. "I'm sorry," he said. "You were so angry. I didn't think you'd want to."

"Yeah, I was angry! I cut my trip short to surprise you and meet your parents, and I find Wren there. Even though I was upset, I made an effort to be polite. You didn't." She let her head drop back and looked up at the getting-on-toward-evening sky. "Ughhh. I hate this. I don't want to rehash who said what, who did what. This is why I don't get into serious relationships. It's so much easier to keep things casual." She waited a beat. "Can you honestly say this is fun?"

"No," he said. "It's not great. I've missed you these past two weeks though." He took her right hand in his left. They looked at each other. He said, "What do you want to do?"

She decided to say the thing they'd been avoiding. "Maybe we should stop seeing each other."

Silence fell between them. Nearby, a toddler screeched. A dog barked and another answered. Food truck smells wafted from the parking lot below. A million lights sparked off the waves. Finally, Jasper spoke. "I disagree. I think we should move in together."

She felt an inexplicable twist in her gut. Irritation? Excitement? Sheer panic? She tried to pull her hand away, but he held on tight. "Are you serious?"

He squeezed her hand again. "As a heart attack."

"That's nice coming from a heart surgeon."

"Like I said, serious." He then added a kicker. "And I think we should get a dog."

· · · · ·

Later, curled up with him in her bed, sandwiches devoured and wine drunk, Liv ran her hand up Jasper's chest. She loved the texture of his skin. The smell of him. The long, lean muscles of his legs and arms. His dexterous fingers. The dip in the middle of his top lip.

She loved all these things about him, but because she didn't know if she actually loved him, she kissed his chest. She was thinking about his proposal to move in together. "You do know we can't get a dog."

She heard him smile in the gloom "Why not?" he asked.

"Because you work long hours and so do I. It wouldn't be fair."

"You have an assistant now."

She propped herself up on an elbow. "Marion's temporary. She's helping me catch up and get things reorganized. Come fall it'll be just me again. If I want Lively Investigations to be successful, then I'll have to make it a priority for the next two, three years. At least."

He propped himself up, too. "It's simple. Move in with me, rent out this place, and use the money to pay for the assistant. Problem solved."

"You want me to give up my apartment."

"Yeah." He chuckled. "That's generally what happens when people move in together."

She hadn't even considered renting her place out. She loved her third floor walk-up. She'd inherited the three-story apartment building along with a nice trust fund from her grandmother. She'd spent a good chunk of inheritance money on repairs and updates and rented out the more basic first and second floors to a paralegal and a professional couple she barely saw.

She'd remodeled and decorated the third floor, however, into her dream apartment. She felt nauseated imagining strangers hanging clothes in her giant walk-in closet, soaking in her fabulous, clawfoot tub, and watching sunsets from the room overlooking the peninsula all the way out to the western hills.

She hedged. "I suppose I could make it a short-term rental kind of place." That way, she figured, she could come back. If she needed to.

"Or not." He kissed her. "I love you, you know."

She pretended not to be moved. "You're just buttering me up for a dog."

"I'm buttering you up so you'll move in with me."

"Thanks for clarifying that."

"You're welcome." He smiled at her. Her heart flipped, and she remembered why she was with him in the first place. He was smart, gorgeous, and fun. Most of the time.

She didn't understand why he had to push her. Moving in together was a big deal. They'd only known each other a few months. She'd only recently adjusted to being in a committed, long-term relationship for the first time in her life. What was the big hurry?

"I need to think about it," she whispered and kissed his oh-so-sexy mouth.

He rolled away from her and onto his back. His voice sounded defeated when he closed his eyes and answered. "I meant it, you know. That thing I said."

"I know you did," she said. "I'm just not ready to say it back."

After a long, uncomfortable pause, he sat up. "I'm going to go, give you time to think. I'm heading to Vegas for a medical conference on Thursday. I'll be back on Monday."

He stood and pulled on his jeans. His stomach was flat and toned despite the fact he hated to run. She figured he did crunches and push-ups when she wasn't around. You didn't get abs and arms like that by accident.

He looked so good, she almost told him she'd changed her mind.

He picked his shirt off the floor and stuffed his arms into it. As he buttoned the shirt, he said, "I'll call you when I'm back. You can give me your answer then. We either need to move forward or we need to stop wasting our time."

She didn't tell him she didn't consider spending time with him a waste. Obviously, he did, though. She went for a breezy tone. "And the dog?"

"Negotiable." He leaned over and gave her a quick kiss. "See you next Monday."

Chapter Twenty-One

• • • • • • • • • • • • • •

"**B**usterdoodle, get off her!"

Van grabbed the dog's wide leather collar and dragged him away from Liv. They were standing in the foyer of Van's home. He'd called her an hour earlier to tell her the police had returned some of Alice's things, including the necklace. Anxious to follow up on the triangle logo mystery, she'd told him she'd be right over.

Now he closed the door and led her through the living room. "Come on into the kitchen. I didn't expect you to drive all the way up here to get the necklace. I could have brought it to your office."

"I didn't mind." Liv followed Van.

The big house was unsettlingly quiet. Busterdoodle, nails clicking on the hardwood floors, made a beeline—dogline—for his dish. He stuck his nose into the bowl and began chomping loudly, flecks of kibble flying out of his mouth in every direction as he lifted his head to look at them before plunging back into the bowl.

"Have a seat." Van pointed to a bar-stool—blue leather with gold nailheads—in front of a marble-topped island. He opened the refrigerator door and pulled out a glass pitcher of what looked like iced tea. "Arnold Palmer?" he asked. "Or I could open a bottle of wine."

"Iced tea sounds perfect, thanks." She glanced around the kitchen. "Your house is very nice. I didn't get a chance to really take it all in last time. I like this marble on the island."

"Thank you. We moved in a couple weeks after we were married. Her parents gave us the down payment as a wedding present."

Liv remembered the devastated couple stooped with grief at Alice's funeral. They hadn't stuck around for the finger sandwiches and chit-chat at Van's afterward. She'd been told they'd flown back to Atlanta that evening. Liv doubted they'd ever be truly happy again.

"That was generous."

"Yeah. I was still paying off student loans. Alice had her heart set on this neighborhood. It's a good school district. Lots of young families in the development. She said the backyard would be perfect for kids. She went on and on about hide and seek and birthday parties, putting in a pool. That sort of thing."

"Kids?"

"We…" His voice cracked. "We, uh, talked about it, and now, it's too late."

Plus he'd told her Alice wouldn't sleep with him. Pretty hard to start a family if that was the case.

An awkward silence stretched a few seconds too long for comfort. Liv sipped her drink and changed the subject. "So, you said the police returned Alice's things to you?"

"They kept some of her clothes, for DNA stuff, I guess, plus her laptop and phone. They returned the necklace, so they must not think it's important. I'm sure it has nothing to do with that strip club."

"You're right. It could be a weird coincidence, but if it's okay with you, I'd like to check it out."

"I don't know." Looking agitated and worried, Van shook his head. "Why not just tell the police?"

She remembered her fruitless phone call to the detective. Karina Briggs wasn't sharing information either.

Liv traced a vein of marble with a red-painted fingernail. "Until I have a chance to look into it, there's nothing to tell them. The similarity of designs could be a coincidence. I mean, triangles are common jewelry elements. Just do a search on Etsy. Even if it turns out Alice *was* involved in that club in some way, it's not necessarily relevant to her murder. The police might already have looked into it and found no connection."

"That's true. They did have the necklace for a while."

"Exactly. I don't want to put myself out there without solid evidence. I have to protect my reputation and the reputation of Lively Investigations. If you don't mind, I'd like to do a little under-the-radar investigating first."

"Yeah, makes sense, I guess. You always did like to do things your way." Van lifted his eyebrows. "So what's the plan?"

"I'll go to the club, ask a few questions, see if I find anything definitive concerning Alice. Was she a regular patron? Who did she talk to? Did she meet anyone there? That sort of thing. If I turn up nothing, I'll have only wasted my own time, not the police's."

Frowning, Van nodded. "Okay."

"Believe me, this is the best course of action."

Buster trotted to her and stuck his big, curly head onto her lap. He really was kind of cute. She gave him a light scratch. He rolled his eyes up at her in a comical expression of bliss.

Her thoughts turned back to Alice and the file she'd shared with Alby. Too bad the police still had the laptop, she thought. She'd love to get her hands on that document, analyze it for details that might correlate to the club.

She'd already researched the tabs Alice had open at the time of her death. Good thing she'd thought to snap a photo of the computer display. The Erotiwritica.com website advertised itself as a free fan fiction page for writers and readers who liked the steamier side of romance. Liv had created an anonymous profile and searched for both Alice and Alby's names, but if they had an account or accounts, they used aliases or handles.

The pole dancing site contained links to many video accounts, some free and some behind a paywall. She clicked through to a few but found nothing out of the ordinary. If Liv had to guess, she'd say Alice used those sites for research. *Maybe the strip club, too,* she thought, but until she talked to some people—and got her eyes on Alice's manuscript again—she wouldn't know for sure.

She glanced at Van and pressed her lips together to keep from blurting what she knew. As much as she wanted to tell him about Alice's writing, she couldn't risk him saying something to his lawyer or the cops about her snooping around the crime scene. For now, she'd keep the information to herself.

Instead, she said, "I know it's not my so-called jurisdiction. I'm just a P.I—not law enforcement—but I really want to help bring Alice's killer to justice if I can. I mean, I feel responsible in a way."

"You're not responsible for what happened," Van said on a sigh. "I also know you won't let it drop just because I said that. You haven't changed that much since high school. Once you fixate on something, nothing can get in your way. What was that guy's name? Donny Dobson, aka D-Cent?" Van snorted. "Famous white, teen rapper from South Portland, Maine. You girls were so into him."

Liv rolled her eyes. "Give me a break. I was sixteen and he had an online following."

Van's grin widened. "Whatever you have to tell yourself."

"Moving *on*." She let the word hang for a second. A thought occurred to her. What if Alice wasn't just going up north to write—she'd obviously had time to work on her book at home—but because she was scared?

Liv looked at Van. "You said it seemed odd that Alice would take two weeks off to go to the chalet. What if she was hiding from someone? Someone who was threatening her?" She frowned, thinking about the kind of people one might meet at a club like The Golden Triangle. "If I'd talked to her before that night, maybe she would have confided in me about any trouble she was in. I could have advised her, helped her contact the police."

"The *trouble* she had was getting involved with my brother." Anger suffused Van's face. "If Alice was messed up in that strip club, you can bet Alby had something to do with it! I always suspected there was something off about his big Wall Street deal. Who gets that rich, that quick?"

Interesting. "Is there anything that makes you think he was involved in illegal trading or some other criminal activity?"

"No. I just know Alby. Did you know he cheated all the way through high school?"

Liv raised her eyebrows. "Seriously?"

"Yup," Van said. "Paid some kid to write all his papers. Alby threatened to beat me up if I told our parents. The thing is, he was smart enough to write them himself, but he always took the easy way out. He had everyone fooled. He pretended to be so easygoing and charming, but he was dangerous if someone got in his way. Or told him no. Alice found out the hard way, I guess."

Liv remembered her conversation with Emsley. "What about Alby's ex-wife? Do you think she had suspicions about his financial affairs or, uh, romantic ones?"

"Emsley liked that Alby subsidized her work. I'm not sure she cared much about him or how he made his money as long as he paid for her studio and materials." He paused. "You know, I did ask her once if she'd ever seen Alice and Alby together."

"Oh, yeah? When was that?"

"Not long before I hired you. I saw Alice getting into his car after work, remember?"

Liv nodded.

"Well, that afternoon, I went to Emsley's studio to ask her if she'd ever heard any rumors about the two of them, and she said no, it was news to her. She said something like, 'The wife is always last to know' or something like that." He shoved himself to his feet. "The necklace is upstairs. I'll get it for you."

Liv stood, too. "Could I use your powder room?"

"Of course. There's one off the laundry room. You remember where it is."

Oh, yes. I remember. My mother will never let me forget.

The laundry room was as she remembered it. She flicked on the lights, wandered toward Alice's desk, and examined the bulletin board hanging above it. A grocery list had been tacked onto the board along with an advertisement for a vitamin supplement, a brochure for a local OB-GYN & fertility clinic, and a takeout menu from a local Italian restaurant.

She was distracted by the menu—so many yummy dishes!—and her mouth watered thinking about spaghetti carbonara and garlic bread. She pulled out her phone and snapped a photo of the phone number. Maybe she'd stop by on her way home and grab some takeout for dinner. She'd cue up some *X-Files* or *Alias* episodes and open a bottle of Barolo. Or maybe she'd watch Anthony Bourdain's *Parts Unknown*. Good Italian food plus a bad-boy chef turned culinary adventurer? Heck, yes.

Stomach rumbling, her eyes dropped to the desktop. It held an old-fashioned Rolodex for phone numbers, a pad of note paper, and a ceramic pen holder shaped like a frog. Magazines, books, and a small floral notebook were stacked on one side. Curiosity getting the better of her, Liv flipped open the notebook.

Her breath caught when she realized the notebook contained a handwritten list of Alice Ferguson's passwords. At the chalet, Alice had been using a cloud-based writing program for her story. The police still had the laptop, but it occurred to Liv that with the right password, she could log into Alice's drive and examine what Alice had been working on the day she was killed.

She heard the dog bounding into the kitchen, most likely ahead of Van.

Liv snatched the small, spiral-bound book, hurried to the adjacent powder room, and locked the door. Balancing the notebook on the sink's counter, she snapped photos of passwords.

It was just a *smidge* unethical, she told herself, as she flipped pages and focused the phone's camera on the handwritten list. She wanted to help bring Alice's killer to justice. Sometimes you had to bend the rules a little to get stuff done.

A better person would ask permission first, Liv thought as she snapped away. *But then again, I'm no angel. What Van doesn't know won't hurt him.*

On her way back to the kitchen, she dropped the notebook on top of the stack of books and magazines and hoped Van didn't notice anything out of place.

Buster bounded up to her when she reappeared in the kitchen. Van had poured himself a glass of whiskey and was staring out into the backyard through the breakfast nook window.

Hearing her, he turned and held out a black velvet jewelry box.

"Here's the necklace. I put it in the box so it wouldn't get tangled." He shook the ice-cubes in his glass. "I had a thought when I was upstairs. Want to hear it?"

"Sure," she said.

"Maybe a client gave it to her." He sipped the drink. "Like I told you, she worked with the immigrant community. She was always driving someone to an appointment or going to one of the kids' teacher conferences to help out, even on her off hours, and she took them to the grocery store and the pharmacy, places like that. Maybe this was a gift. Like a thank you or something."

Liv considered. "Could be."

"She cared a lot about the community and her job. She was so smart. She would have made more money doing something else, but she felt passionate about her career and the people she was helping."

"I wish I'd met her. She sounds like a good person."

He gave her a bleak look. "She was. Why'd she have to get mixed up with my brother?"

"I don't know." Liv squeezed the velvet box in her hand. "Hopefully they'll catch him soon, and you'll get some answers. Meanwhile, I'll keep poking around, see what I can find out."

"She shouldn't have been with him. Even if she was in trouble, she should have talked to me. I would have taken care of her. I was her husband. Not him."

"I'm so sorry, Van." She gave him a sympathetic hug. She knew what it was like when someone you cared about deceived you, how stupid and gullible you felt when the truth came out.

He pulled away and gave her a sad, grateful smile. "I'm okay. Thank you."

She hitched her bag higher on her shoulder. Busterdoodle trotted to a side door off the kitchen. The dog stared at the door and whined.

Van stood. He moved toward another door off the kitchen. "Someone needs his after-dinner walk, and you're ready to head home, I can tell. Come through here."

Curious, Liv followed man and beast into a mudroom connecting the house and garage. One door led to the back yard, another to the garage bays. A third opened to the driveway. The floor was tiled in practical cream and brown ceramic squares. Bins for recyclables lined one wall. Gardening tools hung on hooks above a small potting bench. Another set of hooks held jackets and other outdoor gear.

Van reached for a red leash dangling on a hook. A yellow rain slicker hung next to it. Matching yellow rain boots stood on a rubber mat along with a pair of pink rubber gardening clogs and a grass-streaked pair of women's cotton sneakers. A large Red Sox hoodie hung beside a soft-looking, knee-length cardigan in light gray.

Buster sniffed the sweater, whined, and then sat and looked expectantly at the leash.

Liv inhaled, too. The faint scent of floral perfume and gardening soil lingered in the room. She felt as if Alice might slip into the mudroom, pull on the sweater, step into the clogs, and head out to the garden beds to prune some rose bushes or something.

Sadness filled Liv's chest. How did Van deal with these kinds of daily reminders? She'd almost prefer to be single and alone her whole life than feel that kind of pain.

Van hooked the leash to the dog's collar. "Okay, let's go, Buster."

Outside in the driveway, he gave her a one-armed hug and thanked her for stopping by. "Let me know if you find out anything," he said.

Driving away with one arm propped in the rolled-down window, Liv glanced in the rearview mirror. She could see Van trudging along the sidewalk, head down, slightly gimpy, Busterdoodle trotting at his side.

A few lights glowed in the windows of nearby houses. The sound of crickets carried in on the sultry air, and a few yellow-green fireflies flashed here and there above the grass of shadowy, perfectly-manicured lawns. Man and dog looked forlorn beneath the decorative street lamps lining the sidewalk.

It was, she thought, one of the loneliest sights she'd ever seen.

Chapter Twenty-Two

• • • • • • • • • • • • • •

Back at her apartment, sated on rich pasta and full-bodied wine, Liv streamed a playlist of Albinoni violin and oboe concertos and settled onto her couch with her laptop and a mug of rose petal-infused black tea.

A cross-breeze through the open windows swept the day's heat and humidity from the room. Wearing light cotton pajama bottoms and a lacy lavender camisole, Liv sipped the tea and contemplated the fact that she didn't mind being alone in her apartment. In fact, she enjoyed it.

Jasper had texted to say he'd reached Vegas, but that was all. No mention of the ultimatum. Good thing, she thought, because she had no idea what her answer would be. Was she prepared to give up her private space in order to save her first serious relationship? The man was in such a hurry to lock it down, she thought, and that made her nervous.

She cracked open the velvet jewelers box and withdrew Alice's necklace. Gleaming in the lamplight, it swung from her thumb and index finger, a piece of basic, gold-plated jewelry, nothing expensive. She held the triangle charm between her fingers like a talisman and tried channeling Alice Ferguson, drawing on what Van had told her and what she'd observed at the lake.

I'm Alice. I'm in Carry Over. I'm wearing this necklace. I'm working on a writing project. Something steamy. Van doesn't know I'm writing erotica, but when I told him I was going to the chalet to write, he was dismissive rather than curious or supportive. In fact, he seemed suspicious. I was happy to get away. We haven't been intimate in awhile. I'm not interested. I have other things—or someone—on my mind.

I spend my days at the lake writing upstairs in my bedroom, tending the flower beds around the chalet, swimming and sunning myself on the dock. After a few days, Alby joins me. We shop for groceries. Back at the chalet, we drink some wine and eat some cheese, and one of us washes the dishes. That night, in the great room in front of the big windows, we fight about something. The affair? The story? Something about Alby's business dealings?

When he goes upstairs, I turn off the lights. I sneak out to the woods with a lantern for some reason. When I come back into the kitchen, I go upstairs and change into my nightgown. Later that night, I go downstairs. Someone attacks me. I reach for the knife in my chest, gasping for breath, and then... nothing.

Liv shivered, remembering the way Alice's fingers clutched at the silky fabric of her nightgown. Had Alby confronted her in the kitchen? They'd been drinking wine. Two bottles by the number of corks, though only one empty in the trash, oddly. Maybe they'd argued, and in a rage, he grabbed the chef's knife and stabbed her. Realizing what he'd done, he may have panicked. People had seen them together at the market. He had no alibi, so his only choice was to run.

She imagined him sprinting upstairs, gathering his things— missing the shirt under Alice's bed—and driving into Canada on some logging road he knew. *Hell on the suspension,* she thought, *but what were shocks and struts in the face of a murder charge?*

Liv sipped her tea. A lover's quarrel. A murderous impulse. Most women were killed by men they were close to. Most stabbings were crimes of passion. Alby was the last person with whom Alice had contact. Therefore, he was the likeliest suspect.

Still, she thought, most of this was mere speculation on her part. There were other scenarios, far-fetched, maybe, but possible.

Someone else could have confronted Alice in the kitchen that night, killed her.

And Alby slept through the whole thing? That seemed unlikely.

She ran through scenarios. He might have left sometime after Liv went to bed but before the murder. Or he might have been killed or kidnapped, his car driven away by the assailant or assailants. He could be alive now, held captive somewhere, or dead and dropped in the deep Maine or Canadian woods. Or drowned and sunk to the bottom of the lake. Had the authorities considered dragging Duckbill Pond? Who could have wanted Alice—and possibly Alby—dead and why?

The sharp edges of the charm bit into her palm as she fisted her hand around it. So many questions remained unanswered at this point, but what did she know for sure? Mainly, that Alice had been keeping secrets. First, about her writing. Second, about meeting Alby in Carry Over. And third, about sharing the novel document with him. Without context, the facts and Liv's speculations about them were just stories she was telling herself.

She held the necklace up so it turned and gleamed in the lamplight. The necklace had been returned to Van, so the detectives working the case didn't think the charm was significant to the murder investigation. If Liv's hunch was correct, though, and Alice had been using the strip club for her research, Alice might have inadvertently seen something illegal going down. Some low-life, squirrelly and paranoid, might have followed her to Carry Over and killed her before she decided to talk.

Feeling excited about this theory, Liv logged onto The Golden Triangle's website. It had only two pages. The first was a home page with a listing of hours, a few photos, and a location map. The second was a contact page for sending an email message to the club. Very basic.

She studied the charm in her hand, comparing it with the club's logo. Impossible to miss the similarity. Next, she enlarged each photo from the site in case any of the dancers highlighted wore similar triangle charm jewelry, but nothing showed up.

Giving up on the club's site, Liv opened the web-based writing program Alice had been using. Consulting the passwords she'd photographed from Alice's notebook, Liv signed on. She scanned through the list of files and folders, focusing on the most recently-opened documents. One jumped out at her. It was labeled *Calliope & The Viper's Den*.

Liv checked the last modification date. Alice had saved the document the day before Liv discovered her body in the kitchen. Setting her mug of tea aside, Liv opened the document and began to read. Bingo.

The story, written in diary form, centered around a nineteen-year-old college girl named Calliope Caine who takes a job dancing at a club called The Viper's Den. Calliope's a virgin, a former high school cheer captain with years of gymnastics and dance training behind her. After being caught up in the college party scene—including an attempted sexual assault at a frat party that she barely escapes—she loses her scholarship. Desperate to stay in school, Calliope's lured into the industry by a girl she meets at yet another party. She's told she can make crazy money—enough to pay for tuition, textbooks, and an off-campus apartment. Calliope decides to try it out. As the story progresses, Calliope transforms from good girl to fallen angel.

Liv read with increasing excitement and even a little shock at the graphic material. She sat back, face flushed, gratified to discover she wasn't as *quite* as naughty as she thought she was.

Alice had thrown everything into the mix: sleazy clientele, Russian mobsters, devious divas, copious drugs and alcohol, and prostitution. Every chapter included some form of sex act. This wasn't your average *50 Shades of Twilight* fan fiction, Liv thought, gaping at the screen. Alice's super-steamy erotica bordered on pornographic.

At least there was a well-crafted story holding the plot together as well as a likable—if flawed—main character.

Alice's manuscript ended in the middle of the chapter, just as Liv remembered. She looked up from the screen, drummed her fingers on the laptop, and mused about the mysterious Alice Ferguson who hid a secret, erotica-author persona beneath her bland, social-worker exterior.

Why had she kept her writing a secret from her husband? Was she embarrassed by the erotic content? Or did it have more to do with their relationship and trust?

Van had been wrong about one thing, Liv realized. Alice had been *very* interested in sex. Maybe she was more enthralled writing about it than engaging in it with her husband, but she'd been anything but blasé.

Liv skimmed through the manuscript a second time and took some notes. She found nothing in the manuscript about a necklace. The few pieces of jewelry mentioned tended toward the spiked or clamped or inserted variety. The document created more questions than answers.

She stared at the screen. What plans did Alice have for the story? Hoping to sell the story to a publisher? Or simply sharing on the erotica fan fiction site for fun?

She sat up, galvanized by a thought. Maybe this wasn't Alice's first book.

On a hunch, she searched "Alice Ferguson Erotica" and several variations on the name. She followed several trails but couldn't find any correlation to file names on Alice's computer. Dead end.

She scanned Alice's computer files one more time, but nothing jumped out at her as relevant. She tried to log onto Alice's email, but Alice hadn't included that password on the list and without resorting to hiring a hacker, Liv probably wouldn't be able to read them. She wondered if the police had managed to get them and what of interest, if anything, they'd discovered.

She briefly considered looking at Alice's—and by proximity— Van's bank accounts as those passwords were listed, but her conscience finally reined in her curiosity. Since she was dead,

Alice's finances might be fair game, but Liv wouldn't snoop into Van's bank statements. There were some lines she wouldn't cross.

What lines had Alice crossed, thought? She'd kept this writing project a secret from Van. Why? Did she think he would disapprove? Was she embarrassed to share that side of herself with her husband? Why share it with Alby?

She shut down the laptop and stared at the mysterious triangle charm. Now that she'd read the manuscript, she believed her original hunch had been correct. Alice must have been researching the club as background for her character Calliope's sexcapades.

She returned the necklace to its velvet box.

Most likely Alice had gone to The Golden Triangle for research and somehow procured the necklace. Or maybe the story followed the experience, not the other way around. Alice could have used the club for other reasons—romantic rendezvous, sexual curiosity, a dare or girls night out—and the idea for the story came to her.

No way to know at this point which came first, the club or the story or the necklace, but it was obvious, thanks to the story's plot and the triangle symbol, that they were connected. And somehow Alby Ferguson was involved.

She retrieved her pen and scribbled another note about other elements of Alice's story that might coincide with the club.

The mafia angle, for instance.

She bit the end of the pen, recalling the car registered to the strip club, Zebri LLC, and Anthony and Leo Zee. Were the two men mixed up with the mafia? Was The Golden Triangle a front for money laundering, drug dealing, or some other underworld operation?

Liv got to her feet and walked to the windows to look down over the city. Getting into Alice's files had left her with more questions than answers, but, if she were being practical, she had no reason to pursue the case any further.

The police were investigating the murder. She should put the Ferguson murder aside and concentrate on her current cases. She

NIGHT MOVES · 143

should return the necklace to Van in the morning and move on.

She should, but she knew she wouldn't.

Curiosity mixed with guilt got the better of her. With Jasper in Vegas, Ashleigh caught up in her pregnancy, and Marion in the office ready, willing, and able to pick up the slack, Liv figured she could spare a few hours to follow her nose.

She looked at her notes and grinned.

Tomorrow was Ladies Night at The Golden Triangle. She'd blend in with the clusters of women looking for cheap well drinks, no cover charges, bachelorette shenanigans, and girls night out carousing. Nobody would think twice about a slightly-hardened woman in a tad too much makeup strolling up to the bar, maybe asking a few questions, especially after a couple strong drinks. She'd keep her eyes out for triangle charms and European jawlines while sucking down a couple of martinis.

She perked up just thinking about it. It had been awhile since she'd indulged her taste for disguises and undercover operations.

She moseyed down the hall to her walk-in closet and flicked on the light. Clothing rods, lingerie drawers, wig stands, and shoe racks lined three walls of the space. A yellow, tufted ottoman held center stage. When she ran her fingers along her collection of vintage scarves, the faint scent of Chanel No.5 puffed from them.

Casting a critical eye over her collection of wigs and clothing, she considered her disguise options. She narrowed her eyes, putting together the perfect look for a night out at an establishment of questionable repute. Her mother would die of embarrassment if Liv happened to be recognized. The disguise had to be perfect. She bounced a little on her toes in anticipation.

This time tomorrow night, she'd be incognito at The Golden Triangle.

Wearing Alice's necklace.

Chapter Twenty-Three

• • • • • • • • • • • • • •

The electronic beat of dance music blasted from the club's shadowy interior. Liv nodded at the bouncer, entered the room, and sashayed across the industrial carpet on her black stiletto heels.

Multicolored lights illuminated the stage's white plastic surface. Gold strip lighting ran along the deep purple walls.

The place smelled of some type of cloying perfume—most likely pumped in through the ventilation system—and pheromones. Patrons relaxed in faux-leather chairs as topless servers delivered trays of drinks to the glossy-black tables.

The servers wore black satin miniskirts with ruched white tulle bustles in the back. Gold lamé bow-ties encircled their necks. In their mile-high purple platform shoes and satin garter belts with little golden triangle charms dangling at their thighs, the girls swayed from table to table. Their sultry smiles didn't quite reach their kohl-rimmed and heavily-lashed eyes.

Men slid tips into the garter belts. Strippers in various costumes performed lap-dances for the men willing to pay for the extra service. A few groups of women—out on a lark for ladies night—raised glasses of champagne or cocktails and scoped out the nearby males who could not be less interested in the "civilian" population, at least this early in the evening. A couple of big-armed bouncers in tight, black tees watched from the edges of the room.

Liv observed this scene through rimless, pink-tinted glasses.

The dancers and servers—most appeared to be in their late teens to early twenties—came in all shapes and sizes. They strutted on killer heels, seemingly desensitized to the pain. She didn't know whether to pity them or admire them for their stamina.

Liv looked for necklaces like Alice's but saw none. The little charms on the servers' garters matched the design, however. She fingered the triangle charm hanging in the vee of her black-and-pink striped silk shirt and wondered if anyone would notice it and if they did, then what? Nervous excitement sent a tingle up her spine.

She loved being undercover. It wasn't always necessary, but it was fun and gave her a bit of helpful anonymity. Tonight, she'd paired the midriff-baring striped blouse with black satin shorts and strappy, black stilettos. A long, black wig covered her pixie cut. With the addition of the rose-tinted rimless glasses and plum-black lipstick, she looked vampish, sophisticated, and a little hardened. Perfect for the venue.

She walked to the bar. A pony-tailed bartender with tattoos on his neck and arms gave her the once-over. "'Getcha?"

"Vodka martini," she said. She glanced at the bottles behind him. "Top shelf. Dirty."

"Good choice."

"I bet you say that to all the ladies."

"Only the ones who don't order $5 well drinks."

"Uh-huh." She tapped the bar with her talon-like press-ons and smiled. "Make it very cold, three olives, thanks."

His eyes dipped to her chest, lingering on the necklace. "You got it."

A minute or two later, he slid a cocktail napkin imprinted with a gold-foil double triangle symbol in front of her and set down her drink. "What's the name on the tab?"

"No tab tonight." She drew a ten and a five from her black, quilted-leather bag. "Thanks very much."

She turned her back to the bar and sipped her drink. A dancer strutted and preened on the stage. She was young and athletic-looking with inch-long false eyelashes and thick, glitter-crusted lips. She pranced to the pole, hooked her leg around, and leaned back. As if in ecstasy, she tossed her head and shook a cascade of reddish-brown hair. She then swung herself onto the pole and executed a series of graceful moves. As a finale, the dancer slid headfirst toward the floor and caught herself just in time with only the grip of her thighs.

If I tried to do that, Liv thought, *I'd end up in a full-body cast. Or a coma.*

The performer bent seductively to pick up the tips tossed onto the stage by the audience. The Golden Triangle's patrons drew all types, Liv noticed.

Young guys in jeans, high-end sneakers, and gold chains. Business-type guys in suits and power ties. A few middle-aged dudes in khakis and golf shirts, pink-nosed after a day on the links.

Liv spied a group of women all wearing little black dresses except for one in a dyed-black wedding gown and matching veil. On her wedding day, walking down the aisle in her beautiful, white gown and dreaming of happily ever after, the woman couldn't have imagined she'd end up here, at a sleazy strip club, recently divorced, her dress dyed as dark as her dreams.

Feeling cynical, Liv carried her drink to a tall table at the back of the room and slid onto the bar-height chair. The glitter-lipped girl left the stage and the next song started. Another performer bounced toward the pole. She carried a giant lollipop in her hand. A baby-pink gossamer see-through nightgown floated over her g-string. She wore her dark hair in high, little-girl ponytails, and she'd plastered glittery heart stickers onto her face. She slowly licked the lollipop, eyeing the audience, and tossed it to the side.

Grasping the pole with both hands, she hunkered down on pink platform heels. She spread her knees on either side of the brass, moved up and down suggestively, sticking her tongue out between smiling teeth. Though she looked like jail-bait with her petite body and perky, cheerleader ponytails, the dancer was probably at least eighteen, maybe even closer to twenty-one or twenty-two.

At least, Liv hoped so.

Liv made a face and chomped on an olive, told herself not to be judgmental. Life didn't give everyone the same chances. Dancing offered more lucrative pay than waiting tables or working retail for minimum wage. She understood how tempting it might be to get into the life.

You'd tell yourself it was just for a year or two, that you'd save your money while you looked for a better job, that you might as well capitalize on your looks and body while you were young.

Maybe you'd been abused or traumatized, and in your mixed-up head stripping felt like taking control. Maybe you knew it was dangerous, but convinced yourself you could handle it.

How hard was it to get out, she wondered? To get out unscathed?

Finishing off her drink, Liv surreptitiously scanned the room for anyone wearing a double-triangle necklace. A server appeared at her elbow, and Liv ordered a second martini. When the woman returned, Liv thanked her.

"No problem." The petite, dark-haired twenty-something tucked Liv's money away. "Let me know if I can get you anything else."

"Hold on a sec."

The woman raised an eyebrow. Liv held out her phone to display a photo of Alice. "I'm supposed to be meeting this woman here tonight. We met online. I hope she didn't stand me up. Have you seen her anywhere?"

The server peered down at the screen. "Not tonight, but she's been here a few times. I think she's friends with Ivy."

"Ivy?"

"One of our dancers. She's working the VIP lounge tonight. Maybe your date's in there."

Liv followed the woman's gaze toward a doorway curtained by purple swags of cloth held back by golden cords. Liv grinned as if she really hoped to hook up. "Cool! Guess I'll check it out. Thank you."

"You have to be a member to get into the VIP area." The server's dark-lashed eyes traveled to Liv's chest. She winked. "But I see you're all set."

Liv put a hand to her chest and felt the necklace. *Aha!*

She gave the woman an extra five. "Thanks for letting me know." She left her drink on the table and wove her way to the curtained doorway.

She found herself in a hallway covered in a gaudy black and gold wallpaper. Wall sconces bracketed gilt-framed mirrors. Black and white nude photographs hung in spaces between the mirrors. *Your basic whore-house chic*, Liv thought.

A man and woman walked ahead of her, the woman wobbling on very high platform heels and holding onto the man's arm for balance. They made their way past two unisex bathrooms and continued to the end of the hall where a huge man, six-foot-six and three-fifty at least, stood guard in front of a quilted-leather door.

Liv observed as the woman hooked a finger into the neckline of her dress and pulled out a chain. A gold charm dangled from the woman's index finger. The man flashed a keychain, presumably with the same double-triangle logo. The guard checked his clipboard, nodded, and opened the door. The couple stepped inside.

Liv sauntered toward the guard as if she knew what she was doing. She held Alice's necklace on one fuchsia-tipped finger, double-triangle swinging from the chain. "Good evening," she said.

The bruiser barely glanced at the charm. "Name?"

Her heart pounded. She pasted a bored expression on her face. "Alice Ferguson."

She tried to think of what she'd say if the bouncer knew Alice and accused her of impersonation, but he didn't even look at her, just ticked off Alice's name on his clipboard without comment and stepped aside to let her pass.

She was in.

Chapter Twenty-Four

• • • • • • • • • • • • • •

A miasma of cloying perfumes, sweat, and the subtle but unmistakable undertone of sex hit her nostrils. Music with a heavy, bass beat thrummed and pumped in a sexual rhythm.

She scanned the room wishing she had a photo of Ivy, whoever she was, *whatever* she was, to Alice. She'd just have to hope someone would point her in the right direction.

Business appeared to be slow. The lounge was smaller than the main room out front. Instead of tables, banquettes rimmed the walls, each booth furnished with purple velvet curtains that could be pulled across the front for privacy. Couples, small groups of men, and one or two solitary patrons lounged in the booths and watched the stage show or interacted with dancers. Two sets of curtains hid activity from public view.

Liv made her way to a button-tufted chaise in the middle of the room where a seating area of faux-Victorian sofas, chairs, and cocktail tables faced the spotlit, black-lacquered stage. She lowered herself onto the purple velvet chaise. A few curious faces turned her way, but returned their gazes to the tableau onstage. Oversized crystal chandeliers with pink-hued, low-wattage bulbs hung from the ceiling but provided limited illumination. Atop the gleaming black lacquer was a structure made of metal, something like a cross between a cage and playground equipment. In and around black metal bars, three women moved and writhed against each other in the spotlight.

They wore outfits made of black lace, leather straps, and thigh-high platform boots. The music beat on, minutes passed, the steam went up several notches as the girls feigned sexual acts…or were they pretending? It wasn't easy to tell.

Liv surreptitiously scanned the room.

A woman wearing nothing but a g-string, gold sandals, and a delicate gold masquerade mask carried a bottle to a private booth. A well-dressed man loosened his tie and leaned back against the cushions. The woman flicked the curtains closed.

"Good evening. Complimentary glass of champagne?" A blonde with long, straight hair and smoky, shadowed gray eyes, held out a flute.

"Thank you." Liv took the champagne.

"Can I get you anything else?" The girl, who looked maybe eighteen, gave her a suggestive smile.

"Maybe. Is Ivy available?"

Irritation shadowed the girl's face. "Ivy's busy, but I'm right here, sweetie, and ready to party."

Liv shook her head. "You're lovely, but I'm looking for Ivy."

The girl popped a hip and pouted. "She's not here tonight."

"I thought you said she was busy."

"Whatever." The girl tossed her hair and turned her attention to a trio of guys to Liv's right.

Liv arranged herself on the chaise and sipped the champagne. It was cheap and barely chilled. She made a face and set it on a round cocktail table. A minute later she caught sight of the blonde whispering to a tall, brown-skinned girl on the far side of the stage. They both looked toward Liv and then away, huddling together to continue their conversation.

The second girl slipped inside a door painted to blend with the dark walls. Liv saw a quick flash of light from the open door before it closed again. The blonde returned to serving complimentary bubbly and plying her tastier offerings.

Meanwhile, the dancers on stage finished their performance,

exiting through some curtains at the back of the stage. Liv stood and made her way toward the unmarked door near the stage. She'd sneak out back and locate the dressing room, try to find Ivy and ask her about Alice. She hesitated for a moment, glancing around, and seeing nobody looking her way, reached for the handle.

A heavy-scented cologne, something expensive with a hint of Oud, alerted her seconds before fingers closed around her upper arm. A low, menacing voice rumbled next to her ear. "This isn't a public exit."

Liv tried to pull her arm away, but the fingers tightened. Liv twisted her head and her eyes widened behind her rose-tinted lenses. Her assailant was the man she'd seen twice before—at Jorgies and the club's parking lot. His chiseled cheekbones, dark-stubbled jaw, and slick European-style haircut were unmistakable.

She decided to play dumb. "S-sorry," she stuttered. "I guess I got turned around. All this champagne." She giggled and pretended to stumble. "How do I get out?"

"This way."

Keeping a firm hand on her arm, the man led her through the room toward the entrance. He steered her out the door, past the bouncer, and down the hall toward the club's main room.

"Your VIP membership has been revoked *Ms. Ferguson*," he said, pulling her toward the door. The way he said the name, together with the look in his weirdly-light eyes, told her he knew she wasn't Alice. "Don't come here again."

Liv decided to brazen her story out. She dug in her heels in front of the bar. "Now wait a minute! I paid for my membership!"

Heads swiveled, but unperturbed, the man let go of her arm and wiggled his fingers. "Give it over."

She widened her eyes behind her glasses. "What?"

"Don't be stupid. The necklace."

Drat. "Okay, fine." Pouting, she reached behind her neck to fumble with the clasp. She dropped the charm into his palm. He closed his fingers around it. She tilted her jaw upward. "I expect a refund."

"I have no idea who you are or what you're doing here, but you are *not* Alice Ferguson." He tightened his grip. "In fact, I heard she died. Pity. She asked a lot of questions, too."

Liv repressed a shiver. He caught the bartender's eye and gave a slight nod of his head in her direction. Deciding caution was the better part of valor, she lifted her chin and stalked out of the club. Good thing she'd gone in disguise. She didn't want that guy—or anyone associated with him—to recognize her out in the wild. He hadn't been fooling around.

Whatever Alice had stumbled into here, Liv thought, it had got her killed. She was sure of it.

•   •   •   •   •

The next day, Marion knocked on the open door of Liv's office and carried an armful of files to the credenza. "Did you call Scarlett, Dean & Brace about that process service job?"

Liv looked up from her computer where she'd been looking up mentions of The Golden Triangle and its owners on the internet, searching for clues that the mafia, Russian or otherwise, might be involved. She thought about contacting Karina Briggs again, but decided against that move. All she had was a wild theory without evidence. Liv figured the police still liked Alby for Alice's murder. He had opportunity and a possible motive, and he'd fled the scene. He certainly looked guilty.

"Yeah. I'm heading out in a few. The defendant's spooked. She hasn't been seen at home or work in over three weeks."

"Do you know what it's all about?"

"A civil lawsuit is all I know. People get wiggy. Can't blame them, I guess." Liv shut her laptop and pushed away from her desk. "Defendant's got a sister in Cape Elizabeth. I'll stop by the firm for the paperwork and then zip over to Cape to take a look-see. Maybe we'll get lucky first time out."

Marion, looking stylish in a pair of colorful palazzo pants and sleeveless top, grinned.

Liv raised her eyebrows. "What?"

"You said 'we'll' not 'I'll.'"

"Huh. Well, I guess I feel like you're part of Lively Investigations now. It won't be the same around here when you go to law school in the fall."

"I'll miss it, too. It's been fun. Even more interesting than I thought it would be."

The two women fell silent.

Suddenly, Liv brightened. "I have a thought. Would you be interested in going to an art gallery opening with me tomorrow night? Jasper's at a conference, so I need a date. You'll be able to finally meet my friend Ashleigh and her husband, Trevor. I thought I'd use the opportunity to ask around about Alby Ferguson, find out if anyone's been gossiping about him and Alice."

Marion's smile widened even further. "Are you asking me to help with actual investigation work?"

"Not officially. I don't have a case anymore, remember? This is strictly off the books. However, if we're at the art show and happen to ask a few nosy questions, who will stop us? What do you say?"

"Sounds like fun. What questions should I ask?"

Liv reached into her drawer for a fresh legal pad and held it out to Marion. "Drop those files. Grab a pen. Sit down. I'll fill you in. "

Chapter Twenty-Five

• • • • • • • • • • • • • • •

Later that afternoon, feeling good about Marion and Lively Investigations in general, Liv headed out on the process service job. She drove across the Casco Bay Bridge and wound along Rt. 77 toward Cape Elizabeth. She navigated several side streets and parked a couple houses down from the defendant's sister's modest home.

It was a real Maine cottage, not one of the summer places the one-percenters occupied. Small dormer windows graced the second floor of the cozy, white-painted 1800s cape. Baskets of red geraniums hung from hooks in the screened front porch. Bisecting a yellowing lawn, a brick walkway led from the crushed gravel driveway to the porch.

Liv scoped out the vicinity. Across the street, colorful birthday balloons bobbed above the mailbox, and a large inflated bouncy house and decorated table took up a good portion of the front lawn. No guests yet. The street remained quiet other than the sounds of birds and buzzing insects. The sounds of summer.

Liv, wearing large, dark sunglasses and a plain t-shirt, peered at the white cottage. She'd thrown a neon yellow vest printed with the words "PUBLIC WORKS DEPARTMENT" into the passenger seat along with an official-looking clipboard to which she'd attached the legal documents.

Noting that the defendant's Subaru wasn't in the driveway, she decided to wait for an hour or until the party started across the street, whichever came first. Sweat popped out on her neck. She rolled down the windows to get a cross-breeze and sipped a bottle of water to stay hydrated.

As a catering service car rolled into the driveway across the street, her phone rang. She glanced at the screen and pressed the answer button.

"Hi, Ash. What's up?"

A middle-aged man and woman got out and carried trays toward the side door.

"Don't hate me." Ashleigh pleaded through the phone.

Liv rolled her eyes behind her shades. Things had been a little strained between them ever since the baby boutique thing. Ashleigh'd missed yoga class that week, and Liv had stewed all through the routine. Yoga had been Ash's idea. Liv went along with it to spend time with her best friend, but she'd rather be kick boxing or cross training.

After class, when she phoned to make sure everything was okay, Ash had given Liv a vague and unsatisfying answer about feeling tired and falling asleep on the couch. She'd promised Liv that she and Trevor would be at the art opening on Saturday.

Liv had been looking forward to seeing both of them, but now she sensed a cancellation forthcoming.

Ashleigh's anxious voice brought her back to the present. "Liv? You there?"

A light blue Subaru Crosstrek approached the cottage from the opposite direction. Liv tensed as the car neared. "I'm here."

"It's about the art opening. We aren't going to make it."

"Yeah, I figured." Liv sighed. "Hold on a sec."

The Subaru continued past the house. She relaxed and pushed her sunglasses up her nose. "False alarm," she said.

"I'm so sorry about the gallery. We were looking forward to it, but my mother called to tell me my aunt's throwing me a surprise family baby shower at my house tomorrow afternoon. Apparently, Trevor knew weeks ago. We have an agreement to always tell each other about surprise parties, but this time he decided it would be fun to, quote, make an exception, unquote."

"Uh-huh."

"But then today my mother started to worry about the state of my bathroom tiles and dust on my window blinds—you know how she is about cleaning—and she called a few minutes ago so that I'd have time to quote, spruce things up, unquote. So now I'm calling Merry Maids for an emergency deep cleaning. Windows to appliances and everything in between. It's gonna cost an arm and a leg, but the last thing I need is all the aunties gossiping about my quote, big britches, unquote and dirty sink drains."

"You're big on the quote-unquotes today."

"Hello. Surprise shower and Franco-American aunties. I'm allowed." Ash sighed. "So, are we okay? I know I've been flaky lately, but you know your friendship means the world to me."

"We're okay. You're preggers. That gives you a couple passes. Double because it's twins." Liv picked at a chipped nail. "I can't imagine your house is that dirty, though. You were the neat one in college. I used to throw stuff on the floor just to make you crazy."

"It's only bad if you know where to look, but you know how the women in my family are about housekeeping. Obsessive is not too strong a word." Ashleigh hesitated. "I don't suppose you'd like to change your plans and come to the shower? It's family, but you're family to me. I'd love for you to join us."

Liv snorted. "I love you, but no. We'll do a nice brunch thing closer to your due date. No surprises, I promise. Besides, I've already asked Marion to go with me to the opening."

"Okay. Um," Ashleigh hesitated again. "There's something else."

Liv closed her eyes behind her glasses. "Let me guess. Yoga."

"I know I talked you into taking Benson's class, and I hope you continue to go because I think it's good for you, but I'm switching to a different studio. This one's geared toward expecting women and mothers with babies."

"Uh-huh."

"I wasn't intending to switch—I figured I could just modify the moves with Benson—but then I went back to Poppie & Porpoise to get those adorable onesies—you remember them, so cute—and while I was there, I started talking to this woman who swears by the Mommy-Too-Bee class, spelled T-O-O B-E-E. Isn't that sweet?"

Silly's more like it. Liv restrained herself and sipped her water, rapidly warming to the temperature of lukewarm spit.

Ashleigh gushed on. "It's closer to my neighborhood, so it will be convenient when the babies are here. I called just to get on the waiting list, and surprise! They had an opening and no one on the waiting list, so I took it." She said this in a defiant tone of voice, so Liv knew Ash felt guilty. "You should keep going to Benson's class without me. It's good for you."

Liv made a face. What could she say? Her best friend was four months pregnant with twins. Life rolled on. Things changed. She understood, but her heart squeezed just the same. "I do love Benson," she said. "I know we're not supposed to objectify the man but that particular man is a *very* fine object."

"Good! Then you'll keep going. It really centers you, and even though you complain about it, I know you secretly like the way—"

Liv interrupted. She wasn't in the mood for Ash's cheerleading. "No, if you're done, I'm done."

"—the way you feel." Ash's voice petered off. Then, "I'm so sorry, Liv. I'm sorry you're quitting yoga, and I'm sorry for disappointing you. We'll still hang out. Maybe not as often, but we will. You'll see."

"I'll be fine. Listen," Liv sat up as the blue Subaru cruised by again in the other direction. "I have to go. I'm on a job right now. I'll call you later."

"Okay, but…"

Liv pressed the end button. She blinked teary eyes, hating herself for wanting to cry. It wasn't the end of the world. It was just yoga class, not the end of her friendship.

Though it sorta felt like it.

She took a deep, steadying breath to clear her head and tracked the car as it pulled into the crushed stone driveway of the white cottage. When a woman wearing dark glasses and a wide-brimmed straw hat emerged, Liv slid into the yellow reflective vest, grabbed her clipboard holding the legal documents and a pen, and scrambled from her car.

The woman, spotting Liv, jumped back into the Subaru. She started the engine, and the brake lights came on.

Liv stood behind the car, tapped the trunk, and waved. She held the vest with the big "PUBLIC WORKS DEPARTMENT" lettering away from her body and smiled. She saw the woman check her rearview mirror and move the gear shift into park. As Liv made her way to the driver's side, the woman cautiously rolled down her window.

"What's going on?" the woman asked. Her eyes, shadowed by green-lensed sunglasses darted back and forth.

"Are you Donnatella Castro?" Liv asked, pen poised, pretending to check her clipboard.

"No, that's my sister. I'm Carmelina Castro."

"Great." Liv pulled the papers from the clipboard. She handed them through the window. "You've been served."

The woman let out an expletive. She threw the papers out the window where they fluttered to the ground. She then put her car in reverse and spun out. Liv jumped back as gravel sprayed across her legs. The Subaru swerved back and forth, straightened, and shot out of the driveway. It roared across the street, onto the neighbor's lawn, and struck the bouncy house.

The structure deflated, air hissing out of multiple punctures. A woman and three kids ran screaming out of the house. The littlest kid collided with a caterer who was carrying a huge sheet cake. The cake flew into the air and landed with a splat.

The woman in the Subaru shifted into drive and took off, knocking over the mailbox with the balloons. As Liv, the mother, the kids, and the caterers looked on, mouths open, Carmelina blew through the stop sign a few yards away and disappeared, dragging a piece of bouncy house behind her.

The littlest kid sat down to eat cake off the lawn. The older kids wailed. The mother yelled a string of four-letter words worthy of a sailor on leave, and the caterer picked up the cake platter and held it up like a shield, backing away from the scene.

Liv picked up the stapled papers and put them on the porch step, her job completed. Now all she'd have to do was sign an affidavit of service. She drew off the vest and strolled back to her car. When one of the kids yelled and pointed up, Liv tilted her head.

There, against the bright, blue Cape Elizabeth sky, a balloon drifted, yellow as lemon meringue pie. Over the modest houses. Over the massive summer cottages. Over the farms and village shops and the ribbon of road tracing the edge of the Cape. Over the marshes and rocky shoreline and out to sea.

Chapter Twenty-Six

•••••••••••••

"I'm going to start mingling. Are you feeling up to this?" Liv gave Marion a questioning glance. They were standing near the entrance of The Gretchen Nolan Gallery, a small and tasteful space located on one of the Old Port's uneven cobblestone streets. The sun had set, and the air had cooled just enough to be comfortable. Sorbet colors of orange, pink, and yellow lingered in the sky. Seagulls circled above the nearby waterfront.

Marion nodded. "I'm a little nervous, but don't worry. I have a plan. If anyone asks, I'm going to say I'm a graduate student interested in learning more about Portland's art scene. I hope I don't look too out of place." She wore a sleeveless black dress, cinched at the waist with a slim belt. The flowing, ankle-length skirt ended in a deep, lacy, scalloped edge. She'd dyed the ends of her dark hair turquoise blue and added a clip-on nose ring for good measure.

"You look perfect." Liv smoothed the front of her asymmetrical, one-shoulder pink shift and tightened her fingers around her small pearl-colored clutch. "I'll find you in an hour to compare notes. Good luck."

Marion held up crossed fingers and headed toward the other end of the gallery. Liv wandered from painting to painting and surveyed the upscale scene. The Gretchen Nolan Art Gallery boasted an industrial ceiling with the usual exposed black pipes and fittings. These elements contrasted with walls painted stark white. A gleaming hardwood floor provided a touch of warmth. There were no frames on the windows. Everything looked clean, crisp, spare. A minimalist's dream.

Except for the art. Liv stopped in front of a particularly rich, glowing piece. She drank in colors and textures reminiscent of Rococo but constructed with modern, abstract swishes, layers, and feathering. It was almost like being drawn deeper and deeper into a Watteau or Goya, a way to experience the painting as if from the cellular level where color particles bounced in random patterns—macro form unfathomable—within the deep, interior space of the composition.

"She's fabulous, isn't she?" a familiar female voice cooed behind her.

Wren Osborne, mousy brown hair twisted into an elegant chignon and tiny body swathed in an oversized cream shirt and cream silk pants from The Row, slid beside her. Wren clasped her hands together under her chin. "I've bought two already."

"Good for you." Liv couldn't keep the sarcasm out of her voice. Wren ignored it.

"They're for my new condo. I went ahead and bought my own place." She quivered with excitement. "All the walls are greige right now, but I'm going to paint them as soon as I move in next week. I want color, color, color!"

"Do you have your overalls and stir-sticks? Can't do much painting without stir-sticks."

"Hilarious. Of course I'm hiring a service." Wren looked at Liv from the corner of her eye. "How's Jasper? I haven't seen him around the hospital this week."

"You're spending a lot of time at Sharon Med these days. Are you volunteering as a candy striper or something?"

"I'm on the Ladies Auxiliary gift shop committee. I'm surprised Tiffany didn't tell you. She encouraged me to take the position." Wren giggled. "I just love your mom."

Figures. "Tiffany has her moments."

"Anyway, I'm in charge of organizing the gift shop volunteers, making sure they're trained, helping with recruitment. It's very rewarding."

And puts you in contact with eligible doctors. "That's great, Wren."

Liv turned back to the painting and told herself to play nice. At least Jasper hadn't been in contact with Wren since he left for Vegas. "Didn't Alby Ferguson show this artist at his gallery last year?"

"Maybe?" Wren leaned close to Liv and stage-whispered, "Poor Alby. Isn't it awful about his sister-in-law? There hasn't been much in the news, but everybody's talking about it, especially since Alby's been who-knows-where all summer. Almost a missing person." She wrinkled her tiny, upturned nose. "You don't think he had anything to do with the murder, do you?"

"It's probably a coincidence."

"I guess." Wren slid another sneaky glance her way. "Are you still friends with Donovan? I know you were close when we were all in high school."

Wren stepped to the next painting. Liv followed. "Why do you ask?"

"He's had his share of bad luck lately, hasn't he? First his job. Then his wife murdered. I wonder how he's holding up, that's all."

"I've seen him a couple of times. He's managing." Liv paused. "What do you mean about his job?"

Wren turned to face her, surprised. "Oh, you didn't hear? He was fired six months ago."

"No, you must be wrong. He…" Liv's voice trailed off. Near the gallery's entrance, Agent Colin Snow grinned at her and waved.

Wren noticed her staring and whipped her head around. "What?"

"Nobody. Er, I mean, nothing." Liv turned her eyes back to Wren. "I'm going to get a glass of wine. Congratulations on your condo. I'm happy for you. Really."

Wren looked astonished. "Thank you, Olivia."

Liv waded into the crowd, trying to track Snow. Several people stepped into her line of sight. Determined to confront him this time, she wove around clusters of art enthusiasts and scanned the room for the cocky FBI agent who seemed to pop up at the oddest moments in her life.

Finally, she spotted him speaking to a stylish middle-aged woman wearing an orange floral dress and turquoise cat-eye glasses. Liv recognized her as Gretchen Nolan, the owner of the gallery.

Gretchen was one of the horde of Brooklynites who'd abandoned New York in recent years for Portland's less-pricey, less-crowded, but still-arty charm. People like her brought style, culture, and money to the city while simultaneously displacing regular Mainers who could no longer afford the increasing rents and home prices. Yin and yang.

Liv headed in their direction, weaving in and out of the crowd, but by the time she reached Gretchen, Snow had melted away. She took a long, slow look around the entire space, but he was gone.

·   ·   ·   ·   ·

An hour later, Liv and Marion settled into a back table at El Gordito Burrito to compare notes. Salt-rimmed margaritas sweated in front of them. A mariachi band played on the rooftop bar, and the sounds of trumpets, violins, guitars and vocalists drifted down the open stairwell. Groups of people young and old made their way from the bar and dining room to the roof, attracted by the upbeat music and laughter.

Marion's face was flushed, her eyes bright as she recounted her evening. "So, I asked about Alby, like you wanted. Nobody's heard from him in weeks. General consensus is that he's fled to Europe or some hideaway he likes to go to in South America. Nobody seems to know where exactly. I heard both Brazil and Chile. They think he vamoosed in order to get away from his ex-wife who, according to everyone, has been cray-cray ever since the divorce, telling everyone how Alby cheated her, gave her nothing in the settlement, et cetera. Supposedly, she's convinced Alby pressured the art community to blackball her and basically ruined her entire life and career."

"Take a breath, Marion."

"Sorry. According to several people I spoke with, nobody will show her work, so maybe she's not totally delusional about the blackballing. I don't know why he'd do that to her. It's kind of horrible, isn't it? I mean if he gave her nothing in the divorce, why ruin her chances to make a living for herself, too? No wonder she's acting crazy."

Remembering Emsley's drunken rant at Alice's funeral, Liv said, "We don't know he's dissing her in the art community. Maybe they won't show her work *because* she's acting crazy, not the other way around. When I talked to her, she seemed angry and bitter, not surprising since Van told her that Alice and Alby had been having an affair. Without any real proof, I might add." Liv lifted her margarita and licked a bit of salt from the rim before sipping. "Did anyone mention seeing the two of them together? Alice and Alby, I mean?"

Marion shook her head. Her fake nose-ring gleamed in the low light. "Nope. From what I could gather, Alby's been dating a couple women, one a filmmaker and the other a life coach. I saved their names in a note." She waved her phone. "I'll send them to you."

"Perfect. And anything else about Alice?"

"Nothing scandalous except for her murder, of course." Marion looked uncertain. "Someone did say they heard Emsley ranting about Alice at a dinner party one night several weeks ago. She said some pretty nasty things, apparently."

"Like what?"

"Like calling her a sneaky little bitch-in-heat." Marion met Liv's eyes over the rim of her margarita glass. "Who didn't deserve to live."

• • • • •

"Hey, I brought you a coffee. Tall and iced with cream and sugar." Van knocked on the doorframe and entered her private office carrying two large plastic cups in a cardboard holder.

Startled, Liv looked up from her computer. It was Monday. She was working on the Raptor case. Marion had the day off so he'd walked through the reception area and had shown up at her door unannounced.

She frowned. "Oh, hey. Did we have an appointment?"

Van crossed the room and set one of the coffees on her desk. "No. Just I thought I'd stop by and say hi. No assistant today?"

"Uh-uh." She shook her head. "Just me, holding down the fort." Liv grabbed the coffee and pointed with it toward the chair in front of her desk. "I wanted to talk to you, anyway. Have a seat."

He folded his tall frame into one of the chairs in front of her desk and crossed one leg over the other. "Did you find out something about the necklace?"

"Quite a bit, actually." She filled him in on the details.

By the time she finished recounting her evening at The Golden Triangle, his face had turned a blotchy red. "You're saying Alice had a VIP membership to a kinky sex room at a strip club? I don't believe it, Liv. There must be some mistake. She was a social worker, not a sex worker!"

"I know this is difficult."

"Y'think?" Van closed his eyes. "So my wife had a fetish for watching strippers. Unbelievable."

"I don't think so. Or that wasn't the whole reason for the membership."

His eyes popped open. "Then what?"

"Okay. I also found out Alice was writing an erotic novel. Or trying to." She noticed the question on his face and waved her hand at him. "Never mind how I know." Liv wasn't ready to tell Van about the password pilferage. "What's relevant is, the story's about a young woman who gets a job as an exotic dancer at a seedy strip club not unlike the one in Fallbrook."

Van absorbed the news in silence. Then he said, "A novel? Wait a minute—you're saying she really did go to the chalet to write?"

"Seems so. The book's pretty detailed. I think Alice was going to the club to research her novel."

"I can't believe this. Why would she keep it a secret from me?"

"I don't know." She hesitated about the manuscript, but decided it was time. Maybe he'd opened Alice's computer. Maybe he already knew. "There's one more thing, and you aren't going to like it. Alby had access to Alice's manuscript, as well. My guess is they were writing it together, or maybe he was going to help her get it published. Something." She sipped her coffee and made a face. Too much sugar. "Either way, it looks like he was involved."

"So they were sleeping together and writing together." Van set his coffee on the desk. "This is so messed up. Have you told the police?"

"Not yet. If I get anything solid I'll contact Briggs."

Van's phone buzzed. He looked down at the screen. "Speak of the devil, this is Briggs now. I should take it."

"Yes, of course. Do you want to go in the other room for privacy?"

Van shook his head and put the phone to his ear. "Donovan Ferguson." His face went pale as he listened. "Okay," he said. "What?" His eyes went big and round. "Wait a minute, what?" He listened some more, his face slack with shock. "Okay. Thank you. Bye." His hand shook as he ended the call. He looked up at her with a hollow look in his eyes.

Liv felt a chill roll over her. "What did she say?"

"They found Alby." Van slumped back against the chair. "He's dead."

Chapter Twenty-Seven

• • • • • • • • • • • • • • •

On the Channel 11 Evening NewsHour with Neva Chapelle, the newscaster arranged her pug-like features into a look of grave concern. Butterfly-sized fake lashes swept down over her protruding eyes as she glanced at her notes. Behind her, a photo of Alby hovered against the dark blue tones of the station's screen. Not a strand of caramel and chocolate hair shifted out of place as she raised her head and fixed her gaze on the camera.

"In breaking news tonight, the body of Albert Ferguson of Portland has been found in Carry Over, Maine, an unincorporated township in the western part of the state."

A stock graphic of an ambulance, stretcher, and crime scene tape filled the screen behind the newscaster's head. "State police officials are calling the death accidental. Ferguson, who has been missing since July 19, was wanted for questioning in connection with the murder of his sister-in-law, Alice Ferguson. That investigation is still ongoing. We will continue our coverage of the story as it develops. In other news…"

Liv switched off the broadcast. Did accidental mean unintentional? When Van got the phone call in her office, he'd told her hikers had found Alby's car at the bottom of a ravine off an old tote road leading through paper company land from Carry Over to the Canadian border. The police hadn't told him whether or not foul play was suspected, only that they'd be looking into everything closely.

Had Alby lost control of his car while fleeing the scene of the murder, she wondered? Or, wracked by guilt after killing Alice, had he crashed on purpose? And how would this new development impact the murder investigation?

Liv considered contacting Briggs, but decided the detective was unlikely to tell her anything. Instead she tried Van's phone. The call went to voicemail, so she left a message asking him to call her if he heard anything new, and then she wandered into her kitchen to check on the *caponata Siciliana* she'd put together for a light dinner.

She didn't want the vegetables to get too mushy. Jasper, who'd returned from Vegas that afternoon, was due to arrive at six. She didn't want *anything* going soft tonight.

●　　●　　●　　●　　●

"You outdid yourself, Liv. The beautiful table. The delicious food. You, looking totally gorgeous." Jasper raised his glass. "Thank you for the perfect homecoming."

"Oh, it gets better than caponata," she said. She'd set the table with a white tablecloth, a red candle, and her great-grandmother's green 1930s majolica plates. The setting sun cast the room in mellow light while Ella Fitzgerald crooned about having the world on a string. She gave him a meaningful smile. "Just you wait."

"Delayed gratification has its benefits." He sipped his wine. "What's new at Lively Investigations?"

She blinked, surprised he wanted to talk about her work. "Well, they found my client's brother dead in a ditch, for starters." She filled him in, leaving out her adventures at The Golden Triangle. Some things were best unmentioned.

He plucked a square of feta from a little bowl shaped like a leaf. "Do you think he did it? Murdered Alice Ferguson, I mean?"

"Most likely. For a while I had another theory that Alice might have gotten messed up with the mob—long story—but since the police have actual crime-scene evidence and the only thing I have is a hunch, I'm going to let it go. I have plenty of paying clients to keep me busy. I shouldn't be wasting time chasing after clues *pro bono*, no matter how intriguing."

"How's your assistant working out?"

"She's a lifesaver. I'll hate to see her go when school starts in a few weeks."

"Couldn't she stay on part-time?"

Liv spread a piece of bread with the caponata and set the knife on her plate. "Unfortunately, no. She's excited about law school. I'm not going to try to talk her out of pursuing her dreams even though I think she'd make an excellent investigator."

Jasper's eyes met hers. His dark hair was tousled, and he'd left the top button of his shirt undone and the sleeves rolled up. He looked relaxed, elegant, and so sexy, she wanted to dive across the table.

Might be dangerous considering the lit candle, she thought, smiling a little.

He held her gaze. "I'm glad things are going well. I hope you don't feel like I'm trying to kill your dreams, Olivia. I really do want you to be happy. And safe."

And locked in. Suddenly she felt uneasy. She'd been excited about the candles, the meal, reuniting with Jasper. She'd missed him while he'd been away, but now their problems rushed in on her like a cold, rogue wave, extinguishing her passion and energy.

She felt herself withdraw, like that wave, pulled back to her own dark sea.

He didn't notice her change of mood. "I was going to wait until after dinner to talk about this." He drew a tiny, velvet, draw-string bag from his pocket and set it in front of her. "But I can't wait."

Her fingers trembled as she opened the bag. A shiny house key attached to a Tiffany & Co. heart keyring dropped into her palm. Her breath caught. She raised her eyes to meet his, prepared to let him down easy. "Jasper..."

"Wait, there's more." He slid his phone across the table. "Fox thinks you should say yes."

"Fox?" Liv glanced at the phone screen. A pair of sad brown eyes stared up at her from a sweet little brown and white face with brown floppy ears.

"I think that's what we should name him. He's a beagle rescue from a medical testing puppy mill, and he needs a forever home. Let's do this, Liv. You, me, and Fox Hounderson Mulder."

She huffed out an exasperated breath. "Not fair, Jasper Temple! You know I can't resist a good *X-Files* reference—and those sweet, sad eyes. What a cutie!"

"Well?" he prompted.

Saying nothing, she put the key onto the tablecloth, stood, and began to clear the plates. He followed her to the sink, stood behind her, and put his hands on her hips. He kissed the top of her head. "Is that a yes?"

She felt a rush of heat and affection that surprised her. She turned and put her arms around him, leaned her head against his chest.

Should she do it, give the living together with a rescue dog thing a try? He felt so good, and when she looked up and stared into his eyes, her insides went warm and liquid. So what if underneath it all an ice-cube of dread remained unmelted by all that heat?

He gave her a lingering kiss. When they came up for air, he said, "You have to admit, he's pretty cute."

She stood on her tiptoes and nipped his earlobe. "He is. Let's get naked and talk about it later."

He removed her arms from his neck and stepped back. "Uh-uh. I need an answer first."

The ice cube expanded. She avoided his eyes. "I need more time."

"I have to know we're moving forward, Liv."

"I'm not ready."

"When will you be ready?"

"I don't know." She sighed. "Seems we're at an impasse."

"Seems like it."

She lifted her hands and let them drop. "So what do we do?"

Silence stretched between them. Jasper tilted his head down and rubbed the back of his neck. He stood silent for a moment and then looked up. His blue eyes drilled into hers. "Tell me something. Do you think you'll ever want to marry me?"

Those eyes hit her like a punch. Anxiety fluttered in her chest. The urge to run filled her entire body. She crossed her arms to hold herself in place. "How can I know that? It's so soon. Only a few months. The whole idea of marriage, well, I've seen all the ways people can hurt each other, the damage they inflict on each other, the mistrust and cheating and recriminations. Seems simpler to be together without the legal paperwork. I know I love you. You love me. Why does every love story have to end in a wedding?"

"Every love story doesn't." He gave her a rueful smile. "But I want that with you. The engagement ring. The church wedding. The house. The dog. The kids. The grandkids."

Liv shook her head. "But, Jasper, I never said I wanted those things. We've barely been together long enough to have this discussion. You're pushing me!"

"I know." He took a step closer to her. "I thought I could convince you, especially if you moved in with me. I thought you'd see how good it could be. I'm very persuasive."

The scent of his cologne filled her with longing. She slid her arms around him. She hooked her hands together behind his back. She put her face against his chest.

"If it's any consolation, you almost did."

His body tensed and then relaxed again. "Ah," he murmured into her hair. "I guess I have your answer."

"I'm sorry."

"Me, too."

Ella crooned on the stereo. They swayed together until the end of the song, and after one long, final kiss at the door and promises to remain friends, she shut the door softly behind him. She stood there and listened to the sound of his feet stomping down the stairs and the door slamming behind him.

Because nothing had gone the way she'd expected that night, she changed into her favorite silk pajama bottoms and a camisole and popped the champagne for herself.

Drinking from the bottle, she wandered into the sunroom. She plopped into a chair and stared across the peninsula, street lights and traffic lights and the last soft blush in the western sky fading into indigo and a rising crescent moon.

She considered calling Ashleigh, but she wasn't in the mood for advice or even consolation. She sighed and tipped the bottle again and replayed the evening in her mind, wondering if she'd made a mistake or narrowly escaped a box she never wanted to be stuck in. Ella sang *Take Love Easy,* and the lyrics brought tears to her eyes.

Damn, she missed him already.

As she stared out over the city, her cell phone buzzed. Her heart sped up. Maybe he'd changed his mind. She picked it up and squinted at the screen. It was a text from Van.

"Got a copy of Alby's will. He never changed it after he and Emsley split up."

Head woozy, she typed back. "Does that mean what I think it does?"

"Yes." Van responded. "She gets everything."

Chapter Twenty-Eight

• • • • • • • • • • • • • •

"What are we talking about here? Stock portfolio? Life insurance? Bank accounts?"

Two weeks after the discovery of Alby's body, Liv stood talking to Van in front of his garage next to a beat-up white pickup. She wore dark sunglasses with a white crocheted midi dress from Draper James and three-inch espadrilles tied at the ankles. Her new favorite Kate Spade pink and white floral tote swung from her shoulder as waves radiated from the paved driveway in the sweltering August heat.

"All of the above. In total it comes to just over ten million." Van let out a mirthless laugh. "He wasn't exactly the Jordan Belfort he pretended to be, but who am I to talk? I spoke with Emsley this morning, and she's still in shock over the whole thing. Poor girl really loved him, I guess. That surprises me more than the will. Of course, the gallery's also an asset, and Emsley can sell it or keep it, whatever she decides to do."

"Ten mill isn't nothing. If she's careful and invests well, she should be more than comfortable." Liv's dark glasses slid down her nose. She pushed them up and watched Busterdoodle race around the front lawn in manic figure eights.

"Hey, dude! Do you have something to put over this desk?" Standing in the bed of the truck, a guy who looked to be in his early twenties maneuvered several pieces of furniture into place. Van had introduced him as Travis, the dog-walker. About the same height as Van and bare-chested in the noonday sun, Travis wore a pair of faded red cargo shorts and yellow work boots. A man-bun secured his sun-streaked brown hair. Tattoos decorated much of his well-muscled body.

Liv tilted her nose to look at him over the top of her glasses. She murmured to Van, "Where did you find this guy? Hot Bods R Us?"

"Dunkin' Donuts."

"Wow. Talk about an extra shot of espresso!"

Van snorted. "He's a barista but also gigs himself out for dog-sitting and odd jobs. Buster loves him. He helps me out with stuff like this once in a while."

"Mmmm. Nice tats."

"You like that? Hold on a sec. I need to grab a blanket." He jogged in his slightly rocking gait toward the open doors of the garage while Liv checked her phone. Sweat ran down her neck. Speaking of coffee, she could go for an iced latte right about now.

She'd stopped by to check on Van and get the scoop on Emsley's stroke of good fortune. For someone who just lost a brother, Van seemed to be doing okay. Maybe he was still in denial. Or maybe he'd felt so angry and betrayed he didn't care.

She worried about him. He'd been through a lot of trauma the past couple of weeks. How much could a person take before they broke?

When Van returned, he hopped into the bed and helped Travis wrap the desk in a gray and red plaid blanket. They began to secure the furniture with bungee cords.

Liv pushed her glasses up her nose again. "Isn't that Alice's desk?"

Van glanced over. "Yes, it is… was." He cast a critical eye at a cord hooked into one of the truck's ring anchors. "I'm not sure that's going to hold," he said to Travis. "Let's use ratchet straps. Check in the garage, will you? I think they're hanging on the pegboard."

"Sure, dude." Travis jumped down and walked to the house.

Busterdoodle, tongue hanging out, trotted after him. Liv stared at man and dog and thought, *Nice. Very nice.*

Van sat down on the tailgate and wiped the sweat from his face with the inside of his tee-shirt. She gave him an appraising look. His abs were taut and his arms looked almost as muscular as Travis's. He wore a pair of stained, ragged jeans, ripped on one thigh, and a faded Three Days Grace concert tee.

When he wasn't dressed in khakis, she mused, he looked like a completely different kind of person. Stronger. More capable. Not at all the beige and boring guy who walked into her office several weeks ago.

"So what's up with the desk?" she asked.

He said, "I'm selling it. The rooms upstairs are full of French Country and American Colonial antiques that Alice and I picked up over the years. It was one of our things, going to auctions and flea markets on the weekend. We'd get up early, grab a nice breakfast somewhere, spend the day poking around and looking for good stuff."

"That sounds like fun."

He nodded. "It used to be. This winter, when we needed some room, I sold a few of our extraneous pieces through one of those online marketplaces. In the process, I learned how to buy and sell on the site and researched fine furniture repair techniques. I even started picking up damaged pieces for cheap, fixed them, and sold them online for a small profit. I didn't make a lot, but it was something to do in my spare time."

She thought about the money he'd paid her to investigate Alice. At the time she hadn't known he'd lost his job, and he still hadn't told her. In fact, Liv might not have accepted his money—or the job—if she'd known he was strapped for cash.

Still sitting on the tailgate, Van looked bashful. "You might not believe this, but I actually enjoy researching design styles and using traditional techniques and tools. Turns out I'm good at it."

"You're a craftsman at heart, then. Good for you."

"I've been thinking now that Alice is gone, I might turn it into a real business. Forget engineering. I could sell this place, get something smaller with a workshop, invest in a delivery van so I don't have to keep borrowing Travis's truck."

"But, Van. Alice's desk? Isn't that a sentimental piece?"

His eyes filled with tears as he nodded. "It is, but it's too small for me to use and it makes me sad to look at it, so I put it up for sale this week. A woman in Gull's Haven bought it. A bureau and chair, too. She wants them delivered this afternoon." He rubbed tears from his face and shrugged. "Sorry for the waterworks."

"No need to apologize."

He took a deep breath. His shoulders relaxed. "It's a nice ride up there. Do you want to come along?"

He looked so eager, she almost said yes, but she only had Marion for a couple more weeks and needed to make the most of that time. She wanted to finish the Raptor worker's comp case, in particular. The insurance company's lawyer called the day before asking for an update. She'd promised to do some surveillance this week and get back to them. "Tempting, but I have to head back to the office." She hesitated. "Can I ask you something before I go?"

"Sure."

"When you hired me to investigate Alice and Alby, why didn't you tell me you'd lost your job?"

Van's face flushed. "Ah. I wondered when you'd call me out on that." He waited a second or two before answering. "Holt & Compton restructured back in January, and I was one of several managers they let go. After telling everyone what a great company they were and how lucky I was to have landed there, when they downsized me, I felt humiliated." He threw her a quizzical look. "Alice was the only person I told. How'd you find out, anyway?"

"Word gets around. Someone who figured I already knew mentioned it." She frowned. "You didn't even tell your parents? Wouldn't they have helped you out financially if you'd asked them?"

"Alice wanted me to, but I couldn't deal with them. You know how it is with the parental disappointment."

"Unfortunately, I do."

"Right. So I thought I'd find another position before they found out. We all had to sign an NDA, so I figured no one would be talking about it and I'd have time to secure a new gig and get back on my feet. Once I found a job, I'd tell them I'd decided to move on to a better company. Best laid plans, I guess." He sounded bitter.

"No luck, huh?"

Van hopped down from the truck. He slid his hands into his pockets. "With my experience and references, I expected at least a couple of job offers. But nope. Not a single one in months despite several good interviews and call-backs. I know my references were solid, and I think my experience speaks for itself. Maybe the companies are looking for diversity hires. It was hard to explain to Alice why it was taking so long."

"So, the layoff put a strain on your relationship?"

"Of course. How couldn't it?" He leaned against the tailgate. "Alice loved this house. She loved her job. She wanted to start a family. Then all of a sudden, I didn't have a job and couldn't seem to get another one. She knew if something didn't change soon, we'd have to sell the house and put kids on hold indefinitely." His eyes watered again. "I guess she thought Alby could give her everything I couldn't."

"That's terrible, Van. I don't know what to say."

"It's like some Greek tragedy, right?" He tried to laugh, and failed. "It sucks, you know? You do all the right things. You pay attention in school. You work for the grades. You get into a good college and graduate with honors. You start work for a company you believe in. Figuring you're right on track, you find a nice girl and marry her. You buy her the big house she wants in the suburbs, go antiquing on the weekends, hang with the neighbors, and start talking about kids. You get promoted. You're on track. You believe that because you've done all these things they told you to do and followed all the rules, you'll be successful and happy."

"That's the party line, for sure."

"Turns out, it's all a lie. You do everything right, *everything*, and find yourself a widower at thirty with no job, savings depleted, forced to sell your furniture to pay the astronomical mortgage on a house you never really wanted for a wife who cheated on you with your perfect older brother who had all the money and respect, not earned through hard work but because of some sleazy Wall Street deal and a lot of charm. So you're right. I could have begged my parents for a loan, but I didn't want to see the contempt on their faces. It was bad enough seeing it on Alice's every day. Then I found out about her and Alby… and ugh. They're both dead thanks to him, and I'm left here picking up the pieces. I can't think about it any more, Liv. My life's a total wreck."

"I'm so sorry, Van. About all of it."

"No. I'm the one who's sorry. I didn't mean to lay all that on you. I loved her so much and I failed her and pushed her into my brother's arms. And then he killed her." Van shook his head. "I wanted to give her everything, and I ended up with nothing. Absolutely nothing. My parents are right. I'm a loser."

She put a hand on his arm and squeezed. "It's not your fault. Alice decided to have a relationship with Alby. *She* did it. Not you. You should give yourself a break."

"And now you're pitying me, too." He sounded angry. "At least I've hit rock bottom. I have nowhere to go but up."

Travis strolled from the garage, red and blue straps in his hands, Buster at his side. "Got 'em!

Van shoved himself away from the tailgate. "I'll feel better once the murder investigation is over. Then I can put all this behind me and get on with my life. Finally."

Chapter Twenty-Nine

• • • • • • • • • • • • • •

When Liv returned to the office, still troubled by her conversation with Van, Marion handed her a slip of paper. "Call about a security consult."

Liv took it. "Thanks. Anything else while I was gone?"

"No, I've been—" The phone rang. Marion answered it. "Lively Investigations. Yes, hello Mrs. Lively. She just stepped in." Marion looked up. Liv made a cutting motion with her hand. "Oh. Sorry. I'm wrong. I thought she was here, but she must have sneaked past me." She listened. "No, she's not telling me to tell you she's not here. No… okay. Okay. Okay, I'll buzz you through."

Marion made a face at Liv and mouthed, "Sorry."

Liv rolled her eyes. "Give me a second." She strode past the reception desk and into her office. She tossed her floral tote on one of the chairs in front of her desk and plopped into the one behind her desk. She lifted the handset when the phone rang. "Hi, Mom. What's up?"

"You haven't been answering your phone!"

"I was on the road. Driving and talking on a cell is against Maine law. Did you call for a reason or just to update me on the most recent way I'm ruining my life?"

Liv crossed her legs as she booted up the laptop on her desk. Things had been strained with Tiffany ever since Liv told her about the breakup. No surprise there. What was surprising was Tiffany continued to call Liv every other day, bugging her about getting her nails done or making sure she made her annual gynecologist appointment and warning her to wear sunscreen especially on her chest.

"Did you use that Clé de Peau Beauté cream I gave you? You don't want to get to be sixty with a wrinkled, spotted decolletage, Olivia. Take my advice. SPF 50. You'll thank me later."

"Yes. I've been using it. Was there something else you wanted?"

"I assume you'll be at brunch this Sunday?"

"Only if you promise me you won't be setting me up with any more doctors."

"Oh, believe me, I wouldn't waste my time." There was a pause. "You know he's seeing Wren Osborne again, don't you? He brought her to the Sternheimer's anniversary party last night. It was a lovely evening. They had this wonderful jazz quartet outdoors under a tent and the most glorious floral swags from Broadturn Farm. When you get married, we should seriously consider them for flowers." She paused. "*If* you ever get married."

Wren and Jasper. No surprise there. Liv's heart twisted a little. "I hope it works out for them."

"Yes. Well." Tiffany paused for a second. "Your father and I will see you on Sunday, then."

"Yes. Right after church."

"What?"

"Kidding, Mother. I'll see you on Sunday for coffee, crepes, and criticism."

"I don't criticize! I offer good advice!"

"Bye, Mom," Liv laughed. "And, Mom? Thanks for calling and checking on me. I'm doing fine. You don't need to worry."

"You're welcome." Tiffany's tone softened. "See you, Sunday."

•   •   •   •   •

Two hours later, Liv finished a detailed background check and emailed it to her client. She logged into the new case management system Marion had installed and marked the job as finished. On Friday, Marion would run a report that would automatically generate invoices for all completed cases that week.

Liv leaned back in her chair and stretched. The program was freakin' genius.

Since it was nearing time for Marion to go home, Liv wandered out to the reception desk. Her assistant, dark hair piled on top of her head in a messy bun, head stuck close to her computer screen, didn't look up. She glanced from the screen to a document at her elbow, made a mark on the paper with a pencil, and then went back to the screen.

Liv asked, "Whatcha doing?"

"Oh!" Marion jerked upright and put a hand to her face. Her cheeks flushed red. "You startled me! I'm just checking something. I wanted to be sure before I bothered you with it, but now that you're asking..."

Intrigued, Liv stood behind her assistant and peered at the screen. "Is that Alice's novel?"

"Yes. Remember how you asked me to read it? Well, I did. At first all I noticed was the story and the structure and where it needed to be tightened up and the story's really good but there were some places I thought were confusing and... never mind." She waved her hands. "That's me wearing my editor hat. I realized that I needed to be looking for clues for a murder case, not critiquing like I would in a creative writing seminar. So I went through it a second time, taking notes about the characters, assuming they could be real people or based on real people, and the situations. You know, the crimes. I thought I'd then check the news for recent crime stories and see if anything matched up."

Impressed, Liv nodded. "I've said it before, you'd make a good P.I."

"Thank you! Anyway, something interesting popped out at me. Take a look." Marion pointed at her screen. "This is the scene in Alice's book where Calliope and Nikolai are arguing."

"Okay."

Marion then tapped the print-out on the desk. "This is a copy of your surveillance notes from Carry Over, the part where you observed Alice and Alby arguing in front of the chalet's windows. Each of these check marks indicates where the two match up."

Liv leaned closer. Marks danced across the page. "That's quite a few checks."

"Yup. Alby and Nikolai both clutch their heads. Alice and Calliope each throw something at their man. Both women turn and walk away. Both men put their hands on the women's shoulders. Both couples then embrace." She tossed Liv a satisfied smile. "The scenes are almost an exact match. That's more than a coincidence, right?"

Liv straightened. She stared across the room, replaying in her mind the argument she'd witnessed that night from the dock. She closed her eyes as the implication hit her. Alice and Alby, working on the chapter, might have been acting out the scene to get it right. Not fighting. Liv's report of an argument must be partly why the police believed Alby murdered Alice. If they hadn't actually been fighting, well, it didn't exonerate Alby, but it certainly weakened the evidence.

Which meant The Golden Triangle theory about a mafia hit might not be so far-fetched.

She met Marion's eyes. "I need to call Briggs right away. Excellent work, Marion. I totally missed this."

"Do you think this changes anything in regards to the police investigation?"

"I don't know. Possibly." Liv tapped her upper lip with her index finger, her mind spinning. "It's late. You should go home for the day. Tomorrow I'm taking you out for lunch, okay? This was really, really good work. I'll let you know what the police say."

•   •   •   •   •

Detective Briggs sounded skeptical when Liv told her what Marion had discovered. "I don't know, Ms. Lively. I think you're reading too much into this."

"No pun intended?" Liv paused for a reaction, but there was none. "Uh, there are too many similarities for it to be a coincidence, don't you think?"

Briggs went silent again. "It's hard to say. Could be the argument inspired the scene and not the other way around, right?"

"I guess so. Yes."

"Either way, I don't think it changes anything. The medical examiner ruled Ferguson's death accidental. His injuries were consistent with a car crash involving a driver not wearing a seatbelt. Cause of death: TBI. Traumatic brain injury. He'd been drinking. We gathered forensic evidence at both scenes that point to Ferguson as Alice's killer. I shouldn't share this, but between us? Albert Ferguson's fingerprints were on the murder weapon and we didn't find any unexplained, foreign DNA in the chalet. We'll be sending our report to the District Attorney shortly, and I expect the case will be officially closed sometime this fall."

Liv gripped her phone. "So it's all wrapped up in a tidy, little package, I guess. What about the strip club? Will you look into it at all? I have witnesses that say Alice frequented the place, and there's definitely criminal activity going on there. If she saw the wrong person doing the wrong thing…"

Briggs sighed. "You know the majority of female homicide victims are killed by men they know."

"Yes, but that doesn't mean in this case…"

"Ms. Lively, let me stop you, okay? While I appreciate your enthusiasm and concern, I'm convinced Albert Ferguson killed his sister-in-law and died in a vehicular accident while fleeing the scene of his crime. You're wasting my time and yours going down this particular rabbit hole."

"But if they weren't actually arguing…"

"Thank you, again, for your concern. I'd love to chat," Briggs's tone implied just the opposite, "but I have another call coming in. Goodbye, Ms. Lively." The detective ended the call.

Liv dropped her phone onto her desk. "Ugh!" she said out loud. She leaned back in her chair and looked out the window. Gigantic banks of pink-tinged clouds piled on the horizon, the accumulation of the day's humidity promising an evening storm. Maybe the detective was right, and she was chasing after a phantom theory. Just because Alice spent time at The Golden Triangle didn't mean she'd been targeted by someone in the criminal underworld.

What did she know, anyway? The police had access to forensic and ME reports, traffic camera footage, and phone records, not to mention interviews with Carry Over residents who must have seen Alice and Alby together at the market and who knows where else.

All she had was a hunch. And a dirty book.

She put her feet up on the desk and crossed her ankles, wondering if she should waste any more time on a case for which she wasn't being paid and the police had already decided to put the bed. But then she visualized Alice Ferguson lying behind the kitchen island, pretty nightie hiked up her thighs, and that big chef's knife sticking out of her chest, fingers reaching for the blade, eyes wide open in shock and fear.

She frowned, picturing the scene. Alice's scratched legs. The triangle necklace at her throat. The lantern on the kitchen island. The landline phone on the wall behind her.

The phone. Liv dropped her feet to the floor. Electrical power had gone out in the storm that ripped through Maine that day. Trees fell on electrical wires, pulling them from poles, knocking electricity out as the storm blew through the state. Transformers blew, sparking and booming.

But there were other wires besides the electrical ones. Liv bet if she called the phone company, they'd tell her the land lines had gone down in Carry Over, as well. Most people didn't notice so much because everyone used cell phones, but if your house didn't get cell service, you'd be dismayed and inconvenienced to discover your landline service cut off. You'd feel pretty isolated. Insecure. Unreachable.

The electricity that afternoon, she remembered, had only been out for a couple of hours, but that didn't mean the phone lines had been repaired at the exact same time. Maine was a big state and Carry Over in a sparsely populated area. Not a high priority for the phone company.

Suppose Alice had wanted to make a phone call but the landline was down. The chalet itself sat in a dead spot, but maybe Alice knew of a place in the woods where she could get a bar or two. Liv imagined Alice checking the landline phone for a dial tone and, hearing none, slipping her shoes on and tromping out to make a call, lantern swinging in her hand.

Liv stared ahead while her mind raced going over all the events of that evening in Carry Over, testing for flaws in her theory and finding none. Alice, she was sure, had gone out into the woods to make a phone call that night.

The question was, who did she contact and why had it been so important that she'd risk mosquitos whining in her ears and scratchy branches scraping at her bare legs just to talk to them?

Chapter Thirty

• • • • • • • • • • • • • •

Sure she was on the right track, Liv grabbed her cell phone and pulled up the photos she'd taken of Alice's notebook. Scanning the list, she found the password for Van and Alice's cell phone account and signed-in on the service's website.

Seconds later, the Fergusons' account loaded onto the screen.

The account displayed two phone numbers. One she recognized as Van's. She chose Alice's and clicked through several option drop-downs to the month-by-month log of ingoing and outgoing calls. Her fingers hovered over the mouse pad.

There it was.

She sat back, hands tingling. She recalled her own actions that night, how she'd stood on the dock with her binoculars, watching the chalet. She heard the quiet lap of water against the dock and the call of the loons. She watched the argument in front of the big glass doors, the lights in the rooms going out one by one, and the bobbing light of a lantern passing through the trees next to the chalet.

Alice had carried the lantern into the woods around 9:30 p.m., and now Liv knew why. For a cell phone signal.

She jotted down the phone number that matched the date and time. Who had Alice needed to call so desperately that she'd trudge out to the woods in the night with a lantern?

Not Van. It wasn't his number. Not Alby. He was in the chalet. Someone else then.

Liv studied the phone record. Whoever Alice called that night, the conversation had lasted only a few minutes. Liv scrolled through the record and noticed many calls to and from that same 207 number with a three-digit prefix she didn't recognize.

She picked up her phone and dialed. An automated message announced the number she had reached was not available. Undeterred, she logged into her favorite reverse phone search program and typed in the nine-digit number. She copied the information.

She stared at the notepad. The phone connected to that number was registered to someone named Maralynne Goff. Goff lived in a small town way up on the Maine coast. Another phone number was listed for the address.

No time like the present, she thought, punching the number into her cell.

"Hello?" The woman's voice on the other end sounded wary, as if she expected a robo-call.

"Hi, is this Maralynne Goff?"

"Yes…"

"Great. Hi," Liv said again. "My name is Olivia Lively. I'm a private investigator down in Portland looking into a case, and a cell phone registered to your name came up. I'm wondering if I could ask you a few questions?"

"Uh, I don't know. What was the number?"

Liv told her.

"My daughter Kayla uses that phone. Is she okay?" Maralynne's voice sounded tense.

"I was hoping to speak with her. I take it she isn't home?"

"Are you sure you're not the police?"

"I'm a private investigator. Why? Have the police contacted you?"

Maralynne sighed. "Yes. A couple weeks ago. They also wanted to talk to Kayla. I told them I hadn't seen her in awhile. She's working down in Portland this summer. Is she in trouble?"

"I'm not sure, but I'm doing my best to fit it all together. You said you haven't seen her all summer. Is that unusual?"

"Not really. She's going to school at Longfellow College. Just finished her second year. She's studying French so she can teach high school when she graduates. She got a job down there in Portland and decided not to come home over summer break."

"When was the last time you saw Kayla?"

Maralynne hesitated. "I'm not sure why you are asking me all this. Please, if you know something, tell me."

"I really don't know much, Ms. Goff. I'm calling because I believe your daughter spoke to the wife of one of my clients a few weeks ago. I just want to talk to her. If you could tell me anything that would help me locate her, I'll be sure to let her know you'd appreciate hearing from her"

Marylynne breathed into the phone for a few seconds. Liv tensed, expecting the other woman to end the call, but finally Maralynne took a deep breath and said, "Christmas. That's the last time I saw my daughter in person. She drove up and spent a few days. I thought she seemed tired, finals and everything, but I wasn't overly concerned. I was hoping she'd stay longer, but she said she had to work. I thought she had a college work-study job, but she said no, she'd found something else, waitressing maybe? She never really gave me the details."

"Does she live on campus?"

"Not this year. She got an apartment with some friends. Over near the airport." Maralynne hesitated again. "This is going to make me sound like a bad mom, but I've never seen her place. I don't drive long distances—my eyes are bad—and she discouraged me from visiting. She said there wasn't a place for me to stay because of her roommate. I—I didn't push it. You have to let them fly out of the nest, and she's always been pretty independent."

"Of course," Liv soothed. "Sounds like you respected her boundaries. Not all mothers do, believe me. When's the last time you spoke with her?"

NIGHT MOVES · 189

"After the police called, I got hold of her. She assured me that everything was fine and it was just something to do with a lost wallet or purse or something. I haven't talked to her since then. Like I said, she's busy."

"Okay. Just one more question, if you don't mind. Did Kayla ever mention someone named Alice?"

"Alice? No." A pause. "Was she someone from the school?"

"I'm not sure what connection they had. That's what I'm trying to find out. And to do that I need to find your daughter. Would you be willing to share her last known address?"

"I'm not sure…" The woman sounded shaky.

"I understand. Why don't you take a few minutes and check out the website for my agency. It's called Lively Investigations. I'm at the office right now. If you feel comfortable, just call the number listed. That way you'll know I'm legit."

"Okay. What's the web address?"

After Liv told her, Maralynne hung up. Liv Ten minutes later, the landline rang. Liv picked it up. "Lively Investigations. This is Olivia Lively."

"Okay, I guess you're who you say you are," Maralynne said. "You'll let me know when you find her, right? Just so I know she's okay?"

"Absolutely. I'll tell her you're concerned and suggest she call you, as well."

"All right." Maralynne gave her the address, and Liv wrote it down. Maralynne sounded choked up when she added, "She's only twenty, Ms. Lively. I hope she hasn't gotten herself into trouble. Please call me as soon as you find her."

"I will. You have my word."

After ending the call, she punched Kayla's address into her map app, grabbed her bag, and headed out the door. If the police tried to reach Kayla two weeks ago, that meant they'd also checked Alice's phone records. Since nothing had come of it, Briggs must have determined the call wasn't important to the case.

Still, intuition told Liv to follow this lead. For some reason, on the night of her murder, Alice decided to contact twenty-year-old college-student Kayla Goff. She'd traipsed out into the Maine woods in the middle of the night, braving mosquitos and raccoons and who knows what else. Within a few hours of that call, someone plunged a knife into Alice's chest.

Coincidence? Possible, but not improbable, she mused. She'd know more after she located Kayla Goff.

• • • • •

Liv sped down 295 to the Westbrook Street exit. The exquisite voice of Maria Callas singing Bellini's *Casta Diva* poured from her speakers like a stream of liquid silver. Liv hummed along as storm clouds piled into the sky and darkened to an ominous gray and purple. The first fat raindrops fell as she hooked off the exit and followed her GPS to the address Maralynne had given her.

She turned into the parking lot of The Villas. The modest apartment complex looked vaguely Tuscan with orange roof shingles and tall Cypress trees planted between the buildings. All five two-story buildings boasted yellowish cement walls that had been pebbled to create an impression of stucco. No shutters graced the windows.

Liv cruised slowly through the lots looking for Building Five. The pavement in the parking lots needed to be re-cracked and sealed. Cars and pickups occupied most of the numbered, white-lined parking spaces in front of the buildings. A few listless Adirondack chairs faced a weedy duck pond, and three kids played next to a rusty swing set. One broken seat dangled by a chain.

As the clouds opened up, the two biggest kids raced toward the nearest building, the little one lagged behind them.

She found the building and parked along the grass of the playground area. A set of wide, cement steps led to an entrance on the west side of the building. She ran through the rain to the steps and checked the names on the buzzers beside the door. Finding one labeled Goff, she pressed the button. No answer. She pressed it again. Still nothing.

Next she tried the button above it. The rain began to fall harder. Her white embroidered dress absorbed the water. Soon she'd be sopping wet and weighed down. "Come on, someone answer." Overhead, thunder rumbled.

Great. She turned to go.

"Yeah?" a female voice crackled through the intercom.

"Yes, hi. I'm a friend of Kayla Goff's. She told me to meet her here but she's not answering. Do you mind letting me in?"

"Yeah, whatever." The door buzzed, and Liv grabbed the handle and pulled.

Grateful for the stupidity of people—you don't just let strangers into an apartment building because they ask you—she jogged up the stairwell to the second floor and made her way down the hall looking for apartment 2-C. A dried flower wreath hung around the peephole. Liv took note of the floral welcome mat—Kayla cared enough about her surroundings to invest in pretty décor—and knocked on the door. "Kayla? Are you there?"

Nothing. She put her ear to the door, but did not hear any noise from inside. She knocked again. Still no answer.

Unwilling to give up yet, Liv slid to the apartment next door where she could hear what sounded like a video game playing at top volume. She knocked and then pounded on the door. Finally, the game stopped and a middle-aged woman wearing sweatpants, a baggy Sea Dogs tee-shirt, and a pair of bright pink Crocs knockoffs answered. "What?"

"Hi. Sorry to bother you. I'm Olivia Lively. I'm looking for Kayla Goff, your next door neighbor? Have you seen her today?"

"Not sure when I saw her last. Maybe a week or two? She keeps weird hours." The woman started to close the door.

Liv braced it open with her hand and scrabbled in her purse for a business card. "Just another second, please. I'm a private investigator. Her mother's worried about her. If you do see her, can you call me?"

The woman rolled her eyes and took the card. "Sure." She glanced at Liv's hand on her door. Liv removed it, and the woman shut the door. A few seconds later, the video game started up again.

She knocked on a few more doors, but no one answered. Discouraged, she trotted down the stairs. She looked up complex's leasing office number and called, but all she got was a recording saying the office would open again at nine the next morning.

Rain and wind whipped at her hair and clothing as she dashed across the parking lot toward her Corolla. A giant clap of thunder followed a flash of lightning, and her espadrilles splashed through the inch of water suddenly covering the parking lot. She yanked the driver's side door and slid inside, soaking wet and more than ready to go home. She looked through the rain-blurred windshield at the building and counted windows. Most glowed with light but not the one in 2-C.

It was a blackened eye staring unseeing and unblinking at the brute force of the storm.

Chapter Thirty-One

• • • • • • • • • • • • • • •

After a rejuvenating night that included a long soak in her claw-foot tub, a couple glasses of wine, and sleep soothed by the sound of the rain, Liv woke the following morning excited to start her day.

As much as she wanted to head back to the Villas to check for Kayla again, her calendar pinged her with a reminder about the Raptor case. She'd promised Francine Larabee a report by the end of the month, and with all the distraction of the Ferguson case, she'd fallen behind. She decided to spend the morning watching Raymond Booker's house. All she needed for Raptor was one good video of him using his supposed inoperable hand, a detailed report about the coworkers she'd interviewed, and the photos she'd gleaned from social media.

When she was done with Booker, she'd circle back to The Villas.

Because she might be cramped up in her car for hours on surveillance, she took a fast, invigorating run around Back Cove and returned home to shower and change.

She chose to go simple: jean shorts, a plain white tee covered by a pink sweater, and a matching baseball cap. She packed a simple black backpack with a water bottle, snacks, and her usual spy gear—cell phone, binoculars, camera with zoom lens, and camcorder—and set out.

Portland sparkled after yesterday's cleansing storm. She cracked the window to let in the fresh, salty air and zipped up Brighton against inbound downtown traffic and navigated Booker's Fallbrook neighborhood.

Liv found Booker's house with no problem. He lived in a split-level ranch on a street of similar houses built in the 1950s. It was a solidly blue-collar neighborhood within walking distance of the mill, the Catholic church, and Main Street. People here mowed their fenced-in backyards once or twice a week, planted pansies along the walkways, and placed Virgin Mary statues on the front lawn. Azaleas and rhododendrons provided some privacy between properties.

She spotted Booker's Chevy Tahoe parked in front of Booker's garage and parallel parked across the street. Thirty minutes into her surveillance, Booker accepted a DoorDash delivery. With her camera, Liv zoomed in on the McDonald's bag and snapped a couple pics for the fun of it before slumping back in her seat, already kind of bored.

She set her camera aside and gave herself two more hours before she gave up for the day.

An hour later, she perked up. The sound of metal clanking against metal rang through the air. She rolled down her window to listen. The sound could be coming from behind Booker's house, but she couldn't see the back yard from this angle.

She slouched further when another pickup turned into the driveway. A man she recognized from Booker's social media emerged. The medium-build dude with a drooping Sam Elliott mustache and a bandana tied around his head carried a large, gray toolbox to the side of the house, turned the corner, and disappeared.

Liv grabbed her camera and opened the Corolla's door. She eased herself from the car, slid her phone into the back pocket of her shorts, and draped the pink sweater over the arm holding the camera, hiding it from view in case any nosy neighbors had their eye on the street.

Exuding "homeowner out for a stroll around the neighborhood" vibes, she walked up the sidewalk, passed ten or so driveways, and stopped at the first cross-street. She strolled to the opposite sidewalk and headed back toward Booker's. As she neared his house, she slowed, peering into his backyard.

Beneath a makeshift carport built of two-by-fours and blue tarp, a bass fishing boat sat on a trailer. She slowed some more. Booker and his friend stood at the back of the boat. Booker reached into the boat near the engine and pulled out what looked like a black hose. The friend said something and nodded.

Liv crouched on the sidewalk. She dropped the sweater over the camera and pretended to retie the lace of her sneaker while watching the two men. Booker, using his left hand, braced himself and leaned into the boat with his right, screwdriver in hand. *Perfect.*

She stood and pretended to stretch, twisting on her waist from side to side while scouting the landscape for cover.

Glancing left and right to make sure nobody spotted her, she jogged to a neighbor's yard and situated herself behind a mature rhododendron with thick, dark leaves. She tied the pink sweater around her waist and lifted the camera, squinting through the viewfinder into Booker's backyard.

The camera recorded as Booker and his friend grabbed hold of either side of the engine, and she zoomed in on Booker's supposed useless left hand. He gripped the engine block with no apparent trouble, and the two men lifted the engine off the boat and placed it on a workbench made of sawhorses and planks.

She continued to record as Booker straightened and reached into his pocket. She blinked and lowered the camera when he lifted a cell phone to his ear. He stiffened and swiveled his head right and left. *Uh-oh,* she thought, tensing. Booker's gaze landed on the rhododendron. "Hey!" he yelled and began to run toward her.

The neighbor must've ratted her out. She dashed from behind the rhody and sprinted toward her car.

"Stop!" Booker yelled, sounding furious.

She glanced back as he crossed his small front lawn in three giant strides. She skidded next to her car, threw open the door, and slid inside. As she slammed the door and started the engine, he loped across the street, yelling obscenities. In her rearview mirror, she saw him reach for the rear door handle, but she ground the car into drive and pressed the gas pedal to the floor. Her tires squealed, no doubt leaving black marks on the pavement, and Booker's hand slipped from the handle as she picked up speed.

At the sign, she came to a full stop and glanced in the rearview mirror again. Booker's friend joined him in the middle of the street, hands on hips, both of them staring at the rear end of her car. She wondered if they could read her license plate.

Doesn't matter, she told herself. She had the evidence her client needed. She'd write her report, send it and the images to the insurance company's lawyer, and instruct Marion to email the invoice. She hit the gas, turned left, and made her way toward Brighton.

She slid a pair of shades over her eyes, turned her radio to WCYY, and rolled down the window while *Just Like You* by Three Days Grace streamed from the speakers. A smile crept across her face.

Sometimes she really loved her job.

• • • • •

She didn't love it so much, though, when she had to deal with people like Banjo Foster.

"I can't let you in." The Villas' manager, triple chin rippling in a most unpleasant way, shook his head. "Wouldn't be right."

"Look, here's my private investigator's license, my driver's license, and the text from Kayla's mother sending me her photograph. She hasn't heard from her daughter in over a week, which is really unusual, and Kayla's neighbor says she hasn't seen her, either. I just want to make sure she's not lying in there sick or injured."

Banjo smelled like an overripe banana and sweaty armpits. He wore an electric blue jogging suit, white socks, and leather sandals. His long, stringy hair flowed to his shoulders and framed a puffy, pasty-white face pocked with old acne scars. She felt a little pity for the poor guy.

After checking in at the office following her successful surveillance, she'd driven over to The Villas and tracked the manager down in the complex's leasing office. It was a cluttered space with a couple dented filing cabinets, a beach-scene calendar tacked to the wall, and a string of lights in the shape of red jalapeno peppers.

Banjo, three-hundred and twenty pounds at least, took up most of the room's real estate. She tried not to breathe through her nose. "Her mother's worried sick about her," she said.

Banjo fixed her with an unpleasant stare. "Then I should call the police."

"Okay. You can do that. Call the police and residents might take photos and post about it on social media. Might even get some media people sniffing around. Maybe even make the 6 o'clock news. Not the sort of thing The Villas' owners would appreciate, am I right?"

Banjo grunted. He squished a pink, flying-pig stress ball in his meaty right hand.

Liv, sensing an opening, hurried on with her pitch. "Instead, you could accompany me to Kayla's apartment, unlock the door, and keep an eye on me while I check the premises. No drama. A couple of minutes and you can forget I was ever here." She picked at a nonexistent hangnail. "Now if you choose to go with the police, there will be questions and reports and probably a big headache for you. But if that's what you want…"

"Okay. Fine."

He threw the pink pig onto his desk and lumbered to his feet.

She followed him to the parking lot where he settled his bulk onto a yellow electric scooter. "I'll meet you there," he said and puttered off, knees like wings on the side of the scooter and hair rippling behind him.

A few minutes later, they reconvened in the dim hallway outside Kayla's apartment. When Banjo swung the door open, she flitted past him and into Kayla's sad little one-bedroom flat. The door opened into a windowless kitchen with a small, white-painted table and two matching chairs. A small bathroom and a living room opened off the kitchen. A doorway led from the living room to the bedroom.

"Kayla? Are you home?" Liv called, knowing no one had been there for a while because of the musty, closed-up smell. The sink was empty except for one plate with a few crumbs and a butter knife with a smear of what looked like dried grape jelly on it.

"She's not here. Let's go." Banjo shifted from one hippie-sandaled foot to the other and rattled his keys.

"Hold on a second. I'm going to check the other rooms."

Bango heaved a big sigh and looked up and down the hall. "Hurry up."

Liv peeked into the small bathroom which was cluttered with makeup, brushes, a collection of fake eyelashes, and used makeup remover pads. She took note of glitter sparkling on the floor and sink and a vanilla-scented candle perched on the edge of the tub, but nothing else caught her attention. It was just the usual mess of a college student's bathroom.

In the living room, she found a jumble of magazines, glasses half-full of liquid, vape cartridges, and crumpled takeout napkins. Liv glanced back toward Banjo hovering in the doorway. "Just a few more minutes!"

Scanning the space, she noticed a small bookcase tucked beside a faded, floral armchair with a large brown stain on one arm. She walked over to inspect the contents of the shelves. Paperback novels of famous French writers—Colette, Flaubert, Camus, and

Simone de Beauvoir—sat next to hefty French textbooks. Tucked next to a collection of Victor Hugo essays was a slim, white volume of *The Story of O* by Pauline Réage. More candles, a framed photo of a terrier-type dog wearing a kerchief around its neck, and a jar of pennies sat on top of the shelf.

When she stepped back, Liv's foot nudged something. She scooched down to retrieve a framed photo that had fallen from the shelf, and her eyebrows lifted when she saw the picture behind the glass. Three young women mugged for the camera on what looked like a stage.

The girls posed in slinky, tight dresses and mile-high platform shoes. Their dark-rimmed eyes seemed heavy with fake lashes, and they all wore beauty-contestant sashes across their bodies. Behind them, Liv could see a familiar-looking triangle symbol embossed in gold on a deep purple stage curtain. A banner across the top of the backdrop read, "First Annual Golden Triangle Miss Venus Pageant."

So, Liv thought. Kayla Goff danced at The Golden Triangle. Not all that surprising. She peered closer. Two of the girls looked familiar from the night she went to the club, one dark-haired and the other bleach blond. The third girl she recognized as Kayla Goff from the pic her mother, Maralynne, had texted. Liv's eyes slid to the lettering on the Kayla's sash.

Written in glittery gold script was a name. *IVY.*

Chapter Thirty-Two

● ● ● ● ● ● ● ● ● ● ● ● ● ●

Facts tumbled into place like numbers in a combination lock. Liv inhaled sharply.

Ivy, Alice's connection at the club, and Kayla Goff, the young woman Alice called from Carry Over the night she died, were the same young woman. And now Kayla appeared to be missing.

Liv pulled out her camera and took a picture of the photo before rising from her crouch. Alice's manuscript described mafia ties and human trafficking. What if she'd based her book on reality? Alice was known to have befriended Kayla, aka Ivy, who worked as a dancer at a strip club. Kayla may have revealed some of the details Alice included in her novel, details Anthony and Leo Zee and whatever organization they were part of didn't want broadcast into the world.

Liv's thoughts raced as she considered what to do next. She didn't care that this wasn't a paying case anymore. Bad things must be going down at The Golden Triangle. Every instinct told her Kayla Goff was in trouble, that Alice had stumbled onto something dangerous, and whatever she'd learned had gotten her killed.

Liv didn't have anything against exotic dancing. As far as she was concerned, adults could do what they liked as long as they weren't hurting anyone or being hurt. She did, however, have a thing against criminal activity and—Liv remembered the seamier stuff going on in Alice's novel—human trafficking. And, of course, murder.

She hadn't been able to save Alice, but if she acted fast, there might be time to rescue Kayla from death—or a fate worse than death.

"Hey, are you 'bout done in there?" Banjo yelled from the hallway.

"Couple more minutes," she called back. She walked quickly to Kayla's bedroom. Discarded clothes covered the floor. The bed was unmade. A few wigs on wig stands sat on top of a dresser. Liv strode to the dresser and pulled open the drawers. No underwear or nightclothes in the top drawer, just a few padded bras in various colors, and one workout bra. In the middle and bottom drawers she found sweatpants, leggings, a few heavy sweaters, and jeans but no tee shirts or shorts.

She crossed the room and opened the closet door. She ran her hand along skirts, blouses, and dresses—both regular and costume-type—but also a lot of empty plastic hangers that clacked together under her fingers. On the left side hung a winter coat, black wool, and an old ski jacket with a faded Sunday River tag attached.

Seeing no suitcase or duffel bag, the empty drawers and bare hangers, Liv felt slightly better. It looked more like Kayla'd gone on vacation than like an abduction. Where would the dancer have gone, though?

A jumble of shoes littered the floor. Liv crouched to inspect the footwear. High-heeled sandals. Platform performance shoes in various glittery and vinyl shades. No sneakers. No flip flops or sandals. She picked up a platform-heeled boot covered in purple glitter. A double triangle charm dangled from the zipper.

She was about to put the boot down and snap a photo of the closet when something tucked inside the boot caught her eye. She reached in and pulled out a business card. Alice's face smiled up at her. The card named the social work agency for which she worked. Liv flipped the card over. Handwritten in pen was a phone number Liv didn't recognize.

Mindful of the apartment manager fuming in the hallway, Liv slipped the card into the pocket of her shorts and made her way through the apartment. "Okay, she's not here," she told Banjo as she brushed past him.

"No duh," he said. "Should I call the police?"

Good question.

Liv thought about the empty underwear drawer, the cool weather clothes left behind, and the bare hangers. "No. I'm pretty sure she's gone to stay with friends. You've been a lifesaver today, Mr. Foster. If you hear from Kayla, tell her to call me." She reached into her bag, the Spade again, and handed him her business card.

"If you ever need anything, you know, like a private investigator, give me a call. I owe you one."

• • • • •

Once she got back to her car, Liv snagged Alice's card from her pocket and dialed the number.

"Hopeful Harbor Women's Center," a woman's clipped voice said.

Liv recognized the organization as a Portland women's shelter. "Uh, yes. Hi. My name is Olivia Lively. I'm a private investigator here in Portland. I'm hoping to speak to a young woman by the name of Kayla Goff. She may be going by the name Ivy. Her mother is very worried about her, and has asked me to find her. Is there anything you can tell me?"

"I'm sorry. I can't share information about who may or may not be staying with us."

"I get it." Liv thought for a moment. "If I give you my contact information and you do happen to see Kayla, would you ask her to call me?" Liv hesitated. "Tell her it's about Alice."

"Alice Ferguson?" The woman sounded alarmed.

"Yes. Did you know her?"

The woman took a second before answering, her voice careful.

"We were so sorry to hear of her passing. She was a friend to the center in many ways." The woman cleared her throat. "What's your phone number?"

· · · · ·

A couple hours later, Marion poked her head into Liv's office. "I'm heading home for the afternoon unless you need anything?"

Liv glanced up from her computer. She felt better now that she knew Kayla was safe at the women's shelter, and the urgency she'd felt regarding The Golden Triangle had eased. She still intended to investigate, but she'd been able to put that case to the side in order to wrap up loose ends on the Raymond Booker worker's comp case. It had been a long day.

She gave Marion a smile as she raised her arms over her head and stretched. "I'm all set. In fact, I just finished up this report on the Raptor thing and was about to hit send." She let her arms fall and tapped her mouse pad. "There."

She leaned back in her chair and studied her assistant. Marion looked like a punk princess in her pink Docs, black leggings, and a Pixies *Here Comes Your Man* tee shirt with the bull terrier image on it. She'd dyed the ends of her hair bright pink and wore a bunch of 1980s thin, black rubber bracelets up one forearm.

"Love your look," Liv said. "What do you have planned for tonight?"

Marion grinned. "Nothing definite yet. I've been working on my romance novel most evenings, but there's a good band playing at the Arrow & Song tonight. I'm thinking about meeting with some members of my old writing cohort. Want to join? They'd love to see you. I even think Cooper might show up."

Liv considered the invite. Cooper Tedeschi, soon-to-be published novelist, had asked Liv to help him that spring in an academic plagiarism scandal. His lawyer, Patrick Ledeau, had told her Cooper'd signed a three-book deal with a large indie press that specialized in sci-fi and fantasy. Liv couldn't be happier for him.

"You know, that sounds like fun." She thought about Kayla/Ivy and The Golden Triangle. "I have to follow up on a lead I got today, but maybe I can give you a call later? Would it be too weird since I'm your boss now?"

Marion rolled her eyes. "You're only my boss for another week."

"Don't remind me."

"We'll find someone to take my place. I'll post the ad soon as you give me the go ahead. Hint. Hint."

Liv pretended to pout. "I'm not ready, but you're right. I shouldn't put it off any longer. It would be better if you train the person before you leave. I just keep hoping you'll change your mind."

"I know." Both women fell silent. Marion perked up. "Did I mention it's a really good band?"

Liv laughed and made a shooing motion with her hand. "Get out of here. Post the job tomorrow. And yes, I'll meet you at the Arrow. Eight sound good?"

"Yay! Perfect. Byeeeee."

Liv laughed again and shook her head. She straightened her desk, turned off her computer, and took a satisfied look around. Lively Investigations was running smoothly thanks to Marion's excellent organizational skills allowing Liv to concentrate on her cases. Money now flowed in at a steady rate. She'd turned in the Raptor report, so the company's defense lawyers would take it from there.

Work-wise things looked bright. Sadly, she couldn't say the same for her personal life. Whenever she thought about Jasper, she felt a pang of loss. Yin and yang, she mused. Maybe her breakup represented some sort of cosmic balance in the universe.

Thinking she might consult Ash on the topic, she reached for her phone, but then she remembered their last conversation and dropped her hand. She'd had a good day. A productive day. Forget girl talk. What she needed was a celebratory five o'clock somewhere martini to celebrate the completion of the Raptor case.

An ice-cold vodka martini with three olives and just a hint of brine.

Lucky for her, she knew just the place to get one.

. . . . .

The beefy guy at the door didn't react when Liv strolled into The Golden Triangle.

She'd changed into a pair of white jeans, a slinky green satin camisole, and green stilettos. She covered her short, dark hair with a red wig cut in a cute bob. Subtle makeup transformed the contours of her face. She chose a nearly-nude lipstick instead of her usual red. Using a brow pencil, she thickened her brows to Cara Delevingne proportions and swept dark eyeshadow over her lids before adding a pair of amber rimless glasses.

At four o'clock on a weekday, business was slow. Liv scanned the room for Anthony Zee, and not seeing him, strolled to the bar. When she caught the bartender's eye, he winked and reached for the Tito's on the top shelf.

Her smile faltered. *Darn,* she thought. *He recognized me. I must be slipping.*

She settled onto one of the low-backed leather stools, crossed her legs, and watched him pour the vodka into a shaker. "How's it going?" she asked.

"Fine and dandy," he said. The shaker rattled in his hand. "One olive or two?"

"Three."

"Three then." He grinned. "I like the red hair. It suits you."

"Just mixing things up."

"Uh-huh." He poured the icy vodka into a martini glass, speared three olives on a pick, and slipped it into the glass. "Or are you trying to avoid Teddy?"

"Teddy?"

"The bouncer, remember? Bald head. Built like The Rock? He

escorted you out last time." He slid the drink toward her. "Nervy, coming back. You must like this place."

She gave him a twenty. "Actually, I'm looking for someone. A dancer by the name of Ivy. She wouldn't happen to be here tonight would she?"

"Nope. Hasn't been around for a while."

"Okay, thanks. And thanks for the olives...?" She waited for his name.

"Dawson."

"Thank you, Dawson."

He winked at her again. "My pleasure."

Liv carried her glass to a table next to a group of fancy-shirt-and-tie types and took a seat. The dancer on stage picked up some dollar bills and tucked them into her garter before prancing off stage. Another girl took her place. The music changed. Liv sipped her martini and, using her teeth, pulled one of the olives into her mouth. Yum.

"Hey, how's your day been, sweetie?" The dancer who'd left the stage smiled down at her.

"Not bad." Liv reached into her cross-body bag and held out a five. "Nice moves up there."

The young woman smiled. She put her foot on the chair next to Liv, flashing her thigh at eye level. She wore a pretty red garter with white lace to match her lingerie look. "Thank you, sweetie. Don't be shy. Tuck 'er in there."

Liv placed the bill on the table. "What's your name?"

The dancer grabbed the five, fleeting annoyance crossing her pretty features before the mask fell back into place. "Amie. What's yours?"

"I'm Olivia. Can I ask you a question, Amie?"

The dancer put the tip of her tongue between her teeth. "Sure you can, sweetie."

"I'm curious about your dancing. Did you have to take lessons to learn how?"

"Oh!" Amie looked surprised. "I did take a few lessons on the pole. It's not as easy as it looks. As for the other stuff, I took dance as a kid. Ballet. Tap. Hip-hop. So I had a base, and now I practice and watch videos, you know, to get new ideas. And I watch the other dancers. We teach each other sometimes. Would you like me to show you some moves right now?" She ran a fingertip up Liv's bare arm.

Liv put another five on the table. "I'd rather keep talking. Can you sit down for a minute? Is that allowed?"

"Sure. For a minute." Amie sat, tucked the bill away, and crossed her legs, swinging one satin, sky-high heel.

"So," Liv smiled widely, attempting to look friendly, "I've heard a lot about places like this. Not always great stuff. Let's say I'm interested in trying it myself. Do you feel safe working here?"

Amie shrugged. "Sure. I mean we dance, we talk to people—guys mostly—and they're pretty respectful, most of the time. Some get grabby, and that gets old, but if it's bad, the bouncers have a word with them. You just have to get used to people looking at you a certain way, you know?"

"Like how?"

"Oh, I don't know. Like you're nothing but a pretty piece of meat, not a person." Amie giggled. "Or maybe more like a piece of cake. Fluffy and sweet, a little sticky. Something they'd like to run their tongues over."

Liv smiled. "You're clever."

"I'm getting my master's in communication. I'm going to graduate debt-free thanks to this job. It's better than working retail or waiting tables, believe me. I've tried both. This keeps me in shape, pays great, and I like the uniform." Amber winked.

"Ha! Well, good for you." Liv sipped her drink. "What about the VIP room? Are you okay with that, too?"

Amie's smile faded. "No one's doing anything they don't want to do."

"You sure about that?"

The dancer pasted a fake pout onto her face and batted her false eyelashes. "You're so sweet to care. Enough about me. What do you do for work?"

Liv pulled out a twenty and a pen. "I find people, among other things. Right now I'm looking for Ivy. You know who she is?"

Amie nodded. "Sure."

Liv wrote her phone number on the back of the bill. "If you see her, tell her I've been in touch with her mother and she's worried about her. If Ivy calls me and tells me you're the one who gave her the number, I'll be back with a couple more of these, okay?"

Amie took the twenty and stood. "Sure. I'll do that, sweetie." She blew Liv a kiss and strolled away to solicit the bros at the next table.

Liv scanned the room one last time for a glimpse of either Ivy or the management. She briefly considered checking the restrooms, but decided not to press her luck.

Figuring she'd accomplished all she could that night, Liv downed her drink, stood, and wove through the tables to the door. She waved at Dawson who nodded at her while mixing drinks for a couple of older dudes standing at the bar.

Feeling satisfied with her work, she emerged into the cool evening air. The breeze smelled of fried food from a nearby fast-food chicken place, coffee from the Dunkin' next door, and the faint funk of the Raptor mill a few miles away.

As she walked toward her car, a tall woman approached, headed toward the club. A *familiar* tall woman with platinum-blonde hair plaited into a long braid down her back and dark, Jackie O glasses concealing her eyes.

Liv put her head down and continued toward the Corolla. She got into the car and stared out the window as Emsley Ballard-Monihan, Alby Ferguson's ex-wife, disappeared inside the club.

Chapter Thirty-Three

• • • • • • • • • • • • •

Suddenly, fall was in the air.

It happened at the end of every August. The heat evaporated in the evenings creating a delicious briskness. Sunsets grew more colorful, striking sherbet bands of orange and rose. The first maple leaves turned red. Dusk settled earlier over the Portland skyline, and in the mornings, mist rose off the Atlantic in the cooler air.

On Sunday, Liv dressed for brunch with her parents. Once a month they convened for brunch at the Portland Regency Hotel, attendance mandatory barring a deathly illness or a European vacation. Lucky for her, she loved the lobster eggs benedict and the scones if not the parental grilling about her life. She expected today's questioning to be brutal considering her breakup.

She chose to go casual in her white jeans, pairing them this time with a navy and white striped boatneck top, a navy blazer, and her navy pumps. She'd just added gold hoops to her ears when her phone buzzed.

Glancing at the screen and not recognizing the number, she frowned. "Olivia Lively," she said as she held the phone in one hand and squirted some Chanel No. 5 onto her neck with the other.

The caller sniffled but remained silent.

"Hello. This is Liv," she said again. "Can I help you?"

"H-hi. Yeah, this is, um, Kayla. Kayla Goff." She sniffled again. "Can you tell me what happened to Alice?"

• • • • •

The young woman sat at the corner table at Buoy Bagels. Nervous fingers twisted the coffee cup back and forth. Her shoulder length brown hair, streaked with blonde highlights, looked dirty and shapeless. She wore a pair of gray-lensed aviator sunglasses and a yellow Longfellow College sweatshirt over black workout pants and a pair of cheap flip flops.

"Hi, Kayla?" Liv said as she walked toward the table. "I'm Olivia."

The girl nodded and pushed strands of lank hair over her ears.

Still full from eggs benedict, Liv took the seat across from her, and placed her red leather bag on an empty chair. "Do you want something to eat? My treat?"

At 1:00 p.m., the bagel shop bustled with customers, but it was nowhere as busy as it would have been earlier in the day. Freshmen had arrived on the Longfellow campus for orientation weekend. Clumps of jittery eighteen-year-olds crowded around most of the small tables. They talked too loud and laughed too long, trying to hide their insecurities. Behind the counter, Ruth offered them motherly smiles along with her comforting sandwiches and coffee drinks.

Kayla shook her head. "No, thank you."

Polite, Liv thought. Spooked but polite. "Okay."

Liv caught Ruth's eye behind the counter and made a tipping motion with her hand. Ruth nodded. She knew Liv's coffee preference, and Liv knew Ruth wouldn't mind bringing it to the table. She searched Kayla's face. "So, are you okay? Safe, I mean?"

Kayla twisted the cup again. "Sort of. For now. I'm scared though. After what they did to Alice."

As gently as she could, Liv asked, "Who, Kayla?"

"Tony and Leo."

"Anthony and Leo Zee?"

Kayla nodded. She looked back down at the cup, her shoulders hunched as if she wanted to hide.

Ruth approached the table with Liv's coffee. "Heah ya go, hun," she said. Kayla's shoulders hitched. Ruth caught Liv's eye with a questioning look on her face.

Liv gave a slight shake of her head. Ruth nodded and bustled away.

Liv removed the lid from her coffee to allow the steam to escape. "Why do you think the Zee brothers had something to do with Alice's death?"

Kayla sipped her coffee, her shoulders still hunched. "Their real name is Zhebrovsky. They're cousins, not brothers. Anyway, they freaked out about her talking to me. I told them it was for a book, that she wasn't a cop or anything, but that made things worse, I guess? I mean, she's dead. It had to be them trying to cover stuff up."

"Stuff. Like what's going on at the club?"

"I don't want to talk about that."

"That's fine." Liv waited a beat. "How did you and Alice meet?"

Kayla scratched the back of her hand, drawing blood. She winced and pulled her fingers away. Liv handed her a napkin and Kayla pressed it to the scratch as she talked. "She came into the club a couple of times, and we started talking. She told me she needed to make some extra money and wanted to publish some books. She had this idea for a story about a dancer but didn't know anything about it and would I be willing to sit for some interviews for background or whatever. She got a VIP membership, for research she said. She also told me she had an investor backing her book project. So we met up a few times outside the club, and I told her about the job and my life and how I got into stripping and everything. She was really nice about it."

"Did you consider her a friend?"

"I mean, sort of, I guess? It was more like she could tell there was a lot going on in my life, some things not so great, and she got me to open up to her. She tried to give me advice and encouraged me to quit the club and go back to college."

"Go back? Did you drop out?"

Kayla's mouth trembled. "Last year. I couldn't tell my mom. That's why I haven't been home. She'll be able to tell right away. She's always been able to do that, and she'd be so disappointed. She's so proud of me, always telling her friends about how I'm going to be a teacher. If she knew I was stripping, it would kill her."

"So you left college. That's why you moved into the apartment."

"Yeah. I told her it was cheaper than the dorm and that I had roommates so she couldn't visit." Kayla sipped her coffee again and slumped in her chair. "I feel awful lying to her. I've totally screwed up my life. I just wish I could go back and make a different decision, you know? It was stupid to work at the Triangle, but at the time it seemed like a good idea."

Liv nodded slowly. "Believe me, I know all about how bad good ideas can be. What's it like working for the Zhebrovskys?"

Kayla picked at the sleeve of her sweatshirt. "At first I thought they were okay, but they aren't nice guys. That's why Alice worried about me. She gave me the number of the shelter and told me the women there would help me get away from the club and start over. I was scared, though. I'm still scared. Anthony and Leo, they'll mess me up if they find me."

"Why would they hurt you?"

"I owe them…" Kayla realized she'd said too much and clammed up. She looked ready to bolt.

As gently as possible, Liv said, "Why do you owe them, Kayla?"

Kayla sighed. "Okay. I guess I'll tell you because you're a detective, right? You can help me?"

"I'll certainly do my best."

The girl nodded, looking younger than her twenty years. Gradually, as Liv asked questions, she got the whole story. Kayla told her about going to a college party one night and meeting a girl who seemed to have it all: great clothes, perfect body and hair, an apartment off campus. When Kayla told her she'd been a dancer and cheerleader in high school, the girl told her she could make a ton of money dancing and introduced her to the Zees.

At first, Kayla planned on saving the money for tuition, but by the end of the spring semester, she'd missed too many classes and her grades fell. She lost her financial aid, and she hadn't saved as much as she'd planned.

The other dancers told her if she got breast enhancement surgery, she could make a lot more money, so she borrowed money from the Zees for a boob job, took on more hours at the club, and moved into the apartment. The plan was to re-enroll at Longfellow as soon as she paid the Zees back and saved enough for tuition.

Listening to her story, Liv suspected Kayla owed the Zees not only for her surgery, but also for drugs. When Liv asked whether or not Anthony and Leo were involved in criminal activities, Kayla confirmed that, yes, the Zees trafficked drugs and girls.

"How's the business run?"

Kayla explained that the dancers "rented" the stage from the club, paying ten percent of their earnings. Because these earnings were considerably higher in the VIP room, the Zees pushed the dancers to focus on upselling VIP memberships and offering high-priced services. Kayla confirmed that customers paid for sex of all kinds, and that the women were forced to perform lewd acts on stage as "advertisement" for these services.

"What if a dancer refuses to go along with it? Are they fired?" Liv asked.

"That's not how it works," Kayla said. Her mouth hardened. "They get dancers hooked on drugs. Oxy. Meth. Coke. Anthony won't sell them any more if they don't go along with the sex stuff. Sometimes they get physical with us, too."

"Like physical and sexual assault?"

She nodded. "Yes. Sometimes."

"And you told Alice all of this?"

Kayla nodded again.

Shocked by what she'd heard, Liv wondered why the authorities hadn't shut the place down. It was obvious to her that The Golden Triangle operated as a criminal organization. She thought about the way Karina Briggs brushed off her information and suspicions. Were the police being paid off? Seemed like a stretch. Something that only happened in thrillers and police procedural television shows.

"Have you ever seen anyone at the club or with Anthony or Leo that looked like some sort of organized crime?"

Kayla's eyes went wide. "I don't think so. I mean there are some guys that come up from Boston with the drugs. Or maybe down from Canada. I'm not really sure."

"Have you interacted with any of them? Zhebrovsky sounds Russian or Eastern European. What about these outside guys? Same?"

"I've, uh, performed for some of them, but I can't say they seem like Russians or anything." She started twisting her cold cup of coffee.

"But you think the cousins might have killed Alice?"

"The last time I talked to Alice, she called me on my old phone. I got rid of it after I heard she was killed and picked up a burner at Walmart. Anyway, she didn't sound scared or anything, just asked me if I'd contacted the shelter and told me to let her know if and when I decided to make a change. Then I heard on the news she'd been killed."

"That must have scared you."

"Yeah. Tony and Leo started giving me a really rough time, telling me I better keep my mouth shut about Alice and me being friends and her being a member of the club. They told me if I talked to anyone, they'd hurt me so bad I'd never be able to dance—or maybe even walk—again."

"So you went to the shelter?"

"Yes. I was afraid if they'd killed her, I'd be next. They didn't want her to blab to the police, and now I'm sure they're looking for me. If they find me—if they find out I've been talking to you—that'll be real bad. I can't go to the police. I can't go to my apartment. I'm terrified. I just want all this to go away."

Kayla started to cry. Tears leaked out from behind the shades. She wiped them with the sleeve of her Longfellow College sweatshirt. She sounded more like a kid homesick at summer camp than a hardened stripper when she looked up at Liv and pleaded, "I just really, really want to go home."

Chapter Thirty-Four

• • • • • • • • • • • • • •

"Has Kayla called yet?" Liv had her phone on speaker while she painted her toenails a classic, shiny red. Monday morning's rays fell through the sunroom windows, highlighting the dancing motes of dust particles in the air and reminding her that an ounce of furniture spray was worth a pound of Tiffany disapproval. "She promised me she'd call you as soon as she got back to the shelter."

On the other end of the call, Maralynne Goff's voice vibrated with tension. "No. She hasn't contacted me. Are you sure she was all right when you saw her?"

Liv let her left foot drop to the floor and put her right on the coffee table. "She looked tired and stressed, maybe a little thin." *Or strung out,* Liv thought, but no need to go there with the girl's mom. "But otherwise, safe and sound. Darn. I was sure she'd get in touch with you."

"Should I worry?"

"Try not to. I'll clear my schedule today and track her down."

After she ended the call, Liv screwed the cap on her polish and sat back in her chair, brooding as she gazed over the city. She considered her options. First, call the shelter. Second, check Kayla's apartment in case she'd decided, against all reason, to go back there. If that didn't pan out, she'd hit the Triangle when it opened its doors at eleven. Maybe one of the dancers or bartenders knew of a friend Kayla/Ivy might go to for help.

Liv reviewed the events of the past few days. She was forgetting something. Something about the strip club…

"Emsley!" Liv bolted out of her chair. How could she have let Alby Ferguson's widow slip from her mind? She'd look for Kayla— Liv felt a spurt of irritation that the girl hadn't cared enough about her mother to make a quick phone call—but first she needed to find out why Emsley had been at The Golden Triangle.

She grabbed the polish, walked down the hall with her toes in the air so as not to smudge, and slid her feet into a pair of cherry-colored TKEES flip-flops. She pulled a navy tee-shirt dress over her head, smoothed it to her knees, grabbed her keys and red tote, and zipped down the hill to Coffee by Design for her morning caffeine fix.

While waiting for her order, she called Marion to say she'd be in a bit later than expected. It was Marion's last week. Liv had enjoyed meeting up with the Longfellow MFA gang at the Arrow & Song. Cooper hadn't showed, though. He called Marion to say he was behind on his edits.

Still sporting a little goatee and a big attitude, Ethan scoffed. "Once a douche, always a douche."

Marion countered. "At least he has a publishing contract, which is more than the rest of us can say."

Ethan flushed. "Whatever." He drank Gneiss Rocktoberfest lager throughout the evening and then teased Marion about her pink hair. He shut up about *that* when the band's drummer strolled over on break and asked Marion for her number.

Served him right, Liv thought. Boy needed to grow up and take Marion, who he obviously liked, out to dinner and a movie.

Now, still waiting for her coffee, she instructed Marion, "If Kayla Goff calls, find out where she is. And tell her to phone her mother."

"Will do. Do you want me to call the employment agency today about my replacement?"

"I guess you should," Liv said. "Any calls come in?"

Marion ran through a short list of phone messages left on the answering machine overnight. None seemed urgent. Liv told her to get more info on two and said she'd handle the rest herself later.

Liv disconnected the call and frowned. She hated to see Marion go. She'd make an excellent apprentice investigator if only Liv could lure her away from law school...

But no. She couldn't—wouldn't—do anything to squelch Marion's or any other woman's dreams. *We need to stick by each other*, she thought, remembering her mother's recriminations at brunch. *Too bad Tiffany never got the memo.*

"Cafe mocha to go." The barista set the paper cup on the counter. "Have a good one, Liv."

"You, too. Thanks." She carried the coffee to her car and, shoving thoughts of Marion's departure from her mind, sped off to find Emsley's Pine Point studio and hopefully get some answers about what she'd been doing at the Triangle.

· · · · ·

Liv parked the Corolla along the small cross street a block from the ocean and raised binoculars to her eyes. Across the road, a sign reading "Emsley Ballard-Monihan Designs" swung from a tapered, pink granite post topped by a weathered brass bell that gave the entire piece a vaguely-phallic vibe. Two round, bushy shrubs at the base didn't help.

She shoved the binoculars into her bag and approached the property. Overgrown beach roses fronted the sidewalk, and tall maples cast the lawn and cottage in gloom.

A narrow cobblestone driveway led from the sign to a one-story outbuilding whose old, mossy shingles peeled up at the corners. A three-story cottage, covered in weathered-gray cedar shakes, faded into the shadows except for the window casings and front door. These had been painted a bright, surprising green. A vintage

Triumph roadster, faded blue, sat on a gravel area in front of the house.

Liv tapped on the front door and waited. Nothing. She knocked louder. Still no answer. A slow tapping noise broke the stillness, a steady *tink, tink, tink* from the outbuilding.

She crossed the drive. A stone hand, giant-sized, topped an iron post. The index finger pointed to the side of the outbuilding facing the house. She navigated the uneven cobblestones to a door. When she knocked, a female voice yelled, "Come in!"

Liv twisted the door knob and entered. The smell of dust and marijuana hung in the air. Stone sculptures, pieces of metal, and handmade tool benches cluttered the space. In the center of the room stood Emsley, tall and gangly in a pair of baggy overalls, a sleeveless ribbed tee, and yellow steel-toed work boots. She wore clear safety goggles over her eyes, and her long, pale hair fell in two braids over each shoulder.

She held a chisel in one hand and a hammer in the other. Beside her, a piece of flecked granite six feet tall and three feet wide loomed.

Liv stepped forward. "Hi, Emsley. I don't know if you remember me. I'm Olivia Lively, a friend of Van's. We talked at Alice's funeral reception."

Emsley transferred the chisel to the hand with the hammer, managing both easily in her large, strong hand. She removed her goggles and gave Liv a pale, narrow-eyed stare. "I remember. Can I help you with something?"

"I hope so." Liv fixed her eyes on Emsley's face. "What can you tell me about The Golden Triangle?"

The artist looked alarmed. Then embarrassed. Then resigned.

She turned her back to set the tools on a bench, and stood motionless for several seconds. When she whirled to face Liv, two bright spots flamed on her otherwise pale cheeks. She clenched her fists and yelled, "Stupid idiot!"

Startled, Liv blurted, "Who?"

"My ex-husband, of course." Emsley looked up at the ceiling. She took a couple of deep breaths. Her chest heaved. "I'd kill him if he weren't already dead." Seconds ticked by. Finally, Emsley's fists unclenched and her shoulders dropped. She turned her pale eyes to Liv's. "Do you want some tea? I need some tea. Come on."

Emsley took off out of the studio in long strides. Liv followed her across the cobblestones to the house. The door led into an old-fashioned kitchen that looked as if it hadn't been updated since 1956. An electric teakettle sat on the old, yellow Formica counter. "Water's already hot." Emsley opened a tin canister painted with cabbage roses and plopped two bags of tea into a pair of pottery mugs and brought them to a yellow-painted table in the corner. "Have a seat."

The smell of bergamot rose on the steam from the mugs. Outside, a cardinal called, a flash of red at a bird feeder in front of the window.

"This was my family's summer place," Emsley said, perching on one of the antique farmhouse chairs. "My great-grandparents built it back in the 1920s, and for decades all the aunts and uncles and cousins shared it. We had Fourth of July celebrations here and family reunions. Birthdays. When Alby and I got married, he bought out my mother and my uncle so I could make it my studio."

"That's nice."

Emsley snorted. "Not so much for my cousins. They still haven't forgiven me. The place was falling apart, though. No one else wanted to take on the repairs, so whatever."

She shrugged. "If we hadn't done something the town would have condemned it sooner rather than later. You wouldn't know it from looking, but we already made a lot of big, unsexy improvements. Jacked the house off the old dirt cellar. Poured a new cement foundation. Installed new wiring. Insulated for winter temps. Replaced the furnace. The roof was going to be next. We've got squirrels in the attic. Some water damage."

"Mmm," Liv said. The place did give off a whiff of Gray Gardens.

"So what about the strip club?"

Emsley looked into her mug and let out a deep sigh. "I don't know how you found out about it, but okay. Here's the thing. Alby fancied himself a savvy investor. An 'angel investor' he liked to call himself when he was showing off. Certain snotty, arty types ate it up. They sucked up to him because he'd lived in New York and was supposedly 'somebody.'"

"Somebody?"

"You know what I mean. When someone moves here from New York or L.A., everyone fawns all over them, like their big-city gloss is gonna rub off or something. Like they're more important and impressive than regular Maine people."

Liv thought Emsley sounded bitter. "But Alby's from Maine."

"Yeah, but he left after high school. He lived that big Manhattan life for a while and cashed in before moving home. Once back, he got involved in the art and culture scene. Donated to the symphony, the theater, the opera, and the museums. He opened the gallery in order to promote artists he liked. Didn't hurt that he looked like a movie star and could charm the spots off of a leopard. They lapped him up like cream."

"Is that how you met? The gallery?"

Emsley twitched a shoulder. "He saw one of the pieces I'd entered in a competition, and he gave me a show. We dated for a few months—whirlwind romance, artist and gallery owner, a lot of social buzz—and he pulled me into that clique. At first I loved it. Later, not so much. It made me claustrophobic."

Liv nodded. "I get it."

"After we married, I found out Alby was investing in all kinds of small businesses. Some he talked about. Others no. He fancied himself some kind of financial genius, but really he was losing money." Emsley twisted the mug in her long fingers. "He kept investing even though he really couldn't afford to. People would come to him with these offers, and it made him feel important. It was like an addiction, I guess."

"Did you ask him to stop?"

Emsley nodded. "We fought about it. A lot. It got nasty, and then I guess he fell in love with Alice. Next thing I know, we're divorced and I'm a social pariah. Nobody wanted anything to do with me after we separated. I couldn't get anyone to show my work. Basically, I was blackballed."

"Sounds rough. And unfair." Liv sipped her tea and brought the conversation back around to the money. "So, Alby invested in The Golden Triangle?"

Emsley nodded. "I found out after he died. Turns out he never got around to changing his will after the divorce. I inherited everything. Believe me, I was as shocked as everybody. Van and my in-laws, well, I think they expected to get something. I'll let them take Alby's personal things, of course. Some of the art. They can pick what they want, but I'm keeping the cash and stocks. I figure I earned it, dealing with his infidelity and the divorce and all."

She jutted her chin and Liv nodded. "Go on."

"Okay, anyway, I was going through paperwork last week when I discovered Alby had invested a hundred-thousand for a percentage of The Golden Triangle. I don't want *anything* to do with that place, so…" Emsley's voice trailed off.

"So, you went to the club to talk to them about divesting."

Emsley looked startled. "Yes. How did you know?"

"Doesn't matter. How did it go?"

"I met with the owners, Anthony and Leo. I offered them the chance to buy me out for half of the original investment. It's a great deal for them, so of course they agreed. My lawyer drew up the paperwork. We signed and they wrote me a check yesterday. I'm out."

"Do you know if Alby ever went to the club? With Alice or without her?"

Emsley shrugged. "No idea."

"How did you find out they were having an affair?"

"Van told me."

"When?"

"After Alice." A shadow passed over Emsley's features. "The police questioned me about Alby, and later that day I drove over to see Van, and he told me about the affair."

"Do you believe Alby was capable of killing Alice?"

"If he did, he wouldn't have wanted to face the consequences. That's why he drove down that ravine."

Liv raised her eyebrows. "You think Alby killed himself? The police called it an accident."

"Oh, please." Emsley twisted the cup again. "My husband knew all those old tote roads. He learned to drive on them when he was twelve or thirteen years old. Van, too. Gavin taught them in an old Jeep he kept up there."

She let out a sad laugh. "Once a bear got into it when the boys forgot a couple peanut butter and jelly sandwiches in a lunch bag overnight. That's one of the stories Alby liked to tell. Anyway, my lawyer told me the coroner's report said he'd been drinking that night, but I know Alby. He never passes out. Not like that. He's never been a black-out drunk, either."

Emsley slumped in her chair, and her voice wavered as she blinked back tears. "He must have killed Alice and then drove into that ravine on purpose out of guilt. Stupid, stupid, *stupid* man."

Tragedy and loss clung like humidity in the confines of the old-fashioned kitchen. "I'm sorry for your loss, Emsley," Liv murmured. "I can see you loved him despite everything. And I'm sorry for interrupting your work. I appreciate your being willing to talk to me about these very painful topics. I'll see myself out."

Emsley nodded.

When Liv returned to her car, she listened to a frantic phone message from Ashleigh. "Liv, I need you. It's all a mess. Zoo animals? What was I thinking? It's all wrong. Or maybe not! I don't know. You have to come over and talk me off this ledge." Ashleigh paused. "And bring Cheetos."

Chapter Thirty-Five

• • • • • • • • • • • • • •

"Helloooo. I come bearing gifts!" Trudging up the center staircase in Ashleigh and Trevor's early 1800s Pellham home, Liv carried a pineapple and strawberry smoothie in one hand and a bag of Cheetos in the other.

"I'm in here," Ashleigh called from a room down the hall.

Liv noted the beautiful new carpet runner on the stairs and the fresh, peach-colored paint on the hallway walls. Ashleigh, who in college always finished papers two weeks early instead of waiting to pull an all-nighter like Liv, was predictably in her nesting phase several months in advance.

Liv, following the smell of paint and turpentine, entered the last room at the end of the hall, and her mouth fell open.

A large rug in soft greens and creams lay on top of the old, pumpkin pine floor. Two cribs dressed in the green bedding Liv remembered from Poppie & Porpoise hugged one wall. Painted on the other wall, a pastiche of gender-neutral zoo animals wearing sunglasses and goggles and jewel-toned top-hats cavorted amongst bizarre, spotted flowers, twisted trees, and lollipops in a mural that could best be described as Willy Wonkaesque.

"Ashleigh!" Liv gasped. "What have you done?"

Her friend, blonde hair in a ponytail, paintbrush in hand and splotches of vermilion and chartreuse on her face, was sitting on the floor staring at the mural. She looked up at Liv with wide blue eyes. "Is it horrible? It's horrible, isn't it?" She looked at the wall again.

"What was I thinking?"

Liv approached Ashleigh the way she'd approach a nervous animal. Softly and deliberately. No swift moves.

When she was close enough, she took the brush from her friend's hand and gave her the smoothie in its place. "Here. I picked this up at that new shop we saw the other day." She sat beside Ashleigh and tossed the bag of cheesy twists into her friend's lap. "And here are the Cheetos you requested." She gazed at the wall along with her friend. "So. Tell me what inspired this, this… I don't even know what to call it."

"I was bored!"

"Has Trevor seen it?"

"Nooooo." Ashleigh sipped her drink. "Mmm, this is good. Mango?"

"Strawberry."

"Oh, right." She held up the clear plastic cup. "Pink. My taste buds are all screwed up from the pregnancy hormones." She sipped again. "Mmmm, Trevor's been away for a couple of weeks on some big project down in New Jersey or Maryland or West Virginia or wherever, and I kept looking at this big blank wall and thinking babies needed stimulation, so I got out my sketch book…" She looked sideways at Liv. "Remember how I used to talk about illustrating children's books?"

Liv nodded.

"Well, I started drawing, and these funny, weird characters kind of showed up, so I thought, why not make a mural? I ordered some paint and brushes and… *voila!*"

"But how did you know how to make a mural?"

"YouTube."

"Ah."

Ashleigh sipped again and tilted her head at the wall. "Is it really bad? Am I going to mess my babies up for life?"

Liv put a hand to her chin and gave an exaggerated nod. "Yes. Definite psycho killer training material here." She glanced at

Ashleigh's horrified face and laughed. "I'm kidding! It's actually kind of cool, plus I hate you because do you have to be so perfect at every single thing?"

"You really think it's good? I've lost all perspective."

"I love it. The babies will love it. I don't know about Trevor, though. He's always been a bit on the bland side," Liv teased.

Ash snorted. "Only compared to the losers you like to date."

Ouch. Liv closed her eyes. *Really* ouch.

Ashleigh put a hand on Liv's arm. "OMG, Liv. I'm sorry. That was horrible. I meant it to be funny, but it wasn't. I'm so, so sorry."

Liv ignored the sting in her heart. It was one thing to think these things herself. It was another to know that her best friend thought them, too. She hid her pain behind a small smile. "That's okay. It's probably just the fumes getting to you."

Ashleigh shifted around to face Liv and crossed her legs. "No, it's not okay. I've been a total B lately. It's the hormones or something. I've been all wrapped up in this pregnancy and not thinking about how it's affecting our friendship. You mean the world to me. You know that, right?"

"I guess."

"No guess. You have to know I want you to be part of my life and the babies' lives. Dill and Scout will need their Auntie Liv to give them books I think are too old for them, tell them gross-out jokes because I just don't find them funny, teach them how to make water balloons, and buy them junk food on the sly because you *know* I'm going to be obsessed with making homemade, whole foods, highly-nutritious meals."

Ashleigh ripped into the bag of Cheetos and popped three in her mouth. "See? They already crave this stuff. I made boxed mac and cheese last night and ate the entire thing out of the saucepan while watching reruns of *Gilmore Girls.*"

"Dill and Scout?"

"Placeholders."

"Ah." Liv reached into the bag and took a handful. She lifted one toward Ash. "Well, here's to babies who like junk food."

Ashleigh picked out another one and tapped it against Liv's. "And to being friends forever." She chomped the Cheeto and raised her hand. "Now help me up, please. I have to pee."

· · · · ·

Because she was in Pellham already, Liv considered stopping in to see Van on her way back to the office but decided against it. She'd already spent the morning talking to Emsley and now the better part of the afternoon with Ashleigh. She'd told Marion she'd be back in time to go over the job listing for the online employment site, so she headed back down I-295 to Lively Investigations.

The rest of the afternoon and evening passed uneventfully. After her meeting with Marion, she finished some paperwork and went for a long, sweaty 10K run before ordering a pepperoni pizza, watching a couple *Alias* episodes, and going to bed early with the novel Ashleigh had pushed into her hands at the door, gushing, "It's *so* good. You *have* to read it. And then maybe you'll come to book club with—"

"No. I will not be joining your bougie book club. I will, however, take the book." Liv tapped the cover where a well-muscled man wearing not much more than a kilt, and a beautiful woman who looked like English aristocracy clung to each other in a passionate clinch. "I need something to take my mind off Dr. Hottie, and this might do the trick."

"I'm really sorry things didn't work out with Jasper. I can't believe that Wren Osborne!"

"I appreciate your loyalty, but it's not Wren's fault." To Liv's surprise, she realized she meant it. "Jasper and I didn't have the right stuff for a long-term future, that's all. We're looking for different things in a romantic relationship. I miss him, but not enough, if that makes sense."

"I guess it's better to find out now rather than later."

"I think I tried him on for size the way you'd try on a designer dress. You know it's not quite your style, but part of you wishes you were the kind of woman who could pull it off, so you wrestle yourself into it in the changing room. You look at yourself in the mirror and know you'll never be able to rock a Stella McCartney or a Gucci even though you'd love to and you know lots of women who look stunning in their designs."

Ashleigh sighed. "I love Gucci."

Liv had smiled at her friend. "I know you do, sweetie. I'll call you next week, if not sooner. Thanks for letting me borrow the book. I'll give it a try."

By eleven p.m. that night, she was on page 125 and totally hooked.

She growled with annoyance when her phone buzzed, interrupting a very steamy scene taking place beside an icy Highland loch.

"Please come get me!" The young woman's whisper was tight with urgency.

"Kayla?" Liv sat up in bed. The book slid to the floor. "Where are you?"

The call ended.

Liv dialed back. "Pick up, pick up," she whispered. The ringing stopped as the call connected. Her shoulders relaxed. "Thank goodness! Are you okay?"

"Stay out of it," a man said. In the background Liv heard the pumping beats of a popular R & B song. Once again, the call went dead.

She stared at the phone in her hand. Why was Kayla at The Golden Triangle?

She considered calling 911 but hesitated. What was she going to say? That a stripper who worked at The Golden Triangle had called Liv for a ride? That the guys who ran the place didn't seem very nice and—shocker—one of the dancers had told her she'd engaged in some illegal sexual activities on the premises?

She had to do something, though. Liv pictured Alice Ferguson's wide-open eyes, her fingers reaching for the knife in her chest, the gold charm dangling at her throat.

Liv shuddered. She should have gone over to check on Alice that night, but she hadn't. She'd have to live with that bad decision the rest of her life. Now another woman was in trouble—a young woman Alice had been trying to help.

Liv thought of Kayla, hunched over her coffee. Fearful. She thought of Maralynne Goff waiting for a call that never came, listening for a voice she'd never hear again.

Liv might not be a mother, didn't want to be a mother, but still she could imagine the unspeakable pain of that loss.

Her jaw tightened. She'd stood by once, and the unspeakable happened. She wouldn't make the same mistake twice.

Scrolling through her contacts, she found Karina Briggs's number. The detective's voicemail picked up. Liv left a message and hoped the detective got it in time. "This is Olivia Lively. Someone connected to Alice Ferguson's case just contacted me. A young woman named Kayla Goff. She goes by the name Ivy sometimes. She's in trouble. I'm heading to The Golden Triangle in Fallbrook to find her. I might need your help. Please call me as soon as you can."

She ran to her closet and shimmied out of her silk PJs. She dug through her drawers looking for simple, dark clothing—the kind she wore for night-time surveillance. There'd be no fancy disguises tonight. This was a rescue mission, pure and simple. She needed comfort, ease of motion, and low visibility, not short skirts, low-cut blouses, and high heels.

She pulled on a pair of snug black jeans, a long-sleeved black tee, and sturdy combat boots, also black. She strapped on her belt holster, checked to make sure her Sig P365 handgun was loaded, and slipped the gun into place.

She grabbed the necessities and shoved them into her pockets. Phone. Keys. Chanel *Rouge Coco* lipstick. She retied the special paracord laces on her boots. Finally, she took a quick look in the mirror and touched a pinky to the dip in her upper lip where the deep red shade had smudged just a tad.

Checking the safety on her Sig one last time, she headed out the door.

•   •   •   •   •

The Triangle was hopping. Cars, trucks, and even a few minivans filled the parking lot.

Raptor Paper's three-to-eleven shift had just ended, she realized, and for guys on swing schedules, midnight might as well be five o'clock.

Liv pulled the Corolla into the lot. She parked as close as she could to the side front of the lot. Beside her, a meaty-looking F-350 provided a bit of cover. The heavy bass of R & B vibrated the seat beneath her every time someone opened the door to the club. She grabbed a small pair of binoculars from the go-bag she kept in the passenger seat footwell and focused on the entrance.

She didn't recognize the bouncer, but he looked like a former NFL player who'd taken one too many knocks to the noggin. Big, but cross-eyed.

She trained the binocs on the side of the building. A line of scraggly oaks and maples separated the property from the Dunkin' Donuts drive-thru lot next door and cast shadows on the driveway that led to the back service area of the club. A small, dented sign attached to a perforated metal post read "LOADING DOCK" with an arrow pointing behind the building.

The corners of Liv's mouth turned up. Where there was a loading dock, there was a way in.

Chapter Thirty-Six

• • • • • • • • • • • • • •

Liv waited until a group of men distracted the bouncer, and like a cat-burglar, she exited the car and crouch-walked into the shadows of the scraggly trees. Once past the corner of the building, she crossed the driveway and hugged the cheap vinyl siding of the club. It stretched, windowless, long, and low to the back service area.

Behind the building she found a small, paved parking area, two dumpsters, and a pile of broken pieces of furniture most likely destined for a landfill. A sagging chain link fence separated the lot from the adjacent property. Several sulfur-yellow lights illuminated the area, creating weird shadows.

She assessed the club's back entrance. Attached to the building, a two-foot high concrete slab acted as a loading dock. On the left side of the slab, a concrete ramp with a blue iron railing fronted a flaking, blue-painted steel door. Somebody had stacked wooden pallets on the slab next to a closed, garage-style bay door.

Liv crossed in front of the dumpsters and jogged up the ramp to the door. Hoping for a lucky break, she tugged on the handle.

Finding it locked, she hissed in frustration and grabbed the metal handle on the garage door. If she could raise it a couple of feet, she could slide beneath it into the building, hopefully unnoticed. She yanked. It, too, refused to budge.

A quick jog to the other side of the building revealed another blank expanse of siding. No doors or convenient windows to jimmy open. Hidden for the moment in shadow, she contemplated the logistics of simply strolling through the front entrance. Her sexy black jeans and good lipstick could work if she worked it. Once in, though, she'd have to find a way to the back because she had a feeling Kayla wouldn't be working the front room tonight.

She ran through her options. She could wait out front at the bar and hope the police showed up, causing a distraction. She could try to charm and bribe the bouncer at the VIP door. She could ask a dancer or maybe that bartender, Dawson, to help her find Kayla. She could try to make a distraction in the parking lot—maybe set off a bunch of car alarms—and slip inside when customers streamed out to see what was going on. None of these choices seemed ideal, but Kayla needed her and she couldn't do a thing from outside.

She'd almost made up her mind on the car alarm option when she heard a rusty squeak followed by women's voices and the flick of a lighter. She peered around the corner of the building. On the loading dock, two dancers wearing platform shoes and skimpy outfits stood on the concrete and smoked cigarettes. One wore a puffy coat draped over long limbs clad in silk lingerie. The other pulled a long cardigan sweater tight around her torso as she bounced lightly on her heels. The scent of cigarette smoke drifted in the air.

Liv waited as the girls chatted about the other dancers and their clients, the good tippers in the front, and the creeps to avoid in the VIP lounge. If they'd come out, they'd go back in again, she reasoned, and she'd make her move. After a few minutes, the door opened. A man stuck out his head. "You're up, Patti. Get your ass back inside," he said, and disappeared.

"Jerk-face." The woman in the coat threw her cigarette to the concrete and crushed it beneath a shoe before slipping into the club.

The other woman stood half a minute longer, smoking her cigarette down to the filter. She peered out at the bleak landscape, left arm encircling her waist, right arm bent, fingers holding the cigarette to her lips.

Liv wondered what the woman thought about, staring out into the night. Was she lonely? Did she dream of one day settling into a more boring, suburban life? Or did her ambitions stretch more toward snagging a wealthy lover or husband? Did she enjoy her job or merely tolerate it? Did she hate the men who gazed at her for their own sexual pleasure? Or did the act of arousing them feel powerful?

She supposed similar questions had fascinated Alice Ferguson, leading her to The Golden Triangle and her tragic, brutal demise.

Liv sidled closer to the ramp as the dancer turned toward the door, withdrawing a key from her cardigan pocket. The young woman threw the door wide and stepped inside. The door began to close behind her.

Sprinting up the ramp, Liv snagged the handle just in time. She held it open just a sliver and listened to the retreating hollow clomp of the dancer's heels crossing a wooden floor. Liv counted a slow ten, and, holding her breath, slotted herself sideways into the building.

She found herself in a spacious storage room stacked with pallets of beverages and lined with industrial shelving containing jars of olives and cocktail onions, containers of juices and mixers, citrus fruits in produce boxes, and non-perishable items like paper towels and liquid soap. Naked light bulbs lit the space. Gouges and dirt marred an old, pinewood floor.

She hustled through the room and emerged into a hallway lit by flickering fluorescent rectangles. Crouch-stepping along the ugly, musty, industrial carpet at her feet, she noticed a dull silver walk-in cooler on her left. A few steps further, a door stood open on the right. She approached, held her breath, and peeked around the frame.

No one there, she discovered. Just basic office furniture and a few filing cabinets. The room smelled like cigarettes and perfume overlying the same musty mildew scent as the hallway. Behind the faux glitz of the bar and VIP room, the place was a dump.

She didn't linger long. The more time she spent snooping around the club, the more likely it was she'd get caught. She scurried past the office and continued down the hall until she found herself at the black-painted service door of the VIP lounge. Three short stairs led up to the backstage. Sultry music played on speakers beyond the heavy, purple curtains bisecting the stage floor. Glancing to her right, she spied a door marked with a "Dancers Only" sign, presumably the dressing room.

She reached for the handle, but before she could slip inside, the service door opened. The volume of the music increased, and a man stepped into the hall.

She froze, recognizing Anthony Zhebrovsky.

His eyes widened when he spotted her. "What the f—!"

He lunged, but she evaded him with a quick move and sprinted back toward the storeroom in hopes of escaping capture.

She careened around a shelving unit and raced toward the door. Just as she flung it open, he tackled her at the knees. The door swung shut and smacked her on the head. She tried to stand but couldn't get her footing. Anthony scrambled to his feet. When he reached for her, she rolled to the left, got on her hands and knees, and crawled away from him.

Swearing, he grabbed her ankles, and yanked her backward by her boots.

Her face and palms scraped on the splintery floorboards. Ignoring the pain, she kicked her right foot free and blasted her boot into his kneecap. He went down with an outraged howl.

Unfortunately, he landed on top of her. Her breath whooshed from her lungs. Grunting, he pressed his other knee into the small of her back. She twisted, reaching for her Sig, but he was too fast. He snagged her wrists and pulled them together behind her back, wrenching her shoulders.

"Let go of me!" she yelled, struggling in his grasp.

She wriggled and twisted, but he managed to keep hold of

her wrists. With a guttural expletive, he hauled her to her feet. She held back a scream. Her shoulders felt as if they were being wrenched from their sockets. Her skinned face and palms burned, but if anything, the humiliation of being discovered and caught stung worse than her physical pain.

Incensed and frustrated, she glared at him. Instead of rescuing Kayla, she'd managed to get herself caught, too.

"Let's have a chat, shall we?" Anthony said, breathing heavily as he shoved her toward the hallway and perp-marched her into the office. He kicked the door behind them and pushed her into a chair in front of his desk.

She popped up, but he placed his hands on both her shoulders and pushed her back down. Then he slapped her, hard, across the face. He hesitated a moment then slapped her again, harder.

Cheek and mouth throbbing, she straightened her head to look at him. Holding his eye, she licked the briny, metallic taste of blood from her cut lip, and smiled. She hoped she looked crazy enough to give him second thoughts about keeping her captive.

Liv guessed he'd become immune to crazy, because he didn't react.

"Don't move unless you want more," he said as he pulled a cell phone from his pocket. Watching her, he pressed the phone to his ear and growled, "Office. Now. We've got a problem." He paused, listening to whoever it was on the other end. An exasperated look crossed his face. "Just get down here."

Chapter Thirty-Seven

● ● ● ● ● ● ● ● ● ● ● ● ● ●

Liv, sensing an opportunity, jumped from her chair and reached for her gun. He dropped his phone and tackled her again, this time smashing the back of her head against a shelving unit filled with athletic trophies.

Reeling, she grabbed one of the trophies and swung the heavy marble base. It connected with his head. Zhebrovsky grunted, backpedaled to catch his balance, and nearly toppled.

Staggering and dizzy herself, she reached once again for the Sig.

From the corner of her eye, she caught motion in the doorway just before a strong hand encircled her wrist. In a deft movement, she was relieved of the gun. She glared as Dawson, the bartender, checked the safety and tucked the Sig into the back of his waistband. He stepped away from her and gestured toward the chair. "You'd better have a seat."

Another man, a beefier version of Anthony that Liv recognized as his cousin Leo, rushed into the room. "What's going on, Tony? Who's this chick?"

Anthony, who'd recovered enough to smooth his hair and straighten his tie, nodded at Dawson. "Thank you for the assist, man. Leo and I will take it from here. Please return to the front."

Dawson nodded and turned toward the door.

"But first give me the gun." Anthony held out a hand and snapped his fingers. "Actually, find something to restrain her with and bring it back here. Bitch nearly bashed my head in."

Dawson handed the Sig to Anthony who pointed it at Liv as he moved around his desk and sat in the ergonomic office chair behind it. Leo loomed over her. His paunch pressed into the back of her head as he held her shoulders with beefy hands.

Her head ached where she'd hit the shelf, and the right side of her face burned from where the skin had been scraped off. Her mouth throbbed. *I'm sure going to look cute in the morning,* she thought. *If I make it to morning.*

She licked more blood from her lip and lifted her chin. "Where's Kayla Goff?"

"I'm asking the questions here, not you."

She narrowed her eyes while her brain ran through possible escape scenarios. She wished she'd left the Sig at home. It had only served to make her situation more impossible. Getting shot wouldn't help Kayla.

Anthony smiled, his eyes void of emotion. "I can see the wheels turning in that pretty little head of yours. I wouldn't try anything if I were you. I have a few questions, and I suggest you answer them."

She tensed, ready to fight, but remained motionless.

Anthony's chair squeaked as she adjusted his weight against the back, trying to look nonchalant and in control. "Who are you, and what's your business with Kayla?"

She shrugged but said nothing.

Leo cuffed her ear with a meaty palm. "Tell us your name."

"Puddentain."

It took him a couple of seconds before her sarcasm sunk in, but he eventually got there. "You think you're funny?" Leo cuffed her again, harder this time. Pain exploded in her right ear.

She twisted her head to glare at the goon. "Cut that out, you Neanderthal. I'll talk."

She faced Anthony again. "I think we've gotten off on the wrong foot. I'm not here to cause you any trouble. My name's Olivia. I'm a friend of Kayla's. She called me for a ride, said to meet her out back."

She jerked her head to indicate the back of the building and immediately wished she hadn't because she went dizzy again. Idiots probably gave her a concussion. "Anyway," she continued, "when Kayla didn't show up, I figured it wouldn't hurt to try to the door. It was unlocked. You really ought to be more careful about your security around here. So I came inside, no biggy, and I was heading for the dressing room to find Kayla when I ran into you instead. Lucky me."

She reached a finger to her lip and dabbed at it, wincing. "Didn't your mother teach you it's not nice to hit girls?"

Before Anthony could answer, Dawson entered the room. A pair of fuzzy purple handcuffs swung from his fingers. "These ought to work."

Anthony scowled. "Are you f-ing serious? Where's the zip ties?"

Dawson shrugged and threw a pair of tiny, silver keys on Anthony's desk. "We're fresh out. I couldn't find any duct tape around, either. So I got these from one of the girls. Don't worry. They're real cuffs." He held a bracelet in each hand and yanked. The chain held. "These are good quality. Sturdy. See?"

Anthony waved the gun. "Okay. Whatever. Put them on her."

Dawson grabbed one of her wrists and snapped the cuff around it. Liv snorted. "You've got to be kidding me."

Dawson repeated the action with her other wrist and moved so that his body came between her and Anthony. He caught her eye and then glanced down. He tapped his index finger on a minute knob on the cuff and then looked into her eyes again. His eyebrows lifted just a smidge.

Liv's spirits lifted. For some reason, Dawson was on her side. She had a suspicion it wasn't just because she was a good tipper and better flirt, but she didn't have time to figure it out now. She only knew she had an unexpected ally and felt a wash of relief. Not only for her sake, but also Kayla's.

What he *didn't* know was that she was familiar with cuffs—especially the fuzzy, sexy kind. It was reassuring, however, to know she had an ally in the building, whoever he really was and who he worked for. She gave him a nearly-imperceptible nod.

For theatrics' sake, she pretended to struggle. "Ouch! You didn't have to put them on so tight. Hey, what are you doing now, Handsy?"

Dawson ignored her as he felt her pockets and withdrew her lipstick, phone, and car fob.

"She's all yours," Dawson told Anthony after he'd patted her down and placed the items on the desk. "No I.D."

He gave her a last, fleeting glance and exited the room.

Anthony set the gun on the desk in front of him. "You're quite the little nuisance. Last time you were here, I told you to stop nosing around. You should have listened. Now, what are you really doing here?"

"I told you. I'm Kayla's friend, and she asked me to pick her up." She lifted her hands and shook the fuzzy purple cuffs. "Just get her and we'll be on our way. Oh, and I want that lipstick back. It's Chanel."

Anthony picked up the lipstick, opened it, rotated the tip up and down. "Nice try, cupcake. I already know that coked-up, little skank's been telling fairy tales to some reporter or novelist. That's bad enough. Now we got to deal with you, too. What are you? Undercover cop?"

Liv decided to go with a version of the truth. "Not a cop. A private investigator. My name's Olivia Lively. I run an agency called Lively Investigations. Check it out online, and you'll see I'm telling the truth. Kayla's mother hired me to find her. That's it. No cops. No Feds. I'm just a local P.I. trying to make a living, same as you. Let Kayla and me leave, and we'll both forget this ever happened. I promise. You'll never see or hear from either of us again."

Anthony shook his head. "Though I'd like to believe you, it's too risky."

Leo, who now hovered in front of the door, said, "This is out of our league, bro. Felix will be here in about an hour. I say we let him decide what to do with the two of 'em."

Liv's skin crawled. She considered popping the cuffs and attempting escape, but with two against one and the gun still in Anthony's reach, she didn't like her chances. She decided to keep him talking, throw him off kilter, and hope for a better chance. "Felix? Is that who killed Alice Ferguson?"

Anthony frowned. "Who?"

"You know. The writer. The one Kayla was talking to. That's what happened, right? You found out Kayla was talking to Alice and Alby Ferguson about your business and you arranged to have someone follow them to Carry Over and kill them. I'm thinking that someone was Felix, but I could be wrong. Maybe you and Tweedledum over there murdered them yourselves."

Anthony looked at her like she was crazy. "Ferguson? The finance guy? And the dead chick up north? We had nothing to do with that." He looked at his phone and then at his cousin. "Felix just texted. He just got off the pike. Put her in the cooler for now."

Leo grabbed her arm, yanked her to her feet and into the hall. Liv, not liking the sound of that cooler, unlocked her knees and dropped toward the floor. Leo lost his grip on her arm. She rolled onto her back and kicked toward Leo's knees with her Doc Martens, but he managed to avoid them. He moved to her left, reached down to clamp a meaty hand on her elbow, and hauled her upright. "Stay on ya' feet, or else."

He shook her, hard. Her head whipped forward and backward a couple of times. She felt her eyes cross as she tried to regain her equilibrium. She'd have to get checked for a concussion after this for sure. "Or else what?"

He was dumb as a post, but somehow he intuited the one threat she'd take seriously. "If ya' don't cooperate, I'll hurt Kayla." He grinned. She didn't like the look in his eyes, and she knew why when he added, "More than she already is."

Liv allowed him to lead her to the walk-in cooler she'd noticed on her way in. He opened the door and gave her a shove. She stumbled inside as the door slammed shut. Total darkness enveloped her.

Her claustrophobia kicked in. For a moment, she panicked. Her lungs constricted. Her head felt wobbly on her neck. Panic like ice-cold acid raced in her veins. A scream gathered deep in her lungs as she held her breath and stumbled forward, losing her balance and nearly falling.

She let out her breath and held herself still, willing herself to focus. *I will not lose it.* Remembering a technique Ashleigh had taught her, she closed her eyes—harder to tell in the dark—and inhaled through her nose for a four-count, held her breath for another four-count, and let it out on yet another four.

Her panic subsided a bit. She started again, but her breath whooshed out of her lungs when she heard a whimper to her right. Her heart thudded.

"Kayla?" Liv whispered into the darkness. "Is that you?"

Chapter Thirty-Eight

• • • • • • • • • • • • • •

L iv heard a low moan but nothing more.

"Kayla, it's Liv," she said. "Hold on for a few more minutes, okay? I'm going to get us out of here." More for her own benefit, she added, "We just have to remain calm."

Kayla moaned again.

Liv took stock of the situation. The air inside the cooler was chilly but not cold, and she couldn't hear a fan. At least the unit wasn't being used for refrigeration.

Lucky for her and Kayla, Liv knew how to escape a cooler. Her fear of small spaces had prompted her to research things like dumpsters, vehicle trunks, and vintage refrigerators. She'd even asked Ruth if she could inspect the walk-in at Buoy Bagels. Ruth, surprised but amenable, showed her the hardware on the inside and handed her a copy of the user manual to take home.

As long as the Zees hadn't blocked the door from the outside, she'd get them out, but first, she needed to free her hands from the fuzzy purple cuffs. With her left fingers, she felt for the little knob concealed beneath the fuzz on the right cuff. She pressed and the cuff clicked open. Letting out her breath, she pulled it from her wrist and quickly did the same with the left. She let the furry, purple restraints thunk softly to the floor.

"Okay," she told Kayla in a calm, soothing voice. "My hands are free. Make a noise so I can find you." Another whimper came from a spot ahead and to her left. Dropping to her hands and knees, Liv crawled until she felt Kayla's leg. "Okay, I've got you. Are you hurt?"

Kayla tried to talk around whatever they'd gagged her with. "Uhmmmm-hmmm."

Liv felt Kayla's ankles and discovered a plastic zip tie holding them together. It would be impossible for the girl to run or even shuffle.

"Listen," Liv said. "I need you to work with me so we can get out of here as quickly as possible. Can you lean forward and touch my hands on your ankles?"

Kayla shifted and let out another little groan. Liv felt cold fingers on hers. Kayla's wrists had been bound with another zip tie. Liv slid her fingers up Kayla's arms to her shoulders and finally to her face. The Zees had gagged her with some kind of cloth. Liv hooked her fingers into the material and gave a tug.

Kayla gasped as the gag slipped off her mouth. Voice choked with tears, she whispered, "What are they going to do? Are they going to kill us?"

"No." Liv said, keeping her voice steady. "We'll survive this if we stay calm and use our heads, okay?"

"Okay." Kayla sniffed. "I can do that."

"I know you can. Let's take this one step at a time, all right?" Liv put more confidence into her voice than she felt. After they escaped the cooler, they'd have to find their way out of the club before Felix, whoever he was, showed up. "Take a few deep breaths and get your oxygen level up while I check the cooler door."

"What if you can't open it?" Kayla's voice rose to a higher, near-hysterical pitch.

"I'm pretty sure I can do it," Liv said. "I need you to trust me and do exactly what I tell you. If you can, we'll make it." She hoped she wasn't kidding herself. "Pull yourself together, and get ready to move. I'll be right back."

Liv stood and groped for a wall. Using a shelf edge as a guide, she made her way around the cooler until she reached the front, right corner of the unit. With her fingers crab-walking the wall, she felt for the door's sealed edge. "Where are you?" she muttered to herself as she groped in the dark. Finally, she found a lever. "I think I found the safety latch," she told Kayla.

She pulled up on the handle and pushed against the door. It gave way, and a bit of light and air flowed into the interior of the cooler. Liv's shoulders dropped with relief. "Got it," she whispered.

Liv adjusted the door, leaving it open a sliver. She hoped one of the cousins didn't decide to check on them in the next few minutes. She peered into the corner of the cooler and saw Kayla huddled in a protective ball, her hair in a tangle around her shoulders.

Even in the gloom, Liv could see that Kayla's face was a mess. Black mascara tracked her cheeks. One eye was swollen shut, the other wide with fear. Her neck looked mottled and bruised, her mouth swollen and crusted with dried blood. She was dressed for work in a costume of fancy corset top, a matching thong, thigh-high fishnet stockings, and patent leather platform shoes. A zip-tie held Kayla's wrists together in front of her body.

Liv bent one knee to unlace one of her boots. She slipped the paracord from the eye holes and poked one end of the cord through the zip tie around Kayla's wrists. "Put your elbows on either side of your knees and hold your hands as steady as you can. Ready?"

Kayla nodded.

"Good." Gripping both ends of the cord, Liv sawed back and forth against the zip. "Almost there," she said through gritted teeth. "Keep pulling your wrists apart."

It only took a few seconds to burn through the plastic tie. It broke with an audible snap and fell to the floor.

"It worked!" Kayla whispered, rubbing one wrist.

"Yeah, it's a pretty cool trick," Liv said, running the cord through the tie around Kayla's ankles and repeating the operation. Soon the second tie fell to the floor. "Do you have circulation in your feet?"

Kayla rotated her feet, shook them in the air. "Prickles. Kind of numb." She hit her thighs with her fists and moved them up and down. "Legs, too, but I'm pretty sure I can walk."

Liv quickly relaced her boot. She stood, reached down, and hauled Kayla to her feet. She held the young woman's eyes with hers. Her voice, when she spoke, was grim. "Try to run."

·　·　·　·　·

The two women sprinted down the hall toward the storage room. Liv pointed toward the door leading to the loading dock. They clattered across the wooden floor.

Liv pushed the door open a few inches, hoping the coast was clear. The red lights of a small delivery truck flashed as it backed up to the dock. The driver braked and cut the engine.

Liv's stomach dropped. *Too late.*

She held up a hand to signal Kayla to wait and watched as a man emerged from the passenger side of the truck. He was short but stocky. Close-cropped gray hair formed a ring around his bald scalp. Felix, she presumed. Drug dealer? Probably. Russian mafia? Maybe. He carried a large, black duffel bag toward the ramp.

Liv eased the door closed and pulled Kayla to the side of the room. "Someone's coming," she whispered. "Get behind those." She pointed to a stack of pallets filled with beverage cans. As Kayla ducked into the shadows between the pallets and the shelving unit behind them, Liv scurried toward the door leading into the club. She found the electrical switch, and cut the lights.

The room wasn't totally dark because the door to the hallway was open, but that made the shadows in the room seem that much deeper. With just seconds to spare, she shoved several shrink-wrapped, twelve-roll paper towel packages from a bottom shelf, wriggled into the space, and pulled a few in front of her.

A key turned in the lock. She heard the door creak open, and the man with the duffel bag muttered, "Jerks can't even turn on the friggin' lights." Liv peered at him as he made his way through the room. The duffel bag swung from his right hand. Liv held her breath until he disappeared and then waited a few seconds longer. When the coast seemed clear, she pushed the towels out of the way and scrambled to her feet.

"Let's go!" she whispered to Kayla.

They sprinted to the door.

Liv put a hand on the push bar. "Listen," she said. "There's a driver in a delivery truck backed up to the dock. Do you think you can climb over the railing and drop a couple feet in those shoes? Without rolling an ankle?"

Kayla reached down, pulled off the platforms by the straps, and threw them away from her. They thumped when they hit the floor.

Liv winced, thinking of broken glass and who knows what else littering the parking lot. "All right then. Stick close to me. Here we go."

They slipped through the door, scurried onto the cement dock, and reached the railing to their left. Keeping an eye on the truck, Liv scrambled over the railing and jumped onto the pavement near the corner of the building. She looked up at Kayla and motioned for her to hurry.

Kayla clambered to the other side of the railing but hesitated at the top. "I'm not sure I can do this in my bare feet after all," she whispered.

Liv remembered Kayla's cheerleading background. She webbed her fingers together and said, "Go down backward. Step into my hands."

Kayla nodded. She held onto the bottom of the railing and did as Liv instructed. Seconds later, they ran across the pavement to the shadows of the trees and scurried toward the front parking lot. "This way!" Liv led Kayla to her car, hoping the girl's feet were okay and remembering just as she reached the Corolla that her fob—and her favorite lipstick—were still on Anthony's desk.

She'd left the car unlocked in case she'd needed a quick getaway. It would provide cover, at least for a few minutes until Anthony came out of the club and clicked her key fob. If he was smart enough to think of it. She didn't want to wait around to find out.

"Quick, get in," she told Kayla as she opened the driver's side door. "Scramble over." Liv followed Kayla into the car and shut the door. Their chests heaved as they caught their breath.

"Open the glove box," Liv said. "There's a phone."

Kayla did as requested and handed over the burner Liv kept for emergencies. Liv dialed 911. When the operator responded, Liv said, "My name's Olivia Lively. I'm a private detective working on a missing person's case. I'm at The Golden Triangle in Fallbrook. Another woman and I were abducted, restrained, and held against our will. We managed to escape. We're hiding in my vehicle in the parking lot, but I don't think we'll be safe here for long. Our abductors also took my gun, so they are armed. There's a truck parked at the loading dock. One man exited the truck and entered the building. Another is still in the truck. I think it might be a drug delivery."

The operator said she'd notify officers in the area and asked if Liv wanted to stay on the line, but Liv disconnected the call. She turned to Kayla. "I'm going to pop the trunk. Keep your head down."

Liv exited the car, went to the trunk, and fumbled through her collection of odd clothing items she kept in there for on-the-fly disguises and emergencies. She grabbed a baseball cap, a hoodie, jeans, and a ratty pair of sneakers before easing the trunk closed.

She drew the cap onto her head, slid back into the driver's seat, and dumped sneakers ans jeans into Kayla's lap. "Put those on."

Liv kept watch, scowling over the dashboard, for the Zees or Felix. The adrenaline rush made her feel shaky. And feeling shaky made her angry. She felt a flush rise to her cheeks. This was the second case this year that involved a writer. What was it about literary ambitions that got people into so much trouble?

This time, the answer seemed obvious. Of all the possible topics in the world, Alice Ferguson—mousy social worker by day and erotic novelist by night—decided to write a book about the drug dealers, strippers, and the mob. *Why not a cozy mystery?* Liv fumed. *Or an Amish freakin' romance?*

When Kayla finished tying the sneaks, Liv handed her the dark hoodie. "I'm in the mood for a coffee," she said in a falsely cheerful tone. "How about you? Dunkin' sounds good, right?"

Kayla blinked at her as if she'd lost her mind. "I, uh, guess so."

"Look, the police should be here soon. In the meantime, I think we'll be safer next door. Anthony has my fob."

Kayla's already pale face went a shade whiter. "Coffee's perfect," she managed to say.

Liv smiled. The girl had spunk, she'd give her that.

When a pickup jacked up on monster wheels and sporting green and purple lighting rolled into the parking lot, Liv reached for the door handle. "Walk, don't run. We'll attract less attention that way. Don't look back. We'll be okay."

They wove through the cars to the edge of the parking lot and made it to the sidewalk. Cars zipped in both direction along the busy four-lane road. Keeping their heads down, the women crossed the Dunkin's drive-thru lane, and reached the door without incident. Liv pulled the pink D-shaped handle and motioned Kayla in front of her, and they stepped inside. As the heavenly smell of coffee and sugar enveloped them, Liv felt some of the tension ease from her body.

"Go to the restroom and wash your face," she told Kayla. She reached into her pocket for cash. "I'll order coffees."

When Kayla emerged, face scrubbed clean, she sat down across from Liv in a booth in front of the window. She started to lower her hood.

"Keep the hood up," Liv said. She pushed a large cup across the table. "Drink the coffee. There's sugar and cream in it. It will help stabilize your adrenaline."

"So, we just wait here until the police show up?" Kayla said, her shoulders hunched near her ears. Her eyes looked spooked.

"Yes. We wait."

Kayla pried the lid from the cup. She took a tentative sip, and her shoulders relaxed. "Mmmm. That's good."

"Do you want a donut or something?"

Kayla shook her head. Her hand trembled as she lifted the cup to her mouth again.

They drank their coffee in silence. Other customers came and went, but no one took any interest in the two women beside the window. Liv wanted to ask Kayla how she'd ended up back at the club and in the clutches of the Zees, but the girl looked shell-shocked. Liv decided questions could wait.

After a few minutes, sirens whooped next door. Liv and Kayla peered out the window. The flashing lights of law enforcement vehicles lit up The Golden Triangle parking lot. A black SUV pulled in behind the Portland and state police cars, and a familiar figure in a jacket with the letters FBI on the back walked toward the club.

"Should we go over?" Kayla asked. The bruise around her swollen eye looked dark against her pale skin framed by the black material of the hoodie.

"Not yet. Let the police do their job. I will, however, make a call."

Liv punched numbers into the burner. It struck her that she'd memorized this particular number without even realizing it, and she wondered, briefly, what that meant, if anything. Through the window, she watched Colin Snow pull a phone from his pocket and slap it to his ear.

"Snow," he said.

Liv couldn't help but smile. "Hello, Agent. What are you doing at The Golden Triangle?"

After a surprised pause, Snow let out a short laugh. "Lively," he said. "I should have known you'd be involved in this cluster." He looked left and right, scanning the parking lot. "Where are you?"

"Next door," she said. "Want a Boston cream?"

He spotted her in the window and lifted a hand in greeting.

She waved back. "Hey, can you do me a favor?"

"What kind of favor?"

"No biggie, really. When you get in there, my cell phone and car fob should be on top of the desk in the back office. Lipstick, too. Can't miss it. Just grab the stuff for me, okay?"

"Sure, anything for you, babe."

"Cool, thanks."

He waited a beat. "Or maybe I *won't*. It's a crime scene, Lively."

"Just the lipstick? Please? It's Chanel."

"Sorry, but no."

"All right, all right. It was worth a shot."

She ended the call and shook her head at Kayla. "Men. They just don't understand the importance of the perfect shade of red lipstick."

Kayla, who was staring at her in something like awe, said, "You know FBI agents?"

"Just the one." Liv winked at her. "Now, since we have some time, and I'm sure I'm going to be oh-so-fascinated by this story, why don't you tell me why you were back at the club tonight after you told me you were through with that life?"

Kayla looked startled. "I don't—"

Liv cut her off. "Uh-uh. No excuses. Start with you deciding to go back to the Triangle. End with you in the cooler. I'm gonna drink this delicious java while you talk." She pointed around her cup, now three-quarters full. "Go."

Chapter Thirty-Nine

• • • • • • • • • • • • •

As Liv listened—occasionally asking Kayla to elaborate—the story came out.

After a few days at the women's shelter, Kayla changed her mind. She missed the money. And, yeah, she admitted to Liv, the drugs. She figured she'd apologize, promise to pay back what she owed, and pick up where she left off, but she was in for an unpleasant surprise. Anthony, deciding to make an example of her in front of the other girls, ordered Leo to rough her up. And not just a little.

"He really hurt me," she said, shaking. "I knew right then I'd made a huge mistake. When Leo finished with me, Anthony and Leo left me in the dressing room and told me to get dressed. They couldn't put me on stage, not with my eye like this, but they said I could take care of some guys who weren't too picky about a face as long as my mouth worked."

Liv felt her insides heave a little. "That's when you called me for help."

"Yeah, but one of the other girls heard me, and I guess she ratted me out to Leo. He told Anthony, and when he figured out I was planning on leaving again, he took all my stuff—my I.D., my phone, my debit card, everything. They started talking about that guy Felix and how I'd work off my debt in Boston. That's when they tied me up and put me in the cooler.

"I thought I was going to die. Or worse. You know." Kayla

stared at Liv with hollow, shocked eyes. "I don't think girls come back from Boston."

Both women fell silent contemplating possible scenarios. Liv said, "Maybe it's better not to think about what ifs and finish our coffees."

Kayla looked down at the table.

When they'd drained the last of their drinks, Liv told Kayla it was time to go. "We'll walk over to the parking lot and talk to the police, or Agent Snow if he's there. We'll probably end up at the station giving statements, but you might need medical attention first. I'll be with you as long as they'll let me. Ready?"

Kayla nodded, but hung back, reluctant. "I'm scared."

Liv nodded and put a steadying arm around the younger woman. "You'd be stupid if you weren't, but the worst is over now. Let's go."

·   ·   ·   ·   ·

The next morning, Liv filled Marion in on the events of the previous night. Liv's face and palms still throbbed, but she thought with some satisfaction about the kick she'd landed on Anthony Zee's knee.

"I can't believe Kayla went back to the club," Marion said. "How much of Alice's story was based on facts, do you think?"

"Plenty—" Before Liv could explain further, the phone at the reception desk rang.

"I'll get it." Marion jumped from the couch and snagged the receiver. "Yes, she's right here. Please hold." She pressed a button and raised her eyebrows at Liv. "It's Detective Briggs."

"I'll take it in the other room."

Liv strode into her office and plopped into the chair behind her desk. She crossed her denim-clad legs and swung one of her blue pumps. She wore a soft, French blue cardigan—comfort clothing, she called it—and had knotted a pretty blue and white striped scarf around her neck to hide several bruises that had popped up overnight.

There wasn't much she could do about the scrapes on her face besides a little antibacterial lotion. She thought longingly of her lost Chanel lipstick. Next time she saw Colin Snow, she'd tell him she was launching a formal inquiry into the tube's location. She didn't want to think too closely why that thought cheered her up.

Outside the window, the sky was clear blue, the kind you get in Maine on the best September days. One yellow leaf flew past on a gust of wind. Autumn was in the air.

The landline phone buzzed. She lifted the receiver. "Good afternoon, Detective Briggs. I was going to contact you this afternoon, but you beat me to it! I was right about the Zhebrovskys, wasn't I? They got spooked about Alice's questions and had her followed to Carry Over and killed to make sure she wouldn't write about them."

"Actually, no."

Liv uncrossed her legs and sat up. "No?"

The squeak of an office chair assaulted Liv's ear. Briggs's voice was frosty. "Ms. Lively, I hope you realize how irresponsible you were last night. You should have let us handle the situation with Kayla Goff."

"Okay, but…"

"You nearly screwed up a year-long, multi-agency investigation. Portland and state police, coordinating with the FBI, have had their eye on the club for months. The Zhebrovksys will most likely be indicted on drug and prostitution charges, not to mention your assault and kidnapping, but there is absolutely no connection to the Russian mafia or the Ferguson case. Their supplier, a guy operating out of the Boston area, is involved with a Mexican cartel. Low on the food chain."

Liv swallowed. "So, Felix isn't…"

"Not a Russian gangster. No."

"What about the Zhebrovskys?"

"Anthony and Leo Zhebrovsky are third-generation Russian-Americans. Their paternal grandfather immigrated from Belarus and settled in Fallbrook to work at the paper mill in the 70s. The cousins grew up in Fallbrook, led the high-school football team to two state championships, dropped out of UMaine after a couple of years, and came back to Fallbrook to go into business together. Zero connection to the mob."

Liv absorbed this information for a moment with a sinking stomach. Alice's plot line had been fictional. At least that part of it.

"Okay, so they aren't Russian mafia. That doesn't mean Felix, or someone else who works for the cartel, didn't murder Alice and Alby Ferguson. Or maybe the Zees did the dirty work themselves. They seemed plenty capable of violence last night interrogating me at the club. Kayla had been talking to Alice about some pretty incriminating stuff. If they thought Alice was an undercover cop or even an investigative journalist—"

Briggs interrupted. "Forget it, Ms. Lively. You're barking up the wrong tree here. They have solid alibis for the night Alice Ferguson was killed. They hosted a big party at the club. We have photos from multiple sources—not to mention one undercover investigator's testimony—to prove it. All the evidence points to Albert Ferguson as Alice's killer."

Liv swallowed the bile rising in her throat. She'd been so sure. Mortification brought blood rushing to her face. The scrapes on her cheek throbbed. "I guess my theory was wrong," she said. "I'm sorry I wasted your time. I really thought I was on the right track."

"You should have let the pros handle it."

That stung. "Okay, I hear what you're saying, but you know what, Detective? I'm not sorry I got involved. A young woman needed help. If I hadn't *interfered*, Kayla Goff would have been abducted last night. The van was there. The driver was there. Felix was there. She would have been sent down to Boston to be trafficked, raped, tortured, or who knows what. She might have disappeared for good. Or her body might have been found months or even years from now, out in a swamp or a shallow grave in the woods somewhere. So, yeah. I'm glad I went to the Triangle last night. You got your guys. Maybe you should be thanking me."

Briggs's voice grew louder. "You'll be lucky if you're not charged with obstruction. From now on, let the police handle the criminal investigations. Stay in your lane."

Briggs ended the call.

Fuming, Liv slammed down the receiver and crossed her arms. Last night, though dicey, was a win from her point of view. Who cared what snotty Detective Briggs said! The raid by police and feds had been successful. They'd arrested the bad guys, and most likely the Zees and their collaborators would be charged, tried, and put away for their crimes.

Most important, Kayla had a chance at a better life. After giving her statement to the authorities, Kayla had been examined at the hospital and then admitted to a local rehabilitation facility. Kayla's mother, Maralynne, sobbed on the phone when Liv called to tell her the news. "Thank you so much for saving my baby," she told Liv. "You're an angel."

"I'm really not," Liv laughed, embarrassed. "I'm just happy it turned out okay and your daughter's getting the help she needs."

Liv knew something about mistakes. She knew that not only could you survive them, but you could also make better choices next time around.

But, given the choice, she'd make this one all over again.

Chapter Forty

• • • • • • • • • • • • • •

New morning. New month. New season.

Liv dumped the dregs of her morning coffee into the sink and thought about the interviews for new assistants scheduled that week and how everything seemed to be wrapping up all at once after a sticky, troubling summer that had, at least, ended on a high note for Lively Investigations.

The Raptor case was over. The day before, Francine Larabee called to tell her that Booker had dropped his lawsuit. "We are very pleased with the job you did on this investigation," Francine told her. "You can expect a bonus check in the mail next week."

Liv invited Marion and Patrick Ledeau to a celebratory dinner at Scales where they inhaled briny oysters, succulent mussels swimming in broth, and seared scallops bathed in a rich, creamy sauce, all mopped up with chewy bread and washed down with an excellent bottle of *Moreux Sancerre Les Bouffants* from the Loire Valley.

With summer over, the Raptor case complete, her off-the-books investigation of Alice Ferguson's murder at a dead end, and Marion starting law school, Liv smelled the change of season in the air. It reminded her of pencil shavings and Crayola crayons and the scent of new books. And the faint whiff industrial cleanser drifting from the janitor's closet.

She ambled toward her closet day-dreaming about cozy sweaters, librarian glasses, and pumpkin spice lattes.

She froze when her doorbell buzzed. "And apparently I'm going to be late for the first day of school," she grumbled as she stomped back toward the kitchen to check the monitor. She peered at the screen, and then reared back, heart thudding.

She pressed the intercom button. "Jasper? Is everything okay?"

"I need to see you. Can I come up?"

She buzzed him in.

Still in her pajamas and robe, Liv held the door open as Jasper lugged a cardboard box into the entryway. Crisp, cool, morning air followed him in.

"What's in the box?" she asked, shutting the door behind him.

He gave her a sheepish look. "Just some stuff you left at my place. A couple books. A toothbrush. A pair of sneakers." He reached in and pulled out a black, lacy bra and lifted his eyebrows. "This."

A break-up box. Fantastic.

She grabbed the bra and then the box, cradling it in her arms. "Thanks. Um, do you want to come in? I was just going to get dressed, but if you want some coffee or tea or anything…"

"Sure," he said, shrugging out of his leather jacket. "Coffee sounds good."

She stared at him.

He stared back. "What?" he said.

"I was just being polite. I drank the last of the pot already."

"No worries. I'll make another while you get dressed. Unless you don't want to get dressed quite yet." His eyes fell to her mouth. And lingered.

She narrowed her eyes. "What does that mean?"

"It means you look good. Tousled. Irritated." He stepped closer to her. His eyes, dark blue and intense, met hers. "Nice PJs."

Feeling herself softening, she tightened her grip on the box and glared. "You did not come here to seduce me. You're a surgeon. You're smarter than that."

He took the box from her arms and set it on the floor. "No, but now that I'm here, it seems like a pretty good idea."

When he moved toward her, she straight-armed him. "No. We had the big talk. We decided to break up. We moved on."

"I haven't moved on." He took a step back, though. He put his hands in the pockets of his khakis and grinned at her. "Okay, back to plan A. I'll make the coffee. You get dressed."

"Plan A was you bringing me my stuff and leaving. Don't you have to work or something?"

"Day off." He moved into the kitchen and began rooting around in her cupboard. "Decaf or regular?"

She snorted. "As if I'd have decaf in my house. I'm beginning to think you don't know me at all." She picked up the box and lugged it down the hall. Flinging open the door of her walk-in closet she sank down onto her tufted, yellow ottoman, took a deep breath and mouthed the word, "Wow!"

A million thoughts flooded her mind, all of them contradictory, as she stood again and kicked the box under the ottoman. After a few minutes of deep breathing, she took stock of the situation.

There was a man in her kitchen. Not just any man. Jasper.

She hugged her bathrobe to her body and listened to the sounds of cupboards and drawers opening, water running in the tap. Aches and pains still throbbed in her shoulders, legs, face, and ribs. A mere forty-eight hours earlier, she'd been in hand-to-hand combat with a strong and lethal guy.

She didn't have it in her to fight an emotional battle, too.

The smell of coffee set off little pings of dopamine in her brain. Or was it serotonin? Some Pavlovian chemical, anyway, that drew her like a moth to a cappuccino-scented candle and overrode the fight or flight response triggered by Dr. Hottie's presence in her apartment.

Why had he come here, knowing their life goals weren't compatible? She wanted to get over him and move on with her life, not drag out this uncoupling over weeks and months.

A spurt of irritation prodded her to do something. She couldn't hide in her closet forever. She needed to get him out of her apartment before she did something foolish. Like falling back into bed with him.

The best defense, she thought, was offense. And by that she meant clothes.

She dressed in her conservative French blue, button down shirt and stretchy black pants. After sliding her feet into a pair of open-toe kitten heels, she finger-combed her hair and reached for her Chanel lipstick before remembering it was gone.

If there was a moment calling for the perfect shade of red lipstick, it was this one.

She made her way back to the kitchen. Jasper poured coffee into one of her favorite mugs and slid it across the counter toward her. The rich smell of dark roast hit her nostrils. She lifted the cup to her lips and sipped. Heaven.

Jasper nodded approval. "You look gorgeous. As always."

She cut to the chase. "What are you really doing here, Jasper?"

"I heard you got into some trouble the other night."

She froze. *How had he heard that?*

"Do you have a mole inside the police department or something? Geesh!" She walked with the coffee into her sunroom. He followed behind.

"I wanted to make sure you were okay. I mean, I figured you were, but I wanted to see for myself. This is why..." He shook his head and took a gulp of coffee. "Never mind."

"This is why you wanted me to reconsider my private investigation career."

"You have to admit, what you did—what you do—is dangerous."

"Yeah, the situation wasn't ideal, I admit. But a young woman needed my help. It all worked out fine."

"This time."

She recalled the purple handcuffs, the dark cooler, Kayla huddled in the corner. Luckily, she'd had an undercover ally in the building. She wondered who Dawson worked for. State police? FBI? She'd probably never know.

He'd possibly saved her life, though. If Leo or some other bouncer had tied her up with a zip, things could have ended up much worse for her. She considered Karina Briggs's phone call. Even if the Zhebrovskys weren't Alice's killers, they weren't nice men. They worked with a drug cartel, trafficked women, and who knows what else.

Jasper lightly touched her elbow. His face looked concerned. "Hey, Liv. Are you all right?"

"What? Yes. I'm fine." She shook off his hand and sank into one of the floral chairs. "I should have called the police before I rushed into the rescue. I didn't think. It could have cost me."

Jasper took the other chair. He crossed one ankle over his knee. "I'm impressed."

"By what?"

"Admitting your mistake."

"Believe me, I'm aware when I screw up. Mistake should have been my middle name."

"I wouldn't go that far. I like the name Rose." Jasper sipped his coffee. "So the girl? She's okay?"

Liv nodded. "I think so. She was a little battered and shaken up, but I think she'll be okay. She's getting the help she needs at a rehab facility. Her mother will be here today or tomorrow."

"And the Ferguson thing? How's your friend doing?"

Liv shrugged. "Last time we talked, Van still seemed broken. Grieving. Even though his wife betrayed him—with his brother no less—I think he still loves her. The police said they're wrapping up the investigation, and maybe that's for the best."

She shifted in her chair and her shoulders protested. She tried not to wince. "I really thought there was a connection with the strip club. That's how I ended up in that sticky situation at The Golden Triangle. I guess I was chasing mirages, letting myself get influenced by an unpublished manuscript Alice Ferguson was writing. I'm not sorry though. I saved a young woman from a truly horrifying future."

He stared at her cheek. "You have bruises, Liv. I hate that. Hate the risks you take. What if something…" His voice trailed off.

"I know." She let out a shaky laugh. "It will be awhile before I take on any more cases for old friends, I can tell you that."

He met her eyes. They stared at each other for a long moment. She felt herself falling into that familiar, blue gaze.

He cleared his throat. "Uh, I hope you know how much I admire your courage, your strength, and your persistence. You're so good at what you do. If only…"

"If only I'd take less dangerous cases."

"Yeah" He gave her a tender, questioning smile. "I don't suppose you'd consider becoming a forensic *accountant*?"

"Huh. That's an idea. Let me think." She pretended to consider it, tapping her chin. "No."

She placed her mug on the side table. Her heartbeat sped up. She missed him. Missed this. Maybe, now that they'd taken some time apart, he'd reconsider his ultimatum and pick up where they left off before Wren, before the key, before the dog. "Um, Jasper, maybe we should talk about…"

His phone beeped. "Hold that thought," he said and pulled it out of his pocket. He frowned as the other person spoke.

She listened to his side of the conversation. It was the hospital. One of his patients needed to be assessed. She picked up her coffee again and gulped it down. He ended the call. "Well, looks like I have to go to work."

"So I gathered. No rest for the weary. Thanks for bringing my stuff."

"No problem. I'll call you later. I'd like to take you out to dinner. No strings, just a couple of friends talking *X-Files* and aliens. What do you think?"

She thought it was a terrible idea. Which is why she was tempted to say yes. Because she was the queen of terrible ideas and bad boyfriends. "I don't know. Can we leave it at maybe?"

"Sure," he said. "Let me know."

She walked him to the door. He grabbed his coat on the way out and started down the stairs.

"Hey!" she called. When he turned to look up at her, she said, "Did you really think I'd sleep with you just because you brought me my toothbrush?"

He laughed. "I took a long shot. I'll call you later, okay?"

He didn't wait for an answer. He whistled as he went down the two flights of stairs, opened the outside door, and disappeared. She leaned against the doorframe, put her head back, and closed her eyes.

• • • • •

That afternoon, finding herself unable to concentrate at the office, Liv pulled into the parking lot of the rehab clinic and made her way inside. She signed in at the desk, and a nurse led her to a room on the first floor. The place smelled like antiseptic, air freshener, and Brussels sprouts. Gross. The nurse knocked and stuck her head in the door. "Hi, Kayla. You have a visitor."

Liv entered the small, spare room. Kayla, sitting on the edge of her narrow bed and staring out the window, looked over her shoulder when Liv entered the room.

"How are you doing?" Liv said. She put her bag on the floor and took a seat in the chair next to the bed.

She noted the cheap, mint green paint on the walls, the thin, washed-out pink blanket, the single pillow. A bedside table held a plastic cup and box of tissues. No reading material or electronics in sight. "This place is pretty basic, huh?"

"It's not the Cormorant, that's for sure." Kayla tried to smile. She winced and put a couple fingers to her cut and swollen lip. "They won't even give me an aspirin."

"The Cormorant? Have you stayed there?" Her heart thudded then went back to normal. Memories of her many trysts with Rob Mickelson at the fancy, downtown Portland hotel caused

Liv to do her own wincing.

"Only once." Kayla shrugged. "Some clients from the club invited me and a couple other girls to party with them. Basketball players. They had a limo. They'd booked the penthouse suite for the weekend. It was, um, wild." Kayla's voice and eyes drifted away. Her shoulders slumped.

"Have you spoken with your mother?" Liv asked.

"She's coming to see me tomorrow. Her friend's gonna give her a ride." Kayla's voice cracked. "I don't know how I'm going to face her. She must be so ashamed of me, so disappointed."

"Disappointed maybe. Ashamed? I don't know about that."

Kayla's face scrunched as she turned toward Liv and folded her legs into a criss-cross on the bed. "Of course she's embarrassed! I was supposed to go to college, get my degree, and become a teacher. Instead I'm a stripper in rehab. I screwed up everything. All my plans. All her plans."

"You made some mistakes."

"Big mistakes!"

"Okay, yes, big mistakes." Liv agreed. "But that doesn't mean you can't do better in the future. You have your entire life ahead of you."

"I'm young and stupid, you mean." Kayla's voice was bitter.

"Not stupid." Liv took a deep breath. "And guess what? Even when you aren't so young anymore, you're going to make mistakes. We all do. What's important is that you learn from your mistakes and do better the next time." Liv grimaced. "Unfortunately, life keeps handing you different situations all the time. Gives you plenty of opportunity to screw up again. You aren't the only one, trust me."

Kayla met her eyes. They shimmered with unshed tears. She whispered, "Thank you."

The nurse returned and informed Kayla her group session was starting. Kayla stood. She followed the nurse from the room but turned and looked over her shoulder and gave Liv a little smile and a wave.

Liv waved back. Satisfaction created a little glow in her chest. She didn't know for sure that Kayla would end up having a decent life—that would be up to Kayla—but because of Liv she had a chance. It felt good.

She exited the building and stepped into the warm afternoon sun. Just as she reached her car, a voice called to her from the next row. "So, Lively, you got messed up in another one of our cases. You sure are a pesky P.I."

Colin Snow always popped up at the weirdest moments. Liv pushed her sunglasses up her nose as he walked toward her. "How've you been, Agent?"

"Oh, you know. Sleepless nights. Long stakeouts. Tons of paperwork." One corner of Colin Snow's mouth turned up. "I miss your chamomile tea."

"Celestial Seasonings, my friend. You can find it at any supermarket." She put a hand on her hip. "We seem to be running into each other a lot. Is that a coincidence?"

"What else would it be?"

"Why didn't you say hi at the gallery the other night?"

"I did. Didn't you catch my wave?"

"You know what I mean."

"Let's just say I wanted to keep a low profile."

Liv's eyebrows shot up. "Oooh, intrigue. What's going on there? Art forging ring? Money laundering operation?"

"You know I can't tell you that. It's good to see you, though. You look great." The compliment and his admiring gaze sent a tremor rippling across her stomach. "Want to go somewhere and grab a bite? Drinks and an early dinner?"

Liv shook her head. "Tempting, but I can't."

"You're still with the doc then." His voice was bland but the sharp look in his eyes betrayed his keen interest.

"Actually, no."

"Then he's still an idiot."

Liv grinned. He'd said that once before, months ago, when

she'd needed to hear it. "We just didn't work out. Not that it's any of your business."

"I wouldn't mind making it my business." The gleam in his hooded eyes set off another ripple. "I'm in town for the next couple of days. If you change your mind about dinner or a drink, here's my card." He held it out.

"I have one already." She wasn't about to admit she had his digits memorized.

"I have a new phone number."

"Well, Agent, if you insist." She plucked it from his fingers and, with a sly look, tucked it into her bra.

He put a hand to his heart and said, "Ooh, you're killing me, Lively."

"I think you'll live."

"Oh, I almost forgot this." He gave her that little crooked smile that never failed to set off a little quake in her nether area, and reached into his jacket pocket. She caught the gold and black case he flipped toward her. "You're welcome."

He turned and walked toward his SUV, a bounce in his step and a whistle on his lips. The man, she thought, was much too charming for his own good. Or hers.

"Thank you, Colin," she whispered, feeling strangely light and happy, as she tucked the Chanel lipstick into her bag.

Chapter Forty-One

• • • • • • • • • • • • • •

Several days later, Liv exited the looming brick edifice that housed the downtown law offices of Scarlett, Dean, & Brace and headed toward the waterfront. She'd met with Gordon Brace, one of the founding partners, about investigating a defendant's background in a big medical malpractice case.

They wanted any dirt she could dig up: personal, medical, financial, legal, online history, and political leanings. The works in other words. Up until now they'd used her for process service work. This felt like a step to the next level professionally.

All her hard work had begun to pay off, she thought. She strode down Pearl Street, head high, a smile lifting the corner of her mouth as she made her way back to where she'd parallel parked the Corolla. It was all coming together. Except for hiring a new assistant.

Two days ago, she'd given Marion a parting bonus and wished her all the best.

"Let's stay in touch," Liv had said. "I know you'll rock law school, but if you ever change your mind, there's always a place for you at Lively Investigations. I mean it. In the meantime, I'm thinking drinks at the Arrow & Song should be a regular thing."

Marion gave her a brief hug. "I'll hold you to that, you know."

Liv hugged her back. "Good. And if you ever need my help, with anything, call me."

"I will. Thanks for everything, Liv. See you later."

As Liv made her way toward her car, a chilly breeze skittered up the narrow street from the water. She shivered and buttoned the red wool coat she wore over a navy Long Wharf Supply Co. sweater and dark jeans. The day had gone gray, the overcast sky threatening afternoon showers. The screeching of a seagull reminded her of the crows at Duckbill Pond and then, of course, Alice's staring eyes.

The Maine State Police were closing the case. She'd been sure she'd been on the right track with The Golden Triangle angle, but ultimately that theory didn't pan out. Like Van, Anthony and Leo Zee provided solid alibis for their whereabouts the night of the murder.

She knew she should let the case go—what good could come of worrying it to death?—but something seemed off. She just couldn't put her finger on it.

What did she know? One, Alice and Alby had been collaborating on a book manuscript based on her research at The Golden Triangle. They had supposedly argued the evening Alice was killed, providing motive and opportunity. But Liv suspected the so-called argument she'd witnessed had been a scene re-enacted from Alice's novel, not an actual conflict.

Two, the night she was murdered, Alice sneaked out to the woods to make a telephone call to Kayla—aka Ivy—because the phone lines were still down due to that afternoon's thunderstorm. Later that night someone—presumably Alby—stabbed her in the kitchen.

Three, after committing the gruesome crime, an intoxicated Alby packed all his belongings and fled the scene, possibly attempting to get into Canada unnoticed. Out of control, he'd driven his car off a logging road into a ravine, accidentally killing himself with a blow to the head.

Liv shivered and stuck her hands in the pockets of her coat. Her thoughts circled back to the question of Alby and Alice's relationship. Certainly, Alby Ferguson had means and opportunity to kill his sister-in-law, but the motive remained murky. Had they been lovers? It's what Van had hired her to find out, and she still couldn't say for sure. Why would he kill her? The question of motive gnawed at her, a tiny insect boring into her brain.

If not Alby and not the Zees, who else might have a reason to kill Alice? Or in a fit of passion or jealousy might lose control and commit the unthinkable, horrific act?

Two names popped into her mind. Van, the suspicious husband, and Emsley, the jilted wife. But the police had Van's video alibi for the night in question, and she assumed the detectives had likewise cleared Emsley as a suspect.

This was silly, she scolded herself. The police know what they're doing. Karina Briggs said they had forensic evidence. *Let it go and move on!*

Deciding she could use a bowl of steaming seafood chowder, Liv continued on past the Corolla and emerged onto Commercial Street not far from Gilbert's Chowder House. She entered the warm and cozy space hung with fishing nets and ships wheels and other waterfront kitsch but decided to sit outside. She chose a gray picnic table on the patio and ordered chowder served in a bread bowl and a Shipyard Pumpkinhead in honor of the season. The server brought the beer.

Liv raised it to her lips and stared at the water. Seaweed floated here and there. Lobster buoys hung on gray-painted wharf-side walls and someone had stacked lobster traps of various colors behind nearby buildings.

Seagulls screeched and wheeled over the wharves sticking out into Casco Bay near the ferry terminal. Once upon a time, the Portland waterfront had a whiff of fish guts and catered to the calloused-handed crews of fishing vessels who plied their trade for long hours and then drank in dive bars up and down Commercial Street.

This was before Liv's time, of course, but the history lingered, and the city had protected, somewhat, the "real" working waterfront while also catering to the development of hotels, condos, chi-chi retail shops, touristy places, and pricey restaurants.

Still, authentic places like Gilbert's hung on. Liv loved it all—high-end, low-end, and everything in between. She loved her city. She loved her Munjoy Hill neighborhood, gentrified now, but retaining a certain character in its architecture.

The server brought the soup bowl along with a plastic spoon and packet of oyster crackers. Liv spooned a chunk of haddock into her mouth. A couple at the next table argued about who would pay the bill.

Money, Liv thought. People were always arguing about money. Worrying about it, figuring out who had more of it, calculating how to get more for themselves. She wasn't immune. She'd agreed to take Van's case because he'd offered her cash. A lot of cash. Particularly a lot of cash for a man who had been out of work for eight months.

She spooned up another chunk of potato and fish but hesitated as something Kayla told her rose to the surface of her mind. Confiding in Kayla in order to get her to answer questions for her novel, Alice said she wanted to write and publish a book because she *needed to make money.*

Liv lowered the spoon into the chowder. When Donovan hired her, he'd lied to her about his job. When she'd caught him loading furniture into his dog-walker's pickup, he'd told her that refurbishing and selling vintage and antique furniture online was a hobby, something to keep him occupied between professional jobs.

But what if he actually needed the money? What if Alice and Donovan Ferguson had been on the verge of bankruptcy or losing their house? What if he'd gone to Alby for a loan, knowing he often invested in businesses, and Alby, always competitive, had refused? And then Alby had seen Alice and Alby together and suspected they were having an affair. How angry would that make a man? Angry enough to kill?

Out on Casco Bay, a ferry sounded its horn, and she stared into the distance watching the seagulls swirl above a fishing boat's wake. The sound brought her back to reality. Maybe she'd been reading too many true crime novels and Scottish historical romances. Whatever story she was making up in her head, it didn't fit the facts. Van had been at home in Portland the entire night Alice had been killed. He'd walked Busterdoodle at midnight, caught on his neighbor's security camera, investigated and confirmed by the police.

Which brought her right back around to Alice and Alby and their supposed affair.

She sipped her beer and thought of all the reasons people cheated on their spouses, all the reasons married couples split up. If Van and Alice had been struggling financially, that would have put a strain on their relationship. Wanting to start a family and frustrated with Van's lack of employment, Alice may have decided to trade up, turning her affections to her wealthy, attractive, and recently-divorced brother-in-law.

Liv rotated her shoulders, easing the sudden tightness in them. This was crazy, thinking about a dead case when she had other, paying, jobs to work on. Still, those loose ends bothered her. For her own peace of mind, Liv needed closure. If she could find someone other than Van to confirm that Alice and Alby had been sleeping together—just one person who knew Alice's intentions in Carry Over—she'd put the case out of her mind for good.

Who would know something like that about Alice?

Liv pulled out her phone and logged onto Alice's social media. Once again, she scanned the bland photos, the silly memes, the random recipes. As she'd remembered, Alice hadn't interacted with many friends, at least online. Liv blew out a frustrated breath and moved her thumb to close the app. At the last second, her eyes fell on Alice's employment link, and she paused, thumb hovering.

For the first time, it occurred to her that Alice might have talked to one of her co-workers about her marital problems. At

NIGHT MOVES · 271

this stage, she figured it couldn't hurt to ask.

Warmed by the chowder and beer, she paid her bill and left Gilbert's, heading toward Preble Street where Alice's employer, Immigration Empowerment for Women, rented office space. As she strode past the Old Port's trendy retail stores, bars, and restaurants on her way up the hill toward Congress, she felt a tingle of excitement, the thrill of the hunt. If she hadn't been so distracted by The Golden Triangle connection, she might have thought to do this sooner.

The Immigration Empowerment for Women office on Preble Street was housed in a three-story, gray stone building with many windows and a decorative cornice. One of the city's major homeless shelters was nearby, and a few unhoused people loitered on the corner, huddled against the damp, chilly wind. Liv pushed the door open, entered the building, and jogged the stairs to the second floor. A receptionist greeted her with a welcoming, if quizzical smile. "Good afternoon. How can I help you?"

"I'm hoping to speak to someone who worked with Alice Ferguson."

The woman looked startled. "Oh. Well, what is this about?"

"I'm a private detective and friend of the family. I'm trying to answer a few questions about the time leading up to Alice's death. Is there someone I can talk to?"

"Hold on. Let me check."

The woman picked up the phone and spoke in hushed tones. She replaced the receiver. "Ms. Stamos will be out in a minute. If you don't mind waiting…" She pointed to three chairs clustered around a small table.

Liv nodded. "Thank you." She took a seat and looked out the tall windows at the street below.

"Hello? I heard you wanted to ask some questions about Alice." A pleasant-faced woman in her early to mid-forties approached. She wore a cream linen smock over black leggings and a pair of red Dansko clogs. Honey-colored hair swung to her shoulders.

Liv jumped to her feet and introduced herself. "I'm Olivia Lively. As I told your receptionist, I'm a private detective looking for some answers regarding Alice's state of mind prior to her death. I promise I won't take too much of your time."

"I'm Reesa Stamos. Actually, I saw you at the funeral. I can't tell you how upset we are about what happened to Alice. Everyone loved her here. She made a big impact on the community and our clients."

Liv noticed the receptionist listening from the front desk. "Can we go somewhere more private to talk?"

"Sure. Come to my office. This way."

Reesa led Liv past a couple of doors and ushered her into a small cubby of an office. She sat behind the basic desk, and Liv took the chair in front of it. Liv noticed a nameplate with Reesa's name followed by the letters LCSW. "So you're a social worker, like Alice?" Liv asked.

"Yes. We started at IEW the same week. I'd been working for the state for a few years, and she was just out of her master's degree program. Like me, Alice was a case manager, helping our clients navigate the systems: housing, employment, food assistance, and legal support. Everyone loved her." Reesa took a deep breath. "It's impossible to believe that she's gone, and no one has told us anything about what happened."

"Just to be clear, I'm a private detective. I'm not with the police or any other law enforcement agency. I became involved as a favor to the family. *Before* Alice's death."

She swallowed a lump that rose to her throat. For some reason she found herself wanting to open up to Alice's colleague. "Actually, I'm the one who discovered her body. The whole thing is haunting me."

Reesa's expression softened with pity. "You found Alice? I'm sorry. That must have been awful. What do you need to know?"

Chapter Forty-Two

• • • • • • • • • • • • • •

"Did Alice ever talk to you about her marriage?"

Silence fell over the room. The ticking of a small analog clock on Reesa's desk filled the space. "We told each other things in confidence." Reesa fell silent again. She looked down. Cleared her throat.

"Take your time," Liv said.

Reesa looked up with a sad smile. "I'm sorry. This is hard, talking about her like this." She tucked a strand of blonde hair behind her ear. "I don't suppose it matters now, but I feel as if I'm betraying her."

"I understand. It's awful what happened to her. I'd like to find out why someone would brutally cut her life short, and I'm thinking she might want someone to know the whole truth of what transpired, even if it can't bring her back."

"She would. That sounds like Alice." Reesa nodded. "To answer your question, yes, she talked about her marriage. Quite a bit, in fact. She didn't have a lot of friends, not close friends, and I think she felt safe sharing that part of her life with me. She knew I'd be discreet."

"What did she say?"

"Things were definitely not good. Not for the last few years, anyway. After her husband lost his job, things got even worse."

"Not good in what way?"

"He—her husband—was always after her to quit her job.

Because she was smart and well-educated, he thought she should pursue a more lucrative career. Alice loved her work. She enjoyed meeting new people, helping them find employment and navigate the healthcare and welfare systems, and finding after-school programs and daycare for the kids. She listened, she empathized, and she knew the ropes inside and out. She was sharp and caring and effective. Really good at her job. It bothered her that her husband didn't appreciate or value what she did."

"Did they argue about it?"

"I suppose they did. She mentioned 'discussions' and 'angry words' a few times. Nothing physical or anything like that. I asked her once if he was emotionally abusive, and she hesitated before saying no it wasn't like that. She told me he had issues with his family and felt less-than in comparison to his brother, and she thought he felt pressured to prove he was successful, too."

That sounds like Van, Liv thought. "You said it got worse when he lost his job? How so?"

"Oh, just more pressure, I guess. Money got tight, and he kept bugging her to find a better-paying job. He threatened to sell their house, but Alice had her heart set on raising a family there. That's when Alice got the idea to write and sell books online under a pen name. She started researching how to make money self-publishing steamy romance novels."

"Did she say Van was on board with this venture?"

Reesa made a face. "She didn't tell him. It was a secret. She wanted to prove she could do it first. She ran into some trouble, though…"

"What kind of trouble?"

"Well, I'm not exactly clear on the details, but she said she wanted to publish her own books. Do it right."

"What did she mean by that, do you know?"

"It had to be a *real* business, she said. There would be start-up costs. She couldn't use money in the accounts she shared with her husband, so she went to his brother to ask for a loan. It had to be super secret because of the way Donovan felt about him."

Liv sat forward. "Alby Ferguson gave Alice a loan?"

Reesa shrugged. "Sort of. She said he wanted to be an investor in the business, which meant he'd own part of it. I think she regretted it because afterward she complained about how her brother-in-law wouldn't leave her alone. He demanded to be involved in everything, including the book she was writing. He convinced her to write actual erotica, not regular romance. He told her he'd done the market research, and it would be the best way to break in."

Liv's mind whirled. This sounded like the action of a control freak. Control was a big factor in homicides, especially sexual homicides. She said, "This fits with what we already know about Alice's murder. Go on."

"Okay, so he even wanted to write the books *with* her, like a co-author. He didn't trust her to do a good job by herself and it stressed her out. But what could she do? He was financing the whole thing. He started pressuring her to hurry up and finish the first book so they could move forward."

Pieces of the puzzle began to fit together in Liv's mind. "Do you think Alice and Alby were having an affair?"

The other woman's eyebrows shot up. Her hair swung as she emphatically shook her head. "Alice and her brother-in-law? No way. Alice loved Donovan despite everything. That's why she wanted to make the publishing business work." Reesa tucked the wayward strand of hair again. "That, and she desperately wanted to have a baby. Another problem between her and Donovan, actually."

"He didn't want kids?"

"Oh, I think he did, but Alice said he had some, uh, issues in that department." Reesa looked embarrassed.

A profile of Van started to form in her mind. Low self-esteem. Employment problem. Frustration over finances. Sibling rivalry. Possible impotence.

She put her fingers to her temples. "Hold on a sec," she said. She ran through the scenario in her mind. Donovan pressures Alice to quit a job she loves so she can make more money. He's let go from the engineering firm and loses his confidence. She's trying to get pregnant, but now he can't perform. Then, he tells her he's going to sell the house she loves. He's too proud to ask his family for help. Her life's falling apart.

Thinking money will solve all their problems, she gets the idea to write and sell romance novels. To do it right, she needs to write fast and she needs start-up money. She asks Alby to finance the venture. As a seasoned angel investor, he agrees, but only if she makes him a partner. He then insists they work on the first manuscript together.

Alice and Alby conduct research at The Golden Triangle. Alice meets Kayla and tries to help her leave the club and go back to school. Alice and Alby decide to complete their first book over a two-week period at the family chalet. Van, believing his wife and brother-in-law are having an affair, hires Liv to investigate. She agrees.

Something goes terribly wrong. Alice ends up dead. And Alby does, too.

Liv let her hands fall to her lap. "This is seriously messed up."

Reesa looked thoughtful. "You know, when people saw Alice, they thought she had it all. A handsome, well-off husband from a good family. A beautiful house in an exclusive neighborhood on the coast. Access to Portland's social and art communities. But she had real problems to deal with. It wasn't easy for her. And then..."

"And then she ends up murdered."

Reesa nodded, hanging her head. Her hair fell around her face. She swiped at tears on her cheeks and raised her head. "Do they know who did it?"

"They think they do. And after what you've told me, I think they're probably right."

"It was her brother-in-law, right?"

"I can't say for sure," Liv said, "but I'm sure the police will make a statement soon." She gathered her bag and stood. "Thank you so much for sharing all this, Ms. Stamos. It's helped me to see the bigger picture."

"Actually, I think I needed to talk about it. Alice's death has been weighing on my mind, too. I miss her a lot. She was a good person."

Liv held out a business card. "If you think of anything else, or if you ever need a private investigator for anything, business or personal, give me a call. I'll be happy to help."

Reesa waved Liv's card and smiled. "I might hit you up for a donation or something when we have our next fundraiser."

Liv smiled back. "Do that."

With a final good-bye, she left Reesa in her office and made her way back to the street.

As she walked to the parking garage where she'd left her car, questions swirled in her mind.

Had Alice really expected to make money publishing her own romance novels? Why hadn't she told Donovan about her business plans? Was she afraid he wouldn't support her and would, instead, pressure her to find a more lucrative job? Or was she afraid she'd fail?

She recalled her conversation with Van in her office the day he hired her. Alice had, in fact, told him she was going to the chalet to write. His attitude while disclosing this fact to Liv had been dismissive. She'd even called him on it. He'd made some comment about how he was a good husband.

But was he?

Considering what Reesa told her, Alice most likely believed Van wouldn't support her new venture. Liv knew how it felt to have a dream, to have a burning desire to build something of your own.

She also knew how it felt when the people closest to you didn't support your ambitions. Her parents didn't. They considered her choice of career a failure on their part. And hers. Even Jasper, nice guy though he was, undervalued Lively Investigations not only as her means of making a living but also as her passion.

Everything that had happened since Donovan Ferguson walked

into her office highlighted the same problem women faced—no matter what their class, race, or marital status. Even in this more enlightened era, certain hypocrisies permeated society and impacted a woman's relationships, careers, ambitions, and ability to reach her full potential.

Society had improved, yes, and many women built impressive careers. They started multi-million-dollar companies and amazing brands, and they somehow managed to "have it all"—at least from the outside looking in.

But even in the 21st century, women paid a price for their successes.

Marriages failed. Children and career sucked energy and time, leaving little in reserve for personal growth and pleasure. In general, men didn't sacrifice as much of their work and personal lives and interests for child-rearing as women, and those who did, well, society acted as if they deserved a medal for it. Women, on the other hand, faced scrutiny and criticism, either for not putting enough time and energy into her children or her career.

The Mommy Wars raged on.

Look at Ashleigh and Trevor, she mused. Both wanted children, but only one quit her job to raise them. This person happened to be the one whose body incubated the babies, nourished them, grew them from her own bones and blood. Because of biology, women would *always* end up giving more in service to the miraculous—creating new life out of nothing but a few random cells floating in some gooey fluids.

And men—having no *actual* power over reproduction and resenting women because of it—invented rules that *gave them* power over women's bodies and fertility.

All over the world, every single day, women and girls were forced into marriage, forced into sexual servitude, forced to endure pregnancies they didn't want or seek, and forced to give birth to babies they didn't want because some man, unable to tolerate a woman's one power greater than his, made a law.

In Liv's opinion, if a woman decided to prioritize her career over her relationships, to put herself and her dreams first rather than subsume them to society's expectations, she should not feel guilty. Having babies demanded incredible sacrifice of mind, body, and spirit. That's why it should be the woman's choice. Always.

This, Liv realized, was what Jasper couldn't grasp. She might have loved him. She gave herself credit for opening herself up to the possibility of love and a close relationship, but it was okay that the relationship ended.

The traditional marriage and life he envisioned appealed to some women. She didn't blame them for wanting it. It just wasn't what *she* wanted.

She simply didn't recognize herself in the role he wanted her to fill.

With this sudden clarity of insight, she straightened her shoulders and strode down the Portland streets feeling lighter and calmer than she had in days.

As she drove toward her office, she contemplated Van, Alice, Alby and their tangled resentments and desires. After what she'd learned, she was satisfied that Alby and Alice's weird, secret relationship had been about finances and writing, not sex. Somehow, it ended in tragedy.

Whether arguing about money, the book, or her reaction to his meddling in her writing process, Alby lost his temper, grabbed a knife from the block, and killed Alice. Or maybe he'd actually fallen in love with her and, rebuffed, struck out.

Van had said it once. Alby didn't like to lose.

She took the I-295 on-ramp and headed to Pellham to talk to Van about what she'd learned. They'd probably never know for sure what happened that night in Carry Over, but Van deserved to know the truth. Alice had loved *him*, not Alby. Maybe knowing Alice had remained faithful, at least sexually, would give him some peace.

And she'd be able to put the case behind her.

Chapter Forty-Three

● ● ● ● ● ● ● ● ● ● ● ● ● ●

By the time she reached Pellham, the clouds opened up in earnest releasing a deluge of pent-up rain. The wipers on the Corolla thwapped back and forth at a frantic pace as Liv turned onto Van's street.

As she neared the driveway, she noticed Van walking Busterdoodle. They trudged through the rain, Buster straining at the leash and Van head-down.

Idly, she noticed he wasn't limping much. In fact, he wasn't limping at all. He had one hand in the pocket of his raincoat, hood up, water dripping off the edge in a steady stream. She tapped her horn and waved. He looked up, and something about the face peering out from beneath the hood of the raincoat seemed wrong. A weird feeling washed over her.

She signaled and turned into Van's driveway to wait.

Keeping an eye on man and dog in her rearview mirror, she rehearsed what she'd say to her old childhood friend. A rap on the window startled her.

A dark, looming figure stood close to her door. She tensed, heart thudding, as a tall man bent to peer into her window.

When she saw who it was, she twisted in her seat to look out the back window at Busterdoodle and the person walking him.

If Van was standing beside her car, who was that walking the dog?

Feeling disoriented, she turned back to face the window and Van's smiling face. Making a shooing motion with her hand, she swung open the door and stepped out. She punched him on the arm. "You nearly gave me a heart attack!"

Van, dressed in dark wool pants and a dark-gray sweater, held an umbrella in one hand. He grasped her elbow with the other. "I spotted you from the living room window. This is a nice surprise. Come inside before you get wet."

They walked toward the open mudroom door. Rain pattered on the umbrella above them. "Wait a minute," Liv said. She stopped and peered toward the end of the driveway. "Who's that walking Busterdoodle? I thought it was you!"

Van glanced back. "Oh, that's Travis. He took Buster to the dog park this afternoon. Come on inside, and I'll open a bottle of wine." He deposited the dripping umbrella in a stand in the mudroom and led her into the kitchen. "Your timing is impeccable. I was just making osso buco. Maybe I can entice you to stay for dinner."

As they entered the kitchen, the rich scent of meat, onions, tomato, and spices made her mouth water. "It smells delicious. Since when have you been such a gourmet cook?"

"There's a lot you don't know about me. I'm a total disciple of Giada De Laurentiis." Van crossed to the built-in wine rack near the refrigerator and pulled a bottle from a space near the top. "This is a nice Dolcetto. I think it will pair nicely with the beef. Have a seat." Standing behind the kitchen island, he pointed at the blue and gold bar stools on the opposite side.

She watched as he uncorked the bottle, snagged glasses, and poured a couple inches into each. She lifted hers. "Salute," she said.

"To friendship," he replied. They clinked their glasses together. There was something watchful in his eyes despite the casual expression on his face, the friendly smile. She opened her mouth to bring up the subject of Alice when she heard commotion in the mudroom.

Busterdoodle barreled into the kitchen. He tore around the room greeting Liv and Van, water dripping off his curly coat. Liv laughed and brushed at her jeans. "He's full of it today."

Having shed the rain gear in the mudroom, Travis appeared with a grubby-looking towel in his hands. As Buster trotted past him, Travis grabbed the dog's collar and proceeded to rub the towel over his coat while Buster trembled with repressed energy. "Sorry, dude," Travis said. "Almost done."

When he was finished, Travis threw the towel over his shoulder and hooked a thumb toward the door. "Thanks for letting me use your gear, man," he said to Van. "You were right about the rain."

"No problem," Van said as they all watched Buster pick up a braided toy and shake it like a maniac. "Did he behave at the park?"

"Yeah, he was chill. I'll see you tomorrow, right?"

"If you could be here by ten that would be great."

"I got you." Travis nodded at Liv. "Nice to see you again."

"You, too," she said, voice faint. Until this moment, she hadn't realized that Van and Travis were nearly the same height and weight. Travis, however, was ten years younger, wore his longish hair in that sexy man-bun, and didn't have a gimp knee. She sneaked a look at the tattoos on Travis's muscled arms. He wore a loose white tee-shirt with a pair of aged, ragged jeans and work boots. Totally hot, in a Kevin Bacon in *Footloose* kind of way.

Forget Alby, Liv thought. *If I'd been Alice, I might have gone for the dog sitter.*

She sipped her wine and watched Travis as he strolled to the mudroom and disappeared. She let out a little sigh, and a moment later she heard one of the garage doors rattle. "Is my car in the way?" she asked Van.

"No, you're fine. He can swing around you."

If only, Liv thought and then felt guilty for objectifying the poor guy.

Standing between the island and the stove, Van turned to check the food. He grabbed a pair of tongs, and when he lifted the lid on a large ceramic pot, fragrant steam puffed into the air. He flipped the meat and replaced the lid. "It'll be another hour or so. Want to listen to some music?"

"Sure."

He punched some buttons on his phone and the smooth notes of a saxophone filled the room. "Nice choice," she said as he refreshed her wine glass. "Jazz is perfect for a rainy afternoon."

She'd been listening to Ella Fitzgerald ever since the breakup, but she didn't mention that to Van. She wasn't here to talk about her love life. She needed to tell him what she'd learned about Alice and Alby. If only she could figure out how to broach the subject.

Buster flung his toy and chased it, skidding on the tile floor and landing on his butt, and then looking up at them, goofy and embarrassed. Liv laughed. "Guess he still has plenty of energy even after his playdate." She wondered about something and decided to ask, if only to put off the more uncomfortable conversation. "I don't know much about dog ownership. You hire Travis to walk him even when you're home?"

"Sometimes. If I'm working on a piece of furniture and don't have time to do it myself. Plus Buster loves him, and Travis enjoys spending time with him. Those two have formed a kind of a mutual admiration society. Alice used to joke about it."

Van leaned a hip against the counter across from her and picked up his wine. He looked handsome and comfortable in this setting, not the band geek she remembered from high school. Yet, she realized, inside the man that awkward and insecure boy still pulled the strings.

Too bad, she thought, because he had so much going for him. Good looks. Intelligence. Health. Family connections. A college degree. It was a shame he let his resentment and jealousy of his older brother color every other aspect of his life.

"That's cute." Liv glanced at Busterdoodle who began twirling himself in a circle, chasing his tail. She laughed. It might be nice, she thought, to have a dog to greet you at the end of the day—no expectations beyond a bowl of chow, a few minutes of play, and a run in the rain.

Her thoughts jumped to Jasper and the little mutt he wanted

to name Fox Hounderson Mulder. She didn't want the man, but suddenly the dog didn't seem like a horrible idea. Except for her weird work hours. That's where a tall and tattooed dog walker came in. "Does Travis ever dog-sit overnight?"

Van's expression turned wary. "He has a couple of times when I've had to be away overnight. Why? Are you thinking of getting a dog?"

"Maybe," she said. "My latest ex-boyfriend wanted us to get one, but I'm not sure I'm a dog person."

Van expression smoothed. "Come over and visit Buster and me anytime. I bet he'll win you over. I can hook you up with the breeder whenever you're ready."

As if he understood, Buster trotted over and sat beside Liv's stool. She reached down to scratch behind one of his ears. "You're a good boy, aren't you, Buster?"

Buster thumped his tail.

Van grinned. "He likes you."

She slumped on her stool, put her chin in her hand. "Maybe I should forget men and get a dog instead. My troubles would be over."

"Oh, come on! We aren't all that bad. We don't bring in fleas. We don't roll in stinky stuff on the lawn. We don't need to be walked in the middle of the night."

"That's nothing compared to emotional blackmail, mommy issues, and weird sexual hangups." She twirled her wine glass. "Like Renee Russo's character says in *The Thomas Crown Affair*, 'Men make women messy.'"

Van pretended to wince. "You women are hard to please sometimes."

Liv knew he was joking but felt a spurt of anger just the same. She frowned, remembering what Reesa had told her about Van's and Alice's troubles in the bedroom and his pressuring her to bring in more money and threatening to sell the home she loved. Now he was joking about how *women* expected too much?

She played with the stem of her glass. "I'm sorry I showed up this afternoon without calling first. I wanted to tell you something." She hesitated. "Before I do, can I ask you a question?"

"Shoot."

"When you were laid off, how did Alice handle it? I mean, she must have felt some pressure as the sole income earner."

Van's face paled. He answered, cautiously choosing his words. "She was, uh, supportive at first, but then things between us got… tense. Like I told you. She began pushing me away. I—I think that's when started her affair with Alby, but I can't, uh, say for sure."

Except she hadn't, Liv thought. *At least not according to Reesa.*

The wind picked up outside, slashing raindrops against the windows as the skies darkened into evening. "About that. I did some further investigating into Alice and Alby's relationship. I wanted to tie up loose ends for you now that the police are wrapping up their investigation."

Van tensed. "And?"

"Alice wasn't sleeping with your brother." She studied his reaction. He looked confused and then angry. A vein throbbed in his neck. She said quickly, "I talked to someone Alice confided in. She was pretty sure."

"Listen, Liv. I don't care what that person told you. They're wrong."

Liv stilled, hearing the harshness in his voice. She stared at him as he spoke.

He continued, "Alby was there, in Carry Over. With Alice. At the chalet. You told me yourself. You saw them. At the store. At the chalet that night. Arguing. What other explanation could there be?"

She reached out and put her hand over his. "I'm so sorry. I know it's hard to talk about, but there's more. I have proof Alice was writing up there in Carry Over, like she told you. A book, in fact. What she didn't tell you is she also wanted to start her own self-publishing company."

Van's fingers twitched beneath hers. "No. No, she didn't."

"Turns out Alby was financing her start-up." Liv withdrew her hand and wrapped her fingers once more around the stem of her glass. "They were working together, not sleeping together. According to my source, Alice loved you. She wanted to do this for you. For both of you. "

"That's why he met her at the chalet? For business? That's a stretch." A funny, almost sly look crossed his face. "Why did he kill her, do you think?"

Liv felt a sudden tremor of unease in her gut. She chalked it up to the trauma of discovering Alice's body. That horrible knife.

She said, "Someone else told me that Alby tended to be intrusive when he invested in businesses. Maybe Alice wanted his money but not his advice. Maybe she told him to leave and they argued. Maybe he bullied her, she fought back, and he snapped. I don't think we'll ever know exactly what happened or why, but the police are closing the case, and I'm doing the same. I don't think there's anything left to uncover."

Van's hand trembled as he wiped it across his mouth. "Okay. Okay," he mumbled. "I appreciate everything you've done, Liv. I still want to pay you what I owe you."

"I told you before, I consider us even." She took a sip of wine and watched the rain lash against the windows. After a few moments, she said, "I know it's cold comfort, Van, but Alice loved you. She wanted to build a life with you. She wanted to start a family with you. Now, at least, you can lay your suspicions to rest and begin to move on."

Van flushed. His voice went rough and harsh. "Really, Liv? Is that what you think? That I'll move *on*?"

Liv recoiled as Van glared at her, his face a mask of pain and something that looked a lot like rage.

Chapter Forty-Four

• • • • • • • • • • • • • •

Van shuddered and swayed. Alarmed, Liv set her wine down on the counter. "Are you okay? You don't look so good."

He rubbed his mouth with a trembling hand. She noticed how his wedding band gleamed, catching the lights above the kitchen island. "I was so sure," he said. "It was killing me, the thought of the two of them going at it behind my back. I hoped I was wrong, but then you called me and said you saw them together at the chalet. It seemed so obvious they were having an affair. Even you thought so, right?"

"I don't know what to say, Van. I told you I couldn't say for sure. There wasn't anything definitive."

"I know. Of course you did. Yes." Tears tracked down his face. He palmed them away with an impatient gesture. His face reddened. "This is just… It's too much."

Liv, heart breaking for her friend, walked around the island. She stood behind him, put her arms around him, held him tight. "It's okay. It's all over now. You know the truth."

He shrugged out of her arms and put some distance between them.

"I'm sorry. Do you want me to go?" she asked.

"No. I'll be okay in a minute." He shuddered again. "Sometimes I feel like my skin's crawling. My doctor says it's anxiety. It will pass. Stay for dinner. Unless you have other plans. I shouldn't assume. It seems to get me in trouble."

"I don't have any plans." She picked up the bottle of wine. "A little more of this, don't you think?"

"Definitely."

A nose prodded her knee. She looked down at Busterdoodle and ran her hand along his curly, beige head. His fur was still damp. She looked into his bright, light-brown eyes.

A dog might be nice. Even if I have to walk him in the rain.

She scratched behind one floppy ear, and Buster leaned his head into her palm. Funny how she'd mistaken Travis for Van earlier. In Van's rain jacket and hood, from a distance, Travis looked just like her friend. Except for the limp. No wonder she'd just about had a heart attack when Van knocked on her window.

She smiled, but then she remembered about the storm that rolled over Maine the night Alice was murdered, and her smile faded.

Goosebumps rose on her arms.

What if the person walking the dog hadn't been Van at all? What if it had been Travis in Van's raincoat, hood pulled up shielding his face?

Liv held herself still as Van gathered plates, silverware, and napkins from cupboards and carried them to the table in the breakfast nook. Outside the rain continued to pour, tapping against the window overlooking the yard where Alice imagined her children at play.

She looked down and told herself she must be wrong.

A drop of wine had fallen on the granite countertop. The ruby red Dolcetto looked like blood. She remembered Alice on the floor of the chalet, the blood on her nightgown, the knife sticking out of her chest. It had been raining that night, too.

Her suspicion grew as various facts gathered in her mind like crows nesting at the end of the day in a tall, dark, lonesome pine.

A wicked thunderstorm had ripped through Maine that night. It traveled north to south from Canada, knocking out power and telephone lines in Carry Over, and rumbling its way toward Portland before heading out to sea.

NIGHT MOVES · 289

Anyone near Portland, walking a dog at midnight, would have needed rain gear.

Van and Travis often traded vehicles so Van could deliver furniture he'd sold online.

Travis sometimes stayed with Busterdoodle overnight.

Today, she'd mistaken Travis for Van.

What if it had been Travis, not Van, caught on the neighbor's security camera that night?

She did a quick calculation. From the time she'd phoned Van that afternoon in Carry Over to the next morning when she discovered Alice's body, Van would have had plenty of time to borrow Travis's truck, drive to Carry Over, confront Alice, and return home by the following morning to meet Travis at Dunkin' Donuts.

Van looked over at her. He looked calmer. "Dinner should be ready soon. I'll throw a salad together. Sound good?"

"Great!" She smiled brightly at him even as her stomach turned. "Can I help?"

"I got it. But here." He opened the refrigerator and withdrew a bottle of olives and a tub of feta cheese. He put olives and cubes of cheese in a little blue pottery bowl and slid it toward her. "Take this. There's a box of matches on the table. Why don't you light the candles?"

"Okay." She carried the dish of olives to the table. She found the matches. Soon two dancing flames flickered and reflected off the bay windows. The rain continued to tap-tap-tap along with the jazz. "This is cozy," she said. She popped an olive into her mouth. "I bet Alice appreciated coming home to nice dinners like this."

He shrugged. "To be honest, she wasn't impressed. Like I said, she could be hard to please. After a while, when I lost my job and couldn't find another one right away, she looked at me like I'd failed her. First with tolerance. Then pity. Then disgust. Like I was nothing. She might have loved me, but she wasn't attracted to me anymore. She tried to hide it, I think. But I saw it. Felt it. I told you before, she wouldn't sleep with me."

Liv thought about what Reesa had told her. According to her, the bedroom problem hadn't been Alice. She murmured, "That must have been frustrating."

He brought two plates of salad to the table. "When I saw her and Alby together outside her office, I jumped to conclusions."

He set the plates down hard. Anger flickered in his eyes. "Freaking Alby. Always the golden boy. Always the winner. You know, it doesn't matter that they weren't having an affair. It doesn't change anything. They kept secrets from me. He gave her money behind my back. I bet that made him feel so special. So important. He couldn't even let me take care of my own wife. I would have found another job. We would have worked it out. She didn't need to go running to him for help."

Liv swallowed. "When I called you that afternoon from Carry Over, told you I'd seen them together, you must have been hurt. Angry, too. Like now."

"I suppose so. I don't really remember what I felt. Let's talk about something else and enjoy our meal. I've been eating alone lately. It's a nice change of pace to have company." He pulled out a chair and held it. "Have a seat."

Chapter Forty-Five

• • • • • • • • • • • • • • •

S he sat.

Van stepped to the stove and plated the osso bucco. He carried the steaming plates to the table and slid one in front of her. A spot of sauce stained one of his rolled up shirtsleeves, she noticed. He sat across from her and picked up his fork. "Please," he said. "Tuck in and tell me what you think."

Liv toyed with her food, but she couldn't bring herself to eat. After a moment she put her fork on her plate.

He scrunched his eyebrows together. "Is something wrong?"

She took another moment to gather her thoughts. "Look, Van. We've known each other a long time. You know I'm your friend, right? That I care about you?"

"I do."

"Okay. So please, don't take this the wrong way. Something's been nagging at me ever since I mistook Travis for you this evening." She looked into his eyes. "If I ask Travis if he stayed here with Busterdoodle the night Alice and Alby died, what's his answer going to be?"

Van froze. His eyes darkened. He set his fork and knife against the edge of his plate. "What are you implying?"

"I'm not accusing you of killing Alice. It's just if you *had* switched vehicles with Travis to deliver furniture somewhere that night, wouldn't it be better to come clean to the police?"

Van hung his head. Seconds ticked by as rain pattered against the window. He remained silent.

"Van?"

He sighed. "Okay. I should have known you'd figure it out after you saw Travis walking Buster today. You're right. We'd switched vehicles, and I'd asked him to dog-sit that night because I was delivering an armoire to a customer in a small town an hour north of Bangor that evening. When I got there, the customer asked me to help her lug it to the third floor of her house. The storm rolled in just as I left her place. When I hit Bangor, I decided to hang out in the casino until it passed. I had cash from the sale, I had a few drinks, and I wanted to get my mind off my situation."

Liv watched him carefully. His story sounded plausible, but she couldn't be sure he was telling the truth. Or what she would do if he wasn't.

"One thing led to another, and by the time I left, it was four in the morning. I stopped at Dysart's for breakfast and realized I left my cell phone in the truck, so I used the payphone to call Travis and let him know I was on my way home. He told me he had a morning shift at Dunkin', and we planned to exchange vehicles there. I drove to Dunkin' and switched vehicles with Travis, bought donuts, and went home."

"Why not tell the police all this when they questioned you?"

"I don't know. It was just easier to say I was home. When the neighbor gave the police the video footage and they assumed it was me, it seemed easier to go along with it." He gave her a weird look. "You aren't going to blow my alibi, are you?"

"I think you should contact your family's lawyer and tell him or her everything you just told me. The lawyer can go with you to the police station and make sure you don't implicate yourself when you give your revised statement. I'm sure if you tell the truth, it will all work out. I'm sure the police will be able to corroborate what you've said. Your customer will make a statement. They'll be able to access the security cameras at the casino. There are cameras on the highway and probably at Dysart's too."

He stared at her, his face unreadable. "And what if I don't? What will you do?"

"Please, Van. You dragged me into this. You asked for my help. This is me helping. Do the right thing."

She tensed, waited. She really wanted him to make the best choice and tell the truth. Otherwise, she'd have to. The rain clicked against the windows. Jazz still played softly from the speakers. The candles flickered on the table. The moment stretched, tension so tight it almost hummed.

Buster clicked toward the door and whined. He let out a sharp bark. Then another.

The noise seemed to snap Van from his fugue. "Okay. You're right. That makes sense, calling my lawyer. You're right. I should have told the truth from the beginning. The police have proof Alby killed her, not me, so I don't need to worry, right?"

Liv let out the breath she'd been holding. "The evidence should clear you, yes."

"Okay, this has been a weird night." Van ran a hand over his face. "Why don't you go into the living room. I'll make us some coffee, and then I'll call my guy."

Liv stood. "You're doing the right thing, Van. I promise."

She settled onto the couch. He'd lit a fire in the fireplace, and she watched the flames dance and crackle. A silver frame on top of the mantle displayed a photo from Van and Alice's wedding, a burnt-down candle and a strand of rosary beads next to it. It looked like some kind of altar.

Liv tried to relax, but tension ran like a cord between her shoulder blades, pulling them tight. She wriggled her shoulders, rolled them, rolled her head.

They'd have their coffee, she told herself, and then he'd call his lawyer. She repeated this to herself like a mantra and watched the flames.

After a few minutes, her eyes widened and her head snapped up. She couldn't hear any sounds from the kitchen. No drawers opening. No coffee maker gurgling. Something was wrong. Very wrong.

Just as she sprang to her feet, the dog barked.

She heard a clatter and a thump. She ran to the kitchen and skidded to a stop. Van slumped against the cupboard next to the stove, feet touching the island, head down, eyes focused on his arms.

"What did you do?" Liv cried.

Blood pumped from long slashes on both Van's forearms. Next to him, Buster licked at the blood on the chef's knife.

"Get away from that, Buster!"

Fear and panic bubbled together, and she recognized the beginnings of hysteria, the odd fight or flight response the situation set off in her amygdala. She rushed to Van's side. She pushed Buster away from the knife, picked it up, and threw it on the counter.

Grabbing two dish towels from the handles of the stove, she pressed them against Van's arms, praying they would staunch the bleeding while she called for help. He raised his head, eyes blank and emotionless. "Let... me... die," he said.

"Shut up," she told him. "You aren't dying." She pulled her phone from her back pocket and dialed 911. "I need an ambulance. Pellham." She gave them the address and shoved the phone back into the pocket.

Buster whined and lay down beside Van as Liv pressed hard on the towels. Blood spread across the material. She needed tourniquets to stop the bleeding.

As she stood, she slipped and fell against the island, catching herself with one hand. Pain shot through her wrist, but she ignored it and sprinted to the mudroom. She grabbed Alice's sweater and ran back to the kitchen. Van had closed his eyes, arms resting on top of his legs. Wincing against the pain in her wrist, she first used one sleeve and then the other to tie the material just below each of Van's elbows.

Van slipped into unconsciousness.

She pulled each tourniquet as tight as she could and waited for the ambulance to arrive.

·   ·   ·   ·   ·

After giving her statement to the Maine State Police, she was released. Ashleigh picked her up and took her to the emergency room at Sharon Medical Center where they x-rayed her wrist. Lucky for her, she had a bad sprain, not a break. They wrapped it, gave her a sling, and told her to ice it several times a day.

Ashleigh asked Liv if she wanted her to call anyone—Jasper or her parents.

Liv shook her head. They'd hear about it through the grapevine, no doubt, but she didn't want to deal with any of them tonight. "No. Just take me home, okay?"

They walked into the rain-soaked parking lot. The hard rain had stopped, but a fine drizzle still fell, chilling their faces and dampening their clothes. The air smelled of woodsmoke and ocean. The faint scent of autumn leaves added a poignant layer to the perfume of fall.

"The season's really changing, isn't it?" Liv said. "I guess summer's over for real."

"Couldn't last forever."

"Nothing ever does."

They got into Ashleigh's SUV. When they reached Liv's apartment, Ashleigh sighed, hands on the wheel. "I don't know exactly what happened tonight—I don't need to know, not now anyway—but I'm worried about you, Liv. You keep getting into these weird situations. I sometimes wonder if you don't seek them out on purpose."

"It's my job, Ash. Stuff like this happens. It could have been worse. At least nobody died tonight."

The ambulance had arrived within a few minutes. They rushed

Van to the hospital where he was stitched up and given blood transfusions. Once they had him stabilized, they put him on psychiatric watch to ensure he wouldn't make another suicide attempt.

The police took Liv to the Portland station and sent a team to process the scene while she gave her statement, including her conversation with Van about the events of the night of Alice's murder. She included as many details as she could remember but didn't share any theories, suppositions, or conclusions. She'd let the criminal investigators take it from there.

Ashleigh nodded. "Okay." Her face glowed green from the dashboard lights. She looked as exhausted as Liv felt. "Do you want me to stay the night?"

"No. I appreciate it, but you should get home to Trevor. I'll be okay."

"Are you sure?"

"Positive. I'll call you tomorrow."

"Okay. Love you."

"Love you, too. Drive safe."

Liv got out of the SUV and watched the taillights disappear down the hill. She felt like she'd been punched all over her body, a reaction to the adrenaline, and her wrist throbbed. When she got inside, she changed into a pair of sweatpants and a comfy sweater, took three ibuprofens, and made herself a mug of chamomile and lavender tea.

She turned on her electric fireplace, snuggled beneath a blanket, and picked up the book she'd started up in Carry Over. After a few minutes of staring at the page and absorbing nothing, she set it aside.

Restless, she wandered to the kitchen. She heated the kettle again and sifted through a stack of mail. A business card slid to the floor. Sighing, she bent to pick it up. As she straightened, she studied the card she'd thrown in the mail basket the other day after visiting Kayla at the clinic. She punched the number into her phone.

He answered on the third ring. "Colin Snow."

"Hey, it's Liv. Are you busy?"

She heard him smile. "Not really. What's up, Lively?"

"Are you still in town?"

"Yeah. I am."

"I've had a very strange night. I don't suppose you'd like to come over and hang out for a while? Just to talk or whatever? I could use the company."

He didn't hesitate. "Give me ten minutes. Do you need anything? Food? Drink? I can pick up something on the way."

"No thanks. I have to warn you, I look like some alley cat's leftovers."

She heard him smile. "You'll always look good to me, Lively. I'll see you in a few."

Chapter Forty-Six

• • • • • • • • • • • • • •

Three Weeks Later:

Sitting at her desk, Liv leaned back in her chair and glanced out the window as a few colorful autumn leaves flew past. From her computer, Debussy's *Prelude to the Afternoon of a Faun* wound like a ribbon of sound, playful and soothing at the same time. A few slim file folders rested in a wire holder on her desk along with her computer monitor, a pen holder, and a silver frame holding a photo of the current love of her life.

The desk itself smelled of fresh lemon polish. So did the credenza. She'd painted the walls of her office a bold, turquoise blue and hung several new pieces of bright, colorful art she'd picked up at local galleries. Her philodendron's leaves shone with glossy, healthy leaves. No spider dared to spin a web in the room.

What a difference a couple months made.

Smiling to herself, she hummed along with the music. She shuffled through a new case, making notations on several items for later research, and slid the folder into the wire holder with the others.

Scanning a pink sticky note with a scribbled reminder to pick up her dry cleaning after work today, she crumpled it and tossed it into the trash bin beside her desk. It held only a few similar scraps of paper and an empty Coffee by Design to-go cup. No smelly takeout containers. No biohazards of any sort.

She stood, stretched, and stepped to the coffee maker on the credenza. Six clean Lively Investigations coffee mugs glazed turquoise with yellow lettering sat in perfect order beside a selection of K-cup pods. She found a pumpkin spice cup and inhaled the scent of nutmeg, cinnamon, and cloves as the coffee dripped into the mug.

Carrying the coffee, she opened the door into the reception area. Marion looked up from her computer screen and protested. "I could have made that for you."

"I know." Liv said. She pointed around the mug to a black and gold L'Or Barista Coffee & Espresso maker. "You just want to use the new machine."

Marion grinned. She'd dyed her hair the color of raven's feathers and wore a short, green velvet dress over black Doc Martens. "That's true."

"Have I told you lately how happy I am that you're back?"

Marion's smile widened. "Only about a million times."

Two days after Van's arrest, Marion had walked into the office and asked if the job was still available.

"What about law school?" Liv had asked.

Marion scrunched her face. "Turns out I'm not that interested in studying law. It was just something to do while I worked on my writing. I realized I'd rather work here. I know finances are tight, but if there's any way you could keep me on full-time, I promise I'll work super hard and make it pay off."

"Let me see if I can figure something out."

An idea had formed as soon as Marion left the office.

Liv had pitched the idea to Emsley over dinner at David's restaurant the following evening. The sculptor jumped at the opportunity to invest Alby's Golden Triangle money in Lively Investigations for a ten percent share in the business.

"You're going to turn this agency into a little gold-mine, I just know it," Emsley told her as they sealed the deal over champagne and crème brûlée.

"Are you sure it's not too weird, considering Van and Alice and Alby and all?"

Both women fell silent.

If Liv hadn't seen Travis walking Buster in the rain, the truth might never have come out.

After several hours of questioning by state police detectives, Van admitted he'd killed both Alice and Alby. Karina Briggs had called the following day to fill Liv in.

As he'd told Liv, Van borrowed Travis's truck and delivered the armoire to the town north of Bangor. Instead of spending the night in the casino, however, he drove to the family's chalet where he confronted Alice in the kitchen and killed her.

When Alby, intoxicated, came downstairs to see what was going on, Van hit him on the forehead with a bottle of wine, knocking him out.

"That's why it looked like he'd died from a blow to the head?" Liv had asked Briggs.

"That and the way he went through the windshield at the bottom of the ravine," Briggs answered, her tone dry. "One kind of overrode the other."

"Ah."

"He got Alby to the Audi. He drove to the nearby tote road and maneuvered Alby into the driver's seat."

"Where he put the car in gear and let it run into the ravine."

"Yes. He ran back to the chalet, got the truck, and returned to Pellham. He'd planned on saying he'd been in Bangor all night, but when the neighbor's video footage showed up, he'd let everyone assume he was the person walking Busterdoodle in the rain."

"A perfect alibi," Liv said. "He almost got away with it."

After thorough questioning, the investigators determined Travis had no idea that his vehicle had been involved. The Fergusons swooped in with their lawyer, and now Van, locked away in a psychiatric facility, awaited a judge's ruling on competency to stand trial.

Sitting with Emsley at the restaurant, Liv broke the silence. "I feel responsible, somehow. If I'd refused to take the case, none of this would have happened. Alby and Alice would still be alive."

Spooning up some of her crème brûlée, Emsley said, "You were doing your job. Van asked you to help. He committed the crime. He covered it up. He lied to you, the police, his parents, and possibly even himself. I'm not saying Alby deserved to die, but sometimes life has a way of evening the score."

"In this case, Van evened the score."

"And now he has to pay for it," Emsley said. "His parents, too. You know if they'd treated Van more fairly maybe things would have turned out different for all of them." She lifted her glass. "I say we concentrate on the future of Lively Investigations."

"You're right." Liv clinked her glass with Emsley's. "Cheers."

The following week, flush with Emsley's cash infusion, Liv set up a 401K and a company health insurance plan, and she hired Marion as a full-time receptionist and P.I. apprentice.

Things had come together in a way she couldn't have imagined at the beginning of the summer.

Now Liv asked Marion, "Is Patrick on his way?"

"He should be here any minute. Emsley, too."

"Why don't you make yourself some coffee, and you can tell me about how your book's coming along while we wait."

As Marion fussed with the new machine and caught her up on the intricacies of her romantic suspense plot lines, Liv settled into a chair in the seating area. She jumped up again when plump, cheerful attorney Patrick Ledeau entered the office. Emsley swept in behind him.

"Hope I'm not late," Ledeau said, moving toward Liv and giving her a brief kiss on the cheek. "Congress and Franklin were all backed up."

"Leaf peeper season," Emsley said, lowering herself onto the couch.

Emsley wore a pair of faded boot cut jeans and a long kimono with a green, orange, and pink floral design. She'd wound her platinum-blonde hair into two knobs on top of her head and carried a portfolio in one hand. The scent of Gucci's Chants for a Nymph perfume clung to her, the notes of frangipani and vanilla perfectly suited to her arty vibe. "I have a meeting with Gretchen Nolan at the gallery this afternoon. She's interested in my new collection. I have some sketches and photos to show her."

"That's fantastic, Emsley! Can Marion get you a coffee or espresso? She's fallen in love with the new machine."

Marion stepped toward the group with a small espresso cup in her hand. She held it out to Emsley. "Way ahead of you, boss. Mr. Ledeau? Coffee?"

"None for me. I've been ordered by my doctor to drink more water." Ledeau waved a trendy glass bottle and frowned at Liv. "Speaking of doctors, how's the wrist?"

"It's good. Just throbs a little once in a while."

"I hope that psycho gets put away for life." He glanced over at Emsley. "No offense."

Emsley waved a large, languid hand. "Not my family anymore. I'd be happy if he never sees the light of day. Who knows when they'll deem him fit to stand trial, though."

Liv ignored a throb of guilt. She was getting better at that. Regret couldn't undo the series of events that had ended with two people dead, and in the end she believed justice would prevail. "Let's get this meeting started," she said, taking a seat on the couch.

Marion settled onto the other end. Ledeau and Emsley took the side chairs. They all looked at Liv, waiting for her to begin.

After her recent brush with sex traffickers, drug dealers, and a McMansion murderer, Liv had taken a week off to contemplate her business. She'd spent her days walking on the beach, reassessing her life and how she saw Lively Investigations operating in the future. With Emsley's cash infusion, she now had options.

Jasper, she admitted as she watched the waves rolling over the sand in long ruffles, had been partly right. She realized that while she could continue to take any and all types of cases, she no longer wanted to.

She'd never run away from danger—it wasn't in her character—but she didn't need to court it either. After a long talk with Patrick, she'd decided to position Lively Investigations as a niche firm specializing in intellectual property and insurance fraud. With Emsley's financial backing and Ledeau throwing work her way and acting as a legal advisor to the firm, not to mention Marion's exceptional organizational skills and brains, she figured the timing couldn't be more perfect to rebrand and relaunch her agency.

She looked around at her team. "Thank you so much, all of you, for believing in and taking a chance on growing Lively Investigations. It's going to take a lot of time and effort—we have a lot of marketing to do, and I'm sure there will be some bumps along the way as I phase out some old aspects of the business—but I'm certain we can succeed. Here's where I see us going…"

They spent the next two hours talking and making plans.

Patrick had a mediation to get to and extracted a promise from Liv that she'd join him for a cocktail later that week. Emsley and Marion spent fifteen minutes chatting about a new exhibit opening downtown, and then Emsley took off with her portfolio for her meeting with Gretchen Nolan. Marion tried to gather the mugs to wash them, but Liv told her to leave them. "Go home and write." She gave Marion a mock-serious school-teacher look. "You have a novel to finish."

When everyone had gone, Liv washed the mugs, stopped to talk to a couple of fiber artists in the Fiber Fox studio, and then she, too, went home.

· · · · ·

Liv opened the door of her Munjoy Hill apartment. Four sets of nails skittered on the floor, and a giant bundle of curly fur launched himself at her.

"Down, Buster, down!" she commanded.

He dropped to all fours and sat, tongue hanging out, goofy as all get-out. She bent over him and gave him a big rub while he wriggled and writhed and tried to lick her face. She laughed and pushed him away, but he came right back, eager for more licking and snuggles. She obliged with a laugh, and his entire body shook with delight and doggy love.

After Van's arrest, someone had to take the dog.

Liv volunteered to foster him until the local animal rescue found a permanent home, but it turned out Jasper'd been right. She'd needed a dog in her life. The following week—sick with the thought that someone else would take him—she filled out the paperwork and brought Buster home with her for good.

All licked out, Buster gave a final shake, trotted to the door, and whined. She laughed again when he stared back at her with a beseeching look in his light brown eyes.

"Okay, let me change, and we'll go for a run," she said.

At the word "run," Buster barked and turned himself in circles before sitting in front of the door again as if he expected her to forget him.

A few minutes later, the pair took off toward the Eastern Prom trail, woman and dog jogging at an easy clip, the ferry's horn sounding across the bay.

Acknowledgments

• • • • • • • • • • • • • • •

Many thanks to Cynthia Brackett-Vincent, Eddie Vincent, and Deirdre Wait of Encircle Publications for giving Olivia Lively a home in the publishing world.

To Sgt. Darryl "Jay" Peary, Jr. (25 years with the Maine State Police), for answering questions about witness interviews. Anything incorrect is my mistake, not his.

To K.C. Brote, author and daily talker-down-from-the-ledges friend. To Carolyn Chute, for all the encouragement over the years. To Kathy Lynn Emerson who suggested there should be a dead body. I ended up with two!

To Sara Cyr Eastman for introducing me to her book club. To Andrea Newland-Lizarraga for helping with the book fair and general encouragement. To all my friends (especially the members of the Stakeout Team) and family for spreading the word and all your generous support and encouragement this year and many years.

Once again and always, to Craig.

About the Author

• • • • • • • • • • • • • • •

Shelley Burbank is a mystery and women's fiction author and journalist based in Maine and San Diego, California. She's a contributing writer to the *Waterboro Reporter* newspaper, and her short fiction has been published nationally in *True Story*, *True Love*, and *True Confessions* magazines. Regional and literary publications include *San Diego Woman Magazine* and *The Maine Review*. *Final Draft*, the first Olivia Lively Mystery published by Encircle Publications (March 2023), was her debut novel. The second in the romantic mystery series, *Night Moves*, released in August 2024. For the latest news, find Shelley on Facebook and Instagram, and visit www.shelleyburbank.com.

If you enjoyed this book,
please consider writing a review
and sharing it with other readers.

Many of our authors are happy to participate in
book club and reader group discussions.
For more information, contact us at info@encirclepub.com.

Thank you,
Encircle Publications

For news about more exciting new fiction, join us at:

Facebook: www.facebook.com/encirclepub

Instagram: www.instagram.com/encirclepublications

Sign up for the Encircle Publications newsletter:
eepurl.com/cs8taP